ASSASSIN ZERO

Assassin Zero

((An Agent Zero Spy Thriller—Book 7)

Jack Mars

Jack Mars

Jack Mars is the USA Today bestselling author of the LUKE STONE thriller series, which includes seven books. He is also the author of the new FORGING OF LUKE STONE prequel series, comprising three books (and counting); and of the AGENT ZERO spy thriller series, comprising seven books (and counting).

ANY MEANS NECESSARY (book #1), which has over 800 five star reviews, is available as a free download on Amazon!

Jack loves to hear from you, so please feel free to visit www.Jackmarsauthor.com to join the email list, receive a free book, receive free giveaways, connect on Facebook and Twitter, and stay in touch!

TABLE OF CONTENTS

Prologue

I can't locate Sara.

That was what Todd Strickland had told him over the phone. Zero had barely been home from Belgium for a full day, after exposing the Russian president as the puppeteer behind an attempt to annex Ukraine with American interference, when he got the news. Strickland had been keeping tabs on Sara ever since she had become an emancipated minor and moved to Florida, but now she had seemingly vanished. Her cell service was cut off and location inactive. Even her roommates at the co-op where she rented a room claimed they hadn't seen her in two days.

Text me her home address, Zero had ordered him. *I'm going to the airport.*

Just shy of three hours later he stood outside the ramshackle house in Jacksonville, Florida, the place Sara had been calling home for a little more than a year. He marched up the cracked concrete steps and pounded on the front door with the flat of a fist, over and over again without pausing, until someone finally answered.

"Dude," groaned a lanky blond teenager with tattoos up and down his arms. "What the hell are you doing?"

"Sara Lawson," Zero demanded. "You know where she might be?"

The kid's eyebrows knit quizzically, but his mouth curled in a smirk. "Why? You another Fed looking for her?"

Fed? A chill ran up Zero's spine. *If anyone who claimed to be FBI had come around, it could mean she's been abducted.*

"I'm her father." He stepped forward, shoving the kid back with his shoulder as he pushed into the house.

"Yo, you can't just barge in here!" the kid tried to protest. "Man, I will call the cops—"

Zero spun on him. "It's Tommy, right?"

The blond kid's eyes widened apprehensively, though he didn't answer.

"I've heard about you," Zero told him, keeping his voice low. Strickland had given him a full briefing while he was en route. "I know all about you. You're not going to call the cops. You're not going to call your lawyer dad. You're going to sit there, on the couch, and shut your damn mouth. You hear me?"

The kid opened his mouth as if he wanted to say something—

"I said shut it," Zero snapped.

The lanky boy retreated to the couch like a kicked dog, taking a seat beside a young girl who couldn't have been eighteen if she was a day.

"Are you Camilla?"

The girl shook her head frantically. "I'm Jo."

"I'm Camilla." A young Latina girl came down the stairs, dark-haired and wearing entirely too much makeup. "I'm Sara's roomie." She looked Zero up and down. "You're really her dad?" she asked dubiously.

"Yeah."

"Then... what do you do?"

"What?"

"For work. Sara told us what you do."

"I don't have time for this," he muttered at the ceiling. "I'm an accountant," he told the girl.

Camilla shook her head. "Wrong answer."

Zero scoffed. *Leave it to Sara to tell her friends the truth about me.* "What do you want me to say? That I'm a spy with the CIA?"

Camilla blinked at him. "Well... yeah."

"For real?" said the blond kid on the sofa.

Zero held up both hands in frustration. "Please. Just tell me where you last saw Sara."

Camilla looked at her roommates, and then the floor. "All right," she said quietly. "A few days ago, she was looking to score, and I gave her..."

"Score?" Zero asked.

"Drugs, man. Keep up," said the blond kid.

"She needed something to even her out," Camilla continued. "I gave her the address of my guy. She went there. She came back. Next morning she left again. I thought she was going to work, but she never came home. Her phone's off. I swear that's all I know."

Zero almost saw red at these irresponsible kids, barely adults, sending a teenager alone to a drug dealer's house. But he swallowed his anger for her. He needed to find her.

She needs you.

"That's not all you know," he said to Camilla. "I want the name and address of your guy."

Twenty minutes later Zero stood outside a Jacksonville rowhouse with grimy siding and a broken washing machine on the front porch. According to Camilla, this was the dealer's house, some guy named Ike.

Zero didn't have a gun on him. He'd been in such a rush to get to the airport that he'd run out the door with nothing but his car keys and his phone. But now he wished he'd brought one.

How do I play this? Burst in, kick ass, demand answers? Or knock and have a chat?

He decided the latter would be a better way to start—and he'd see where things took him from there.

On the third brisk knock, a male voice called out from inside the house. "Hang the fuck on, I'm coming!" The guy that appeared at the door was taller than Zero, more muscular than Zero, and far more tattooed than Zero (who had none). He wore a white tank top with what looked like a coffee stain on it, and jeans that were too big for him, hanging low on his hips.

"Are you Ike?"

The dealer looked him up and down. "You a cop?"

"No. I'm looking for my daughter. Sara. She's sixteen, blonde, about this tall …"

"Never seen your kid, man." Ike shook his head. He had a frown on his face.

But Zero noticed the tiny, almost imperceptible twitch of his eye. A flicker on his lips as he willed them not to scowl. *Anger.* He showed a brief flash of anger at Sara's name.

"Okay. Sorry to bother you," Zero said.

"Yeah," the guy said flatly. He started to close the door.

As soon as Ike was partially turned away, Zero raised a foot and delivered a solid kick just below the doorknob. It flew open, crashing into the dealer and sending him sprawling on his belly to the brown carpet.

Zero was on him in a second, a forearm against his windpipe. "You know her," he growled. "I saw it in your eyes. Tell me where she went, or I'll—"

He heard a snarl, and then a blur of black and brown as a thick-necked Rottweiler leapt at him. He barely had time to react other than to take the force of the dog and roll with it. Teeth gnashed and bit at the air, finding purchase on his arm and sinking fangs into flesh.

Zero clenched his teeth hard and rolled once more, so that the dog was under him, and pushed down, forcing his bit forearm into the dog's mouth even as it tried to clamp down further.

The dealer scrambled to his feet and fled the room while Zero grasped behind him for whatever he could find. The dog wriggled and thrashed beneath him, trying to get free, but Zero pinched his legs together so it couldn't get upright. His hand found a ratty blanket draped on the leather couch, and he pulled it loose.

With his free hand he delivered a single, snapping blow to the dog's snout—not enough to hurt it badly, but to stun it enough that its teeth released his arm. In the half-second before the jaws clamped down again, he wrapped the blanket around the dog's head and relaxed his legs so it could flip over and stand.

Then he whipped the end of the blanket under its body and tied the ends behind its head, wrapped the front half of the Rottweiler tightly in the blanket. The dog thrashed and bucked, trying to get free—and it would, eventually. So Zero scrambled to his feet and dashed after the dealer.

He skidded into a tiny kitchen just in time to see Ike pulling a small, ugly pistol loose from a drawer. He tried to bring it around, but Zero leapt forward and stopped it with a hand, and then snapped it from his grip in a twisting maneuver that definitely dislocated, if not broke, one of the guy's fingers.

Ike yelped sharply and cowered, holding his hand, as Zero aimed the gun at his forehead.

"Don't shoot me, man," he whimpered. "Don't shoot me. Please don't shoot me."

"Tell me what I want to know. Where is Sara? When did you last see her?"

"Okay! Okay. Look, she came to me, but she couldn't pay, so we worked out a deal where she could run my stuff around town—"

"Drugs," Zero corrected. "You had her running drugs. Just say that."

"Yeah. Drugs. It was just a few days, and she was doing okay, but then I gave her a big score of pills …"

"Of what?"

"Prescription pills. Painkillers. And she just ghosted me, man. Never showed up, never delivered. My people were pissed. I was out more than a thousand bucks. And she even took one of my cars, 'cause she didn't have one of her own …"

Zero scoffed loudly. "You gave her a thousand dollars' worth of drugs, and she ran off with it?"

"Yeah, man." He looked up at Zero, his hands up near his face defensively. "If you think about it, I'm really the victim here …"

"Shut up." He gently pushed the barrel against Ike's forehead. "Where was she going, and what kind of car did she take?"

❧ ❧ ❧

Zero took the black Escalade, which he'd "borrowed" from Ike along with his gun, and used the GPS on his phone to drive as quickly as he could to the drop-off point, all the while looking for a light blue 2001 four-door Chevy sedan.

He didn't see one before he reached the delivery point, which much to his chagrin was a local rec center. But he couldn't worry about that in the moment. Instead he thought to himself, *What would Sara do? Where would she go?*

He already knew the answer before he even finished asking himself the question. It floated to him on the salty scent of the air as easily as recalling a memory.

It was no secret in their family that Kate, Maya and Sara's late mother, had a favorite spot in the entire world. She had taken the girls there on three separate occasions, the first time when they were only eight and six respectively, and told them: "This is my favorite spot."

It was a beach in New Jersey, a phrase that would typically make Zero cringe. The beach was too rocky and the water was usually too cold except for two months in the summer, but that's not what Kate liked about it. She just liked the view. She'd gone there every year when she was a little girl, all through her teens, and had a fond and almost unfounded love for the place.

The beach. He knew that Sara would go to the beach.

He used his phone to find the closest ones and drove there like a maniac, cutting people off and blowing lights and overall generally surprised that no cops zipped out from hiding places to pull him over. The parking lots at the beach were only a few rows, long and narrow and full of cars and happy families. But he didn't see any vehicles that matched the one that Ike had described.

He searched three of the largest, closest beaches to Sara's home and work and found nothing. Dusk was falling fast. In the back of his mind he was aware that the US had a new president; the former Speaker of the House had been sworn in that afternoon. Maria was invited there, to the ceremony, and was most likely at some cocktail party by now, full of stuffy politicians and wealthy constituents, sipping champagne and talking idly about a bright future while Zero searched the coast of Jacksonville for his estranged daughter who, last time he'd seen her, had called the police on him and shouted that she never wanted to see him again.

"Come on, Sara," he muttered to the ether as he flicked the headlights on. "Give me something. Help me find you. There must be a ..."

He trailed off as he realized his mistake. He'd been searching public beaches. Popular beaches. But Kate's beach had been small and sparsely visited. And Sara had a thousand dollars' worth of drugs. She wouldn't want to be where people were.

He pulled over to the side of the road and opened the browser on his phone. He frantically searched for less popular beaches, rocky beaches, places that people didn't often go. It was a hard search, and it didn't feel like he was making progress until he touched the "images" tab and then he saw it—

A beach that looked remarkably like Kate's beach. As if it had been molded from his own memory.

Zero headed there at about eighty miles an hour, not caring about police or traffic laws or even other drivers as he swerved around cars going far too slow, people casually heading home for the night and not concerned that their daughter might be dead in the surf somewhere.

He skidded into the tiny gravel parking lot and slammed his brakes when he saw it. A blue sedan, the only car in the lot, parked at the farthest end. Night had fallen, so he left the headlights on and put the Escalade in park right there in the middle of the lot, and he jumped out and ran over to the sedan.

He threw the back door open.

And there she was, looking like both heaven and hell: his baby girl, his youngest daughter, pale-skinned and beautiful, lying prostrate in the backseat of a car with her eyes glazed and half-opened, pills scattered around the floor below her.

Zero immediately checked for a pulse. It was there, though slow. Then he tilted her head back and made sure her airway was clear. He knew that most overdose deaths were the result of blocked airways that resulted in respiratory failure and eventually cardiac arrest.

But she was breathing, albeit shallowly.

"Sara?" he said hoarsely in her face. "Sara?"

She didn't answer. He hefted her out of the car and held her upright. She was unable to stand on her own two feet.

"I'm so sorry," he told her. And then he stuck two fingers down her throat.

She retched involuntarily, then again, and vomited into the parking lot. She coughed and sputtered while he held her and told her, "It's okay. It's going to be okay."

He put her in the Escalade, leaving the doors of the sedan still open with pills all over the seats, and drove two miles until he found a convenience store. He bought two liters of water with a twenty and didn't stick around for his change.

There in the parking lot of a Florida gas station, he sat with her in the back seat, her head in his lap as he stroked her hair, feeding her small amounts of water and watching for any signs that he should bring her to an emergency room. Her pupils were dilated, but her airways were open and her pulse was slowly returning to normal. Her fingers were twitching slightly, but when he slipped his hand into them they closed around his. Zero held back tears, remembering when she was just a baby, when he'd hold her in his lap and her tiny fingers would clench his.

He lost track of time sitting there with her. The next time he glanced up at the clock he saw that more than two hours had gone by.

And then she blinked, and moaned slightly, and said: "Daddy?"

"Yeah." His voice came out a whisper. "It's me."

"Is this real?" she asked, her voice floating to him dreamily.

"It's real," he told her. "I'm here, and I'm going to take you home. I'm going to take you away from here. I'm going to take care of you ... even if you hate me for it."

"Okay," she agreed softly.

And eventually he relaxed enough to realize that the danger had passed. Sara fell asleep and Zero slid into the front seat of the SUV. He couldn't put her on a plane in this state, but he could drive back, through the night if he had to. Maria would get rid of the vehicle for him, no questions asked. And the local authorities would be paying a visit to the dealer, Ike.

He glanced over his shoulder at her, curled in the backseat with her knees drawn up and her cheek on the soft leather, looking peaceful but vulnerable.

She needs you.

And he needed to be needed.

4 Weeks Later

CHAPTER ONE

"You ready for this?" Alan Reidigger asked, his voice low as he checked the magazine on the black Glock in his meaty fist. He and Zero had their backs to a plywood structure, keeping hidden and obscured by the darkness. It was almost too dark to see, but Zero knew that in moments the whole place would be lit up like the Fourth of July.

"Always ready," Zero whispered back. He held a Ruger LC9 in his left hand, a small silver pistol with a nine-round mag, as he flexed the fingers of his right. He had to stay cognizant of the injury he'd sustained almost two years earlier, when a steel anchor had crushed his hand to the point of uselessness. Three surgeries and several months of physical therapy later, he had regained most of its operation, despite permanent nerve damage. He could fire a gun but his aim tended to track to the left, a minor annoyance that he'd been working to overcome.

"I'll go left," Reidigger laid out, "and clear the causeway. You go right. Keep your eyes up and watch your six. I bet there's a surprise or two waiting for us."

Zero grinned. "Oh, are you calling the shots now, part-timer?"

"Just try to keep up, old man." Reidigger returned the grin, his lips curling behind the thick beard that obscured the lower half of his face. "Ready? Let's go."

With the simple, whispered command they both shoved off from the plywood façade behind them and split off. Zero brought the Ruger up, its barrel following his line of sight as he slipped around the dark corner and stole down a narrow alley.

At first it was just silence and darkness, barely a sound in the cavernous space. Zero had to remind his muscles to keep from tensing, to stay loose and not slow down his reaction speed.

This is just like all the other times, he told himself. *You've done this before.*

Then—lights exploded to his right, a severe and jarring series of flashes. A muzzle flare, accompanied by the deafening report of gunfire. Zero threw himself forward and tucked into a roll, coming up on one knee. The figure was barely more than a silhouette, but he could see enough to squeeze off two shots that connected with the silhouette at center mass.

Still got it. He climbed to his feet but stayed low, moving forward in a crouch. *Eyes up. Watch your six...* He whirled around just in time to see another dark figure sliding into view, cutting off the path behind him. Zero dropped himself backward, landing on his rear even as he popped off two more shots. He heard projectiles whistle right over his head, practically felt them ruffle his hair. Both his shots found home, one in the figure's torso and the second to the forehead.

From the other side of the structure came three tight shots in quick succession. Then silence. "Alan," he hissed into his earpiece. "Clear?"

"Hold that thought," came the reply. A burst of automatic fire tore through the air, and then two punctuating shots from the Glock. "All clear. Meet me around the side."

Zero kept his back to the wall and moved forward quickly, the rough plywood tugging at his tac vest. He spotted a blur of movement up ahead, from the roof of the flat-topped structure. A single well-placed headshot took out the threat.

He reached the corner and paused, taking a breath before clearing it. As he whipped around, the Ruger coming up, he found himself face-to-face with Reidigger.

"I got three," Zero told him.

"Two on my side," Alan grunted. "Which means ..."

Zero didn't have time to shout a warning as he saw the human-shaped figure glide into view behind Alan. He brought the pistol up, right over Alan's shoulder, and fired twice.

But not fast enough. As Zero's shots landed, Alan yelped and grasped at his leg.

"Ah, dammit!" Reidigger groaned. "Not again."

Zero winced as bright fluorescent lights came to life suddenly, illuminating the entire indoor training course. Heels clacked against the concrete floor, and a moment later Maria Johansson rounded the corner, arms folded over her white blazer and her lipsticked mouth frowning.

"What gives?" Reidigger protested. "Why'd we stop?"

"Alan," Maria scolded, "maybe you ought to take your own advice and watch *your* six."

"What, this?" Alan gestured to his thigh, where a green paintball had splattered across his pant leg. "This is barely a graze."

Maria scoffed. "That would have been a femoral bleed. You'd be dead in ninety seconds." To Zero she added, "Nice job, Kent. You're moving like your old self."

Zero smirked at Alan, who furtively gave him the finger.

The warehouse they were in was a former wholesale packing plant, until the CIA purchased it and turned it into training grounds. The course itself was a product of the eccentric agency engineer Bixby, who had done his best to simulate a nighttime raid. The "compound" they had been storming was made of boxy plywood structures, while the muzzle flashes were strobe lights placed throughout the facility. The gunshots were reproduced digitally and broadcast on high-def speakers, which echoed in the huge space and sounded to Zero's trained ear almost like real shots. The human-shaped figures were little more than dummies molded from ballistic gel and affixed to dolly tracks, while the paintball guns were automated, programmed to fire when motion sensors picked up movement at varying ranges.

The only thing genuine about the exercise were the live rounds they were using, which was why both Zero and Reidigger wore plated tac vests—and why the training facility was only open to Spec Ops agents, which Zero found himself once again being.

After the fiasco in Belgium, in which the two of them had confronted Russian President Aleksandr Kozlovsky and unearthed the secret pact he had with US President Harris, to say that Zero and Reidigger had landed themselves in hot water would have been a monumental understatement. They'd become international fugitives wanted in four countries for having broken more than a dozen laws. But they had been right about the plot, and it didn't quite seem justified for the two of them to spend the rest of their lives in prison.

So Maria pulled every string she could, sticking her neck out in a big way for her former teammates and friends. It was nothing short of a miracle that she somehow managed to have the ordeal retconned as a top-secret operation under her supervision.

The trade-off, of course, was that they had to return to work for the CIA.

Though Zero wouldn't admit it aloud, to him it felt like a homecoming. He had been working hard the past month, hitting the gym again, target-shooting at the range daily, boxing and sparring with opponents almost half his forty years. The weight he'd gained in his year and a half absence was gone. He was getting better at shooting with his injured right hand. Maria was right; he was very nearly back to his old self.

Alan Reidigger, on the other hand, had resisted at every turn. He had spent the last four years of his life with the agency thinking he was dead, living under the alias of a mechanic named Mitch. Coming back to the CIA was the last thing he wanted, but given a choice between that or a hole at H-6, he had reluctantly agreed to Maria's terms—but as an asset rather than a full-fledged agent, hence Zero's digs of him being a "part-timer." Alan's involvement would be on an as-needed basis, providing support whenever able and helping to train up younger agents.

But first that meant that the two of them had to get back into fighting shape.

Reidigger wiped at the green paint on his pants, only serving to smear it further across his thigh. "Let me clean this up and we'll go again," he told Maria.

She shook her head. "I'm not spending my whole day in this stuffy place watching you take shot after shot. We'll pick it up again after the holiday."

Alan grunted, but nodded anyway. He had been an excellent agent in his day, and even now had still proven himself to be sharp-witted and useful in a fight. He was quick despite the extra weight he carried around his midsection. But he'd always been something of a bullet magnet. Zero couldn't recall how many times Reidigger had been shot in his career, but it had to be approaching double digits—especially since he'd been tagged in the shoulder during their Belgian escapades.

A young male tech wheeled out a steel-topped cart for their equipment while a team of three others went about resetting the training course. Zero cleared the round from the Ruger's chamber, popped the magazine, and set all three down on the cart. Then he tore at the Velcro straps of the tac vest and tugged it over his head, suddenly feeling several pounds lighter.

"So, any chance you've reconsidered?" he asked Alan. "About Thanksgiving. The girls would love to see you."

"And I'd like to see them," he replied, "but I'm gonna take a rain check. They could use some quality time with you."

Alan didn't elaborate, and he didn't need to. Zero's relationship with Maya and Sara had been severely strained over the past year and a half. But now Sara had been staying with him for the past several weeks, ever since he found her on the beach in Florida. He and Maya had been talking over the phone more and more—she had almost jumped on the very first plane when she'd heard what happened to her younger sister, but Zero had calmed her down and convinced her to stay in school until the holiday. This week was going to be the first time in quite a long time that the three of them would all be under the same roof. And Alan was right; there was still substantial work to be done to repair the damage that had separated them for so long.

"Besides," Alan said with a grin, "we've all got our traditions. Me, I'm going to eat an entire rotisserie chicken and rebuild the engine of a seventy-two Camaro." He glanced over at Maria. "How about you? Spending time with dear old dad?"

Maria's father, David Barren, was the Director of National Intelligence, essentially the only man other than the president that CIA Director Shaw answered to.

But Maria shook her head. "My father is going to be in Switzerland, actually. He's part of a diplomatic attaché on behalf of the president."

Alan frowned. "So you're going to be alone on Thanksgiving?"

4

Maria shrugged. "It's not a big deal. In fact, I'm way behind on paperwork, thanks to spending so much time down here with you two idiots. I plan on putting on some sweatpants, making some tea, and hunkering down…"

"No," Zero interrupted firmly. "No way. Come have dinner with me and the girls." He said it without fully thinking it through, but he didn't regret the offer. If anything, he felt a stab of guilt, since the only reason she'd be alone on Thanksgiving was because of him.

Maria smiled gratefully, but her eyes were hesitant. "I'm not so sure that's a good idea."

She had a point; their relationship had ended barely more than a month prior. They had been living together for more than a year as… well, he wasn't sure what they had been. Dating? He couldn't remember ever referring to her as his girlfriend. It just sounded too strange. But it didn't matter in the long run, because Maria had admitted that she wanted a family.

If Zero was going to do it all over again, there wouldn't be anyone else in the world he'd rather do it with than Maria. But when he took a good introspective look, he realized he didn't want that. He had work to do on himself, work to repair the relationships with his daughters, work to exorcise the ghosts of his past. And then the interpreter, Karina, had come into his life, in a too-brief romance that was dizzying and dangerous and wonderful and tragic. His heart was still aching from her loss.

Even so, he and Maria had a storied history, not only romantically but professionally and platonically as well. They had agreed to stay friends; neither of them would have it any other way. Yet now he was an agent again, while Maria had been promoted to Deputy Director of Special Operations—which meant she was his boss.

It was, to say the least, complicated.

Zero shook his head. It didn't have to be complicated. He had to believe that two people could be friends, regardless of their past or current associations.

"It's a great idea," he told her. "I won't take no for an answer. Have dinner with us."

"Well…" Maria's gaze flitted from Zero to Reidigger and back again. "Okay then," she relented. "That sounds nice. I guess I should go get started on that paperwork."

"I'll text you," Zero promised as she left the warehouse, heels clacking loudly on the concrete.

Alan pulled off his own tac vest with a long grunt, and then replaced the sweat-stained trucker's cap over his matted hair before casually asking, "Is this a scheme?"

"A scheme?" Zero scoffed. "For what, to get Maria back? You know I'm not thinking about that."

"No. I mean a scheme for Maria to be a buffer between you and them." For a covert operative who had been living the last four years as someone else, Alan had a brutal candor about him that sometimes bordered on insulting.

"Of course not," Zero said firmly. "You know there's nothing I want more than for things to be the way they used to be. Maria is a friend. Not a buffer."

"Sure," Alan agreed, though he sounded dubious. "Maybe 'buffer' wasn't the right term there. Maybe more like a…" He glanced down at the bulletproof tac vest lying on the steel cart in front of them and gestured to it. "Well, I can't think of a more apt metaphor than that."

"You don't know what you're talking about," Zero insisted, trying to keep the heat out of his voice. He wasn't angry with Alan for being honest, but he was irritated at the suggestion. "Maria doesn't deserve to be alone on Thanksgiving, and things with the girls are far better than they've been in more than a year. Everything is going great."

Alan put up both hands in surrender. "Okay, I believe you. I'm just looking out for you, that's all."

"Yeah. I know." Zero looked at his watch. "Look, I gotta run. Maya's coming in today. Let's hit the gym on Friday?"

"Definitely. Tell the girls I said hi."

"Will do. Enjoy your chicken and engine." Zero waved as he headed for the door, but now his head was swimming with doubts. Was Alan right? Had he subconsciously invited Maria because he was afraid to be alone with the girls? What if them being together again reminded them of why they had left in the first place? Or worse, what if they thought the same thing Alan did, that Maria was there as some sort of protective barrier between him and them? What if they thought he wasn't trying hard enough?

Everything is going great.

It wasn't at all a comfort, but at least his ability to lie convincingly was sharp as ever.

Chapter Two

Maya trudged up the stairs to the second-floor condo that her dad was renting. It was in a newer development outside of downtown Bethesda, in a neighborhood that had been built up over the past few years with apartments and townhomes and shopping centers. Hardly the sort of place she had ever expected her father to live, but she understood that he had been in a hurry to find something available when things fell apart between him and Maria.

Probably before he could change his mind, she imagined.

For the briefest of moments she mourned the loss of their home in Alexandria, the house that she and Sara and her dad had shared before all of the insanity started. Back when they still believed he was an adjunct history professor, before discovering that he was a covert agent with the CIA. Before they had been kidnapped by a psychopathic assassin who sold them to human traffickers. Back when they believed their mother had died of a swift and sudden stroke while walking to her car after work one day, instead of being murdered at the hands of a man who had saved the girls' lives on more than one occasion.

Maya shook her head and swept the bangs from her forehead as if trying to push away the thoughts. It was time for a fresh start. Or at least to give it an earnest try.

She found the door to her father's unit before she realized that she didn't have a key and should have probably called first to make sure he was home. But after two brisk knocks, the deadbolt slid aside and the door opened, and Maya found herself staring for several dumbfounded seconds at a relative stranger.

She hadn't see Sara in longer than she cared to admit, and it was evident all over her younger sister's face. Sara was quickly growing into a young woman, her features becoming defined—or rather, the features of Katherine Lawson, their late mother.

This is going to be harder than I thought. While Maya more closely resembled their father, Sara had always taken on aspects of their mother, in personality and interests as well as looks. Her younger sister's complexion was paler than Maya remembered too, though whether that was a trick of her memory or a result of a detox, Maya didn't know. Her eyes seemed somehow duller, and there were evident dark crescents beneath each that Sara had attempted to obscure with makeup. She'd dyed her hair red at some point, at least two months earlier, and now the first several inches of the roots were showing her natural blonde. She'd had it cut recently as well, to chin level, in a way that framed her face nicely but made her look a couple years older. In fact, she and Maya might very well have passed for the same age.

"Hey," Sara said simply.

"Hi." Maya snapped out of the initial surprise of seeing her dramatically different sister and smiled. She dropped her green duffel and stepped forward for a hug that Sara seemed grateful to return, almost as if she'd been waiting to see how she might be received by her big sister. "I missed you. I wanted to come home right away when Dad told me what happened…"

"I'm glad you didn't," Sara said candidly. "I would've felt awful if you left school for me. Besides, I didn't want you to see me … like that."

Sara slid out of her sister's arms and grabbed up the duffel bag before Maya could protest. "Come in," she beckoned. "Welcome home, I guess."

Welcome home. Strange how little it felt like home. Maya followed her inside the condo. It was a nice enough place, modern with lots of natural light, though rather austere. If not for a few dishes in the sink and the television humming in the living room at low volume, Maya wouldn't have believed anyone actually lived there. There were no pictures on the walls, no décor that spoke to any sort of personality.

Kind of like a blank slate. Though she had to admit that a blank slate was appropriate for their situation.

"So this is it," Sara announced, as if reading Maya's mind. "At least for now. There are only two bedrooms, so we'll have to share a room…"

"I'm fine with the couch," Maya offered.

Sara smiled thinly. "I don't mind sharing. It'd be like when we were little. It'd be … nice. Having you around." She cleared her throat. Despite how often they had talked over the phone, it was painfully obviously how oddly awkward it was to be in the same room again.

"Where's Dad?" Maya asked suddenly, and perhaps too loudly, in an effort to diffuse the tension.

"Should be home any minute. He had to stop off after work and get a few things for tomorrow."

After work. She made it sound so casual, as if he was leaving an office for the day instead of CIA headquarters in Langley.

Sara perched herself upon a stool at the bar-like countertop that separated the kitchen and small dining room. "How's school?"

Maya leaned against the countertop on her elbows. "School is ..." She trailed off. Though she was only eighteen, she was in her second year at West Point in New York. She'd tested out of high school early and was accepted to the military academy on the merit of a letter from former President Eli Pierson, whose assassination attempt had been thwarted by Agent Zero. Now she was top of her class, perhaps even top of the whole academy. But a recent tiff with her sort-of ex-boyfriend Greg Calloway had evolved into hazing and some bullying. Maya refused to give in to it, but she had to admit it made life irritating lately. Greg had a lot of friends, all of them older boys at the academy whom Maya had shown up at least once or twice.

"School is great," she said at last, forcing a smile. Sara had enough problems of her own. "But kind of boring. I want to know what's going on with you."

Sara almost snorted, and then held her hands out at her sides in a grand gesture at the condo. "You're looking at it. I'm here all day, every day. I watch TV. I don't go anywhere. I don't have any money. Dad got me a phone on his plan so he can keep an eye on my calls and texts." She shrugged one shoulder. "It's like one of those white-collar prisons they send politicians and celebrities to."

Maya smiled sadly at the joke, and then cautiously asked: "But you're ... clean?"

Sara nodded. "As I can be."

Maya frowned at that. She knew a lot about a lot of things, but recreational drug use wasn't one of them. "What does that mean?"

Sara stared at the granite counter, tracing a small circle on the smooth surface with an index finger. "It means it's hard," she admitted quietly. "I thought it would get easier after those first few days, after all the junk was out of my system. But it didn't. It's like ... it's like my brain remembers the feeling, still craves it. The boredom doesn't help. Dad doesn't want me to get a job just yet, because he doesn't want me having any extra money lying around until I'm better." She scoffed and added, "He's been pushing me to study for my GED."

And you should, Maya very nearly blurted out, but she held her tongue. Sara had dropped out of high school after she was granted emancipation, but the last thing she needed right then was a lecture, especially when she was opening up like she was.

But one thing was clear: Sara's problem was worse than Maya had realized. She'd thought her younger sister had just been experimenting recreationally, and that the near-OD on pills had been an accident. Yet the opposite was true. Sara was a recovering addict. And there was nothing that Maya could do to help her. She didn't know anything about addiction.

But is that really true?

She suddenly recalled a night, about two weeks earlier, when she'd woken her dorm mate by coming in from the gym at one in the morning. The irritated cadet had grumbled at her, half-asleep, something about being a "workout junkie." And then Maya had stayed up for another hour studying, only to be out on the track for a jog at six the next morning.

The more she thought about it, the more she realized she knew all about addiction. Wasn't she addicted to proving herself? Had she not been chasing a dragon of her own success?

And her father, even after all the tumult of the last two years, had still gone back to the job. Sara still craved the chemical high the way that Maya craved accomplishment and their dad craved the thrill of the chase—because maybe they were all just a family of addicts.

But Sara is the only one that's acknowledged it. Maybe she's the smartest of all of us.

"Hey." Maya reached over and put her hand on Sara's. "You can beat this. You're stronger than you know. I have faith in you."

Sara smiled with half her mouth. "I'm glad someone does."

"I'll talk to Dad," Maya offered. "See if he won't relax a little bit, give you some freedom—"

"No," Sara interrupted. "Dad isn't the problem. He's been great to me; probably better than I deserve." Her gaze swept the floor. "The problem is me. Because I know damn well that if I had a hundred bucks in my pocket and could go wherever I wanted, he'd have to come find me again. And next time he might not get there fast enough."

Maya's heart broke at the obvious torment reflected in her sister's eyes, and then again at the knowledge that there was nothing she could do to help. All she had were empty words of encouragement, which were all but meaningless in the scope of solving her problems.

Suddenly she felt incredibly out of place in that foreign kitchen. They had been through so much together. Growing up. Mourning their mother. Discovering their father. Family vacations and fleeing from would-be murderers. The kinds of things that anyone would assume would bring two people closer together, create an unbreakable bond, had instead created the vacuous silence that ballooned in the space between them.

Was this how it was going to be now? Would the girl before her just continue becoming more and more unrecognizable until they were mere strangers who happened to be related?

Maya wanted to say something, anything, to prove herself wrong. Reminisce about some happy memory. Or call her Squeak, the childhood nickname that hadn't been used in god-only-knew how long.

Before she could say anything at all, the doorknob rattled behind them. Maya spun as the door swung open, her fists balling instinctively at her sides. Her nerves still jumped when it came to unexpected intrusions.

But it was no intruder. It was her father, carrying two grocery bags and taking seemingly cautious steps into the kitchen of his own home at the sight of her.

"Hi."

"Hi, Dad."

He set the grocery bags on the floor and took a step toward her, arms opening, but then paused. "Can I ...?"

She nodded once, and he put his arms around her. It was a ginger hug at first, a hesitant hug—but then Maya noticed, strangely enough, that he still smelled the same. It was an overpoweringly nostalgic scent, a scent of her childhood, of a thousand other hugs. And maybe she was older, and maybe Sara looked different; maybe she still wasn't entirely sure who her father was and maybe they were standing in a new place that she was supposed to call home, but in that moment none of that felt like it mattered. The moment felt like home, and she leaned into it, squeezing him tightly.

Maya tugged open the sliding glass door at the back of the condo, pulling on a hooded sweatshirt against the chilly night air. The condo had no yard, but did have a small deck outfitted with a stubby table and two chairs.

Her dad was in one of them, sipping from a glass of something amber-colored. Maya lowered herself into the other, noting how clear the night was.

"Sara asleep?" he asked.

Maya nodded. "Dozed off on the couch."

"She's been doing a lot of that lately," he said, sounding troubled. "Sleeping, that is."

She forced a light chuckle. "She's always slept a lot. I wouldn't read too much into it." She gestured to the glass in his hand. "Beer?"

"Iced tea." He grinned sheepishly. "I haven't been drinking since going back to work."

"And how's that going?"

"Not bad," he admitted. "I haven't been on any field assignments lately, since I'm taking care of Sara and still getting back into shape."

"I was going to mention that you lost some weight. You're looking much better than ..."

Than the last time I saw you, Maya was going to say, but she stopped herself, because she didn't want to dredge up the memory of that visit, when she'd brought Greg to the house, got angry, stormed out, abandoned Greg there, and told her dad she never wanted to see him again.

"Thanks," he said quickly, clearly thinking the same. "And school is going well?"

She had already told him so earlier, over dinner, but it seemed as if he didn't quite believe her—and she reminded herself that part of his job was the ability to read people. There was little use lying to him, but that didn't mean she had to share either.

"I don't really want to talk about school," she told him plainly. She didn't want to talk about how things sometimes went missing from her locker. Or how boys shouted unkind things at her across the quad. Or the feeling she couldn't shake that it was only the beginning of the torment, that the more she tried to ignore them the more the boys at West Point would escalate.

"Fair enough." Her dad cleared his throat. "Um, there is something I should mention though. I should have asked you first. But Maria had nowhere to go tomorrow, and it didn't seem right..."

"It's okay, Dad." Maya grinned at his awkward attempt to ask her permission. "Of course I don't mind, and you don't need to clear it with me."

He shrugged. "I guess you're right. It's just—you're so grown up now. Both of you. I missed out on some important parts."

Maya nodded slightly, though she didn't feel the need to vocalize her agreement. Instead she changed the subject. "It's a good thing you're doing for Sara. Helping her like this. She sounds like she really needs it."

This time it was her dad who nodded slightly, staring out over the deck at nothing in particular. "I'd do anything I could for her," he said wistfully. "But I'm afraid it still won't be enough."

"What do you mean?"

He took a sip of his iced tea before he explained. "Last week we went to dinner, just the two of us, to this place downtown. It was nice. We talked. She seemed okay. When the check came, I paid with a hundred-dollar bill. And something happened; it was like a shadow passed over her. I saw her look at the money, and then the door, and..."

Her dad fell silent, but Maya didn't need him to explain any further. Now she understood Sara's comment from earlier; she had actually been thinking about grabbing the money and making a run for it. She wouldn't have gotten far with only a hundred bucks, but she was probably thinking in the very short term. Getting a fix wherever she could.

"I'm sure you noticed," her dad continued, "the place is pretty plain in there. I haven't really put much out, because..."

Because you're worried she might steal it. Pawn it. Run off again. The CIA hadn't sent him anywhere in the time that Sara had been living with him, but sooner or later they would—and then what? Would Sara just sit here and wait for him to come back? Or would she be a flight risk, if left to her own devices and demons?

"It's so much worse than I thought," Maya murmured. Then, resolutely and without a second thought she added, "I'm staying."

"What?"

She nodded. "I'm staying. There's only three more weeks of school before Christmas break. I can make up the work. I'll stay here through the holidays, go back to New York after New Year's."

"No," Zero told her firmly. "Absolutely not—"

"She needs help. She needs support." Maya wasn't sure what sort of help or support she could offer her sister, but she would have time to figure it out. "It's okay. I can handle it."

"It's not your job." Her dad leaned over and touched her hand. She nearly flinched, but then her fingers closed around his. "I appreciate the offer. I'm sure Sara would too. But you have goals. You have a dream. You've worked hard for it, and you need to see it through."

Maya blinked, a little taken aback. Her father had never once shown support for her goal of joining the CIA, of becoming the youngest agent in history. In fact, he had often attempted to talk her out of it, but she remained steadfast.

He smiled, seeming to pick up on her surprise. "Don't get me wrong. I still don't like it at all. But you're an adult now; it's your life. Your decision to make."

She smiled back. He had changed. And maybe there was a chance after all to get back to what they once were. But there was still the matter of what to do about Sara.

"I think," she said carefully, "that Sara might need more help than we can give her. I think she might need some professional help."

Her dad nodded as if he already knew it—as if he'd been thinking the same thing himself, but needed to hear it from someone else. She squeezed his hand gently, reassuringly, and they let the silence reign over them. Neither of them knew what would come next, but for now, all that mattered was they were home.

Chapter Three

*W*hoever named New York *"the city that never sleeps"* has never been to Old Havana, Alvaro mused as he wound his way toward the harbor and the Malecón. In the daylight, Old Havana was a beautiful part of the city, a rich blend of history and art, food and culture, yet the streets were jammed with traffic and the air was filled with the sounds of construction from the various restoration projects to bring the oldest part of Havana into the twenty-first century.

But at night... night was when the city showed its true colors. The lights, the scents, the music, the laughter: and the Malecón was the place to be. The narrow streets surrounding Calle 23, where Alvaro lived, was vibrant enough but most of the native Cuban bars closed down at midnight. Here on the broad esplanade at the edge of the harbor, the nightclubs stayed open and the music swelled ever louder and the drinks continued to flow in many of the bars and lounges.

The Malecón was a roadway that stretched for eight kilometers along Havana's sea edge, lined with structures painted sea green and coral pink. Many of the locals tended to snub it because of the staggering tourist population, but that was one of the many reasons Alvaro was drawn to it; despite the increasingly (and irritatingly) popular Euro-style lounges, there were still a handful of places where a lively, addictive salsa beat combated the EDM from neighboring buildings.

There was a joke among locals that Cuba was the only place in the world where you had to pay musicians *not* to play, and that was certainly true in the daytime. It seemed as if every person who owned a guitar or a trumpet or a set of bongos set up shop on a street corner, music on every block accompanied by the rumble of construction equipment and the honking of car horns. But nighttime was a different story, especially on the Malecón; live music was dwindling, losing the fight to electronic music played through computers—or worse, whatever pop hits had recently been imported from the States.

Yet Alvaro did not concern himself with any of that, so long as he had La Piedra. One of the few genuine Cuban bars left on the seaside strip, its doors were still open—quite literally, both of them propped with doorstoppers so that the dynamic salsa music floated to his ears before he stepped inside. There was no line to get into La Piedra, unlike the long queues of so many of the European nightclubs. There was no swarming throng, six deep of patrons vying for the bartenders' attention. The lighting was not dimmed or strobing, but rather bright to fully accentuate the vibrant, colorful décor. A six-piece band played on a stage that could hardly be called such, just a one-foot raised platform at the farthest end of the bar.

Alvaro fit in perfectly at La Piedra, wearing a bright silk shirt with a white and yellow pattern of mariposas, the national flower of Cuba. He was tall and dark-featured, young and clean-shaven, handsome enough by most standards. Here in the small salsa club on Malecón, he was not just a sous chef with grease under his fingernails and minor burns on his hands. He was a mysterious stranger, an exciting indulgence. A tantalizing story to bring back home, or a sultry secret to keep.

He sidled up to the bar and put on what he hoped was a seductive smile. Luisa was working tonight, as she did most nights. Their routine had become something of a dance in itself, a well-practiced exchange that no longer held any surprises.

"Alvaro," she said flatly, barely able to suppress her own smirk. "If it isn't our local tourist trap."

"Luisa," he purred. "You are absolutely stunning." And she was. Tonight she wore a bright maxi skirt, slit high up one leg and accentuating the curves of her hips, with an off-the-shoulder white crop top just barely cresting over a perfect belly button pierced with a stud in the shape of a rose. Her dark hair cascaded like gentle waves over the gold hoops in her ears. Alvaro suspected that half the patrons of La Piedra came just to see her; he knew it was at least true for him.

"Careful now. You wouldn't want to waste your best lines on me," she teased.

"I reserve all my best lines *especially* for you." Alvaro leaned on his elbows on the wooden bar top. "Let me take you out. Better yet, let me cook for you. Food is a love language, you know."

She laughed lightly. "Ask me again next week."

"I will," he promised. "And in the meantime, a mojito, *por favor?*"

Luisa turned to make his drink, and Alvaro caught a glimpse of the butterfly tattooed on her left shoulder. So went the *pasos* of their dance, the steps of their own personal salsa; compliment, advance, reject, drink. And repeat.

Alvaro tore his gaze from her and glanced around the bar, swaying gently along to the rapid and animated music. The patrons were a pleasant mix of music-loving locals and tourists, mostly American, generally peppered by some Europeans and the occasional group of Asians, all of them seeking the authentic Cuban experience—and with a little luck, he would become a part of someone's experience.

Down at the end of the bar he caught sight of fiery red hair, porcelain skin, a pretty smile. A young woman, likely from the States, mid-twenties at best. She was there with two friends, each seated on barstools on either side of her. One of them said something that made her laugh; she tilted her head back and smiled wider, showing perfect teeth.

Friends could be a problem. The redheaded woman wore no ring and appeared dressed to attract, but it would be the friends who ultimately decided for her.

"She's pretty," Luisa said as she set the mojito down in front of him. Alvaro shook his head; he hadn't realized he'd been staring.

He shrugged one shoulder, trying to play it off. "Not nearly as beautiful as you."

Luisa laughed again, this time at him, as she rolled her eyes. "You're as foolish as you are sweet. Go on."

Alvaro took his drink, his heart breaking just a little more each time Luisa spurned his advances, and went in hopes of seeking the solace of a pretty redheaded American tourist. His methods were well-practiced, though not entirely foolproof. But tonight Alvaro was feeling lucky.

He sauntered along the bar, passing the girl and her two friends without giving them a glance. He took a position at a high-topped table in her line of sight and leaned against it on his elbows, tapping a foot rhythmically to the music and waiting, biding his time. Then, after a full minute, he glanced casually over his shoulder.

The redheaded girl glanced back, and their eyes met. Alvaro looked away, smiling shyly. He waited again, counting to thirty in his head before he looked back at her. She looked away quickly. She was watching him. That was all he needed.

As the song came to an end and the bar erupted in applause for the band, Alvaro plucked up his mojito and approached the girl—not too quickly, shoulders back, head high and confident. He smiled at her, and she smiled back.

"*Hola. ¿Bailar conmigo?*"

The girl blinked at him. "I-I'm sorry," she stammered gently. "I don't speak Spanish…"

"Dance with me." Alvaro's English was flawless, but still he exaggerated his accent to seem more exotic.

The girl's cheeks flushed crimson, almost matching her hair. "I, uh…don't know how."

"I will teach you. It is easy."

The girl smiled nervously and—as he expected—looked to her friends. One of them gave her a small shrug. The other nodded enthusiastically, and Alvaro had to keep his smile from broadening into a grin.

"Um … okay."

He held out a hand and she took it, her fingers warm in his as he led her to the dance floor, little more than the foremost third of the bar where the tables had been pushed outward to make room for the two dozen or so likeminded patrons who had come for the music.

"Salsa is not about getting the steps right," he told her. "It is about *feeling* the music. Like this." As the band began the next song, Alvaro stepped forward with the beat, rocking on his back foot, and moving back again. His elbows swayed loosely at his sides, one hand still in hers, his hips moving with his steps. He was by no means an expert, but had been gifted with natural rhythm that made even the simplest *pasos* appear impressive.

"Like this?" The girl imitated his steps stiffly.

He smiled. "*Sí.* But looser. Do like I do. One, two, three, pause. Five, six, seven, pause."

The girl laughed nervously as she fell into step, loosening up as she became more confident in the movements. Alvaro bided his time, not moving in just yet, waiting for the song to end and another to begin before he gently put a hand on her hip, both of them still moving to the beat, and said, "You are quite beautiful. What is your name?"

The girl blushed deeply again. "Megan."

"Megan," he repeated. "I am Alvaro."

The girl, Megan, seemed to loosen up further after that, succumbing to the charm of a dark, handsome stranger in an exotic land. He had her right where he wanted her. She dared to move closer, closing her eyes, feeling the music as he had instructed, her hips swaying with each small salsa *paso* closer and away—not as shapely or pleasant as Luisa's hips, he noticed, but attractive all the same. Alvaro knew from experience not to move too quickly, to let the music and her imagination take its hold first, and then …

He frowned as a sensation trembled through him. It was unusual for the pulse-pounding electronic dance music from the club next door to be heard through the walls, but he could have sworn that he heard it.

Not heard, he realized—*felt*. He felt a strange thrum in his body, difficult to discern and even harder to describe, so much so that his immediate assumption was the heavy bass from the too-powerful speakers of the next-door club. His redheaded dance partner opened her eyes, her face creasing in a concerned frown. She felt it too.

Suddenly the entire club shifted—or it seemed like it did as a wave of dizziness crashed over Alvaro. He stumbled to the side, catching himself on his left foot before he fell over. The American girl was not so lucky; she fell to her hands and knees. One by one the musicians of the band stopped playing, and Alvaro could hear the groans and frightened gasps of La Piedra's patrons, backdropped by the dim pounding of the bass from next door.

Whatever this was, it was affecting everyone.

A powerful headache prodded at his skull as nausea bubbled up within him. Alvaro looked sharply to his left in time to see Luisa fall behind the bar.

Luisa!

He managed two steps before the dizziness cascaded again, sending him stumbling into a table. Glass crashed to the floor as he overturned it. A woman screamed, but Alvaro couldn't seem to locate it.

He fell to his hands and knees and crawled, determined to find Luisa. To get them out of there, even if he had to drag them both along the floor. But when next he looked up, all he could see were vague shapes. His vision blurred. The sounds of the panicked bar fell away, replaced by only a single high-pitched tone. The vibrant colors of La Piedra dimmed, the edges of his periphery turning brown and then black, and Alvaro let himself slump to the floor, nauseous and dizzy and unable to hear anything but the tone before he lost consciousness.

Chapter Four

Jonathan Rutledge did not want to get out of bed.

It was, to be fair, a terrific bed. Fit for a king, as well as king-sized—although, he mused to himself in those early morning hours, perhaps it would be more fitting to call it president-sized.

He groaned as he rolled over and instinctively reached for the empty spot beside him. Strange, he thought, how he still stuck to his side of the bed even when Deidre was out of town. He was astounded by how quickly she had taken to her new position; currently she was on a circuit through the Midwest, lobbying for funding of art and music programs in public schools, while he pushed his face further into a down pillow as if it might drown out the sound that he knew was coming any moment.

And with that, the phone at his bedside rang again.

"No," he told it. It was Thanksgiving Day. The only things on his schedule were to pardon a turkey, pose for some photos with his daughters, and then enjoy a nice, private meal with them. Why were they bothering him at the crack of dawn on a holiday?

A sharp knock at the door startled him. Rutledge sat up, rubbed his eyes, and asked loudly, "Yes?"

"Mr. President." A female voice floated to him through the thick door of the White House master suite. "It's Tabby. May I come in?"

Tabitha Halpern, his Chief of Staff. She couldn't be bringing good news this early, and definitely not coffee.

"If you have to," he muttered.

"Sir?" She hadn't heard him.

"Come in, Tabby."

The door swung open and Halpern entered, dressed smartly in a navy blue pantsuit with a crisp white blouse. She took two brisk steps inside and then paused just as suddenly, casting her gaze at the carpet, seemingly uncomfortable standing over the president while he was still lying in bed in silk pajamas.

"Sir," she told him, "there's been an...incident. Your presence is required in the Situation Room."

Rutledge frowned. "What sort of incident?"

She seemed hesitant to say. "A suspected terror attack in Havana."

"On Thanksgiving?"

"It occurred late last night, but...technically yes, sir."

Rutledge shook his head. What sort of deviants planned an attack on a holiday? Unless..."Tabby, does Cuba celebrate Thanksgiving?"

"Sir?"

"Never mind. Is there time for coffee?"

She nodded. "I'll have some brought up immediately."

"Great. Tell them I'll be there in twenty minutes."

Tabby turned on a heel and marched out of the bedroom, closing the door behind her and leaving Rutledge grumbling under his breath about the injustice of it all. At long last he swung his bare feet out of the bed and stood, stretching and groaning again and wondering, for what must have been the ten thousandth time, how he had ended up living in the White House.

The technical answer was a simple one. Five weeks earlier Rutledge had been the Speaker of the House—and a damned good one at that, if he could say so himself. He had gained a reputation over his political career as a man who could not be bought, who stuck to his moral code and did not sway from his beliefs.

But then came the news of former President Harris's involvement with the Russians and their plan to annex Ukraine. With the incontrovertible evidence of an interpreter's recording, impeachment proceedings went dizzyingly fast. Then, with minutes to midnight before Harris's definitive ousting, the president threw a hopeful Hail Mary for a reduced sentence by implicating his own VP. Vice President Brown folded like a lawn chair, pleading no contest to having knowledge of Harris's involvement with Kozlovsky and the Russians.

It happened in the span of a single day. Before Rutledge had even finished reading the transcript of Brown's testimony, Harris's impeachment was approved by the Senate, and the VP resigned with a trial pending. For the first time in US history, the third man in line, the Speaker of the House, would take the seat in the Oval Office—Democrat Jonathan Rutledge.

He didn't want it. He had assumed that leading the House of Representatives would be the pinnacle of his career; he'd held no aspirations to go any higher than that. And he could have stated those four little words that would have made all the difference—"I decline to serve"—but in doing so he would have been letting down his entire party. The President Pro Tempore of the Senate was a Republican from Texas, about as far right on the political spectrum as one could go in the democratic system.

And so Speaker Rutledge became President Rutledge. His next step would have been to nominate a vice president and have Congress vote them in, but it had been four weeks since his inauguration and he hadn't done so yet, despite mounting pressure and criticism. It was a very careful deliberation to make—and after what the last two administrations had done, there weren't exactly people lining up around the block for the job. He had someone in mind, the sharp California senator Joanna Barkley, but his time in office thus far had been so tumultuous that it seemed controversy and scrutiny awaited him around every corner.

On any given day, it was enough to want to give up. And he was keenly aware that he could; Rutledge could nominate Barkley as his VP, get the vote of approval from Congress, and then resign, making Barkley the first female president of the United States. He could justify it by the whirlwind of events surrounding his rise to the office. He would be lauded, at least he imagined, for putting a woman in the White House.

It was tempting. Especially when waking to news of terror attacks on Thanksgiving Day.

Rutledge buttoned up a shirt and knotted a blue tie, but decided to forgo a jacket and instead rolled up his sleeves. An aide wheeled in a cart with coffee, sugar, milk, and assorted pastries, but he simply poured himself a mug, black, and carried it with him as two stoic Secret Service agents silently fell in step beside him as he strode toward the Situation Room.

That was just one more thing he had to get used to, the constant accompaniment. Always being watched. Never truly being alone.

The two dark-suited agents followed him down a flight of stairs and along a hall where three more Secret Service agents were posted, each nodding in turn and acknowledging him with a murmur of "Mr. President." They paused outside a pair of oak double doors, one of the agents taking a post with his hands clasped in front of him while the other opened the door for Rutledge, granting him access into the John F. Kennedy Conference Room, a five-thousand-square-foot center of command and intelligence in the basement of the White House's West Wing, known more commonly as the Situation Room.

The four people already present stood as he rounded the table to take a seat at its head. To his left was Tabby Halpern, and beside her, Secretary of Defense Colin Kressley. The Secretary of State and Director of National Intelligence were notably absent, having been sent to Geneva to speak to the UN about the ongoing trade war with China and how it might impact European imports. In their stead was CIA Director Edward Shaw, a severe-looking man whom Rutledge had never actually seen smile. And beside him was a blonde woman in her late thirties, professional but admittedly stunning. A glance at her slate-gray eyes lit a glimmer of recognition; Rutledge had met her before, at his inauguration perhaps, but he couldn't recall her name.

How they all had assembled so quickly, dressed impeccably and so seemingly alert, was beyond him. *Bright-eyed and bushy-tailed*, as his mother used to say. Rutledge suddenly felt downright slovenly in his rolled shirtsleeves and loosely knotted tie.

"Please, have a seat," Rutledge said as he lowered himself into a black leather chair. "We want to give this matter the attention it deserves, but there are places we'd all rather be today. Let's get right into it."

Tabby nodded to Shaw, who folded his hands atop the table. "Mr. President," the CIA director began, "at 0100 hours last night, an incident occurred in Havana, Cuba, specifically near the northern harbor shore in an area called the Malecón, a popular tourist spot. In a span of approximately three minutes, more than one hundred people experienced an array of symptoms, ranging from dizziness and nausea to permanent hearing loss, vision loss, and, in one unfortunate case, death."

Rutledge stared blankly. When Tabby had said a suspected terror attack, he'd assumed a bomb had gone off or someone had opened fire in a public place. What was all this about symptoms and hearing loss? "I'm sorry, Director, I'm not sure I follow."

"Sir," said the blonde woman beside him. "Deputy Director Maria Johansson, CIA, Special Operations Group."

Johansson, right. Rutledge suddenly recalled meeting her, as he had thought, the day of his inauguration.

"What Director Shaw is describing," she continued, "is indicative of an ultrasonic weapon. This sort of concentration on a limited area in such a finite period of time creates parameters narrow enough for us to assume this was a targeted attack."

That did little to explain anything to Rutledge. "I'm sorry," he said again, feeling like the dunce of the room. "Did you say ultrasonic weapon?"

Johansson nodded. "Yes, sir. Ultrasonic weapons are typically used as nonlethal deterrents; most of our Navy's ships are outfitted with them. Cruise ships use them as defense against pirates. But based on what we know happened in Cuba, what we're seeing is much larger in scale and more potent than what our military employs."

Tabby cleared her throat. "The police in Havana collected reports from at least three eyewitnesses who claim to have seen a group of masked men loading a 'strange object' onto a boat in the aftermath of the attack."

Rutledge rubbed his temples. *An ultrasonic weapon?* It sounded like something out of a science fiction movie. It never ceased to amaze and confound him the creative ways humans dreamed up to hurt and kill each other.

"I assume you don't believe this is an isolated incident," Rutledge said.

"We would love to assume so, sir," said Shaw. "But we simply can't. That weapon and the people behind it are out there somewhere."

"And the nature of this attack," Johansson picked up, "appears random. We can't discern a motive to target Havana or a tourist destination other than ease of access and escape, which in a case like this generally indicates a testing ground."

"A testing ground," Rutledge repeated. He had never served in the military, nor had he ever been employed in intelligence or covert operations, but he was fully aware what the deputy director was suggesting: this was the first attack, and there would be others. "And I suppose I should also assume that some of the victims were American."

Tabby nodded. "That's correct, sir. Two suffered permanent blindness. And the lone casualty was a young American woman..." She consulted her notes. "Named Megan Taylor. From Massachusetts."

Rutledge was not prepared to deal with this. It was bad enough that he hadn't yet nominated his vice president, a decision he had been floundering on because he didn't trust himself not to resign immediately. It was bad enough that he was under a microscope, from not only the media but practically the entire world, because of the indiscretions of his two predecessors. It was bad enough that China's new and seemingly irrational leader had sparked a trade war with the US by imposing ever-climbing tariffs on the massive amount of exports manufactured there, which was forecast to cause leaping inflation and, in the long term, potentially destabilize the American economy.

It was bad enough that it was Thanksgiving, for Christ's sake.

"Sir?" Tabby prodded gently.

Rutledge hadn't realized he'd been lost in his own head. He snapped out of it and rubbed his eyes. "All right, brass tacks: do we have reason to believe the United States might become a target?"

"Currently," said Director Shaw, "we should operate under the assumption that the US *will* be a target. We can't afford not to."

"Any intel on who's behind this?" Rutledge asked.

"Not yet," Johansson said.

"But this doesn't quite fit the MO of any of our Middle Eastern friends," offered General Kressley. "If I was a betting man, I'd put hard cash on the Russians."

"We can't make any sort of assumptions," said Johansson firmly.

"Given our recent history," Kressley argued, "I'd call it an educated guess."

"We are an intelligence agency," Johansson fired back across the table, even wearing a thin smirk as she did. "And as such, we'll gather intelligence and work on facts. Not guesses. Not assumptions."

Rutledge found himself very fond of the slight blonde woman who refused to back down from a scowling four-star general. He turned to her and asked, "What do you propose, Johansson?"

"Our top engineer is currently devising a method of tracking this sort of weapon. Based on Havana, I would say the perpetrators are most likely to stay close to the water and target a coastal area. With your approval, sir, I'd like to send a Special Ops team to find them."

Rutledge nodded slowly—a CIA operation sounded far more preferable than sounding the horn on the potential for an attack. *Keep it small, keep it quiet*, he thought. Then an idea came, sudden as an actual light bulb coming to life.

"Johansson," he asked, "one of your agents was the guy that cracked the Kozlovsky affair, yes? He found the interpreter and retrieved the recording?"

Johansson was oddly hesitant, but she nodded once. "Yes, sir."

"What was his name?"

"That would be ... well, his call sign is Zero. Agent Zero, sir."

"Zero. Right." Rutledge rubbed his chin. "Him. I want him on this."

"Um, sir ... he's not quite field-ready at this time. He's transitioning back to operations work."

The president didn't know what that meant, but it sounded like an excuse or a euphemism to him. "It's your job to make him ready, Deputy Director." There was no swaying him now; Rutledge knew that this was the right call. The agent had singlehandedly rescued former President Pierson from assassination, and uncovered the secret pact between Harris and the Russians. If anyone could find the perpetrators and this ultrasonic whatever-it-was, it was him.

"If I may," Johansson said, "the CIA has one of the very best trackers in the world at our disposal. A former Ranger, and a highly decorated agent in his own right—"

"Great," Rutledge interrupted, "send him too. As soon as possible."

"Yes sir," Johansson acquiesced quietly, staring down at the tabletop.

"Is there anything else?" he asked. No one spoke, so Rutledge rose from his seat, and the four others in the Situation Room stood as well. "Then keep me updated, and, uh ... try to enjoy the holiday, I suppose." He nodded to them and strode out of the conference room, where the two Secret Service agents instantly fell in step with him.

Always being watched. Never truly alone.

Actually, he realized, he was wrong about that. In the moment it felt quite the opposite—no matter how many people were around him, advising him, protecting him, prodding him in one direction or another, he did feel truly alone.

CHAPTER FIVE

Zero woke to sunlight filtering through the blinds, warm on his face. He sat up and stretched his arms, feeling well rested. But something wasn't right; this bedroom was bigger than it should have been, yet familiar. Instead of a single bureau opposite him there were two, one of them shorter and topped with a mirror.

This was not his condo in Bethesda. This was his bedroom from New York—*their* bedroom, in the house that *they* shared. Before ... before everything.

And when he slowly turned his head he saw, impossibly, that *she* was there. Lying beside him, the comforter pulled halfway up her torso, sleeping peacefully in a white tank top as she so often did. Her blonde hair was arranged perfectly on the pillow; there was a light smile on her lips. She looked angelic. Carefree. Peaceful.

He smiled and settled back down on the pillow, watching her sleep. Noting the perfect contours of her cheeks, the slight dimple in her chin that Sara had inherited. His wife, the mother of his children, the greatest love of his life.

He knew this wasn't real, but he wished it could be, that this moment could go on forever. He reached for her and gently touched her shoulder, running his fingertips along her smooth skin, down to the elbow ...

He frowned.

Her skin was cold. Her chest was not rising and falling with breath.

Not sleeping. Dead.

Killed by a lethal dose of tetrodotoxin, administered by a man Zero had called a friend, a man that Zero had let live. A decision he regretted every day.

"Wake up," he murmured. "Please. Wake up."

She did not stir. She wouldn't, ever again.

"Please wake up." His voice cracked.

It was his fault that she died.

"Wake up."

It was his fault she was *murdered.*

"WAKE UP!"

Zero sucked in a breath as he sat bolt upright in bed. It was a dream; he was in his bedroom in Bethesda, white walls and plain with only one bureau. He wasn't sure if he had actually shouted or not, but his throat was hoarse and a powerful headache was coming on.

He groaned and checked his phone for the time as he came around to reality. The sun was up; it was Thanksgiving. He had to get out of bed. He had to get the turkey in the oven. He couldn't dwell on a nightmare, because that would mean dwelling on the past, and dwelling about...

About...

"Oh my god," he murmured under his breath. His hands trembled and his stomach turned.

Her name. He couldn't remember her name.

For a long moment he sat like that, his gaze darting around the bedspread as if the answer was going to be written there on its surface. But it wasn't there, and it didn't seem to be in his head either. He could not remember her name.

Zero tore the blankets off of him and practically fell out of bed. He dropped to his hands and knees and reached underneath it, pulling out a fireproof security box the size of a briefcase.

"Key," he said aloud. "Where's the damn key?" He scrambled to his feet again and tore open his top dresser drawer, nearly pulling it out completely. He snatched up the small silver key that laid there, amongst balls of socks and curled belts, and flopped to the floor again as he unlocked the security box.

Inside was an assortment of important documents and items—among them his and the girls' passports, his birth certificate and Social Security card, two pistols, a thousand dollars in cash, and his wedding ring. He pulled all of those out and made a small pile on the floor, because none of them were what he was looking for. He paused briefly on a picture, a photo of the four of them in San Francisco one summer, when Maya was five and Sara was three. The woman in the photo was completely familiar; he could hear her playful laugh in his head, feel her breath on his ear, the warm touch of her hand in his.

"What's her goddamn name?!" His voice wavered as he tossed the photo aside and kept digging. It had to be in here. A lot of his things were still in Maria's basement, but he was certain he would have put it in the security box...

"Thank god." He recognized the manila envelope and tore the flap opening it. There was a single sheet inside, printed on thick stock and embossed with the stamp of a New York court. Their marriage license.

His throat ran dry as he stared at the name. "Katherine," he said to himself. "Her name was Katherine." But there was no relief in it; he felt only terror. The name did not register any memories in him or familiarity. It was like a foreign word on his tongue. "Katherine," he said again. "Katherine Lawson."

Still it didn't sound right, even though it was printed right there in front of his eyes in black and white. Had she been Katherine? Had he called her Katherine? Or maybe it was ...

"Kate."

The air rushed out of him in an enormous sigh. Kate. He called her Kate. The memories rushed back, as sudden as a faucet turning on. Now there was relief, but still it was underscored by the very real fact that for those few harrowing minutes, he had absolutely forgotten his wife's name—and that was not something he could write off as an arbitrary lapse.

Zero grabbed his cell phone and scrolled through his contacts. International charges be damned; he needed answers. Switzerland was six hours ahead. It would be early afternoon there, assuming their office was open.

"Pick up," Zero pleaded. "Pick up, pick up ..."

"Dr. Guyer's office." The female voice that answered the call was soft, tinged with a Swiss-German accent. He would have thought it sultry had he not been panicking.

"Alina?" he asked quickly. "I need to speak with Dr. Guyer, it's very important—"

"I'm sorry," she said, "may I ask who's calling?"

Right. "It's Reid. I mean, Kent. Kent Steele. Zero."

"Ah, Agent Steele," she said brightly. "How wonderful to hear from you."

"Alina, it's urgent."

"Of course." Her demeanor changed on a dime. "I'll get him for you, hold a moment."

Dr. Guyer was a brilliant Swiss neurologist, likely among the best in the world—and also the man who had installed the rice-grain-sized memory suppressor in Zero's head four years earlier, which had wiped his memory clean of any affiliation with the CIA. But Guyer had been acting upon Zero's own request, and later he was also the doctor who performed the procedure that restored his memory, albeit belatedly.

The two of them had been in contact on and off over the last year; the doctor had been delighted to learn that Zero's memories had returned and eager to run further tests, but that required a trip to Switzerland, which Zero hadn't had the time or energy to do—though he fully admitted he owed it to him. Nevertheless, if anyone could tell him what was happening in his head, it was Guyer.

"Agent Steele," said a deep voice through the phone, accented and somber enough to suggest they were going to skip the pleasantries. "Alina said you sounded distressed. What seems to be the trouble?"

"Dr. Guyer," Zero said. "I need help. I'm not sure what's happening, but…" He paused as another horrid thought struck him. What if this wasn't a private call? What if someone was listening in? The CIA had tapped his personal lines before. And if they heard all this…

You're being paranoid. Don't become that person again.

Even so, once the thought was in his head, he couldn't shake it. It was best to err on the side of caution, after all. He'd just made his way back into the CIA, and it felt good. Like his life had purpose again. If they heard about this, things could change very quickly for him—and he didn't want to fall back into the listless, fifteen-month depressive episode he'd found himself in before.

"Agent Steele? Are you still there?"

"Yes. Sorry." Zero did his best to keep his voice even and casual as he said, "I'm, uh… having some trouble remembering things."

"Hmm," said Guyer thoughtfully. "Short-term or long-term?"

"I would say more of the long-term."

"And you believe this to be of… concern?" Guyer was choosing his words carefully. Zero wondered if the doctor was thinking the same thing, that their call might be monitored. Someone like Guyer could face a world of trouble for what he'd done—certainly lose his medical license, if not actually face jail time.

"I would say that I think I should schedule that trip to see you sooner than later," Zero told him.

"I see." Guyer fell silent, and in that pregnant pause Zero became certain that the doctor was being as careful as he was. "Well, it so happens that you're in luck. You won't have to come to me; I'm attending a conference next week at Johns Hopkins in Baltimore. I can see you then. I'm sure that one of my colleagues will allow me use of an examination room."

"Perfect." Finally some semblance of relief came. He trusted that the doctor would know what to do—or at least be able to explain what was going on in his head. "Text me the details, and I'll see you then."

"I shall. *Adieu*, Agent Steele." Guyer hung up, and Zero sat heavily on the edge of the bed. His hands were still shaking, and his bedroom floor was a mess of strewn nostalgia.

Maybe it was just a fluke, he told himself. *Maybe the dream rattled me and it was just a brief bout of waking forgetfulness. Maybe I panicked for nothing.*

Of course he didn't truly believe any lie he might tell himself.

But despite whatever was happening in his head, life had to go on. He forced himself to stand, to pull on a pair of jeans and a shirt. He replaced the items back into the security box, locked it, and pushed it under the bed.

In the bathroom he brushed his teeth and splashed some cold water on his face before heading down the hall to the kitchen—just in time to see Maya closing the oven door and setting the digital timer.

Zero frowned. "What's this?"

She shrugged and pushed the sweeping bangs from her forehead. "Just putting the bird in the oven."

He blinked. "You're cooking the turkey? Is that something they teach you at West Point?"

Maya smirked. "No." She held up her phone. "But Google does."

"Well...okay then. Guess I'll just get myself some coffee." He was again pleasantly surprised to find that she'd already made a pot. Maya had always been as independent as she was intelligent, but this almost seemed to him as if she was trying to pull some weight around. He couldn't help but wonder if she was feeling as helpless about Sara's situation as he was; maybe this was her way of showing support.

So he decided to stay out of her way and let her do what she would. He took a stool at the counter and stirred his coffee, trying to push the morning's unpleasantness out of his mind. A few minutes later Sara trudged her way into the kitchen, still in pajamas, eyes partially open, her red-blonde hair tousled.

"Morning," Maya said cheerfully.

"Happy Thanksgiving," Zero chimed in.

"Mmph," Sara grunted as she dragged herself to the coffee machine.

"Still not a morning person, huh, Squeak?" Maya ribbed gently.

Sara grunted something else, but he saw the hint of a smile on her lips at the sound of her childhood nickname. He felt a warmth inside him that wasn't just the coffee; this was a feeling he had lacked for some time, the feeling of truly being at home.

And then, naturally, his cell phone rang.

The screen showed him that it was Maria calling and he winced. He had forgotten to text her the time and address to come today. Then he panicked all over again; it wasn't like him to forget something like that. Was this another symptom of his ailing limbic system? What if he hadn't actually forgotten, but it had been pushed out, just like Kate's name had?

Calm down, he commanded himself. *It's just a little absentmindedness, nothing more.*

He took a breath and answered the phone. "I am so sorry," he said immediately. "I was supposed to text you, and it completely slipped my mind—"

"That's not why I'm calling, Kent." Maria sounded somber. "And *I'm* the one who should be sorry. I need you to come in."

He frowned. Maya noticed and mirrored his expression as he rose from the stool and sought the relative privacy of the adjacent living room. "Come in? You mean to Langley?"

"Yes. I'm sorry, I know the timing couldn't be worse, but we have a situation and I need you in this briefing."

"I…" His first instinct was to refuse outright. Not only was it a holiday, and not only was he still dealing with Sara's recovery, but Maya was visiting for the first time in a long time. Throw in an ample helping of terrifying memory loss and Maria was right; the timing couldn't be worse.

He almost blurted out, "*Do I have to?*" but held his tongue for fear of coming off as petulant.

"I don't want to do this any more than you do," Maria said before he could think of any way to refuse. "And I really don't want to pull rank." Zero read that part loud and clear; Maria was reminding him that she was his boss now. "But I have no choice. This isn't coming from me. President Rutledge asked for you personally."

"He asked for me?" Zero repeated dully.

"Well, he asked for 'the guy that cracked the Kozlovsky case,' but close enough…"

"He could have meant Alan," Zero suggested hopefully.

Maria chuckled halfheartedly, though it came out as barely more than a breathy sigh. "I'm sorry, Kent," she said for the third time. "I'll try to keep the briefing short, but…"

But this means I'm being sent into the field. The subtext was plain as day. And worse, there was no excuse or defense he could give to turn it down. He was under the CIA's thumb for what he'd done, now more than ever—and he couldn't very well say no to the president, who was for all intents and purposes his boss's boss's boss.

"Okay," he relented. "Give me thirty minutes." He ended the call and groaned softly.

"It's all right." He spun quickly to find Maya standing behind him. The condo wasn't big enough for him to actually take the call privately, and he was certain she could ascertain the nature of the conversation even hearing only his side of it. "Go, do what you have to do."

"What I have to do," he said plainly, "is be here with you and Sara. It's Thanksgiving, for crying out loud…"

"Apparently not everyone got the memo." She was doing the same thing he tended to do; attempt to diffuse the situation with gentle humor. "It's okay. Sara and I will take care of dinner. Get back when you can."

He nodded, grateful for her understanding and wanting to say more, but ultimately he just murmured "thank you" and headed to his bedroom for a change of clothes. There was nothing more to say—because Maya knew just as well as he did that his day would be much more likely to end on a plane than it would sharing Thanksgiving with his daughters.

Chapter Six

If anyone were to consider the phrase "Middle America," the images they conjured would likely be shockingly close to that of Springfield, Kansas. It was a town surrounded by gently sloping farmland, a place where the cows outnumbered the citizens, so small that one could hold a single breath while driving clear through it. Some would find it idyllic. Some would call it charming.

Samara found it disgusting.

There were forty-one towns and cities in the United States named Springfield, which made this town not only unremarkable, but particularly uninspired. Its population hovered around eight hundred; its main street consisted of a post office, a bar and grill, a mom-and-pop grocer, a pharmacy, and a feed store.

For all of those reasons and more, it was perfect.

Samara pulled back her bright red hair and bunched it into a ponytail, exposing the small tattoo on the back of her neck, the single simple character for "fire"—which transliterated in Pinyin to Huŏ, the surname she had adopted after defecting.

She leaned against the commercial box truck and examined her fingernails, biding her time. She could hear the music from there, teenagers and young adults playing poorly while marching to the beat of a rattling snare drum. They'd be at her location soon.

Behind her, in the cargo area of the truck, were four men and the weapon. The attack on Havana had gone surprisingly well, easy even. With any luck, the Cuban and American governments would believe it to have been a testing ground, but their weapon had been tested plenty already. The purpose of the Havana attack was much more than that; it was to introduce chaos. To sow confusion. To present the illusion of a fair warning while making the powers-that-be scratch their heads and wonder.

Nearby, Mischa sat on the curb behind the colorful box truck and idly tugged at brown weeds that had made their way through the cracks in the pavement. The girl was twelve, typically sullen, dutifully quiet, and delightfully lethal. She wore jeans and white sneakers and, almost comically, a blue hooded sweatshirt with the word BROOKLYN screen-printed in white letters across the front.

"Mischa." The girl looked up, her green eyes dull and passive. Samara held out a fist and the girl opened her hand. "It is nearly time," Samara told her in Russian as she dropped two objects into the small palm—electronic earplugs, specifically designed to counter a particular frequency.

The weapon itself was unremarkable, ugly even. To see it, most would have no idea what they were looking at, and would hardly believe that such a device was even a weapon—which only worked in their favor. The frequency was emitted by a wide black disc, a meter in diameter and several centimeters thick, which produced the ultra-low sound waves in a uni-directional cone. The most potent of its effects occurred within a range of approximately one hundred meters, but the deleterious effects of the weapon could be felt from up to three hundred meters away. The heavy disc was mounted to a swiveling apparatus that not only held it upright like a satellite dish, but allowed it to turn in any direction. The apparatus was in turn welded to a steel dolly with four thick tires, which also held the lithium-ion bat-tery pack that powered the weapon. The battery alone weighted thirty kilograms, or roughly sixty-five pounds; all together, including the dolly cart, the ultrasonic weapon weighed in at just under three hundred pounds, which was why such weapons were typically mounted on ships or atop Jeeps.

But mounting their weapon on a vehicle would make it far less mobile and far more conspicuous, which was why the four men in the truck were necessary. Each was a highly trained mercenary, but to her they were little more than glorified movers. Had the weapon been lighter, more maneuverable, Samara and Mischa could have handled this operation themselves, she was sure. But they had to work with what they had, and the weapon was as compact as it could be for how powerful it was.

Samara had been mildly concerned about logistics, but so far they had not run into any hitches. Immediately following the Havana attack they had loaded the weapon by ramp onto a boat, which carried them north to Key West. At the small airfield they quickly transferred to a mid-sized cargo plane that took them to Kansas City. It had all been arranged weeks earlier, bought and paid for. Now all they had to do was carry out the careful plan.

Samara meandered casually to the corner of the block as the marching band's music swelled. They were in sight now, heading her way. The box truck was parked at the curb outside the grocer's, two car lengths from the corner where orange cones blocked the road for the parade route.

Samara had done her research. The Springfield Community College put on a Thanksgiving Day parade every year, led by their marching band and following a circuitous two-mile route that started from a local park, wound through the town, and doubled back to the origin. At the forefront of the parade was a young male drum major, wearing a ridiculously tall hat and heartily pumping a baton in one fist. Following them was the tiny college's winless football team, and then their cheerleading squad. After that would be a convertible containing Springfield's mayor and his wife, and after them the local fire department. Bringing up the rear were faculty members and the athletic association.

It was all just so sickeningly American.

"Mischa," Samara said again. The girl nodded curtly and stuck the electronic earplugs into her ears. She rose from the curb and took a position near the cab of the truck, leaning against the driver's side door to avoid the range of the frequency.

Samara unclipped a radio at her belt. "Two minutes," she said into it in Russian. "Power it up." She had taught the team Russian herself, insisted that it was the only language they spoke in public.

An old man in a fleece sweater frowned as he passed by her; hearing someone speak Russian in Springfield, Kansas, was about as strange as hearing a Shar-Pei speak Cantonese. Samara scowled at him and he hurried along on his way, pausing when he reached the corner to watch the parade.

It seemed like the entire town had come out for the event, lawn chairs lined up for several blocks, children eagerly waiting to catch the candy that would be thrown by the handful from buckets.

Samara glanced over her shoulder at the girl. Sometimes she wondered if there was any remnant of childhood left within her; if she observed the other children with longing for what might have been, or if they were alien to her. But Mischa's gaze remained cold and distant. If there was any doubt behind those eyes, she had become an expert at hiding it.

The marching band rounded the corner, horns blaring and drums thrumming, their backs to Samara and the box truck as they marched onward down the block. Young men in jerseys followed on foot—the college's football team, tossing candy into the crowds, kids darting forward and crouching in clusters to snatch it up like carrion birds on a carcass.

A tiny object sailed toward Samara and landed near her feet. She picked it up gingerly between two fingers. It was a Tootsie Roll. She couldn't help but smirk. What an incredibly bizarre tradition this was, the youths of the wealthiest country in the world scrambling over one another to fetch the cheapest of treats tossed idly onto the pavement.

Samara joined Mischa near the cab of the truck, the end facing away from the parade and its patrons. She held out the candy. A flicker of curiosity passed over Mischa's young, passive face as she took it.

"*Spasiba*," the girl murmured. Thank you. But rather than unwrapping and eating it, she stuck it in the pocket of her jeans. Samara had trained her well; she would get a reward when she deserved one.

Samara lifted the radio to her lips again. "Initiate in thirty seconds." She did not wait for a reply; instead she put in her earplugs, a soft but high-pitched tone whining in her ears. The four men in the cargo space of the truck would take it from there. They did not have to expose the weapon; they did not even have to lift the rolling gate at the rear of the truck. The ultrasonic frequency was capable of traveling through steel, through glass, even through brick with little hindrance to its efficacy.

Samara clasped her hands in front of her and stood beside Mischa, silently counting down. She could no longer hear the marching band, or the applause of the parade-goers; she heard only the electronic whining tone of the earplugs. It was strange, seeing so many sights but hearing nothing, like a television on mute. For a moment she thought of that ridiculous adage: *If a tree falls in the forest and no one is around to hear it, does it make a sound?* Their weapon did not make a sound. The frequency was too low to register on a human's auditory spectrum. But there would still be falling.

Samara did not hear the music or the general din of the crowd, and she did not hear the screams when they began either. But mere moments after her countdown reached zero, she saw the bodies falling to the asphalt. She saw the citizens of Springfield, Kansas, panicking, running, trampling one another like so many children clambering for candy. Some of them writhed; several vomited. Instruments clattered to the street and buckets of treats spilled. Not twenty-five yards from her, a football player fell to his hands and knees and spat a mouthful of blood.

There was such beauty in chaos. Samara's entire existence had been based on regime, on protocol, on practice—and yet few knew as well as she did how unreliable all of that could be when mayhem reared its unpredictable head. In those situations, only instincts mattered. It was then that one truly became aware of the self, of what one was capable of. In the chaos that unfolded silently before her eyes, families trampled over their own loved ones. Husbands and wives abandoned their partners in the interest of self-preservation.

Confusion reigned; bodies toppled. The crowd would end up doing more damage to each other than the weapon would do to them.

But they could not linger. She nodded to Mischa, who rounded the cab and climbed into the passenger seat as Samara got behind the wheel and put the key in the ignition. But she didn't turn the engine over just yet. They would give it one more minute—long enough for the fallout of the attack to be considered truly devastating, and leave those who would be pursuing them utterly perplexed by the significance of Springfield, Kansas.

CHAPTER SEVEN

Zero entered the George Bush Center for Intelligence, the headquarters of the CIA, in the unincorporated community of Langley, Virginia. He strode across the expansive marble floor, footsteps echoing as he trod over the large circular emblem, a shield and eagle in gray and white, surrounded by the words "Central Intelligence Agency, United States of America," and headed straight for the elevators.

There was hardly anyone there, a skeleton crew of security guards and a few administrative assistants toiling on paperwork. He was still pretty sour about being called in, being called away from his girls on a holiday, and hoped that the briefing, as its name suggested, would be brief.

But he wasn't about to bet on it.

"Hold the door," called a familiar voice as Zero pressed the button for the sublevel on which the meeting was being held. He stuck out a hand to keep the doors from closing, and a moment later Agent Todd Strickland trotted in beside him. "Thanks, Zero."

"They called you in too, huh?"

"Yup." Strickland shook his head. "Just as I got to the VA hospital, too."

"You spend Thanksgiving with veterans?"

Strickland nodded once, casually, which Zero took as an indication that it wasn't something he wanted to discuss. Todd Strickland was just shy of thirty, thick-necked and well-muscled, still favoring the military fade style of haircut that he'd worn during his time with the Army. His bright eyes, boyish features, and clean-shaven cheeks gave him a youthful and approachable aspect, but Zero knew that behind the façade was a force to be reckoned with, one of the best the Rangers had ever seen. Todd had spent almost four years of his young life tracking insurgents through Middle Eastern deserts, sleeping in sand, climbing through caves, and raiding compounds. He was a fighter, through and through, and yet he'd managed to maintain a compassion that was just as strong as his sense of duty.

"Any idea what this is about?" Zero asked as the elevator doors slid open.

"If I had to guess? Probably the attack on Havana last night."

"There was an attack on Havana last night?"

Strickland chuckled lightly. "You really don't watch the news, do you?" He led the way down an empty corridor. It seemed that just about all of Langley was enjoying the holiday at home with their families—except for them, of course.

"I've been a bit busy," Zero admitted.

"Speaking of, how are the girls?" Strickland was no stranger to Maya or Sara; when the girls' lives were threatened by a psychopathic assassin, the young agent had made a vow that he would keep an eye out for them, regardless of whether Zero was around or not. So far he had stuck to his word.

"They're ..." He was about to simply say "they're good," but he stopped himself. "They're growing up. Hell, maybe grown up already." Zero sighed. "I gotta be honest. If we get sent out somewhere today, I'm not sure what I'm going to do about Sara. I don't think she's well enough to be left on her own."

Strickland paused as they reached the closed conference room door, beyond which the briefing would be held. But he lingered, and reached into his back pocket. "I was kind of thinking the same thing." He handed Zero a business card.

He frowned. "What's this?" The card was simple, ivory, embossed with a website and phone number and the name "Seaside House Recovery Center."

"It's a place in Virginia Beach," Strickland explained, "where people like her can go to ... recuperate. I spent a few weeks there myself, once upon a time. They're good people. They can help."

Zero nodded slowly, a little taken aback by how everyone seemed to see it but him. Maya had already told him that Sara needed professional help, and evidently it was plain to Todd as well. He knew precisely why he'd been blind to it; he wanted to be able to help her. He wanted to be the one who pulled her through it. But he had already known, deep down, that she needed more than he could offer her.

"I hope this wasn't overstepping any boundaries," Todd continued. "But, uh ... I gave them a call to make sure they had space. There's a spot for her, anytime she wants."

"Thank you," Zero murmured. He didn't know what else to say; it certainly wasn't overstepping any boundaries to do something that Zero probably wouldn't have brought himself to do. He stuck the card in his pocket and gestured toward the door. "After you."

He had attended scores of briefings in his time as a CIA agent, and no two were alike. Sometimes they were populated and chaotic, with representatives from cooperating agencies and video conferences with subject-matter experts. Other times they were small, quiet, and confidential. And even though he was certain that this one was going to be the latter, he was still quite surprised to enter the conference room and find only one person seated at the table, a single tablet in front of her.

Strickland seemed equally puzzled, because he asked, "Are we early or something?"

"No," said Maria as she stood. "Right on time. Have a seat."

Zero and Todd exchanged a glance and took seats on either side of Maria, who was at the far head of the long table.

"Well," the younger agent muttered, "isn't this cozy."

"I'm sorry for taking you away from the holiday," she began. "You know I wouldn't if I had a choice." She said it as if it was meant more for Zero; Maria knew precisely who and what was waiting for him at home. After all, she'd been invited as well. "I'll get right into it," she continued. "Last night, an incident occurred on the northern waterfront of Havana, and we have strong reason to believe that it was a calculated terror attack."

She told them everything they knew; that more than one hundred people experienced a wide range of symptoms, and that the proximity of those impacted the worst suggested the use of an ultrasonic weapon positioned near the water's edge. As she explained, her fingertips slid across the tablet's touch-screen, navigating through photos of emergency services in Cuba aiding the victims. Some of them needed support just to stand; others had thin trails of blood running from their ears. A few were carried off on stretchers.

"There was only one casualty," Maria concluded, "a young American woman on vacation. And the weapon was not found, hence our involvement."

Zero had heard of this kind of ultrasonic weapon before, at least something like it, but aside from the tiny sonic grenades that Bixby had cooked up, he didn't have any experience with them. But he had to acknowledge that despite the lack of any visual on a weapon or perpetrators, it did sound very much like a terrorist attack—which only made it more confusing.

"Kent?" Maria prodded. "Penny for your thoughts?"

He shook his head. "Honestly, I'm a little perplexed. Why go through the trouble of building or buying this kind of weapon when a single assault rifle and a few magazines would have done a lot more damage?"

"Maybe it wasn't about the damage," Strickland suggested. "Maybe it was a message. For all we know, the perps could have been Cuban. They targeted a touristy area; maybe they're nationalists, and this was some sort of violent protest."

"It's possible," Maria admitted. "But we need to work on facts—and the only facts we have right now are that American citizens were part of this, one of them is now dead, and this weapon is still out there ... which is where you two come in."

Zero and Strickland glanced at each other, and then Maria. For a minute there, he had started to think that this might have just been an intelligence briefing, keeping them abreast of what had happened in Cuba, but with those few words he now understood what it really meant.

There was no doubt about it; he was being sent back into the field.

"Hang on," said Strickland. "You're saying that *some*one, *some*where in the world, has a fairly portable and powerful sonic weapon, and you want us to what? Just go find it?"

"I understand it's not much to go on..." Maria started.

"It's not anything to go on."

Zero was a little surprised by Strickland's attitude; at heart he was still a soldier, and never spoke that way to a superior, not even Maria. But he understood, because while Strickland expressed indignation, Zero felt a wave of anger. *This* was why he was pulled away from Thanksgiving, from reuniting his family? He felt for the victims of the Havana attack, but his skills were typically put to use stopping nuclear wars and avoiding mass casualties, not to go off on a wild goose chase for a weapon that had claimed a single life.

"We do have something," Maria told Strickland. "A handful of eyewitnesses at the harbor claim to have seen a group of men, four or five of them, wearing some sort of protective mask or helmet, and loading a 'strange-looking object' onto a boat immediately following the attack. The details are sketchy at best, but a few people also reported seeing a woman with bright red hair, possibly Caucasian, among them."

"All right, that's something," Strickland agreed, appearing to shove down any further protests he might have voiced. "So we go to Havana, find out about the boat, who owns it, where it was going, where it is now, and follow the trail."

Maria nodded. "That's the long and short of it. Bixby is working up some tech that should help. And I don't mean to be pushy, but President Rutledge did use the words 'as soon as possible' on this order, so—"

"Can we talk?" Zero blurted suddenly, before Maria could give the official go-ahead for them to act. "Privately?"

"No," she said simply.

"No?" Zero blinked.

She sighed. "I'm sorry, Kent. But I know what you want to say, and I know that if you do I'll likely give in and try to get you off the hook. But this came from the *president*. Not from me, not from Director Shaw—"

"And where's Director Shaw now?" Zero found himself asking heatedly. "At home, I'm guessing? Getting ready to enjoy Thanksgiving with his family?"

"Yes, Zero, that's exactly where he is," she replied firmly. She never called him Zero; coming from her, it felt like being scolded. "Because it's not his job to be here. It's yours. Just like it's not my job to put my own neck on the block for you again and again. My job is to tell you where you need to go and what needs doing." She tapped the tablet twice with a finger. "This is where you're going. This is what you're doing."

Zero stared down at the tabletop, smooth and polished to a reflective sheen. He had foolishly thought that he and Maria could still be friends after all they'd been through. But at the end of the day, this was how it would shake out. She was his boss, and this was what it felt like to have rank pulled on him.

He did not at all like the feeling, not any more than he liked the idea of the president commanding that he be put on this. As far as he was concerned, this was a complete waste of his skills. But he didn't bother saying that.

"Just look at the state of things." Maria's tone softened, but she didn't look directly at either of them. "We've got a trade war on our hands with China. Our ties to Russia are all but severed. Ukraine is less than pleased with us. Belgium and Germany are both still pissed about what they believe was an unsanctioned op last month. No one trusts our leadership—least of all our own people. We don't even have a vice president yet." She shook her head. "We *cannot* allow for the possibility of an attack on US soil, even if it's just a possibility. Not if we can help it."

Zero wanted to argue. He wanted to point out that the efficacy of two men, highly trained or not, was still paltry compared to a cooperative effort of law enforcement agencies. He could understand why they didn't want to make a big public issue out of this, but even so—if they truly wanted to find these people, if they really thought that an attack on the US was likely, they could put out an APB, starting with coastal areas of Florida, Louisiana, Texas, the best estimates of potential targets considering the Havana attack. Have the Cuban government investigate the missing boat. Work together, as they should, to protect their respective citizens and anyone else who might be hurt along the way.

And Zero was about to suggest it aloud too, but before he got the chance, Maria's cell phone rang.

"One sec," she told them before answering with her typical greeting: "Johansson."

Then her face fell slack, and her gaze met Zero's. He had seen that expression before, many times—far too many for comfort. It was a look of shock and horror.

"Send me everything," Maria said into the phone, her voice a hoarse whisper. She ended the call, and he already knew what she was going to tell them before she even said it.

"There's been an attack on US soil."

Chapter Eight

Already? Zero was stunned by the speed with which a subsequent attack had come—he had clearly underestimated the severity of the situation.

But he was even more shocked when Maria told them *where* it happened.

"The attack was on a small town in the Midwest." Maria studied the tablet screen, scrolling through the intel just as fast as it was coming in. "A place called Springfield, in Kansas—population of eight hundred forty-one."

"Kansas?" Zero repeated. If they had gotten all the way to Kansas since the Havana attack, that meant... "They must have traveled by plane."

"Which means this was planned," Strickland added. The young agent stood suddenly, as if there was something he could do in that moment. "But why? What could possibly be significant about a one-horse town in Kansas?"

"No idea," Maria murmured. Then her hand flew to her mouth. "Oh my god." She looked up at Zero, her eyes wide. "There was a parade going on. College kids, families... children."

Zero took a deep breath, working to mentally put distance between the part of him that was a father and former professor, and the part of him that was an agent. "Fallout?"

"Unclear," Maria reported, staring back down at the tablet. "This *just* happened. The first nine-one-one call was twenty-three minutes ago. But..." Her throat flexed in a gulp. "Initial reports from first-responders are claiming sixteen dead at the scene. Though it's likely more."

Strickland paced the short length of the conference room like a tiger waiting to be sprung from a cage. "We can't assume the casualties were entirely the result of the weapon. Some could have been from panic."

"But maybe that's the point," Zero murmured.

"Hang on, we've got a video incoming." Maria tilted the tablet, and both men crowded at her shoulders to see it. She pressed play, and the screen filled with the shaky perspective of someone filming with a cell phone. The scene was of a small town's main stretch, the camera angle directed up the block, catching in its lens the sidewalks jammed with people and chairs on both sides of the avenue.

From around the corner up ahead came a group of young people in green and white uniforms—a marching band, stepping in time with their instruments aloft, the approaching music drowning out the din of applause and cheers.

"They're almost here, Ben!" said a cheerful female voice, presumably the woman behind the camera phone. "Are you ready? Wave to Maddie!"

The camera panned down briefly, showing a little boy who couldn't have been more than five or six, an enormous smile on his face as he waved at the oncoming band. Then it panned back up, showing a group of young men in green jerseys coming around the corner behind the band—a football team, it appeared, tossing handfuls of candy from buckets.

A knot of dread formed in Zero's stomach, knowing that disaster was about to strike.

The transition wasn't sudden. It was slow and bizarre, unfolding over the next several seconds. Zero leaned closer, apprehensive yet rapt as he watched.

First, the camera panned down slightly, and he just barely heard the woman behind it as she muttered, "Does anyone else feel that? What *is* that...?"

Almost at the same time, several members of the band stepped out of cadence. One by one, instruments stopped playing as gasps and confused shouts mingled with the cheers.

A trumpet hit the street. Then a body. Band members stumbled. Behind them, the young men in jerseys keeled. The camera shook terribly as the woman whipped left and right, looking for a source, or perhaps trying to make sense of what was happening.

"Ben?" she shrieked. "Ben!"

Screams rose from the crowd as it surged in every direction. For all of two seconds, Zero witnessed absolute chaos; people running over one another, holding their heads, clutching stomachs, falling over. Then the phone was dropped to the street and the screen went black.

"Jesus," Strickland murmured.

Zero rubbed his chin as he stepped back from the table. He had only been half-right; it was true that a single assault rifle would have done more damage, but this—an invisible force, a hidden weapon, no assailants in sight—this was downright harrowing. It had simply swept through the street like a slow breeze, affecting hundreds of people in seconds. If something like this got out...

"Is this video public?" he asked.

"I hope not," Maria said, clearly thinking the same thing he was. "It came from Springfield PD, which is..." She consulted the tablet again. "Only five officers strong. We'll do what we can on our end, but I doubt they'll be able to keep that under wraps."

"If that gets out, people are going to panic," said Strickland.

"Exactly," Zero agreed as he worked out a theory aloud. "In Havana, they struck at a packed tourist district. In Kansas, a busy parade route. Populated areas that appear random. Maybe they're trying to prove that their weapon is just a catalyst, and that people will do just as much damage to each other as they can do to them."

"So it could be a message after all," said Strickland as he paced the conference room.

It was the only thing that made sense in the moment; an attack on such a small town was an attempt to make their targets appear random in order to sow panic and confusion. "But if that's the case, what would happen if they got this thing into New York City? Or Washington, DC?"

Strickland stopped pacing. "They're practically taunting us. Telling us that the next target could be anywhere. At any time."

"So far local authorities aren't sure what happened," Maria announced. "It doesn't seem like anyone but us is linking it to the sonic attack on Havana—yet."

"But as soon as they do," Zero added, "no one is going to feel safe." He was already imagining it; something as innocent as walking down a busy street and being caught in an ultrasonic blast. Not knowing what was happening or where it was coming from or what to do or how to stop it.

It was a terrifying thought, even for him.

Maria's tablet chirped suddenly. Zero glanced over her shoulder to see an incoming call on the CIA's encrypted server, but instead of displaying a source it simply read, "SECURE."

Maria took a breath and answered. It was a video call; a smartly dressed brunette woman suddenly appeared, looking solemn as a statue.

"Deputy Director," said the woman by way of greeting.

"Ms. Halpern."

Zero didn't recognize the woman's face, but he knew the name; Tabitha Halpern was the White House Chief of Staff under President Rutledge. And he knew the background behind her quite well. She was sitting in the Situation Room, a place he had been numerous times before.

"I have the president here with me," Halpern said. "He'd like a word." She reached forward and swiveled the screen until it settled on Jonathan Rutledge, seated at the head of the conference table. He wore a white shirt with the sleeves pushed to his elbows, a blue tie knotted loosely around his neck, and a world-weary expression on his face.

"Mr. President." Maria nodded. "I'm sorry you had to take that seat twice in one day."

"So you've heard?" Rutledge said, skipping the formalities.

"Yes sir. Just now."

"Is that him behind you? I want to speak to him."

Zero hadn't realized that he was partially in the camera's view—and if he knew that he would be videoconferencing with the president, he would have put on something nicer than a T-shirt and a light jacket. Maria passed him the tablet, and he held it in front of him.

"So you're the one they call Zero," Rutledge said simply.

"Yes sir, Mr. President," he replied with a curt nod. "It's unfortunate that we have to meet under these circumstances."

"Unfortunate. Yes." Rutledge rubbed his chin. There was something about him that seemed... well, to Zero it seemed less than presidential. He looked lost. He looked like a man in over his head. "Have you seen the video of the attack, Agent?"

"I have, sir. Just now. 'Terrible' doesn't quite do it justice, but it's the first word that comes to mind."

"Terrible. Yes." The president nodded, his gaze unfocused and far away. "Do you have children, Agent Zero?"

It seemed an odd question—especially one to ask of a covert operative whose identity was supposed to be confidential, but Zero told him, "Yes. Two daughters."

"Same here. Fourteen and sixteen." Rutledge put his elbows on the table and at last looked Zero in the eye, or his best approximation through a camera. "I need you to find these people. Find this weapon. Put a stop to this. Please. This cannot happen again."

Under even normal circumstances, which these were far from, Zero would not be able to deny an order from the President of the United States. Still, he didn't need Rutledge to implore him to take on the operation. From the time Maria had announced an attack on US soil, he'd already known that this was not something he would be able to turn away from. It was coded into his DNA; if there was something he could do about it, he would do it.

"I will." He glanced over at Strickland and corrected himself. "We will, sir."

"Good. And tell Johansson that you are to have *every* resource made available to you."

Zero frowned at that; it seemed like an odd emphasis to put on the statement, one that was likely meant more for Maria than for him.

"Godspeed," said Rutledge, and he ended the video call abruptly.

Zero passed the tablet back to Maria, who immediately checked for incoming updates on the scene in Kansas.

Strickland sighed heavily. "There's just one problem. Havana's a dead end now, and if they can travel as quickly as they did, there likely won't be anything to find in Kansas either. We have less to go on than we did before."

"That's not entirely true." Maria looked up from the tablet. "An eyewitness in Springfield, an elderly man, reported that he passed a woman on the street just moments before the attack—a white woman with bright red hair. Just like in Cuba. And this man claims he heard her speaking Russian into a radio."

"Russians?" Zero parroted. He shouldn't have been surprised, not after everything that had happened in the last year and a half. But the previous plots had involved secret cabals, huge sums of money, powerful people. This didn't feel at all like the same MO, nor could he ascertain a motive for this kind of attack beyond some sort of revenge scheme.

"Even so," Strickland pointed out, "'Russian redhead' doesn't exactly narrow things down."

"You're right." Maria pulled out her cell phone. "But there's something that can." She pressed a button and then said into the phone, "I'm coming down. I need OMNI."

"What's OMNI?" Strickland asked before Zero got the chance.

"It's ... complicated," Maria said cryptically. "But I'll show you." She rose from her chair, bringing the tablet with her as she headed for the door.

Zero knew that "coming down" likely meant going to Bixby's lab, the subterranean research and development arm of the Central Intelligence Agency. They were already on a sub-level, and the odd engineer was the only one below them—at least as far as Zero was aware.

He also knew by now that he was not going home, not having dinner with his girls. Once they were out in the empty corridor he said, "Hang on. Can I make a call?"

Maria hesitated, but nodded. "All right. But make it quick. We'll meet you at the elevators." The two of them headed down the hall as Zero pulled out his cell phone—as well as the small white card that Strickland had given him.

With his finger on the call button, he changed his mind and instead opened the video calling app, holding the phone in front of him at an angle so his face was in view of the camera.

The line rang only once before Maya answered. Her face was etched with concern, and he could see behind her that she was standing in the kitchen. "Dad?"

"Maya. Something's come up."

"I know," she said somberly. "I've been watching the news since you left."

"It's already on the news?"

"There's a video," she told him. "From someone who was there."

Zero winced. If the video had already leaked, there would be no way to stifle it. By now it was likely on social media, which meant that within minutes it would be viral, if it wasn't already, shared and re-shared on millions of screens.

But if he was judging Maya's expression correctly, she had thought it just as frightening as he had. And if that was the case, she would understand what he had to do.

"Dad, what the hell *was* that?" she asked.

"I can't say," he told her, being purposely vague. "But we need to find the people behind it. Which means I need you to do something for me... and for your sister."

"Of course," she agreed immediately. "Whatever you need."

"Thank you. But first... can you put Sara on?"

"One sec." The screen blurred with movement as Maya passed the phone off, and a moment later Sara looked back at him on the tiny screen, her gaze flat and her voice low. "You're not coming home, are you?"

"Sara. You know there's no place I'd rather be than home with you..."

"Dad," she interrupted, "you don't have to talk to me like I'm a kid."

"Please," he implored, "let me finish. I need to say this, and I don't have a lot of time." He took a breath and gathered his thoughts. "There's no place I'd rather be than home with you—and there's no place I'd rather *you* be than home with me. But you're right; you're not a kid anymore. I can't treat you like you are. We both know that you need more than what I can offer you."

Sara picked up right away on what he was suggesting. "I don't want to go to one of those places. They're not for people like me."

They're precisely for people like you, he thought, but he didn't want to say that and risk turning it into an argument. "This one is," he said instead. "It's a nice place, in Virginia Beach. Strickland recommended it. He spent some time there himself. You trust him, don't you?"

Sara remained silent. He knew she did, but admitting it meant that she was budging on her position. "I want to stay with you," she said at last. "I'm doing better. I don't need rehab."

"You do need it," Zero countered, keeping his voice gentle. "You just don't want it, because..." A thin, sad smile spread on his lips. "Because you're more like me than you want to admit. You think like me. You've done great these past four weeks, but you've always kept an escape route in your head. I've seen it in your eyes. Plotting how to get a fix. Where you might go. How far you could get."

Sara didn't deny it, but she didn't look directly at him, either.

"But that's not you," he continued. "That's the addiction. These people can help. Since you're emancipated, I can't force you to go. It has to be your choice... but I'd like you to try it."

He fell silent, waiting for her response. The faraway look in her eye wasn't defiance, or anger—it was fear. She was afraid of going to a place like that. Maybe, he thought, she was afraid of being forced to acknowledge some ugly truths about herself.

"Okay," she said finally in a murmur. "Okay, Dad. I'll go. I'll try."

He did his best to hold back the sigh of relief and smiled appreciably instead. "Good. Thank you. This will be good for you, I promise. I'll come visit you as soon as I'm able."

She nodded, and he could have sworn he saw the hint of tears in her eyes. But none fell; she wouldn't let them.

"Where's your sister?" he asked.

Maya appeared over Sara's shoulder, evidently having heard the exchange. "I'm here."

"Will you take her?" he asked. "Enjoy today together. Go tomorrow. Take my car."

Maya nodded. "Of course."

"Thank you. The place is called Seaside House. Todd called ahead; there's a spot for her whenever she arrives." He glanced over his shoulder at the empty corridor. Maria and Strickland were waiting for him. "I have to go now. I love you both."

"Love you too," Sara said quietly.

"Be safe," Maya told him.

He ended the call. For a moment he just stood there, wondering if he'd made the right call. Hoping that Sara didn't find a reason to hate him all over again. Painfully aware that it was impossible for the same person to hold the titles of world's best father and world's best covert operative at the same time.

Then he gathered all those thoughts, shoved them aside, and strode toward the elevators to meet up with the other two—and to find out just what the hell this OMNI thing was.

Chapter Nine

Zero was quiet on the elevator ride down to the sublevel that contained the CIA's top-secret research and development department. Neither Maria nor Todd asked about the nature of the call he'd made or its outcome, though he was certain they both wanted to; at one time or another they'd both been close with the girls.

But he was glad they didn't ask. He didn't really want to talk about it, let alone start doubting his decisions again.

The elevator chimed and the doors opened onto a subterranean corridor with cinderblock walls painted gray, windowless and lit with fluorescent lights. Maria's heels clacked against the cold floor, the sound reverberating off the walls, until she came to an unmarked steel door that resembled a vault. She swiped a keycard in the narrow slot near the handle. The electronic lock buzzed loudly as several bolts slid aside, and she pushed the door inward.

No matter how many times Zero had come to the lab, as they called the R&D sublevel's main floor, it was still astonishing to step into. The walls and floor were glaring white, always appearing as if they'd just been polished. Powerful halogen bulbs burned bright as daylight overhead, even though they were deep underground. Tall stainless steel shelves and lengthy workbenches were arranged symmetrically in the shape of a huge H running almost the entire length of the warehouse-size main chamber.

When Zero's memories had returned, he was able to remember just how many times he'd been down there before, to prepare for every op, to gear up for every raid. The familiar scent, a blend of motor oil and a vague antiseptic smell, was downright nostalgic to him.

Maria led the way across the lab's floor toward an indistinguishable hissing sound. As they rounded a corner they found a man in a gray shield mask and thick gloves, bent over the guts of some device that Zero could not begin to guess the nature of. The source of the hiss was the arc welder in his hand, blue sparks cascading from the metal.

"Bixby," Maria called, not wanting to get too close. "Bixby!"

The looked up sharply, apparently startled by their sudden appearance. He quickly turned off the arc welder and lifted the shield of his heavy-duty mask, grinning sheepishly behind it.

"Sorry," said Bixby. "I was just tinkering while I waited."

Bixby was in his early sixties, but no one would have guessed it by his youthful smile and bright eyes. When he wasn't wearing a welding mask, his gray hair was always parted and combed neatly over his black horn-rimmed glasses. It was strange seeing him in the thick leather gloves and mask, while wearing a blue shirt and red tie under a gray vest. The small black smudge of grease on his left cheek only served to complete his dichotomous look.

"Just tinkering, huh?" said Strickland. He glanced around, noticing that no one else was present in the lab—there were usually at least a couple of other engineers or interns about—before asking, "Bixby... you don't *live* here, do you?"

"Of course not," he chuckled. "Why do you ask?"

"Well, because today is Thanksgiving," Strickland said plainly.

"Oh." The CIA's top engineer frowned. "That explains why my brother keeps trying to call me..."

"Bixby," Maria said firmly. "You've seen the report?"

He nodded gravely. "I have. Terrible shame, that. Definitely indicative of an ultrasonic attack, just like in Cuba. Very potent; I daresay more powerful than anything our military is using currently."

"We need OMNI," Maria told him.

Bixby's gaze flitted from her to Strickland to Zero and back to her. "Are you... sure?"

She nodded curtly. "The president said 'every resource.' I know you don't like it. I don't like it either. But we need it."

"Okay. Right this way, Agents." Bixby tugged off the thick leather gloves and, with a wave of his hand, gestured them to follow as he headed toward an antechamber of the lab.

Zero understood now why Rutledge had placed the odd emphasis when he said "*every* resource." Bixby's hesitation could only mean that he and Strickland weren't cleared to know what this machine was—which was strange, because he thought he had the CIA's highest security clearance. But then again, he realized, he of all people should know that behind every secret was usually another secret. No matter what he was told, there was simply no way he knew everything there was to know about the CIA, let alone the US government.

Take, for instance, the lab itself, a veritable labyrinth of rooms and corridors so expansive that it might have run the entire length of CIA headquarters. Zero knew that the halls beyond the main floor held an armory, a firing range, a clean room, a radiation chamber, several other workshops and smaller dedicated labs—and he was still certain that he'd only seen a portion of what was kept down there.

Case in point: Bixby led them out of the lab and past the firing range, down a hall, and through a small robotics lab, pausing at each door to swipe the keycard he kept on a lanyard at his hip. They entered another white corridor, one that Zero was fairly certain he'd never been in before, and strode down its length until Bixby stopped at a place where there didn't appear to be anything at all.

The engineer ran one finger down the wall, feeling for something—a small round indentation, hardly bigger than a dime and veritably invisible unless one knew it was there. He craned his neck and held his eye to it; a blue light flashed, scanning his retina, and a narrow section of the white wall slid aside with a small whoosh.

Zero hadn't even noticed a seam.

"You guys really don't want anyone finding this thing, huh?" Strickland noted.

They found themselves in a chamber no bigger than Zero's bedroom in Bethesda. Three of the walls were lined with rack upon rack of black servers, small lights at the front of each giving the room a bizarre purplish glow, blue wires running between them and bundled impeccably. The room smelled like a hospital, and the collective hum of what must have been a hundred machines made it feel as if the floor was vibrating.

At the far end was a single flat-screen monitor, twice as wide as it was tall, mounted to the wall and displaying a blue background with four simple white letters: OMNI. Beside the monitor was a single black speaker, about a foot and a half in diameter—and if Zero wasn't mistaken, it was vibrating slightly.

Bixby held both arms out in a grand gesture as the hidden door slid closed behind them. "This," he announced, "is OMNI."

"Great," Strickland said flatly. "...What is it?"

Zero frowned as he crouched slightly, holding his ear close to the dark speaker. It *was* vibrating with sound, just barely audible over the collective hum of the servers. It sounded at first like just a dull hiss—but no, he realized. It was voices. Many of them, overlapping one another, each one indistinguishable from the next, like a thousand whispers at the same time.

He pulled away quickly. The sound of it was unsettling.

"What you're looking at is one of the CIA's most closely guarded secrets," Maria told them. "Very few people in the world know about this. So when this is all over, I'd appreciate if you both promptly forgot about it."

"What does it do?" Strickland asked. But Zero already had a hunch. The haunting whispers he'd heard through the speaker were voices—conversations, and possibly ones that were going on at that very moment.

"When Director Shaw came over from the NSA," Maria explained, "one of his first priorities was establishing a closer cooperation between the two agencies. It's no secret that Title Two of the Patriot Act allowed for the surveillance of anyone who is suspected to be involved in terroristic activity. The NSA can tap into any on-network device … phones, computers, tablets, traffic cams, radio frequencies, open-circuit security systems, you name it."

"Sure," said Zero, "as long as the person they're surveilling is a suspect."

"But what happens when we don't have a specific suspect to monitor?" Maria asked pointedly. "What happens when national security is threatened, and the perpetrators could be anywhere?"

"Then … everyone becomes a suspect," Strickland murmured.

She nodded. "Think of OMNI like a search engine for sound. In the event of a pending attack—like we find ourselves in now—it helps us narrow our search. There's an emergency protocol that can only be activated by the president. The NSA opens all available channels, more than a billion devices in just the continental United States, and the results filter through OMNI."

"But like a search engine," Bixby chimed in, "it's not foolproof. We need parameters in order to home in on the results, to get what we want, or else we could end up with a thousand dead ends." He turned to Maria and asked, "So, what are our parameters?"

"Russian chatter," she told him. "Specifically female. Flag keywords that could pertain to the attacks—'sonic,' 'Havana,' 'Kansas,' anything else you can think of."

The wide screen behind them flickered suddenly, the word "OMNI" vanishing and replaced by rapidly scrolling code.

"There's the executive order," Bixby noted. "NSA is active." He pulled a sliding keyboard from beneath the monitor and began inputting the parameters.

Zero was torn. On the one hand, he was grateful they had something to give them a lead, an edge in finding these people, and hopefully before another attack occurred. But on the other hand, the mere existence of something like OMNI felt … controversial wasn't the right word. It just felt wrong.

He was glad to be back with the agency. But more than once before, he had thought about packing up with the girls and going dark, just leaving and starting anew somewhere else. Much like he had told Sara only minutes earlier, they thought alike; he too was always keeping an escape route in mind.

A machine like OMNI would make that very difficult, if not impossible.

The dark speaker hummed louder as Bixby's fingers flew across the keys, narrowing the filtered results from a billion devices. Voices came through a dozen at a time; first in Russian, then decidedly female, vacillating between brief snippets of hundreds of conversations from people who had no idea that the CIA was listening in.

The sound of it made him shudder. He didn't want to be in this room anymore.

"Okay," Bixby announced as he adjusted the settings on his smart watch. "I'll get an alert as soon as we have a viable hit." He turned to Zero and flashed his familiar grin. "In the meantime, let's gear up."

Back on the main lab floor, Zero watched as Bixby laid out an array of gadgets on the stainless steel surface of a workbench. Strickland stood on the other side of the table, though Maria had headed back up to her office with some excuse about paperwork.

There always seems to be paperwork, Zero mused.

"I've got some very cool stuff for you guys," the engineer said proudly. "But first, a few things you should know. This weapon is a high-powered acoustic device that emits 'infrasound,' super low-frequency sound waves that are below the normal limit of what the human ear can detect. You wouldn't hear this type of weapon as much as you would *feel* it. Even at a longer range, one would experience dizziness, nausea, and headaches. At mid-range the possible effects would include all that, plus hearing loss from ruptured eardrums and blurred vision—from the vibration of your eyeballs."

He plucked up a black, kidney-shaped earbud and held it up between his thumb and forefinger. "These are noise-cancelling earplugs that emit a high-pitched frequency, which should be able to combat the long-range effects of the weapon."

"Should?" Strickland raised an eyebrow.

"I'll be honest. They're untested in the field against sonic weapons," Bixby admitted. "But yes, they *should* work—though they won't be able to defend against the more deleterious effects that occur at closer range."

"Which are?" Zero asked. He had witnessed some of them in the video of Springfield, Kansas, but hadn't been entirely sure what he was seeing.

"At the closest range, this kind of ultrasonic weapon could cause permanent hearing loss, blindness, and internal trauma." Bixby said it as simply as a narrator dictating the side effects in a drug commercial. "There's no other way to put it. From what we've seen in the other attacks, the frequency can literally rattle your organs into rupturing."

Zero closed his eyes as an image from the video spun through his head again—specifically the young male football player who had fallen to his hands and knees, spitting blood onto the pavement. He thought of the single casualty in the Havana attack, the young woman, and wondered if that had been her cause of death. It sounded like a horrible way to go.

"If the weapon is anything like what we have," Bixby continued, "the sonic waves would be able to pass through windows and walls, which will make it difficult to locate its source. However, in order to affect the area and number of people that it did, this weapon must be pretty large—bigger than one person could carry, and it would require an external power source. So if you can find it, whoever is responsible will be at a slight disadvantage with mobility."

"But what happens if we find ourselves at ground zero of an attack?" Zero asked. "Or if they realize we're after them and they use the weapon?"

"Ah. That's what this is for." Bixby picked up another gadget, a yellow and black device that looked like a small radar gun with a plastic concave disc facing the front of it. "A sonic detection meter. I adapted this from an industrial ultrasonic leak detector—they use these to find pressurized gas leaks that would otherwise be invisible and inaudible. I recalibrated it to the lowest possible frequency range, so it can at least tell you the direction the weapon is in. At close enough range, it'll pinpoint a location."

"Hang on a sec." Strickland held up a hand. "It sounds like you're saying this thing will only work if the weapon is active."

"Well..." Bixby pushed his glasses up the bridge of his nose. "Yes. That's correct."

Zero frowned. "So in order to pinpoint the location of the machine, we *have* to be in its range—during an attack?"

"Uh..." Bixby chuckled nervously. "I suppose we should just hope that OMNI gets a hit and you find these people first, so it doesn't come to that." He handed the sonic detector to Zero. "Consider it a failsafe."

Zero and Strickland exchanged a concerned glance. They didn't like the sound of that.

"Anyway," Bixby said cheerfully, "the rest of this is your standard fare." He gestured to each item as he rattled them off. "Graphene-reinforced jackets. They'll stop a nine millimeter round at point-blank range, but be careful with anything bigger. Or just try not to get shot in general. These are off-network satellite phones with lithium-ion batteries, fully charged. Ruger LC9 with nine-round box magazine and ankle holster. And of course, the Glock 19, with a seventeen-round magazine and biometric trigger lock. Each is already coded to your thumbprint."

Zero lifted the black pistol, feeling the familiar and welcome weight of it. He had to remember that his aim tracked to the left with his right hand. The raised scars were still prominent, like white-lined henna tattoos, from the injury and multiple ensuing surgeries.

He grabbed up the Glock's magazine in his left, intending to load it—but then he froze.

The feel of the gun was well known, even appreciable in a strange way. But he didn't get that same feeling when he grabbed the magazine. Instead it felt completely foreign to him, and in a moment of searing panic he suddenly realized he had no idea what to do with it.

He had forgotten how to load a gun.

Zero simply stood there, the Glock in one hand and the magazine in the other. He felt eyes on him and glanced up to see Strickland watching him, one eyebrow slightly raised.

"You okay, Zero?"

His expression must have given something away, his undisguised alarm at the sudden failure to remember what to do. Just yesterday he had been on the training course with Alan, expertly loading and reloading, firing rounds into ballistic-gel dummies. Today he was at an utter loss—just like he had been that morning when he had forgotten his late wife's name.

"Of course," he said casually. He turned the magazine over in his hand as if inspecting it, and then set it down again. "Just checking everything out."

"Uh-huh," Strickland said simply. Zero couldn't tell what he might have been thinking, but he didn't say anything further. Instead Todd lifted the other Glock and the magazine, pushed it into the gun until it clicked, and racked the slide. It was a well-practiced move, little more than routine, but one that looked incredibly unfamiliar, even peculiar, to Zero.

What the hell is going on in my brain?

As Strickland pulled the graphene jacket over his shoulders, Zero surreptitiously picked up the gun and the magazine again. He pushed it into the pistol, just as Todd had done, and with some difficulty he pulled back the slide. The resistance of it was more than he thought it would be—or perhaps he had simply forgotten the amount of force required to do what should have been a simple and second-nature task.

But as soon as the slide clicked back into place, the memory did as well. It was as if performing the action brought it back… *Just like riding a bicycle,* Zero thought sourly as he restrained himself from sighing audibly with relief.

What would I do if that happened in the field? In the middle of a firefight?

He should tell Maria, he reasoned. He was compromised. But would she believe him? Or would she think it was an excuse to stay behind, to spend time with his daughters? Even worse—would she have to report it to Director Shaw, and reveal everything that had happened in his past?

He had to do this. And he had to tell himself that it wouldn't happen when he needed it, that his instincts would kick in and take over, as they had so many times before. Even when his memory had been erased his instincts still saved his life on more than one occasion.

He would just have to be careful—and get this done as quickly as possible.

Zero pulled on the jacket and holstered the Glock inside it. Then he strapped the ankle holster and the LC9 to his leg, beneath his jeans, while Bixby packed the rest of the gadgets in a brown messenger bag.

Just as he was finishing, there was a sharp chirp, so loud that it startled Zero, loud enough to be heard clear across the lab. Bixby frowned at his smart watch.

"It's OMNI," he said urgently. "We've got a hit—Russian chatter via a cell phone tower. Talk of an attack." He looked up at Zero and added gravely, "It's time to go."

Chapter Ten

Zero jumped out of the black town car before it came to a complete stop, scooping up the gear bag as he did. Strickland was right behind him as they hurried toward a waiting Gulfstream G650, one of the fastest private jets in the world, its engines already whirring to life.

As soon as the hit had come in from OMNI they'd been dispatched. Zero wasn't even yet sure where they were going; Bixby had promised to update them en route as they tracked the Russian chatter they'd honed in on. A waiting car had taken the two of them straight to a private airstrip just outside of Langley, the jet already there and the pilot on-call for just such an emergency.

The two agents wordlessly jogged to the plane and up the stairway ramp, past the waiting pilot—but then Zero stopped short in the aisle. There was already someone else aboard, looking up at him calmly from a seat at the rear of the jet.

"Maria," he said breathlessly. "What are you doing here?"

"I couldn't in good conscience send you two out on this alone," she said with a small shrug. She had changed her clothes into sneakers and casual wear, and had a gear bag of her own on the seat beside her. "I'm coming with."

Zero threw a glance over his shoulder at Strickland, but the younger agent merely shrugged.

"Are you sure that's a good idea?" he asked, even as the pilot pulled up the ramp and locked the door behind them. "What if you're needed here?"

"For what? A bigger threat than we're already facing?" Maria shook her head. "This isn't negotiable. I'm coming. Besides," she smiled coyly, "if I recall from my *years* of working with you, someone usually needs to save your ass once or twice on these things."

"Ain't that the truth," Strickland muttered as he dropped himself into a seat.

"Well... okay then." Zero took the seat in front of Maria and buckled himself in. It was strange how earlier that morning he had doubted the future of their relationship, wondering how they could ever remain friends when she was his boss—and now he found himself glad, even relieved, that she was coming along.

"There was no paperwork, was there?" he asked over his shoulder.

"Oh, there's always paperwork. I just don't do it."

He chuckled softly, but it was short-lived. "Where are we headed?"

"If you can believe it," Maria said as the jet began a rapid taxi down the runway, "we're going to Las Vegas."

"Vegas?" Strickland asked from the row in front of Zero. "They got to Vegas that quickly?"

"It would fit our theory about them having a plane." Maria scrolled on her tablet, checking the intel as Bixby forwarded it. "OMNI picked up Russian chatter, assumedly female, which definitely mentioned an attack of some nature."

"Oddly enough," Zero murmured thoughtfully, "it makes sense." The more he turned it over in his mind, the more it seemed to fit. "Think about it—Vegas is the number-two most popular tourist city in the US, behind New York. The casinos don't close for holidays, so there'll still be plenty of people on the Strip, and..." He trailed off as a grim realization struck him.

"What? What are you thinking?" Maria prodded.

"Foreigners," he told them. "Foreign tourists that don't celebrate the holiday. That's who's in Vegas right now. That's what makes it an attractive target."

"And attacking foreigners on US soil definitely sounds like these lunatics' MO," Strickland added. "What details we have?"

"Unfortunately, very limited," Maria replied somberly. "They're being careful. The signal was traced to a burner, the first and only call made from it. We won't know if they ditched it unless they use it again. But the call definitely used the word 'attack,' and came from the Strip—specifically the Venetian. Hang on, there's more coming through." She paused briefly before adding: "I've got more of the translation incoming. The call mentioned the words 'rendezvous, illusion, oh-one hundred.' That sounds to me like a meeting and a time."

"We just need to know where." Strickland rubbed his chin as the Gulfstream reached altitude, roaring westward. "Illusion... illusionist? Like a magician? A show, maybe?"

Zero shook his head. It wasn't specific enough; whatever "illusion" meant must have been evident to the recipient of the call. "Illusion," he murmured aloud to himself—not only in English, but in Russian as well.

Where could that mean? He'd been to Vegas twice in his life, the most recent time being almost twenty years earlier, before Maya was even born. He wasn't exactly well-versed in its layout. Hell, last time he had been there, he and Kate had stayed at Treasure Island, which was only a few years old at the time, still new. They had stayed in a room facing the south that looked out on...

"It's not 'illusion'!" he said suddenly, twisting in his seat to face Maria. "It's a mistranslation. It's 'mirage.' As in, the Mirage Hotel & Casino."

"Brilliant. I knew I brought you along for a reason." Maria checked her watch and did some quick calculations. "So the Russians plan on convening at the Mirage at one p.m. At max airspeed and the most direct flight path, this jet can get us there in a hundred and seventy minutes. Which means..." She groaned, deflating visibly. "That we'll have ten minutes *tops* to get there and cut them off."

"No way." Strickland shook his head. "That's not enough time. We need to contact the casino, the local authorities, and make them aware—"

"We can't do that," Zero argued. "If the Russians see an increased police presence, or if the casino evacuates, they might run and we'll lose them again."

"Or worse," Maria added, "they might be inspired to use the weapon prematurely."

"But we'd be avoiding another attack," Strickland countered.

Zero's gaze flitted to the gear bag at his feet. Inside it was the sonic detection meter that Bixby had given him. It was a horrid thought, one that he was ashamed to even entertain—but if they arrived during an attack, at least they could pinpoint the location of the weapon.

He shook it from his head. Strickland was right. Their priority should be to stop it, not to incite one.

"I've got another idea." Maria pulled out her phone and put the call on speaker. "Bixby, can you hack into a Vegas casino's security system and access their cameras without them knowing it?"

"Um..." came the engineer's voice through the phone. "That's, uh, a bit above my pay grade, Deputy Director. But we've got a guy that might be able to. A Danish fellow, name of Tormund."

"Get him on it," she ordered. "I want access to their exterior cameras and casino floor. Reroute them to my tablet."

"It might take some time," Bixby admitted. "You're talking about some of the most secure systems in the world—some of those casinos have better security than *we* do."

"He has two hours," Maria said firmly. "Get it done. Thanks." She ended the call before Bixby could protest further.

"What's the plan here?" Zero asked. "Access the cameras and look for Russians?"

"In a way," Maria replied. "Access the cameras and look for that redheaded bitch everyone keeps talking about."

He nodded. "We'll need a contingency. After all, there are only three of us, and a lot of ground to cover if they split up or try to flee."

"We've got some time to make one," Strickland noted.

Zero settled into his seat, his stomach a knot of blended excitement and dread. Strickland was right; they did have time to plan.

But they had only ten minutes to execute it.

CHAPTER ELEVEN

Sara felt like she had two minds. Even then, sitting in the passenger's side of her dad's SUV with Maya behind the wheel, the day quickly turning to evening as they drove south, she felt it. The second mind. She'd been feeling it for some time now, ever since her dad had found her in the backseat of a drug dealer's car, half-dead and high out of her mind on painkillers.

One mind was hers. That much was clear. She knew who she was, and she knew that what she'd gotten herself into was difficult to come back from. She knew that she shouldn't run or steal or try to get a fix.

But the other one, the second mind that she felt, was different. It was the one that begged for the high. The one that knew she'd be flooded with endorphins from a single hit, the one that remembered all too well how the feeling made the world melt away, erased all the worries and strife and left only the pleasure. It was the mind that told her to run. It was, as her dad had pointed out, the addiction talking—and she didn't like it when that side talked, because it meant that she had to acknowledge that she was, indeed, an addict.

"You know," Maya said quietly beside her. "We don't have to do this today. We can wait until tomorrow, like Dad said."

Sara shook her head as they headed south on I-95. "No," she said quietly. "We can't."

It couldn't wait. The Thanksgiving dinner that Maya had made, the turkey and stuffing and mashed potatoes and cranberry sauce, all of it had tasted like a prisoner's last meal to her. After she had made the agreement with her dad and told him she would give the place a try, everything around her suddenly seemed grayer—and then the other mind, that devious second one, started in.

You could make a run for it. Wait until Maya's asleep, grab what you can, and just leave.

And Sara knew that if they waited until tomorrow, she would try to run. In a moment of lucidity she told Maya that they had to go tonight, after dinner, and drive the three hours south to Virginia Beach. She had to go to Seaside House before she could change her mind.

Maya had agreed, seeming to understand the situation or at least trying to be as supportive as she could. But she couldn't *really* understand, not fully. She didn't know what this was like, and there was no way for Sara to explain it to her.

Even now, even as they headed toward the place that was supposed to help save her, the darkness in her mind told her: *Wait until the next stoplight. Jump out. Make a run for it.*

Maya reached over and gently squeezed Sara's hand. "This is going to be good for you." *You don't need this*, it told her. *You're fine.*

"I looked this place up online. They have a great rating. And it's a really pretty facility." *You'd do better on your own.*

"I bet you'll make friends here," her sister told her.

All they're going to do is convince you there's something wrong with you. That you're broken and need to be fixed.

"Yeah," Sara muttered, though she didn't fully know who she was answering.

"Besides," Maya said brightly, "their program is one of the best on the East Coast. And it's only four weeks—"

"Four weeks?" Sara blurted out. Her dad hadn't mentioned that part.

Maya glanced over at her briefly in concern. "It's not that long, Sara. Some places take a lot longer. It means you'll be home just in time for Christmas."

Sara muttered a halfhearted agreement, though she was suddenly a lot less sure about all of this. Four weeks—that's how long she'd been with her dad, and that had felt like an eternity. An eternity since her last hit. An eternity since Florida.

She thought of Jacksonville, and the ramshackle co-op where she had lived for more than a year as an emancipated minor. She thought of her best friend and roommate, Camilla, the eighteen-year-old Latina who had been teaching her to drive and showed her how to do her eye makeup so that she looked older. She even though of Tommy and Jo, the young couple who lived in the co-op, constantly on her nerves for one reason or another.

Sara hadn't spoken to any of them, not even Camilla, since coming back north. One of her dad's stipulations had been to provide him with all of their phone numbers so he could block them on their shared cell phone account. He didn't want anyone tempting her back to Florida.

Again the two minds crept in.

He was right to do that.

He had no right to do that.

She remembered vividly how it had all started. One morning Sara had been shaken awoke by Camilla because she'd been screaming in her sleep; she still had night terrors about the Slovakian traffickers that had abducted her and her sister. This nightmare was one of the worst she'd ever had; even after waking she trembled from head to toe, barely able to stand let alone go to work. Camilla, in her own way, tried to be a good friend and offered her a half a bar—the street name for a blue oblong Xanax.

It did the trick, calming her nerves at least enough to make it through the day. And it should have stopped there. But the next morning, she realized how much she'd liked the feeling. She wanted another one.

Soon a half a bar wasn't enough. But a full bar made her feel rundown and mute for the whole day, even after work. Then one evening she came home to find Tommy and Jo doing stubby lines off the glass-topped coffee table.

"Want to try it?" Jo had asked her.

"She won't," Tommy had said snidely. He'd always thought of her as a frightened little girl. He had no idea what she'd been through.

Not one to back down, Sara dropped to her knees and put her face to the table and sucked up a thin line of coke from the table's surface. She didn't at all like the way it burned in her nasal cavity. She didn't like the acrid taste at the back of her throat. But less than a minute later, when her brain registered the feeling it gave her, she liked that.

So the cycle went. A bar in the morning, floating dreamily through the day, and a bump at night as a pick-me-up. Though sometimes it was two. Or three. And sometimes she would only get snatches of sleep in a night, a few hours, and she'd need a bump in the morning just to drag herself to work. And then a bar to get through the day. But soon a bar wasn't doing the trick anymore, so Camilla showed her how to use a pill grinder, so she could snort the blue powder instead of taking it orally...

"God," Sara murmured in the passenger seat of the SUV.

"What's that?" Maya asked.

"Oh. Nothing." She hadn't realized she said it aloud. She hadn't really forced herself to think about all of that in a long while. She had been tuning it out—because thinking about was like admitting she had a problem.

You do. You do have a problem.

Dad knew it, and he thought he could help her. He really tried.

Yeah, and now he's dumping you somewhere so he can run off to the CIA.

No, said the other side. *That's not true. What he does is important. More important than...*

Than what? More important than you? More important than taking care of his daughter?

That wasn't fair. She had seen the news, same as Maya. That video...it still gave her chills thinking about it. Her dad had a job to do, and it was stopping people like that. Not being her babysitter. Maya had school. She couldn't expect them to put their lives on pause for her.

"What will you do?" Sara asked suddenly, desperate for something to talk about. Something to take her two minds off the quarrel they were having. "After you drop me off. Will you go back to Dad's?"

Maya shook her head. "No, I don't think so. I don't know when he'll be back. I'll head over to the airport, leave his car in long-term parking, and hop a flight back to New York."

Sara frowned. "Will anyone else be at the school over the holiday weekend?"

"Don't know. I'm sure somebody will be." Maya flashed her a smile and added, "Besides, I'll be home for Christmas break, when you're done. And I'll call whenever I can."

"Yeah," Sara murmured. Maybe her sister did understand, at least a little bit—not about what was going on in her head, but at least part of it. In that brief, fake smile, Sara saw the same kind of loneliness she had seen in the mirror for the past four weeks.

"Hey, if you want," Maya joked, "you're welcome to swap with me. You can go to West Point for the next month and I'll spend some time Virginia Beach."

Sara chuckled halfheartedly, but then she reached over and squeezed her sister's hand. "Thanks."

"For what?" Maya asked.

"For...just for always making me feel like I have someone. Even when I didn't feel like I should have anyone."

"You know I'm always here for you. After what we've been through, we have to stick together." She didn't elaborate—but she didn't need to. "You're a Lawson. You've already proven before that you're stronger than you realize."

"You're right."

I can do this, she told herself.

We'll see, said the dark voice inside her. *When the going gets tough, you'll get going.*

She shook her head, as if she could somehow jar the second mind out of her head. But it was no use. It seemed, at least for now, that it was there to stay.

CHAPTER TWELVE

Zero came to learn the hard way that the pilot of the Gulfstream was something of a maverick—or else just took his job very seriously when Maria told him "as quickly as possible." As the wheels of the jet touched down at Las Vegas' McCarran International Airport, on an unused freight runway outside of the passenger lanes, the air brakes squealed in protest as the Gulfstream ground to a halt. Zero had to put his forearms up to keep from smacking his head on the seat in front of him. He felt the tires shimmy and, for a brief moment, feared the plane would careen sideways. But the would-be daredevil pilot righted it, expertly slowing from a 140-mile-per-hour landing speed to a human's running pace in less than half the tarmac it should have taken.

Strickland was out of his seat before the jet came to a stop, pushing the lever to open the door and lower the ramp. Zero slung his gear bag over a shoulder while behind him, Maria jabbed at her tablet and spoke into a Bluetooth headset, connected with Bixby and a small tech team back at Langley.

"I've got a suspicious person on camera thirteen," she said even as she rose from her seat to follow them off the plane. "Male, red baseball cap, black jacket. Look into it."

It had taken the Danish hacker forty-seven minutes to crack into the Mirage's camera system undetected and link the feed to Maria—twenty-seven cameras in all that covered the entrance, the lobby, the hotel's reception area, and most of the casino floor.

"Nine minutes," Strickland said nervously. He disembarked first, practically jumping down the four stairs from the Gulfstream cabin to the ground, and then jogging toward the car that waited for them.

"I'm driving," Zero called after him. He was beginning to feel it again—the rush of the job. The thrill of the chase. There wasn't adrenaline, not yet; though it would come soon enough, he knew, flooding his brain, numbing pain and exhaustion and leaving only the high...

Oh god, he realized suddenly, though his feet didn't stop moving. *I'm jonesing for it.*

Had he sent Sara to rehab for a habit that he himself was guilty of? Or worse—had he passed it on to her?

What if it's my fault that she's like this?

No. He couldn't think of that now, as he hurtled toward the waiting car. Maria had called ahead and procured an unmarked gray cruiser from Vegas PD, complete with dashboard lights and a siren. The police didn't know the full nature of the request; they just knew that when the CIA asked for something, you gave it to them, which was in addition to the request that they be on standby for what was about to unfold.

"Bixby," Maria said into her earpiece as she hurried after Zero, "alert local PD, tell them to move on the Mirage in... Todd?"

"Eight minutes," Strickland said over his shoulder.

"Thirteen minutes," Maria told Bixby. Zero knew the five-minute cushion was to keep the cops from raining on their parade and potentially frightening off their Russian targets.

She had been the busiest of them on the plane; as soon as the hacker granted her access to the casino's cameras, she initiated facial recognition software to vet every employee they could spot inside the Mirage, including valets, dealers, porters, receptionists, and even custodians. Any suspicious persons milling about were flagged, their faces scanned and their movements tracked by the techs back in Virginia. While she handled that, Zero and Strickland studied the layout of the Mirage and tried to ascertain the most likely places for an attack to occur.

Zero slid behind the wheel of the cruiser. The keys were waiting in the ignition.

"ETA with normal traffic is sixteen minutes," Strickland said breathlessly as he hopped into the passenger seat. "Think you can get us there in half that?"

"Less." Zero shifted into drive before Maria's door was closed and slammed the gas. The cruiser was powerful, a turbocharged V8 engine under the hood, though he wished it wasn't an automatic. He had more control with a stick shift, more power when he needed it.

The car roared down the rest of the runway, skidded onto a short access road, and sped through a gate intended for delivery trucks. The back end skidded, the tires screeching as Zero turned onto the perpendicular road that would lead them to the Strip. Traffic was, thankfully, almost nonexistent. But he knew it wouldn't stay that way as they got closer.

"Seven minutes," Strickland announced. "Take the next right."

Zero spun the wheel without taking his foot off the gas, the cruiser drifting across two lanes and eliciting a series of angry honks from an oncoming sedan. Zero righted the car and course-corrected, missing a sideswipe by a margin of less than a foot.

He felt eyes on him, and quickly glanced to his right to see Strickland frowning at him. "You're grinning like a maniac," he noted.

"I am?" He didn't realize he had been.

"Trust me, that's normal for him," Maria muttered from the back seat.

Zero bit his lip to keep the smile off his face, but he could still feel it tugging at his cheeks. It was the same reason, he imagined, that people dove out of airplanes or jumped off bridges with a cord around their ankles—seeking the thrill. But for him it was doing eighty-five down an urban street with mere minutes to stop a possible terrorist attack.

He was *back*, and it felt good.

Zero swerved around a van going far too slow and flicked on the dashboard-mounted lights, the red and blue flashers visible to other drivers through the windshield. He used the siren as sparingly as possible, giving a small *whoop-whoop* anytime someone got in his way.

Maria grunted as the car mounted the curb, sending her bouncing in the seat behind him. "Jeez, we want to get there alive."

"Any hit on the redhead?" he asked.

"Nothing," she reported. "No sign of her. All the employees we can spot are vetted; doesn't look like it's going to be an inside job." He knew she had been hopeful that they would get a hit on an ID before they even got there; the casino floor made the most sense as a location, which meant they would need to somehow get their weapon out there without scrutiny. Posing as staff would have made that possible.

"Just a—" Strickland started, but he was cut off by a sharp blare of the siren as Zero skidded into the opposite lane and back again. "Just a thought. What if the point of the rendezvous isn't the attack? What if they're just planning it? Then they could be anywhere. Holed up in a hotel room, maybe…"

"Cops will be five minutes behind us," Maria said. "If we haven't found anything by the time they arrive, we'll lock the place down and search every person, every room."

Zero really hoped it wouldn't come to that. Not only would that take hours and involve hundreds of disgruntled people—but it sounded terribly boring, and he was amped up, ready.

"Cut through that lot and make a left," Strickland instructed. "That'll take us onto the Strip, near the Palazzo. Then another left and we'll be less than two blocks away."

"Radio." Maria reached forward and handed Zero a small plastic earpiece, translucent and wireless. He fit it into his ear without taking his eyes off the road as she said, "Stick to the plan. We split up, cover the most likely places for the attack."

"Three minutes," Strickland said.

"Remember, reports said four to six guys, plus the redhead," Maria continued. "Find, incapacitate, and apprehend. Zip ties are in your gear bags. Try your best not to kill anyone."

Zero held back a smirk, fairly certain that the last comment was for him. The cruiser blew through a red light and turned once more, this time onto the multi-lane Las Vegas Boulevard, lined with enormous hotels and sprawling casino properties. But he couldn't appreciate the sights; he kept his eyes forward, cutting the dashboard lights and easing the car forward as fast as he was able without being too conspicuous.

"One last thing," Maria told them. "If you feel *anything* like Bixby was describing, put the earplugs in. Don't take any unnecessary risks."

That comment, Zero thought, was *definitely* for him.

He honked twice and skirted around pedestrians before turning off the boulevard, easing the car under the white archway that announced the entrance to the Mirage, and came to a squeaking halt in the valet roundabout.

"One minute to rendezvous," Strickland said as the three of them jumped out of the car. He flashed his badge at the young attending valet. "Leave it there, and leave it running."

"Good luck," Zero called to his teammates as they split up. Maria and Strickland peeled off left and right, Maria toward the hotel's reception floor and Todd toward the table games as Zero headed straight, plunging into the rows and rows of slot machines, inundated by colorful lights and sounds.

He had never cared much for casinos. He had done enough gambling with life and limb in his career that he didn't need to throw money into the mix. A memory zipped through his head, one that he hadn't thought of in a long time; early in his agent training, he had studied some of the more devious casino tactics. Almost everything about them was carefully designed to have a psychological impact on a person: the lack of windows or clocks so that time has little meaning. The psychedelic patterns of the colorful carpet that jars the senses (and hides stains). The lights and sounds to simulate success. Even the layout of the machines, arranged in a deliberate labyrinthine manner to keep people gambling.

Everything about the casino was a careful manipulation, one that Zero simultaneously found a bit nauseating yet, in a strange way, couldn't help but appreciate.

Focus. The casino was hardly populated. Despite all the noise and constant flashing lights surrounding him, it was still early afternoon on a holiday. He kept his gaze forward and checked his periphery as he strode down a bright-carpeted avenue between two rows of touch-screen slot machines. To his left, a few Asian women in their sixties poked at the screens. To his right, a man sat alone on the row, perched upon a stool and mindlessly feeding the machine. He was a bit scruffy, his face gaunt. He looked like a man who had nowhere else to go on a day like today.

"Nothing here, over," Maria's voice said in his ear.

"Same," Strickland chimed in. "All quiet on the western front. Over."

Zero continued down to the end of the row of slot machines, suddenly unsure of himself. What if he was wrong and the message of "illusion" hadn't meant the Mirage? At the time he'd been so confident, but now he realized there couldn't have been more than fifty or sixty people in the whole casino. It was hardly ripe for an attack.

What if it's about to happen somewhere else in the city, right now?

He rubbed his forehead, glancing around. A young couple passed by him, speaking Spanish in low tones. An elderly woman nearly bumped into him as she rummaged through her purse. A black-haired woman, slim and attractive and wearing a low-cut cocktail dress, glided by and strode down the row.

Zero froze. He sniffed the air, the cloud of scent that lingered in the wake of the raven-haired beauty.

He knew that scent. A moment earlier he never would have been able to name it, let alone place it, but as soon as it hit his nostrils an image snapped into clear focus in his mind's eye: the interpreter, Karina Pavlo, had favored it. The woman he had rescued, briefly loved, and then watched die—she had worn that same perfume.

It was called *Moscou Rouge*. In English, Red Moscow. And that couldn't be a coincidence.

Is that her? Is that the woman we're after? She could have been wearing a wig, or have dyed her hair after being spotted in both Havana and Kansas.

Zero thought fast, digging into his pocket for his phone and putting it to his ear, though he didn't make a call. Instead he said into the inactive device, "Honey, where are you?"

The woman in the black dress lowered herself onto a stool in front of a machine—right next to the scruffy-looking man, though there were plenty of other open machines.

"Kent?" Maria said through the radio. "Do you see something?"

"I'm standing by the slot machines, but I don't see you," he said into the radio and the phone, glancing about as he did and hoping that he looked the part of a husband who lost his wife in the maze-like casino. He watched the woman out of the corner of his eye as she took a hundred-dollar bill out of a black purse, and then set the bag down on the floor between her stool and the man beside her.

"On my way," Maria said, picking up that he was speaking in code.

"Same," Strickland parroted.

"Great," said Zero loudly, "I'll just stay put and you can find me, then."

His ruse seemed to be working; the woman in the dress paid him no mind as she fed the bill into the machine and pulled the crank. The digital dials spun and landed on a bust. She spun again as Zero took a seat at the furthest machine on the row of seven, the phone still to his ear and craning his neck as if looking for someone.

"I'm over by the 'Pharaoh's Treasure' machines," he said. "Are you on your way?"

"This place is huge," Maria said into the radio. "Be there in a minute."

The woman in black glanced over at him then, only briefly, but long enough for him to meet her gaze and for her to smile coquettishly his way. He smiled back, and then looked down at the carpet, the swirling paisley pattern of bright hues that would hide spilled liquor and cigarette ash and even bodily fluids…

The scruffy man beside her rose from his stool and strode away as the woman in black pulled the crank again. Zero frowned—for someone who had been staring so vacantly just a minute earlier, the man seemed to have some purpose in his stride.

Then he noticed that the black purse was no longer on the floor between the two stools. The man had taken it. And Zero knew beyond a doubt that it was no robbery. This was a plan.

"Better yet," he said into the phone as he stood quickly from the stool, "why don't you meet me at the entrance?"

He was witnessing the rendezvous. And he was going to find out what was inside that purse.

CHAPTER THIRTEEN

Zero trailed the man through the casino, keeping about thirty feet between them and maintaining the pretense of the phone to his ear. "There was a hand-off," he said quietly. "I'm trailing the guy now—beard, dark hair, mid to late thirties, scruffy. Seems to be heading toward the exit."

"I can cut him off," Strickland said through the radio.

"Hang on." Zero slowed, moving his lips silently and pretending to have a conversation. Ahead of the scruffy guy came a younger man in a black leather jacket—and as they passed each other, Scruffy slyly slipped the purse to him without missing a step, a quick and practiced move. The young man kept on walking, right toward Zero's location.

"We can have dinner wherever you'd like," he said into his phone as the guy walked past him. "We just have to find a place that's open..." As soon as the man was out of earshot he said quickly, "Second hand-off. Young guy, short blond hair, black leather jacket." Zero started in his direction, careful to appear casual as he did, despite the growing distance between them. "I'll stay on him. Maria, scruffy guy is heading to your position."

"On him," she replied.

"Strickland, find the woman that made the first hand-off. Black hair, black dress, attractive. She should stick out like a..."

"Like a what?" The raven-haired beauty stepped out suddenly from behind a row of slot machines, so abruptly that Zero nearly ran into her. He took a quick step backward.

"Zero?" Strickland said in his ear. "Zero, did you cut out?"

"Like a sore thumb?" The woman stared him down. Her voice was deeper and rougher than he would have imagined—though he was right about her perfume. Her Russian accent was thick. She had her hands clasped in front of her, as if she was hiding something. "Who are you?"

Think fast. Zero cleared his throat, straightened his back, and in his best Russian he said, "I am Alexei Olanov, KGB. We tracked you here. We know you have the weapon. Where is it?"

He was hoping to appeal to the woman's sense of command, but she only smirked. "You are not KGB. I know this because *I am* KGB."

"They must be on him," Maria said in the radio. "Todd, find him."

"On it," said Strickland.

The woman took a step closer, and Zero took another step back. Over her shoulder, the guy in the leather jacket vanished around a corner, and Zero cursed mentally.

"The weapon is already in place," she told him. "You cannot stop it now."

His heart skipped a beat. They were right; there was an attack looming. It was Russian in nature. And it was about to happen.

The woman unclasped her hands briefly and Zero saw a flash of silver—a tiny pistol, small enough to fit in her palm. A Derringer, or something modeled after it.

He could only imagine where she'd been hiding it.

"I ask you again," she said. "Who are you?"

"CIA," he said candidly. If the woman really was KGB, he wasn't about to go for his own gun; she had the drop on him. The graphene in the jacket would stop a bullet that small... unless she aimed for his head. "I've got a dozen agents with me and the police are waiting outside. There's nowhere to go. Put down the gun."

She sneered at him. "A dozen agents, and the police? I do not believe you. Besides... you are too late."

Too late? How could the Russians have known they were on to them? Did they know the CIA was listening in, and baited them with the rendezvous?

All he knew for certain was that he couldn't waste time here. He needed to find the blond guy and whatever was in that purse. He tensed, ready to make his move—when Strickland's voice crackled through his radio earpiece.

"I've got eyes on the woman. Coming up on her three."

Strickland was making his move, coming down a row of slot machines. He wouldn't be able to see Zero from that vantage point... and he didn't know she had a gun.

"Todd, wait—"

The Russian woman's gaze flitted to her right. In an instant she spun, dropped to one knee, and fired off two shots from the tiny pistol.

Strickland yelped.

Gamblers and casino staff screamed. The Derringer was little more than a pop gun compared to the Glock he had in his jacket—but still loud in the enormous room, and still deadly with the right aim.

In the half-second after the second shot, Zero launched himself at the woman, tackling her with his entire body weight. The pistol bounced to the carpet and under a slot machine. They rolled in a heap of tangled limbs, Zero using his inertia to come out on top. But the woman, KGB or not, was as well-trained as she was flexible. She freed one slender leg and snaked it around his neck. With a twist of her hips she threw him to the side and leapt to her feet.

Zero pushed himself up and scrambled to his feet in time to see her kicking off her second shoe, dangerously tall heels. She snatched it up, grabbed the spike of the heel, and pulled it loose.

A concealed knife. A stiletto inside a stiletto.

She flicked it out at him, and then back again, slashing tightly across his chest as he leapt back. A fleeing visitor rushed by him, knocking roughly into his shoulder. He spun as the blade came again, driving for his heart.

He barely managed to sidestep it in time.

The woman kept him on the defensive, maneuvering forward and tightening the gap between them every time he stepped back. He was half-cognizant of people nearby, running for the exit, shouting at each other. He was aware of the radio in his ear and Maria's voice humming, but he was too focused on the knife to heed her words. As much as he wanted to go for his gun, the two seconds it would take him to reach for it could just as easily be an opportunity for her to open his throat.

The graphene, he remembered. The jacket was reinforced with an atomic-scale honeycomb lattice of nanofiber that could stop a speeding bullet by absorbing and dispersing the impact. But he knew the same science didn't necessarily apply to blades; bulletproof vests were not impervious to knife attacks.

Yet he didn't see much of another option. The razor edge of the thin blade sung past his nose, close enough for his breath to catch in his throat.

As the woman twisted her wrist to deliver a thrust, Zero decided to take the chance. Instead of jumping back or stepping to the side, he stood his ground and twisted at the hips, so that his right shoulder was facing her.

The blade tip connected with the fabric. He felt the impact of the stab, stronger than he would have thought the slight woman capable of. He felt the pain of it, spider-webbing out from the impact site. He even felt just how sharp and deadly the knife was, waiting for the moment when it pierced skin and pushed deep into muscle.

But the jacket held. And while his right bicep took the blow, his hand slipped into his jacket and grabbed the grip of the Glock. As he pulled it free he twisted again, and delivered a sharp-knuckled strike to her forearm and the nerve that ran down its length.

The woman cried out. Her fingers opened impulsively and the knife fell to the carpet. Zero kicked it away and aimed the gun at her forehead.

"On the ground," he growled. "Now."

The woman slowly raised her empty hands, palms out. "That was a good trick," she said in English as she grinned. "Let me show you mine." Her face suddenly contorted into an expression of sheer terror as she screamed, in a perfect American accent, "He has a gun! Someone help me! He's got a gun!"

Zero had been so focused on not getting sliced and apprehending the woman that he hadn't been checking his surroundings ... which meant he had not noticed the two men coming up behind him.

Thick, strong arms snaked around him and snapped him into a nelson hold before he could slip away. At the same time, a second man came in and grabbed onto Zero's gun hand, shoving it and the barrel upward. He saw a flash of a red blazer, a black tie.

Casino security.

Then he was off his feet, being shoved to the ground.

"*Oomph!*" He landed roughly on his stomach with a knee in his back and two hundred and fifty pounds of Las Vegas security behind that. The Glock slipped from his grip as the second security officer pulled it from him.

"Gun secured!" the man declared, even as the Russian woman continued to shriek in terror. He had to admit, begrudgingly, that she must have worked hard to perfect her American accent.

"Wait," Zero grunted, "I'm CIA!"

"Sure you are," growled the security man on his back. "Tell it to the police when they get here."

The police. He'd forgotten about them. They should have been there by now—had it been five minutes yet? He'd lost track.

A third red-jacketed guard arrived on the scene. From Zero's vantage point on the floor, he could see a radio in the man's hand. "Threat averted," he said into it. Then to the Russian woman he asked, "Ma'am, are you okay? Did he hurt you?"

"No," she shook her head, breathing hard. "I-I don't know who he is, I've never seen him before in my life!"

"I'm CIA!" Zero tried to argue again. "There is a weapon here, hidden. There's going to be an attack ..."

"Pipe down!" The guard on his back increased the pressure until Zero felt like his spine might snap.

He couldn't move. The guard had him pinned firmly. Strickland was presumably down. "Maria!" he hissed into the earpiece. "I could really use a distraction right about now..."

There was no reply—at least not with words. He imagined she had her hands full with the other Russian, the scruffy bearded guy. But then two shots rang out, clapping like thunder as they echoed around the casino, far louder than the Derringer. Maria's Glock, he was sure.

"Jesus, what the hell's going on here?" the guard behind him shouted in disbelief.

"Stay with him!" the one with the radio commanded. "Don't let him move! You, come with me!" He and the other security guard, the one that had taken Zero's gun, sprinted off toward the source of the shots.

Unguarded, the Russian woman slowly backed toward a row of slot machines.

"Hey!" Zero shouted. "Hey, she's getting away! You need to keep her here!"

"I said pipe down," the guard threatened. He twisted Zero's arm painfully around his back. "Or I'll break it."

Zero hissed a breath through clenched teeth. A broken arm over a bizarre misunderstanding was the last thing he needed—no, that wasn't true. The Russian woman making an escape was actually the last thing he needed.

But then he saw a black boot stepping out from behind a tall machine. Zero twisted his neck at an odd angle in time to see Strickland raise his pistol behind the woman, holding it backward by the barrel like a cudgel. With a single swift blow, the Russian crumpled to an unconscious heap, only a few feet from where Zero lay.

Strickland flipped the gun around in his palm and aimed it at the guard. "Off him, now."

"Whoa, take it easy pal..."

"*Now*," Strickland said again. Zero mercifully felt the pressure release from his arm and his back. He rolled over and quickly got to his feet.

"Thanks. You good? Are you hit?" he asked quickly.

"I'm fine, she got the jacket," Todd replied, not taking his eyes off the guard. "Go find the guy. I'll clean up here."

Zero didn't need to be told twice. He sprinted for the exit, certain that the blond guy would have made an escape once the shooting started. He hit the doors and burst out into the sudden daylight, squinting as he looked left and right. He heard sirens wailing; four police cars were screaming up the street that led to the Mirage.

And beyond them, nearly to Las Vegas Boulevard, Zero spotted a glimpse of a bobbing blond head, striding away quickly.

He gave chase, pumping his legs as fast as they would carry him. One of the police cars careened sideways in the street to block him—perhaps thinking he too was trying to make a getaway—but Zero didn't stop. He jumped, slid on a hip over the hood of the cruiser, and kept right on running.

The blond guy threw a glance over his shoulder as Zero hit the boulevard and immediately knew he was being followed. He broke into a sprint as well. Zero had been training hard the past month, but he had at least ten years on the younger guy. He'd falter before he caught up.

You have a second gun, he reminded himself. The guard had taken the Glock, but he had the backup Ruger on him … somewhere. *Where did you put it?*

It was exactly what he'd feared, that his Swiss-cheese of a limbic system would blot out some crucial knowledge in a time of need. He could not, for the life of him, remember actually stowing the second sidearm anyone on his person—and he couldn't stop and look himself over for fear of losing the blond guy.

So he had to improvise.

"Stop that guy!" he shouted, pointing as he ran. "Somebody stop him! Stop that man!"

Plenty of pedestrians paused, some staring at him curiously and others even looking toward the fleeing Russian, but no one actually tried to stop him.

So much for that idea.

The blond guy threw another brief glance back, and dared to flash a grin at Zero shouting and pointing as the distance grew between them. He did not, however, see the homeless man ahead of him sitting on the sidewalk, who casually stuck out a well-worn brown leather boot.

The young Russian's foot snagged the boot, and for a full two-count he was airborne. He landed on the pavement with his face and shoulder in an impact that even made Zero wince, rolling twice before coming to a stop on his back and not moving.

"Thanks," Zero said breathlessly as he trotted up. He reminded himself to drop whatever cash he had in the homeless man's cup. "Thank you."

"What'd he do?" the man asked gruffly. "Steal somethin'?"

"…Yeah." It was easier than the truth. Zero knelt beside the Russian. His cheek and neck were scoured with road rash and bleeding badly. His shoulder was out of joint. But his eyes were half-open and his breath came shallow and pained; he was conscious.

Zero grabbed the small black purse and checked inside. There were only two objects in it. One was a smart phone. The other was a tube of lipstick. But when Zero pulled off the cap, he saw no wax; beneath the lid was a small plastic safety guard with a red button beneath it.

Familiarity sparked within him, followed immediately by dread. He'd seen things like this before; the CIA regularly hid these sorts of devices into everyday objects like lipstick tubes.

There's a bomb.

Zero grabbed the young man by the lapels of his leather jacket and shook him. "Where is it? Where?!"

The young man's cracked lips parted slightly as he said in a hoarse whisper: "Go to hell." Then his eyes rolled back as he lost consciousness.

"Todd?" Zero shouted into the earpiece. "Maria!"

"I'm here," she said quickly.

"Evacuate the Mirage, *now*. There's a bomb. I repeat, there is a bomb somewhere in the hotel or casino."

"Are you sure?" Strickland's voice came through.

"Pretty sure," Zero told him. "Because I'm holding a remote detonator."

Chapter Fourteen

Zero zip-tied the blond Russian and gave the homeless man a hundred dollars to keep an eye on him until the police could come pick him up. Then he jogged back to the Mirage, where he was denied access due to the bomb threat. At least the fact that he wasn't attacked on sight told him that Strickland had convinced the police and casino security that they were the good guys.

More cop cars arrived, officers setting up sawhorses to keep gawkers at bay while others quickly escorted people out. Zero spotted Maria and Strickland in the crowd and hurried over to them.

"You okay?" he asked her.

She nodded. "I got Scruffy. He's sitting in the back of a car over there. The woman is handcuffed in the back of an ambulance. You're sure it's a bomb?"

He handed her the lipstick tube and she tugged off the cap. "Dammit," she murmured.

"Hey, you the CIA guys?" An older cop with a gray push-broom of a mustache trotted over to them.

"That's right," Maria confirmed.

"We've got EOD en route," he told them. "Once this place is cleared, we'll have to do a full sweep, every floor and every room."

"We may not have that kind of time," Zero said plainly. For all they knew, this bomb threat could have been a diversion from the sonic weapon.

"Hey, this is Vegas. Ain't the first bomb threat we've had," the grizzled cop replied. "We've got a protocol to follow."

Maria glanced past him, at the cruiser that held the scruffy Russian. "Sergeant, can I borrow your car for a few minutes?"

The cop frowned. "You know there's a perp in the back, right?"

"Yes, I do."

He shrugged and passed her the keys, seeming to know better than to ask further. Maria headed toward the car. "Be back in a few."

"There's a third suspect," Zero told the cop, "about two blocks south of here. He's not going anywhere, but you should have someone pick him up as soon as possible."

"I'll put someone on it now." The cop turned and gave the order into the radio.

Zero turned to Strickland, who seemed to be wincing with each breath. "You sure you're okay?"

"I've had worse." He grinned. "The jacket caught both rounds. My ribs are going to be bruised to high hell and it's going to hurt to breathe for a while, but I'll live."

Zero chuckled softly. Now that the adrenaline of the chase was wearing off, he could feel the dull pain from where his bicep had caught the impact of the Russian's knife. He too would be bruised, but he too would live.

Far more concerning than minor injuries was the problem with his memory. He had forgotten, mid-chase, where he kept his LC9—and he still couldn't remember. He searched the jacket's pockets, patted his waist, and finally bent and checked his ankles...

Ankle holster. Of course. As soon as his fingers found the familiar shape, the weight of it there, the recollection surged back as if it had never left.

"Are you sure *you're* okay?" Strickland asked. "I'm not used to seeing self-pat-downs."

"Just making sure I didn't drop anything when those guards tackled me," Zero said with a shrug. He tried to look casual, and hoped that Strickland didn't think anything was amiss— but that was now the second time the younger agent had witnessed his odd behavior. It was only a matter of time before he started asking more probing questions.

As the cops and security continued their evacuation, guiding people out beyond the sawhorses, Zero turned his attention to the nearby police cruiser that held Scruffy and Maria. He thought he'd hear cries of pain, perhaps see some movement behind the tinted windows, but there was none. And after only a few minutes the door opened and she got out. Just before she closed the door again he caught a glimpse of the bearded Russian man—and he looked terrified.

Zero of all people knew that psychological torture could be at least as effective, if not more so in some cases, than physical. It was easier to train a body not to break than a mind.

Maria paused at the sergeant and said, "Tell EOD there's a suitcase bomb in room 803. We have the detonator, but it's still active." Then she headed toward Zero and Strickland, not at all looking pleased.

"What is it?" Todd asked quickly.

"We stopped *an* attack," Maria said dourly. "Just not the one we were hoping to stop."

Zero frowned. That couldn't be right; these had to be the same people. It felt random enough. It was a small team of Russians, with a woman. OMNI had picked up their chatter. Everything fit.

"What's in room 803 that they want to bomb?" he asked.

"Not what," Maria replied. "But *who*. Seems that a former member of Aleksandr Kozlovsky's cabinet is holed up here at the Mirage under a false name while he brokers a deal with our government—Russian secrets in exchange for immunity and a new identity. Russia caught wind and sent these three, a KGB sleeper-cell in the States."

KGB sleeper-cells in the US, Zero thought bitterly. *Just add that to the long list of "last things we need right now."*

"They sent the woman to his hotel room disguised as a high-end escort," Maria explained. "She planted the bomb and stole his phone. Then she passed it off to Scruffy, who had the detonator. He passed off both to the third guy, whose job was to confirm that the intel was on the phone before detonating the bomb."

"What was on the phone?" Zero asked.

"A map," Maria told him, "showing the locations of two dozen secret nuclear missile silos in Russia."

Zero balked. That was significant intel to be keeping on a phone. "Did you know about this?" he asked her.

Maria shook her head. "Must be above my pay grade."

Strickland frowned. "But why wait to blow it? The phone would have been destroyed in the blast anyway, right?"

"Because," Zero said slowly as he worked it out for himself, "if the map was legitimate, any country that could afford it would pay tens of millions for that kind of information. I'm betting these three were going to defect, sell the intel themselves to the highest bidder."

Maria nodded. "And I feel pretty confident that they have no idea about any ultrasonic weapon."

"So this is all a dead end," Strickland muttered.

"We still averted a major crisis," Zero pointed out, though he was feeling much the same way. The group that attacked Havana and the tiny town in Kansas was still out there, and the Russians seemed to have no idea who they were.

"All I know," Maria said as she looked up at the Mirage behind them, "is that we've done all we can here. And I could really use a coffee." She waved down the sergeant, heading over to speak with him before they left.

Zero slung his gear bag over his shoulder. Something about this just didn't seem right. Their assumptions so far, educated or not, were still guesses.

What if the Russians aren't responsible for the sonic weapon at all? he wondered. That was the primary lead from which they were operating; being wrong about that meant going about the entire search wrong. *What if this is a terrorist faction that just has Russian members?*

He didn't voice the thought aloud, since it was little more than a hunch. They were back to square one; they had no leads, no idea who they were chasing, and most importantly, no idea where to find them before the next attack.

CHAPTER FIFTEEN

Maria swirled her coffee with a plastic stirrer, watching the thin rivulets of cream blend into the dark roast, turning it mocha brown. She sat at a small round table in a chain coffee shop not three blocks from the Mirage. She told herself it was important to stay close, in case they were needed again—but the bitter reality was that she had no idea where to go from there.

"Hey." Kent set down a paper cup and emptied a sugar packet into it. "Where's Todd?"

"Stepped out to make a quick call." At his raised eyebrow she added, "His dad, I think. It's still Thanksgiving, you know."

"I guess it is." He sat across from her and watched the steam curl from his cup. He had that distant look in his eye; she'd worked with him long enough to know he was either working out the details of the op, or he was thinking about his kids back home.

"You want to talk about it?" she prodded.

He smiled, but shook his head. "Not really. You?"

"Not really." The truth of the matter was that she didn't understand why she felt so low. They'd missed their mark, but in doing so had stopped another attack. They'd kept a man from getting killed, and possibly some innocent civilians. She should have felt some sense of pride or accomplishment—but all she felt was pending dread. Those people and their sonic weapon were still out there. They could be anywhere. Another attack could be happening at that very moment, for all she knew.

Maria had fully expected a call, at least from Director Shaw and possibly even from President Rutledge, yet her phone remained silent. There was no doubt they were aware of what happened at the Mirage; aware that she and her team had, so far, failed.

That's what it was. That's why she was feeling the way she was. It was the sting of failure, a feeling she wasn't accustomed to.

"I think I'm just struggling to understand these people," she admitted finally. "Their motives. What they're after. Why two attacks so close together, and silence ever since."

Kent nodded slowly. "I think," he said, "that's the point."

"What is?"

"Psychological torture." He had that faraway look in his eye, the one that suggested he'd been thinking about it already. "The locations of the attacks don't make sense to us. But they've managed to prove that they can get into our country, the heart of it, and strike quickly. They don't *have* to rush into a third attack, because now we know what they can do. Just the knowledge of that is enough to scare us. To keep us making guesses and frantically try to find them. I don't think they knew what was happening here today… but I think they assumed we'd move fast and make a misstep."

As frequently and irritatingly as he was right, she understood. She'd just used similar tactics not so long ago on the scruffy Russian. She didn't need to lay a finger on him to get the information she wanted; as KGB, the man was familiar with the CIA black site in Morocco called H-6. To someone like him, Hell-Six as they called it would have been a ghost story.

And all you had to do was make a ghost story a little more real to put genuine fear into someone.

But even if that was the right answer, it was all the more frightening than any that she could discern, because it meant that these people weren't likely to make demands or show their hand. They *wanted* to incite fear and panic.

Kent gestured to the tablet in front of her. "Any more hits from OMNI?"

She shrugged. "They picked up a few suspicious snippets here and there. But the NSA is looking deeper into each, after all… this." They'd been too hasty, assuming that the Russian female they'd picked up was the same one they were after. "Nothing legitimate yet."

She glanced down at the dark-screened tablet, as if she could will it to spring to life with an update, a lead, somewhere for them to go. Getting back on the plane and returning to Langley felt like a waste of time—and she didn't want to face whoever might be waiting for them.

Maria felt his hand on hers, and she flinched, almost pulling her hand away. But she didn't; his fingers felt warm and familiar. He gave her a small squeeze and said, "We're going to find them. We always do."

She nodded, but her mind wasn't on the sonic weapon and the mysterious Russian woman anymore. The warmth from his hand felt like an electric tingle, running up her arm and into her heart. She'd had a lot of complicated relationships in her life, family and friends and former boyfriends, but Kent was by far the most complex.

She very nearly blurted out, *What happened between us?*

They'd been through so much together. They'd come up as agents together; they'd saved each other's lives countless times. They'd been coworkers and friends and lovers. For a while, they were nothing. Then Kent came back from the dead and they were coworkers and friends and lovers all over again.

And now they were...friends? Superior and subordinate? She didn't know. All she knew for sure was that she thought she knew what she wanted—a family and a steady career and a house in the suburbs—but when he was there, sitting in front of her, holding her hand, smiling as if everything was going to be all right—all those other desires and dreams fell away.

"I think," she said slowly, "when we get back, we should talk."

"Yeah? What are we going to talk about?"

"About..."

Her phone rang, and she cursed silently. Not just for the awful timing of it, but because of the stern chewing out that she feared it to be.

But no. It was Bixby.

Maria put the call on speaker for Kent's benefit. "Do we have a hit?" she asked immediately.

"Yes," said the engineer. "Well, no. Sort of."

"Bixby," Maria said sternly.

"Not a hit through OMNI," he explained rapidly. "Something else. The tech team has been sifting through any available data from the Midwestern attack, but there wasn't much to go on; no traffic cams, barely any security footage, nothing useful. But then we realized that a whole bunch of people must have been taking photos and videos with their phones.

"It's taken a better part of the day, but I've been collecting several videos that people were taking of the parade from cell phones. I've extrapolated still images in the moments just before the attack began, and sort of 'stitched' them together into a panorama shot of ground zero. Here, take a look."

Her tablet chimed, and Maria swiped at the screen to open the image Bixby had just sent. It looked eerily similar to the scene from the video they'd watched just after the attack occurred, but on a much wider scale—she could move the image left and right to see the scores of people lining the streets, the storefronts behind them, obscured only by thin hazy lines where Bixby had hastily put together various images.

Kent rounded the table and peered at the image over her shoulder, his breath light on her ear. *Focus*, she told herself. "Looking at it now," she told Bixby. "Is there something we should be noticing?"

"Not at first glance," the engineer said. "But based on the videos I saw—terrifying stuff, by the way—I reasoned that the sonic attack had to have come from *behind* the parade. Zoom in on the upper left quadrant."

Maria did so, using two fingers to expand a quarter of the panoramic image, but all she saw were dozens of blurred faces and the beginning of the marching band coming around the corner. "I'm not seeing whatever I'm supposed to be seeing," she said flatly. It looked like a real-life *Where's Waldo?* to her.

"There!" said Kent suddenly, pointing at a spot in the image. "Zoom closer there."

She did so—and sure enough, she saw what he saw. A flash of bright red hair. A slight figure. The profile of white skin. The woman was partially obscured by two people in front of her, but it was her. Or at least it looked like her.

"Could be our gal," Maria admitted. "Or it could be any redhead that was there this morning."

"This truck beside her," Kent noted curiously. "It looks familiar." The woman was indeed standing beside a box truck, but the panoramic image was taken from at least two blocks away; they couldn't make out the logo. Only the bright green and orange swirl and vague white letters.

But it did look familiar. Maria had seen similar trucks on the highway before, had noticed them in passing. "That's a food distributor, isn't it?"

"Bingo," said Bixby. "That truck is from Stay-Fresh Grocery Distribution. I took the liberty of contacting their headquarters. They do indeed have a truck missing, from a depot not far from Kansas City. They wouldn't have even noticed until tomorrow, with the holiday."

Maria's heart leapt at the lead. "Tell me that truck has GPS."

"Disabled," Bixby told them, "along with the radio. But we have a license plate number."

She mulled it over quickly. There was a good chance that Shaw and Rutledge would disapprove of what she was about to do, but this was no time to check in and wait for authorization.

"These people are smart enough to stay off of phones and radios," she said. "Pull our NSA resources from OMNI. I want them looking for this truck—highway cams, toll booths, gas stations, any likely place. Have them start at Springfield and work out in concentric circles. Find the route they took. And put out an APB to every highway patrol unit in the country."

Bixby was silent for a long moment. "Are you sure that's the right move here…?"

"I'm not going to risk losing them again," Maria said firmly. "Put out the APB with the license plate number—but make sure they do *not* engage. We want a location, and we want them followed if possible, but *no engagement*." The APB was risky enough; forcing the

Russians' hand into using the weapon again would be entirely on her, and she was keenly aware of it. "I want to know the instant we hear anything."

"On it." Bixby ended the call.

Maria stuffed the tablet and her phone back into her gear bag and snatched up her coffee cup. "Let's get back to the jet. I want to be ready the moment we hear something."

"Hang on a sec." Kent held up a hand, his brow furrowed. She knew that look too; he was working on some calculation—or perhaps an assumption—in his head.

"We're not hanging on," Maria argued. "We have a lead and we're going to move on it. They're transporting the weapon in that truck, Kent."

"But why? There are probably a thousand trucks they could have taken. They knew they were attacking a parade, where people would be taking photos and videos, and they chose one of the most conspicuous trucks they could have chosen?"

Maria scoffed in exasperation. "Are you suggesting they *want* to be found? If that was the case, they could have left the GPS intact."

"No," he said pensively. "Not that they want to be found… but not that they *don't* want to be found either."

"That doesn't make any sense. We're going." She led the way across the coffee shop toward the exit, with Kent trailing at her heels. "It could have been a crime of convenience," she said over her shoulder. "I can't imagine that grocery distribution centers have intense security."

"Maybe," he replied dubiously. "But you have to admit, every time we get new information it feels like we're left with more questions than answers."

She didn't like how doubtful he was being. She didn't like his line of questioning, because it made her feel like he was questioning her. This was the right move. She could feel it; they were getting closer.

Strickland pulled the door of the coffee shop open as they reached it. "We're moving?"

"Back to the jet. We've got a lead."

Strickland turned on a heel and followed them as they strode quickly back to the borrowed cruiser. "What have we got?" he asked.

"A needle in a haystack," Kent said lowly.

"That's right," Maria agreed, rather than argue. "And we're going to jump right in and find it."

She mentally dared Kent to say something further. He didn't—but he didn't have to. She knew him well enough to know the words that were right on the tip of his tongue.

Sounds like a good way to get pricked.

Chapter Sixteen

President Rutledge sat alone in the Oval Office—though not behind the desk. He sat in one of the comfortable armchairs arranged in the room's center, four of them facing each other in a circle. He couldn't bring himself to sit behind the desk right now. It required a strength of presence that he simply couldn't muster.

He glanced down at the carpet beneath his shoes and noticed a few stray hairs there. *Are those mine? Am I losing my hair?* It seemed likely enough.

He hadn't pardoned a turkey that day. Instead he relegated the task to his eldest daughter, Hannah. Social media was abuzz about it; some thought it a cute publicity stunt, while others shamed him for the breaking of tradition. But he hardly cared about that.

He was all too aware of the CIA's snafu in Las Vegas. That was the best he could call it; it wasn't quite a failure. After all, they'd saved the life of a Russian diplomat with highly sensitive information, and stopped a bombing from occurring. But as far as he knew, they were no closer to finding the sonic weapon or the people behind it.

The mainstream media had started to link the incident in Havana with what happened in Springfield, Kansas, but without any actual connection it felt largely like sensationalizing. No one had yet mentioned anything about ultrasonic weapons, though there was plenty of speculation that ranged from chemical agents to biological weapons to induced mass hysteria.

Rutledge worried if he made the right choice or not, sending this Agent Zero after these people. From the stories he'd heard, he imagined some kind of superman, had even concocted a vague appearance of what he thought Zero should look like. But then they had video-conferenced, and Rutledge saw that he was just a man; unassuming, older than the president would have thought, fairly ordinary.

Like me. Just a man.

Maybe they were more alike than either would be willing to concede. Maybe Zero was a kindred spirit who had found himself in the right place at the wrong time, and now had insurmountable expectations on his shoulders, too.

There was a gentle knock at the door. Rutledge already knew who it would be.

"Come in, Tabby."

Tabby Halpern entered the Oval Office alone. She frowned for the slightest of moments, seeing him in an armchair instead of behind the desk, but didn't mention it. Instead she said, "Sir. I have an update. We've just received word that the CIA team has a lead, the vehicle the suspects might be using. They're tracking all known channels currently…"

Rutledge waved a hand dismissively. "I don't want to know about leads," he said firmly, firmer than he intended. "I want to know when they're found, or…" *Or when these people do something again.* "I want to know about results."

Tabby nodded once. "Yes sir. Then might I suggest we involve the FBI? They have field offices all over the country. Anywhere these people crop up, they can be there."

Rutledge shook his head. "No. Not yet. If we alert every field office it'll definitely leak to the media."

"Sir," Tabby pressed, "it's their job. In fact, as soon as this became a domestic issue, it should have no longer been a concern of the CIA—"

"Not a concern?" Rutledge rose from his seat. "National security is *everyone's* concern, Tabby. As soon as we involve the FBI, they'll want to involve local law enforcement. Other eyes and ears. It will be impossible to keep the lid on this thing. Do you have any idea what could happen if word gets out about an invisible sonic weapon that could hit anywhere at any time? The panic that could incite?"

He was growing loud. He forced himself to take a breath, to calm. But he didn't apologize.

"Sir," she began. "Jon. You should eat something."

"I'm not hungry," he muttered as he sank back into the chair. He stared at the floor, and those stray hairs on the carpet taunted him again.

Tabby remained, standing there for a quiet moment and seeming to wait for him to acknowledge her again. "Was there something else?"

"Yes," she said. "There are concerns in the administration that you haven't yet addressed the nation after the Kansas attack."

Rutledge sighed. He'd been waiting for a nudge like that. "What am I supposed to say? Do I stand up there and lie, tell the people that everything is fine? Or do I stick to the usual? 'Our hearts go out to those affected by today's terrible tragedy'?" He scoffed. "I won't lie. I never have before, and I won't start now. I won't avoid the truth."

"So instead you'll avoid the podium?"

A flash of anger rushed through him, but he quashed it. He wasn't angry at her defiance; he was angry at his own inability to act. "Yes," he murmured.

There are concerns in the administration.

Of course there were. He wasn't the leader they'd elected, but he was the one they were stuck with now. It certainly didn't help that Secretary of Defense Kressley was rallying cabinet members to his side. The general was so certain that the Russians were behind this that he wanted Rutledge to declare the attack on the Midwestern town as an act of war, which was outright unthinkable.

"If there's nothing else," Tabby said.

"No," he told her. "Thank you." But as she turned to leave him he stood suddenly. "Wait. There is one more thing."

Tabby paused.

"I want to enter the formal nomination for Joanna Barkley as vice president. I want Congress to convene for a vote as soon as possible—tomorrow, if we can."

Tabby Halpern blinked at him. "Sir, I'm not sure that tomorrow will be feasible."

"Why not?" Rutledge demanded. "They've been on my back about nominating a VP for weeks now. We can call for a special session."

He was well aware that he probably sounded like a lunatic. He expected pushback from Tabby, but instead she said carefully, "I'll... see what we can do."

"Good. Thank you. And see if Barkley is at home or not. I'll put the call in myself."

Tabby nodded, and then she whisked out of the Oval Office.

Rutledge paced. This was the right call, the one he had been deliberating for so long. He would nominate Senator Barkley, call Congress to vote for approval—and then resign. Barkley could be the strong hand that the White House needed. She could negotiate the trade war with China. She could quash Russian aggression. And he... well, he wasn't sure what he would do. Retire, perhaps, and enjoy the perks of being a former president.

Suddenly the idea sounded good, so good that he felt as if a weight had been lifted from his shoulders just by thinking about it. His wife could continue to do her charity work. His daughters could go back to their old school and reunite with their friends. The country would be in better hands. It was a win-win all around.

And besides, he mused, by the time Barkley was sworn in, he wouldn't have to go down in history as the shortest president to serve; that honor went to William Henry Harrison, who perished from pneumonia only thirty-one days into his presidency. Even if Barkley was sworn in by Monday, Rutledge would be thirty-two days into his term. He could stick it out for just three more days.

It was such a simple acknowledgment, but as soon as he accepted the fact that he was not cut out for this position, he felt lighter. Almost buoyant.

Then the door to the Oval Office swung open without so much as a knock, and Tabby Halpern's face appeared again, etched with concern.

A knot of dread immediately tightened in his stomach. *Did Barkley reconsider? Did she turn down the offer to be the vice president?*

"Sorry for the intrusion, sir. There's a call for you. It's ... Fyodor Ilyin."

"Ilyin?" Rutledge blinked, certain he had her incorrectly. "*President* Ilyin?"

She nodded.

Never mind the fact that he and Russian President Ilyin had not yet met in person, despite the fact that they'd both taken office at about the same time. An impromptu call like that was highly unorthodox; any communication with the newly minted leader of a nation with which they had strained ties would have been planned, with preestablished talking points and a script of measured responses.

And now Ilyin was on hold for him? In the midst of attacks that felt very much Russian in nature?

"You don't have to take it, Mr. President," Tabby told him. "We can tell him you're not available, buy some time to prepare ..."

"No." As the initial shock wore off, Rutledge felt a sting of shame for his near-giddiness of a moment prior. Regardless of whether or not he was plotting his resignation, he still had to handle things responsibly and diplomatically. "No, I'll take it." He instinctively straightened his tie for some reason. "Is NSA in on this?"

"Yes sir."

"And recording?"

"Of course, sir."

Rutledge nodded and rounded the desk, taking a seat behind it. Tabby hesitated, her head still visible in the narrow opening.

"I can stay if you'd like, sir."

He smiled. "Thank you, Tabby. But I think I've got this one."

"Good luck, sir." She vanished and closed the door behind her, leaving him alone in the office to speak with the Russian president—and whoever else was listening in on the line on either side. It was an eerie thought, how the conversation between two of them might be privy to dozens of other ears. But he pushed it aside and lifted the receiver of the red phone on the presidential desk.

"This is President Rutledge," he said, hoping he sounded authoritative.

"Mr. President." The first word that came to mind when hearing Fyodor Ilyin's voice was "smarmy." His tone was purring and placating. "It is a pleasure to speak with you. I hope you are enjoying your holiday." Ilyin's English was excellent, but his accent was bizarre; not only Russian, but tinged with a British slant, having spent several of his formative years as an ambassador to the UK.

"I was, President Ilyin," he lied. "To what do I owe this unexpected call?"

"I understand there has been an incident."

Which incident? Rutledge almost said. But he realized that Ilyin must have meant the attempted bombing in Las Vegas. "You're referring to the alleged KGB operatives that tried to murder a diplomat earlier today?"

"My people have confirmed that the three perpetrators *were* KGB, once," Ilyin said. "But they defected some time ago. Considering the already-present strain between our great nations, I thought it prudent to contact you directly to explain the situation. The three people that were apprehended today are traitors and profiteers. They do not represent Russia or her interests."

Rutledge almost smirked, for as much as he was able to trust Ilyin at his word. Publicly the man had no known ties to predecessor Aleksandr Kozlovsky—but that held almost no weight, considering that Kozlovsky alleged to have no ties to *his* predecessor, Ivanov, yet had been secretly working toward the same end of annexing Ukrainian oil assets.

"And in the interest of cooperation," Ilyin continued, "I humbly request that you allow us to extradite the three criminals, to be tried in their homeland for their transgressions."

Rutledge winced at Ilyin's stilted lexicon. It was bad enough that his tone was wheedling; everything about the way he spoke made him sound insincere.

"We have no extradition treaty with Russia," Rutledge said plainly. "They committed their crimes here on American soil; they will be tried here, on American soil."

"As you wish," Ilyin said simply. "There is another matter."

"Which is?"

"The Russian man they were attempting to kill," Ilyin said plainly. "He was a collaborator of Kozlovsky's, a traitor to our nation and a fraud. My sources indicate that he is attempting to barter his freedom for Russian secrets. I personally assure you—and your intelligence agencies—that any information he has is patently false."

Of course you would say that, Rutledge thought sourly. Aloud he said, "I'm afraid I'm not privy to those details, but I will gladly pass along the message."

Ilyin was silent for a moment. "Then I thank you for your time, President Rutledge," he said at last. "I look forward to us meeting in person and discussing a brighter future. I can only hope that the circumstances will be more pleasant than this."

It won't be me you'll be meeting. "Of course, President Ilyin. Thank you for your candor." A thought struck him suddenly; an opportunity, perhaps. A long shot, to be sure, but a chance nonetheless. As Speaker of the House, he was known to have a firm hand and stand by his scruples. It was time to do that now. "Wait. There is one more matter."

"Yes?" Ilyin purred.

Rutledge hesitated, choosing his words carefully. "There was a ... another incident, recently, in the American Midwest. Some sort of attack on a small town." He made sure not to mention details about the nature of the attack, or the weapon. "We have reason to believe that the perpetrators might have been native to Russia."

Through the phone he heard Ilyin take a deep, measured breath and release it as a lengthy sigh. "I assure you, President Rutledge, that my intention as Russia's leader is to repair the damage that has been done, not exacerbate it."

"So you have no knowledge of this?" Rutledge pressed.

"You have my word that if there has been any violent reprisal on Americans, the order did not come from me or from anyone in my administration," Ilyin said plainly. "I will further remind you that Russian xenophobia in the United States is at its highest since the Cold War. Is it not?"

It certainly was, but that was no reason to dismiss the testimony of victims and witnesses.

"And finally," Ilyin concluded, "I would like to state in no uncertain terms that if every terroristic event and episode that occurs within your borders is going to place blame on myself and my country ... I think we are due for some very difficult times ahead."

Rutledge clenched his teeth. Ilyin had somehow made his response sound like both diplomacy and a threat at the same time.

"Of course," he said in reply. "Blame was not my intention. We need to be thorough, you understand."

"Thorough," Ilyin mused. "Yes. I understand. With that, I bid you good evening, President Rutledge."

"To you as well, President Ilyin."

Rutledge replaced the receiver, his fingers trembling slightly. He was sure that certain cabinet members were going to disapprove of him so brashly accusing Russia's leaders of the attacks. And worse, Ilyin had given away nothing. If the Russians truly were unaware of the attack, then it meant the CIA was working off a false lead. If the Russians *were* behind it ... well, then Ilyin's vague threat of "difficult times ahead" could mean escalation.

He could only hope that Agent Zero and his team would come through in time.

CHAPTER SEVENTEEN

Zero was doubtful that they would find their missing box truck in the whole of the continental United States, even with a nationwide APB and all their monitoring resources. A thousand things could have happened since the Midwest attack—the perpetrators could have ditched the truck, switched the license plate, boarded another plane, or even (ideally) left the country.

All of which was why he was quite surprised when Bixby's tech team, in cooperation with the NSA, started getting hits on its trail.

No sooner had they boarded the Gulfstream in Las Vegas than Maria announced, "Highway cams on the border between Kansas and Missouri caught a glimpse of them." She turned the tablet's screen for them to see. The photo was blurred with the speed of the grocery truck, but the driver behind the wheel was unmistakably a redheaded woman. "That was less than five hours ago." She alerted the pilot that they were heading east, and to stay at low altitude to avoid the regular air traffic lanes. They had no destination yet.

Two minutes later, another hit came through: a gas station less than a hundred miles down eastbound I-70. Maria squirmed in her seat as she waited impatiently for updates, for a definitive location. Zero hadn't seen her like this in a long time; usually *he* was the obsessed one, the one who had to find the target, complete the op, come hell or high water. Maria was usually the level-headed one.

He couldn't help but wonder why this seemed to have become so personal for her. Maybe because of what she'd said earlier, her failure to understand them and their motives. Maybe she feared she was losing her touch, her ability to get inside their heads and think like the other side.

What does that say for me? he wondered. He thought he understood these people, or at least that they were atypical in the vein of the usual sorts they pursued. Maybe he too was off-base.

Maria's face suddenly lit up like Christmas and she stood suddenly in the narrow aisle of the Gulfstream. "We've got 'em!" she all but shouted. "Illinois state trooper just flagged the truck heading north on I-55!"

"Heading where?" Strickland asked. "Chicago? Indianapolis, maybe?"

"Does it matter?" Maria retorted. "We're going to nail those sons of bitches long before they get there. An unmarked statie is trailing them as we speak. We just have to find an airfield and cut them off." She hurried to the cockpit to confer with the pilot.

Zero wished he could share in her enthusiasm. He was just as eager to stop them, but this felt a lot like it did before—like every time they got new information, there were more questions than answers.

"What is it?" Strickland asked.

"Huh?"

Todd was staring at him. "You've got that pointed look on your face. I can actually *hear* the gears turning in your head. What's up?"

Zero sighed shortly. "Feels strange, doesn't it? They've been so careful so far. They vanished from Havana, snuck into the country, and hopped a plane to Kansas. They've been staying off of all frequencies and phones, and now we just ... find them driving down the highway, plain as day?"

"Look," said Strickland, leaning toward the aisle. "It sounds to me that you're assuming we're dealing with some masterminds here. But let me tell you, from my experience: most of these types aren't brilliant strategists. They're lunatics with bombs and guns—or sonic weapons. You're trying to second-guess their logic like they have some genius plan. But I'm betting they're just psychos with a powerful weapon."

"Yeah," Zero murmured. "You might be right." But he didn't actually believe that. He didn't believe these people were the run-of-the-mill insurgent types that Strickland had dealt with for so many years as a soldier—and he was pretty certain that neither of his team members really understood who, or what, they might be dealing with.

Maria appeared in the aisle again. "We're less than thirty minutes out from Chatham Airfield," she told them. "Bixby's got a bead on the truck via satellite; at its current speed, we should get there about twenty-five miles ahead of it. We'll have a helicopter waiting, and state police will set up a roadblock as soon as we land. Any sooner and our friends might realize that something is up."

She took the seat beside him and stared at her tablet screen, on which was a GPS map with a tiny yellow blip that represented Bixby's approximation of the truck's location. Zero leaned over to look at it—and his frown deepened.

"Maria," he noted, "that highway won't take them to Chicago. It leads north to the capital of Illinois... to Springfield."

"So?"

"So?" he parroted. "So they're headed to another Springfield, just like the Kansas attack? You don't find that strange?"

"Kent, Springfield is one of the most common names in the United States. There's at least forty of them. It's a coincidence."

He shook his head. "You know better than that."

She finally looked up from the screen. "It won't matter," she said firmly. "Because we're going to get to them first."

"Sure," he murmured in agreement. Maybe they were right and he was wrong. These people could have just been lunatics with a sonic weapon and no plan.

But it didn't feel that way to him.

As the Gulfstream descended quickly toward a small private airfield, Maria pulled a long black duffel bag from a rear storage compartment and unzipped it.

"We have to assume these people are armed with more than just the ultrasonic weapon." She pulled out an AR-15 with a scope in place of a carry-handle mount and a shortened stock, and passed it off to Zero.

"That's a little intense, don't you think?" he asked as he took the gun.

"It's modded to semi-auto. We're not shooting to kill, but we don't want any civilian casualties. If they open fire or, god forbid, use the sonic weapon, we need to be ready for that."

The jet's tires found purchase on the tarmac and Maria lurched forward. Zero instinctively stuck out an arm and caught her before she sprawled into the aisle.

"Thanks," she muttered, her cheeks turning pink.

"Is your head clear?" he asked her quietly but sternly.

"Yes. Of course it is. It's just..." She stood and smoothed her hands over her hair. "They attacked kids, Kent. Families. A *parade*. There was no reason for it."

"I know. But we've seen just as bad and worse. We'll get them... but I've got to know that someone's going to be there to save my ass when it needs saving." He grinned.

"Hey, I'm here too," Strickland offered.

Maria smiled thinly. "You've got two daughters waiting at home for you. And you still owe me dinner. Would be nice to have this done before it's too late for all that, wouldn't it?"

He nodded—except he *didn't* have two daughters waiting at home for him. But he wasn't about to say that. "Then let's go get it done."

Strickland pushed open the Gulfstream's door as it skidded to a stop and the three of them hurried out to board the waiting helicopter.

But there was no waiting helicopter.

"Goddammit." Maria hissed as she put her phone to her ear. "Where's the helo?" She winced, and then told them, "It's two minutes out. Coming from an Air Force depot north of here." Into the phone again she said, "Have the troopers set up the roadblock, slow traffic in the northbound lanes."

Zero secured the strap of his gear bag and slung the AR-15 over his shoulder. *This is where it counts*, he told his brain. *Let's not have any short circuits.*

There was a steady *whup-whup* of rotors as a black Bell UH-1 approached rapidly, setting down on the tarmac some yards from the nose of the Gulfstream. They scrambled aboard and the skids lifted off again before Maria could even fit a headset over her ears. She dropped into the copilot seat and gave the pilot the coordinates, and then patched them in to Bixby as Zero pulled on a headset and grabbed a canvas loop in the ceiling to steady himself.

"Bixby, we're about twenty-three miles from target," Maria said as the helicopter roared parallel with the highway. "Is the roadblock set up?"

"They're working on it now," Bixby told them through the radio. "Roadblock is about eight miles from the truck's current location. By my best estimation, they should get snagged in traffic just a minute or two before you arrive."

Their plan was to catch the truck in a traffic jam from the state troopers' blockade, and then fast-rope down from directly overhead, surrounding the box truck and apprehending anyone inside as quickly as possible. But as Zero hung onto the canvas loop in a white-knuckled grip, he glanced up at the sliding door of the helo and let out a small groan of disappointment.

"Maria," he said into the radio. "This helo doesn't have rappelling lines."

"What?" she twisted in her seat and her face fell. "You've got be kidding... Bixby! Change of plan. We're going to need a place to set the chopper down, as close to the truck as possible."

"Um... that could be a problem," the engineer said nervously. "This stretch of highway is largely residential, with a lot of trees and power lines."

"Just find us something!" she barked into the radio. "Twenty miles out."

With the Bell's cruising speed of about a hundred and ten knots and the truck, coming straight toward them at a presumed sixty-five to seventy miles an hour, they'd be on them in mere minutes, even if the roadblock slowed them. But Zero was all too aware that a helicopter landing alongside a highway was not exactly the most inconspicuous entrance. They'd have to disembark and move in immediately, with no hiccups and no surprises...

"Johansson!" Bixby shouted through the radio. "They left the interstate! The truck just turned off I-55, onto... State Route 108, heading westbound."

Maria shook the tablet as if it was an Etch-a-Sketch. "I lost the blip! Can you lock onto them again?"

"Trying..."

Alongside Zero, Strickland shook his head. He didn't need to say it aloud; their plan was all going to hell.

"You know this area?" Maria asked the pilot.

"Yes, ma'am."

"Get us to State Route 108 on the fastest route possible," she instructed. Zero swayed as the helo course-corrected to the southwest. "Bixby, tell me good news!"

"Okay, okay." The engineer sounded frazzled. "The state route runs perpendicular to I-55, so on your current route you'll be on a triangular path and end up about... three miles ahead of them."

"Roger that," Maria breathed. None of them said it, but Zero assumed they were all thinking it—they had no way to stop the truck now that they lost their roadblock. They couldn't very well shoot at it from the chopper; they wouldn't be able to hit the tires from their angle, and even if they could, they might risk hitting civilian vehicles. And they definitely couldn't land the chopper on a populated highway.

But there might be another way. The familiar sensation of tense excitement, that anticipation of adrenalin, bubbled up in his chest.

"There's 108, just ahead," the pilot announced.

"Reduce air speed and get us lower so we can get a visual," Maria ordered. The UH-1 dipped as they soared parallel to the highway, no more than a hundred and fifty feet from the ground, no doubt bewildering holiday commuters. Maria scanned the road through the windshield, looking for any sign of the box truck.

"Bixby," she said, "you have a location?"

"Looks like they're coming up on you," he replied. "Three-quarters of a mile and closing."

Zero's throat flexed. There would be no roadblock, no swooping down on fast-ropes—no element of surprise at all. In seconds the perpetrators in the truck would spot the chopper, and from there they would have no choice but to improvise.

"I've got visual!" Maria shouted suddenly. "Turn us around, keep on them!"

The helicopter's air speed dropped drastically and the tail spun, turning the Bell in a tight one-eighty so abruptly that Zero's feet left the cabin floor for a moment.

"I can keep pace with them for as long as we've got fuel," the pilot said into the radio, "but I hope you've got some plan on how to stop them."

"We should call the troopers back," Strickland suggested. "They can get ahead of them, create another roadblock…"

"No." Zero shook his head. The people in that truck were well aware there was a helicopter on their tail; they couldn't risk waiting longer. "Get us lower. Low as you can."

Maria spun sharply in her seat. "Kent, you can't be serious."

He shrugged in a gesture that he hoped looked confident. "I've done it before." He zipped up his jacket, secured the AR-15 and his gear bag, and then pulled open the sliding cabin door. Chilled November wind instantly swirled through the helicopter.

Zero leaned out precipitously, hanging onto the canvas loop. Below him, he could see the green box truck—and there was no doubt they saw the chopper. The truck jumped in speed, swerving around slower traffic, weaving between the two westbound lanes. Cars in both directions screeched to a halt or pulled over, either baffled over the appearance of the helicopter or trying to get a photo.

"Get right over top of them!" Zero instructed. "And low as possible!"

"You're not *actually* going to—" But the pilot's protest was cut off as Zero pulled the headset from his ears and tossed it over his shoulder. Clinging to the open door, he stepped carefully down onto the skid of the Bell. At least that would reduce his fall by a few feet.

The chopper dipped again. The cold wind raked at Zero like claws. The truck swerved in some vain attempt to outrun a helicopter, and they swerved with it. Zero's right foot slipped from the skid, his body teetering forward over nothing—

A strong hand grabbed the back of his collar. He nodded quickly to Strickland over his shoulder as he regained his footing.

Don't think about it too much.

He'd done it before; he'd once leapt from a helicopter onto the top of a moving train. Though that was of little comfort now. The train had afforded him a lot more runway for error than a sixteen-foot-long box truck.

Just do it.

The truck was closer now; they were about twenty-five feet directly over it. The helicopter wasn't going to get any lower, and the truck could swerve out of the way at any moment.

He let out a breath, and he jumped.

CHAPTER EIGHTEEN

The thing about falling from any significant height, in Zero's experience, was that it always felt like it took a lot longer than it did. The mere seconds that one would fall from twenty-five feet, or fifty feet, or a hundred feet seemed to stretch onward, as if the world had suddenly turned to slow-motion. He knew that it was a trick of the brain, full thoughts forming cogent in his head about every horrible thing that could go wrong on landing.

As he fell from the skid of the UH-1, he forced himself to focus and not think about missing his mark or becoming a bloody skid mark on an Illinois highway. He reminded himself that the momentum of the truck would try to force him backwards, so he would have to propel forward on the moment of impact.

But as his feet touched down on the roof of the truck, knees bending with the fall, the driver slammed the accelerator. The truck lurched forward suddenly, and there was nothing Zero could do to keep from hurtling backward.

He fell onto his back, heels flying over his head, sliding on his stomach, hands grasping out fruitlessly for any hold to stop himself but there were none, nothing but smooth metal. His feet slid out over the rear of the truck, then his knees, his waist. He had no way to stop himself. He was going to career right off the back. Broken bones would be the least of his concerns; the oncoming traffic stopping before they pancaked him was far more worrisome.

As his torso slid out over the back of the truck, something white fluttered in his face and he reached for it, grabbing it in both fists. The muscles in his arms screamed in protest as they went taut. His body swung and slammed painfully into the truck's steel rear door, rattling it in its tracks.

Zero was clinging to a white nylon strap that had been caught in the top of the door. He murmured a quick prayer to whoever was the patron saint of lifesaving strokes of luck; if not for that errant strap, he'd be a dead man.

Despite the searing pain in his arms and shoulders, he held tightly onto the nylon and planted his feet on the back of the box truck, shimmying his way around the corner as far as the strap would afford him—just far enough, thankfully, for his feet to rest of the steel wheel well of the rear passenger tire. The truck swerved into another lane and he nearly lost his footing, but clung tight.

Okay, now what?

If he dared to let go with one hand he could reach for his pistol, possibly blow out a front tire. But the angle would be difficult, and if anyone was in the passenger seat they needed only to glance in the side mirror and they'd see him there.

Not that they didn't already know he was there, thanks to his less-than-graceful landing.

Just as he was about to let go with one hand and go for the Glock in his jacket, he saw movement in his periphery. His gaze darted to the right as something protruded from the passenger-side window—something long, like the barrel of a large gun, but green and tapered to a point at the end...

A rocket-propelled grenade.

The truck swerved right, across a lane and right onto the shoulder. Zero was so focused on the weapon that he wasn't prepared for it and lost his footing, bouncing off the corner of the truck as the nylon strap swung him back to the rear. He smacked against it again, cursing, arms burning.

"RPG!" he shouted. "They have an RPG!"

Panic reached its icy claws into his chest and gripped his heart. He didn't have his radio earpiece in. He'd taken it out after the Vegas op and hadn't replaced it.

He couldn't warn them; he could only hope they saw it too.

The hiss of the miniature missile was impossibly loud, even with the cold wind whipping in his ears. Clinging to the strap for his life, Zero could do nothing but watch, his neck craned awkwardly as the projectile rocketed up toward the helicopter.

The UH-1 veered, but not fast enough. The RPG struck a glancing blow to its tail and exploded, tearing off the rear rotor and most of the tail with it. The helicopter spun wildly, unable to stabilize, losing altitude and speed.

The last thing Zero saw before it vanished behind a roadside copse of trees was a flash of Todd Strickland, through the open cabin door, clinging to a loop in the ceiling while the rest of him was airborne, feet flailing.

He was alone now.

But he still had a job to do.

Anger and adrenaline fueled him in equal measure as he once again set his feet against the rear of the truck and pushed off, swinging around the corner and landing on the steel of the wheel well. The truck swerved left and right, trying to throw him off, but he wrapped the strap tightly around his left fist.

Without giving it a second thought, he let go with his other hand, unzipped the jacket enough to free the Glock, and leaned out as far as he dared to give himself a bigger target as he aimed for the front tire.

He fired once. The report was dulled by the wind and the roar of the truck's engine, but the sparks that flew from the front wheel well told him that he missed.

Your aim is tracking to the left, he reminded himself. He aimed again, compensating for his injury. From the corner of his eye he saw movement again from the passenger window of the truck's cab—a stubby machine gun, and along with it, a tiny hand and arm.

Too tiny, he thought, to have been the redheaded woman's. But he had no time to discern its owner. He focused and aimed again; if he didn't hit it this time, he'd be shredded by machine gun fire in the next few seconds.

The second thunderous clap from the Glock hit home. The front tire exploded; the truck veered right. The machine gun tumbled away from the tiny arm that held it. Zero held on as tight as he could while the truck left the road, careening down a small embankment at around eighty miles an hour.

Each bounce of the tires from the ruts in the ground sent him smacking painfully against the aluminum side. He lost his footing on the wheel well and cried out in pain as his entire body weight strained against the strap, crushing his hand.

He had to let go.

He let the Glock fall to the grass as he reached up for the strap and unwrapped it from around his fist. Then he planted a foot on the side of the truck and half-fell, half-jumped away. He hit the ground hard on his back and rolled with it, tumbling two and a half times before coming to a stop on his stomach, panting.

The truck kept going. Despite the blown-out tire and lack of road, the driver seemed intent to try to regain control. It bounced violently through a field, veering uncertainly. A rearview mirror snapped off against the side of a tree. Zero squinted; there was something white ahead of it. A vinyl fence—a home. A residential neighborhood.

The truck tore through the fence as if it was made of paper and smashed into an oak tree on the other side in a collision so violent the rear tires came off the ground.

Then, finally, there was silence.

Zero pulled himself to his feet, groaning in pain. His arms and shoulders hurt. The bruise around his left hand from the strap was already turning purple. He was certain he would have plenty more bruises to discover later from the tumble off the truck. But still, he had a job to do.

He started in the direction of the truck, through yellow weeds two feet tall—but he stopped just as suddenly. He had taken several reckless risks in just the last two minutes. What point was there in rushing into another one?

Instead he slung the AR-15 from his back. He lowered himself to a kneeling position, more than half of him obscured by the weeds, and brought the rifle's stock to his shoulder. He estimated the truck had stopped about forty yards from where he'd landed. An easy shot.

Through the scope, there was no movement except for the smoke pluming from beneath the hood. He waited and watched as sirens whooped in the distance, growing steadily louder.

Then the driver's side door rattled twice. After a few seconds it was forced open, and a woman fell out of the cab. No, not a woman—*the* woman. She had fiery red hair and fair skin and landed in the grass on her hands and knees, coughing.

Zero studied her through the scope. She wore all black, no makeup, with plain features. If not for her bright hair, she could have easily blended into any crowd. There was blood on the side of her face, but she didn't appear to be seriously injured. This was the woman they'd been looking for. He had no doubt about it. The shot would be easy; nonlethal. Clip her in the shoulder, or a careful hit to the thigh, avoiding the femoral ...

But then the woman stood. She turned back to the cab, and she stretched out her arms. Like she was beckoning someone. Zero remembered the passenger of the truck, the one that had fired the RPG at the helicopter; the one that had nearly shredded him with machine gun fire.

Tiny arms reached out of the cab. The woman stepped forward, pulling her passenger from the wreckage.

It was a child.

It was a little girl, wearing jeans and a blue hooded sweatshirt.

Zero watched through the scope as the redheaded woman cradled the girl in her arms like a mother carried her tired child at the end of a long day.

He still had a shot. He could hit the woman in the leg. The girl would fall, but nothing nearly as bad as the collision she'd just been in. His finger was on the trigger. It would just take a squeeze ...

A memory surged through his head, powerful and intrusive.

You're in Bosnia.

On the second floor of what used to be someone's home, long since gutted by bombs.

You lie on your stomach, the barrel of the rifle barely jutting between broken bricks as you peer through the scope. Waiting. Patient.

Your target rounds a corner four blocks north. He's walking home alone. Eyes cast downward at the ground. You have the shot—

Wait. His face lights up as he spots something on the ground and bends to pick it up. It's shiny. A piece of metal—a coin, perhaps. He looks pleased as he sticks it in his pocket.

You have the shot.

You know from your briefing package that he is nine years old.

Your finger compresses the trigger. You take your shot...

Zero sucked in a breath, backing away from the scope as he snapped out of the memory. No—it felt much more like an experience than a memory. An experience he'd had.

Did I ... did I kill a child?

He wouldn't have. He couldn't have. His gaze flitted back and forth across the tall yellow grass, searching for an answer that wasn't in the weeds. Searching his memory for some indication that it had been a lie, one of the fabrications that Guyer had warned him about. But he found nothing that would confirm or deny the reality of it.

He saw only a boy in the dirt, as a single shot echoed from rooftops.

The Russian. Suddenly he remembered where he was, what he was supposed to be doing. He peered through the scope again and scanned the scene of the smoking truck, the crushed fence, the damaged oak tree.

They were gone. In the moments it took the memory to distract him, they'd vanished.

Zero let the AR-15 fall to the ground. He rubbed his temples as if he could coax something out of them. Was it real? Had he assassinated a boy? And if it *was* real, why hadn't that come back with the rest of his memories?

Was it something he'd repressed, buried so deep down in shame and ignominy that it took another child in his crosshairs to bring it back?

"Kent!" He turned at the sound of Maria's voice to see her hurrying through the tall weeds toward him, a slight limp in her left step. "Are you okay?"

"I'll be fine," he told her as she reached him. "You're bleeding."

"It looks worse than it is." There was a narrow, bloody tear in her thigh, and the leg of her jeans was soaked dark. "Nothing vital, I promise."

Strickland trotted up behind her. He had a couple of abrasions on his neck, but otherwise seemed fine—likely thanks to being airborne when the helicopter went down. "You dropped this," he said, holding out the Glock.

"Thanks." Zero tucked it in his jacket. "The pilot?"

"Broken arm, probably a concussion, but he'll live," Maria said quickly. She glanced past him, at the crashed truck. "Did you see anyone?"

"I did. The woman—the redhead—she was driving. And you're not going to believe this, but … she has a child with her."

"A child?" Maria repeated blankly.

"A little girl, no more than eleven or twelve." Then he added quietly, "They slipped away."

Maria glanced down at the AR-15 lying in the grass near his feet, but she said nothing. If there was a child involved, he knew she wouldn't have been able to take the shot either.

"I'll put out an alert immediately," she said. "They can't have gotten far. You two check the back of the truck—*carefully*. If we have their weapon, this is still a win."

As she got on the phone with the state troopers to set up a dragnet, Zero and Strickland hiked the distance between them and the wreckage. But he already had a sinking feeling at what they would find.

Strickland covered him with the AR-15 while Zero pulled up the rear gate, rolling it to the ceiling with a clatter.

It was, as he suspected, completely empty.

"I don't understand," Strickland said, lowering the rifle. "Was this a decoy?"

"Not necessarily," Zero murmured. It was certainly a distraction—but also more than that.

They wanted us to find this truck.

This was part of their head games.

They wanted us to use our intelligence, our resources, our best technology … and still come up empty-handed.

The only thing that he couldn't figure was the redheaded woman. She was, quite literally, the face of the operation. She couldn't seem to help but show herself. Why did they want her so visible?

And why was there a child with her?

He looked down and noticed that his hands were trembling slightly. He stuck them in his pockets as they hiked back to Maria to tell her the bad news. She was still on the phone, establishing parameters to find the woman—but much like the truck, he already knew there would be nothing to find.

The woman and the girl. The ultrasonic weapon. The inexplicable loss of his skills. And now, the resurfaced memory of an assassination.

Once again Zero found himself left with far too many questions, and no answers.

CHAPTER NINETEEN

"**D**o we really have to do this now?" Sara asked, fidgeting uncomfortably in the chair.

"I'm afraid so." The woman seated across from her smiled warmly. "This is what we call the entrance interview, and it's important that we do it as soon as possible after your admission. You walking through those doors meant you're ready for treatment; we want you to be honest and open with us about your reasons for coming here."

Her dad had been right about one thing; Seaside House Recovery Center was a nice place, though it didn't resemble any sort of house. It was a square, contemporary-style building in beige and soft browns, with lots of windows and skylights and two smaller outlying buildings accessible by covered causeways. They were only a few blocks from the beach; Sara could smell the salt on the air.

Maya had stayed with her long enough to fill out the admission paperwork, and then they'd hugged for a long moment, and then her sister was gone, headed back to New York. A female administrator with a kind face had given her a quick tour and showed her where she'd be staying, which looked a lot like a room out of any halfway decent hotel.

Now she sat in the office of Dr. Mavis Greene, an African-American woman Sara pegged to be near fifty, wearing a small crucifix and a pantsuit as they sat across from each other in matching brown armchairs. There was no desk between them; that was pushed up against the far wall because, as Dr. Greene had explained, "There are no barriers between you and me at Seaside House."

Dr. Greene crossed her legs and set her notepad on a knee. "Sara, I'm just going ask you a few questions about yourself, some of which you may have already answered upon admission—but please, indulge me." She smiled again.

Sara could imagine that some people might see warmth in that smile, but she thought it looked fake. Insincere. Judgmental.

"How old are you, Sara?"

"I'm sixteen."

"Sixteen," Dr. Greene repeated softly. "And I understand you're emancipated. When did that happen?"

"About…a year and a half ago, I guess. Two summers ago."

"Two summers ago." The doctor, or clinical psychologist, or whatever she'd introduced herself as that Sara couldn't quite remember, scribbled notes on her pad after each question. "So you were only fourteen at the time?"

"Fifteen. I'd just had my birthday. It's in the summer."

"In the summer," Dr. Greene murmured.

"I'm sorry, can you… can you stop doing that?" Sara said abruptly. "The repetition?"

The doctor smiled. "I apologize. It's a technique called 'echoing.' They teach therapists and medical professionals to repeat the last few words of a response so the patient understands that we're paying attention."

"I bet some of them find it pretty irritating," she said flatly. She wasn't trying to be openly hostile. It was just that everything about this place felt…manufactured. Forced. Contrived. It felt like an illusion designed to placate people who were trying to escape their real-life problems.

Dr. Greene merely chuckled. "I'll do my best to rein it in." She consulted her notes and then asked, "Sara, can you tell me about the *nature* of your emancipation? I assume it was a falling-out with family?"

She nodded. "Yeah. My dad."

"I understand that these kinds of things can be very difficult to talk about. Would you be willing to share with me what happened between you?"

Sara bit her lip. What was she supposed to say? *My dad was the reason my mom was murdered. He knew who killed her and kept it from us. He let her murderer walk free.*

"No," she said instead. "I don't really want to talk about that."

Dr. Greene nodded slowly. "That's fine. We'll have plenty of time together. You can take as long as you need. However…I do need to ask another difficult question. All I need to know is if the falling-out with your father had anything to do with abuse; that is, emotional, physical, sexual—"

"No!" Sara blurted out. "No. There was no abuse. It was…" She was certain this woman was not going to back down without some kind of answer. "Look, my mom died a while back. Almost four years ago. And my dad, he…he lied to me and my sister about how it happened. He thought he was protecting us."

"But when you learned the truth, you didn't feel protected," Dr. Greene guessed. "You felt angry. Betrayed."

"Yes."

"You felt like you couldn't trust him anymore."

"Yes." *Jeez, what is this woman's degree in?* Sara thought sourly. *Obvious answers?*

She flashed her smile again. "Let's move on. I understand you're here for substance abuse, primarily anti-anxiety medications and cocaine. When did that begin?"

She shook her head. "I'm not exactly sure. Maybe a year ago? It was on and off. I tried to stop a bunch of times."

"But it's hard. That's why you're here." The doctor scribbled a few notes. "I also see here that you've been clean for a month now, which is terrific. Yet you wouldn't be here if you trusted yourself not to go back to it."

Once again, paging Dr. Obvious. But Sara said nothing.

"Sara, it seems to me like your addiction—as with a lot of people in your situation—is a means of escape. I think the best way to go about your treatment is going to be to reconcile the issues with your mother and father, but also to help remind you of what brings you joy. I don't think you need the drugs as much as you need something for yourself, something that makes you want to wake up every morning and greet every day to the fullest. So I'd like to go back a little further, to before your habits started. There must have been something in your life that meant a lot to you; some dream, an aspiration, a goal... Can you think of anything like that for me?"

Sara shrugged, staring at the checkered pattern in the carpet. What did she have? The only thing she could think of before all of this happened was her family. Wait, that wasn't quite true. Before her emancipation, even before she discovered who her father truly was, she'd wanted to be an artist.

"My mom," she said quietly, "she used to restore paintings for a museum. She was really artistic. I think I got that from her. I used to draw a lot, and paint."

"You used to paint," Dr. Greene repeated. Then she smiled and said, "I'm sorry, force of habit. But I think that's an excellent place to start. We have a fully stocked art room here, with just about any supplies you could want. You're welcome to use it anytime."

"Great."

"Well." Dr. Greene glanced at her watch. "I think that's enough for this evening. It's getting late, but we don't institute a curfew here. There's a rec room, with some games and a television and a few computers."

Right. The administrator who had given her the tour had mentioned the TV and computers. Their Wi-Fi network and cable had blocks on them; not just for pornography and that kind of stuff, but also for social media, certain news sites, anything they thought might trigger their patients back into destructive behavior.

"Thanks, but I'm pretty tired," Sara told her as she stood. "Think I'll just head back to my room."

Dr. Greene smiled and shook her hand. "All right, Sara. Thank you for meeting with me. I'll follow up with you in a couple of days—and I really hope to see some of your artwork."

"Yeah," Sara murmured as she headed for the door. "Maybe."

She left Dr. Greene's office and headed down the corridor. It was brightly lit, but eerily empty and just as quiet. She wondered if the other patients—or "guests," as the administrator had called them—were allowed to go home to their families for the holiday.

It was fitting; she was actually just as alone as she felt.

This was a mistake. Just the few minutes in the office with Dr. Greene had shown her that. She could see how some people might be reassured by the doctor's smile, or find her words and tone of voice comforting. But Sara just found her to be sycophantic—a word she didn't realize she'd picked up from Maya until she thought it.

These people couldn't help her. They would try to analyze her, get her to open up with their therapy sessions and techniques. But she couldn't open up to them. What would she say—that her mother had been murdered by a CIA agent? That her father had lied for years about his identity? That she was constantly tired and struggled sleeping because she still had night terrors about being kidnapped and trafficked?

She couldn't be honest with them, which was an oversight not only on her part but on her dad's and Maya's as well. Without honesty, any therapy—and by extension, this whole place—was a waste of time.

Well, she thought, maybe not a complete waste. Dr. Greene sounded right about one thing: she needed to reconcile her mother's death and the issues she still had with her dad if she was going to stay clean.

But you can do that on your own. You don't need this place. You just needed a push in the right direction, and you got one.

You know what you need to do. And that Dr. Greene can't help you do it.

Sara headed for the rear of the building, where the guests' rooms were, which meant she had to pass the corridor that led to the main entrance of the facility. She peered down its length, past the admissions office, past the front desk, to the sliding glass doors that led out into the quickly darkening evening. There was a man there, an older man in a blazer and tie, seated near the doors and poking at a cell phone screen. He wasn't a guard; he was just there to witness the comings and goings and report them to the administrators if necessary.

There was nothing legally keeping Sara here. As her dad had mentioned, she was emancipated, so she could leave anytime she wanted. But the man by the doors would see her, and he would report it, and they would call her father—who, if he wasn't still out there doing whatever it was he was doing, would come for her again.

She couldn't have that, for the same reason she couldn't just call her dad and voice her concerns. He would try to make her stay. No, she needed to get out of this place in such a way that they didn't notice she was gone at first. Maya had left her with fifty dollars in emergency cash, just in case. It should be enough to hop a bus back to Bethesda, she figured. If she could escape unnoticed, and could give herself a three-hour head start, she could make it back home and talk to her dad in person. Convince him that this wasn't the right place for her.

She just had to figure out a way to get out that gave her enough time to do that before anyone knew she was gone.

CHAPTER TWENTY

Zero took no solace in the fact that he was right. The police failed to find the redheaded woman and the little girl with her after the truck crashed. They had expanded their dragnet and continued the search even as night fell, but he knew that there would be nothing to find. She was long gone by now, most likely to rendezvous with the others in her group, wherever the ultrasonic weapon was being kept.

And it was his fault that she had gotten away. He had her in his sights, and he'd failed.

Now he sat alone in a conference room of an Illinois state police department off of I-55, just a few miles north from where he had failed. He stared into the middle distance under the droning buzz of florescent lights.

There would likely be hell to pay over the downed helicopter, the failed roadblock, the truck crashing into a residential backyard. There would be harsh inquiries into how they could have failed, how they had fallen for the distraction.

But Zero wasn't thinking about any of that. He was thinking about the Bosnian boy he had seen in his crosshairs, in his memory. He was thinking about the boy he had killed.

As much as he tried to convince himself that it wasn't real, that it couldn't be real without anything to substantiate it, he simply *felt* it. The memory had come back as if he was actually there; he had smelled an acrid scent of smoke on the air. He saw the boy's genuine smile at finding the coin on the ground in the moment before his murder.

Murder. He might as well call it what it was. Not an assassination; it was murder.

And he couldn't stop playing it over and over in his head.

He heard the conference room door open but didn't look up until he heard Maria's voice quietly say, "Hey. Got you this." She set a white takeout carton on the table. "Chicken lo mein. You need to eat something."

"Thanks," he murmured. "But I'm not hungry."

What if this memory was something that my subconscious was fighting to keep locked away? he wondered. *Maybe even before the memory suppressor. What if this was my own mental block, and not an artificial one?*

"...from the NSA or our tech team," Maria was saying.

Zero blinked a few times and tried to get out of his own head. He had barely realized she was talking. "Sorry, what?"

She frowned at him. "I was just saying, we haven't gotten any new information or leads from the NSA or our tech team. Since we know the woman was here, we've narrowed OMNI's search parameters to a four-state region surrounding Illinois. We can only hope that she tries to contact her team or her people..."

"She won't." Zero shook his head. "They played us, and it worked. She won't let us find her again that easily."

Maria sighed heavily. "I just don't understand. What was the point of it? There hasn't been another attack—not that I *want* there to be one. But there's no purpose to a decoy if there's not something else to distract us from."

"Because that wasn't the point," Zero said simply. "It wasn't a decoy. It was a message."

"Oh? Then what was the message?"

"That they've got the better of us."

Maria scoffed. "You're in their heads? You understand them all of a sudden?"

"Better than you do, yeah."

He knew how it sounded, and he expected her to snap back at him, to get angry. But instead she merely sat down beside him and put a hand on his arm. "I'm as frustrated as you are about this," she said softly.

I doubt it.

"But we're going to find them."

What possible reason would I have had for killing a child? He wasn't that person. He wasn't like John Watson, the man who had murdered Zero's wife simply because the CIA had ordered him to.

The door to the conference room opened again, and Strickland stuck his head in. "Johansson," he said. "Can I borrow you a moment?"

"Sure." She gave Zero's arm a slight squeeze. "Eat something," she told him. "We'll be off as soon as we have a direction."

But he barely heard her words. He was thinking about who else might have known about this new shadow of his past, who he could go to for answers. And he thought he already knew—the very same person he'd just been talking to.

Maria knew more about him than anyone else—possibly more than he knew about him-self. If there was darkness behind him, more darkness than he was aware of, she would be the most likely person to know about it.

But if it's something I didn't want myself to remember, can I trust her to tell me the truth?

Maria closed the conference room door behind her, leaving Kent inside to his thoughts. She was worried about him; he seemed out of it. She had been furious when she discovered that the truck was empty, but Kent had been oddly placid. Ordinarily on an op like this, he would be just as eager and adamant as she was about finding these people—if not more so. But now...

"What is it?" she asked Strickland over the din of state troopers working to find the redheaded Russian woman.

Todd glanced over her shoulder. "Is he okay?"

"Yes. I mean... I don't know. He seems a bit dazed, if I'm being honest," she admitted. "Maybe it was the crash. I told him he should get checked out, but he refused..."

"I don't think that's it." Strickland's gaze flitted to the left. He knew something that he wasn't telling her.

"Explain?" she said curtly.

"He's just been acting strangely." Todd sighed hesitantly. "Back in Bixby's lab, when we were gearing up, he was holding the Glock in one hand, and the magazine in the other... and I swear if I didn't know any better, he had no idea what to do with it."

Maria couldn't help herself; she actually let out a short laugh. It was a preposterous notion. "You're kidding, right? He's loaded a gun a thousand times."

"I know. That's what I thought at the time. But then in Vegas, there was more. He was patting himself down, like he'd forgotten something." To Maria's flat look he quickly added, "I know that it doesn't sound like much. But you saw what happened with the truck and the redheaded woman. At that distance? He could have *easily* made that shot, Maria."

"There was a child," she countered. "I wouldn't have tried to make that shot. Not with a kid in the way. Would you?"

"I don't know. Maybe not." Strickland conceded quietly. "I'm just telling you what I saw."

Maria had to admit that Kent didn't seem himself—but at the same time she had to acknowledge that this was his first time back in the field, in an official capacity, in a long while. He was on the verge of repairing his relationship with his daughters when he got pulled away. There was undoubtedly a lot on his mind, more than just these attacks.

"Is that why you wanted to talk to me?" she asked.

"No, there's something else. State cops impounded the crashed grocery truck and did a thorough search. They found this." He pulled something from his jacket pocket—an older-model flip phone.

Maria frowned as she took it. "You two didn't find it when you searched the truck?"

"It had slipped between the cushions of the driver's seat," Strickland said. "There's no passcode to access it, but I couldn't make anything out. I don't read Russian."

Maria flipped it open and the screen lit up, showing about twenty-five percent battery life remaining. The phone was indeed in Cyrillic, and undoubtedly a burner; the digital screen wasn't even in color.

She checked the contacts first, but there was nothing there. The call log yielded a few results though; numbers, not associated with any names, the most recent of which was dated more than twenty-four hours earlier. She had been right; these people were staying off of phones ever since the Kansas attack.

But still, this was something. More than something. This was the best she could hope for under the circumstances. Then she opened the text messages, and what she read there made her throat run dry.

There was only one message thread, brief and one-sided and sent from an unassociated number that must have been another burner. There were three messages there, in Russian:

Get rid of truck.

Times Square.

We will be waiting.

"Christ," she murmured, a mixture of alarm and excitement rising. "We just hit the goddamn jackpot. We've got phone numbers, and a text message that suggests their next target is Times Square."

"Or it was left there intentionally." Neither of them had heard the conference door open behind them, but suddenly Kent was there, standing in the doorway. "A phone with that kind of information on it was just left behind, no screen lock or passcode?"

"We can't jump to that sort of conclusion," Maria argued. "That woman crashed the truck and got out of there in a hurry, with a child in tow. It's entirely possible she left it behind on accident—"

"We were supposed to find that truck," Kent countered. "They wanted us to see that woman. And by that logic, they wanted us to find the phone."

"You have to admit," Strickland said hesitantly, "it does seem a bit overly fortuitous."

Maria scoffed. She couldn't believe what she was hearing—and from both of them, no less. "It doesn't matter how fortuitous it might be, or what we were *supposed* to find." She waved the phone in front of their faces. "We have phone numbers, and a text that suggests their next attack is going to be in the heart of New York City. I don't need to tell either one of you what sort of fallout we could be dealing with there. We need to move on this, and *now*."

Kent just shook his head. "I don't think this is the right move."

"Then what is?" she shot back. "You want to stay here, hope the cops find that woman before she gets halfway across the country?" She lowered her voice to almost a whisper and added, "I don't know what's going on with you, but I need you to snap out of it and focus, okay? You know as well as I do that we can't ignore this. We have to go, and we have to contact the right people, right away."

Kent didn't argue any further. He didn't even meet her gaze. He merely nodded.

"Grab your stuff, we're going back to the jet," she instructed. "I'll have Bixby track the phone numbers from there, and we'll alert Director Shaw and the president and see how they want to handle this."

Times Square, she thought as Strickland and Kent separated to grab their gear. An incident there would be a thousand times worse than the Midwest attack on any given day. And Kent's strange reluctance to act on it was almost just as alarming. It wasn't like him at all.

Maybe Todd was right, and something was going on his head that was worse than what she thought. Clearly some demon was cloying at his mind. But she couldn't worry about him and the safety of innocent people at the same time. One would have to take precedence— and it meant that Kent would have to take care of himself.

CHAPTER TWENTY ONE

President Rutledge paced the West Wing corridor, his black wingtip shoes barely making a sound on the impossibly clean carpet. It still felt strange, living in the White House; often it felt to him more like a museum than a home, and at times like this, he felt terribly out of place.

He couldn't sit in the Oval Office any longer, or the Situation Room, or even his bedroom—not like he was getting any sleep that night. His top agent, a man named (amusingly enough) Roosevelt, had even suggested that Rutledge be moved to a more secure location until the weapon and the people behind it were found. But he had refused.

He wasn't going anywhere. Not until he had answers. Not until he had results. He needed good news. He needed...

I need to stop being followed.

He paused in his pacing and turned on a heel to face the two Secret Service agents that were following him at about a five-yard distance. "Guys." He smiled as amiably as he could. "I know this is your job, but I'm not going anywhere. I just needed to stretch my legs. Think you could give me some space?"

The pair of agents each nodded stoically. "Yes, sir. Of course."

"Thanks." The two of them strode briskly down the hall and took a position at the far end, from which they could still see him and act if necessary.

And Rutledge paced. For all the presumed power that a president held, he felt rather impotent at the moment. The ultrasonic weapon was still out there somewhere. The people were confused. The media was speculating. The answers were his to give, yet he was adamant about keeping this under wraps for as long as possible to avoid panic. And while all that was going on, Tabby Halpern was attempting to organize a special session of Congress for the following day to vote in a vice president.

Never a dull moment around here. He missed dull moments.

Rutledge reached the end of the hall and, just briefly, he considered making a dash around the corner. Not leaving the White House, but fleeing from his security detail, finding a place that he could truly be alone, even if just for a short while.

Running and hiding. He almost laughed at himself. *You're thinking about running and hiding.*

Instead he turned around to pace back the other way—and very nearly ran headlong into one of the Secret Service agents. Hadn't he *just* asked them to give him a break?

"I'm sorry, sir." The agent held something out to him. A cell phone. "There's a call for you. CIA Director Shaw is on the line."

"Oh." Rutledge patted his own pockets; he'd left his phone back in the Oval Office. "Right. Thank you."

"Would you like to take it in the office, sir?"

"No. This is fine." *Please be good news.* He took the phone, and the agent dutifully backed off as Rutledge put it to his ear. "Director Shaw? This is Rutledge."

"Good evening, Mr. President," Shaw said quickly and flatly. "There's been a development."

Rutledge almost sighed out loud. A "development" was rarely good news.

"I have Deputy Director Johansson patched in with us," Shaw continued. "I'll let her explain what's happening."

"Thank you, Director Shaw," Johansson said. Her voice sounded somewhat distant and tinny. "Mr. President, I'll try to keep this brief. We located the truck and one of the perpetrators, but she managed to elude us—"

"She?" Rutledge couldn't help but ask. He hadn't expected that.

"Yes sir. The weapon wasn't aboard either. But we did recover a cell phone, and on it is a text message exchange in Russian that suggests their rendezvous point, and very possibly their next target, is Times Square."

This time the president did sigh aloud, the air rushing out of him as if he was squeezed. "Times Square. Jesus. Do we know anything else?"

"I'm afraid not," said Johansson. "We don't have a time frame or a more specific location. We're en route now on a jet, ETA about eighty-eight minutes to LaGuardia. But under the circumstances, I have to advise an evacuation."

Evacuate Times Square? On the eve of a major holiday? He imagined that right then most New Yorkers were stuffed with food, or half-drunk on wine ... Would they even leave? "Johansson, we're talking about tens of thousands of people."

"No sir," she corrected. "I'm not just talking about Times Square. I'm suggesting that we evacuate the island of Manhattan, at least as much as possible."

Rutledge put out an arm, leaning against the wall to steady himself. She must have been joking. He wasn't even certain that such a thing was logistically possible. Where would they go? How long would that take?

"If the Russians are serious about striking at Times Square," Johansson continued, "they'll notice an evacuation attempt. That might inspire them to initiate early—or to relocate, and strike another target in the city."

"What if we put the city on alert," Rutledge countered. "Warn people of the possibility, advise that they stay indoors..."

"That won't matter, sir. The frequency the ultrasonic weapon uses can travel through walls, through glass, even through steel."

This was too much. The president knew what he *should* do; he should convene an emergency meeting of the joint chiefs to discuss this, prepare for the worst and determine a course of action. But the thought turned his stomach; he already had too many voices in his ear. He didn't need to contend with the likes of General Kressley, who would no doubt have a differing opinion about how to handle the situation.

"Is Agent Zero there with you?" he asked.

"I am, sir," said a male voice. "You're on speaker, on the jet."

"What's your take on this?" Rutledge asked.

Zero was silent for a long moment, long enough for the president to wonder if he lost the connection. But then he said at last, "I think Deputy Director Johansson is right, sir. We can't ignore this, and we don't have enough information to make any assumptions. In Las Vegas, we didn't evacuate because we had a specific meeting time and place to cut them off; here we're going in blind. We don't even know their motive for targeting..." Zero trailed off for a moment, and then murmured something under his breath.

"Sorry?" Rutledge asked.

"Black Friday," Zero said louder. "Black Friday is tomorrow. Times Square and the surrounding area is going to be packed with people..."

"And most of them don't wait until tomorrow," Johansson chimed in. "A lot of stores open their doors as early as midnight tonight. People are probably already coming in to wait in lines."

"If these people are allowed bide their time," Zero said, "we won't be talking about tens of thousands, Mr. President. We'll be talking about *hundreds* of thousands."

Rutledge didn't know what to say—other than Zero was right. He had hardly given a thought to the biggest shopping day of the year, or the fact that Fifth Avenue alone would be jammed so tightly with bargain-hunters that traffic would be at a standstill.

"What do I do?" he heard himself asking.

"Evacuate," said Zero firmly. "Start with Times Square—42nd Street up to 47th, and Third Avenue over to Seventh. After that, we go block by block, or even borough by borough."

"I'll have to call in the National Guard," Rutledge murmured. "Alert the NYPD."

"And it might be time to involve the FBI," Johansson added. "There are only three of us. We'll need help if we're going to find these people."

"Yes," Rutledge agreed simply.

"We'll be there as quickly as we can. Make the calls, sir. We'll take it from there." Johansson ended the call, but Rutledge continued holding the phone to his ear, longer than necessary. Finally he let his arm fall slowly by his side. He felt dazed, almost numb. More of his hair was falling out on the spot, he was certain.

He needed to call Tabby Halpern and get her to start making the necessary arrangements for the evacuation of New York. But for a moment he just stood there and struggled to gather his thoughts. The country needed leadership—but all he could think of was his former zeal for resignation.

Now he stood on the precipice of what could very well be one of, if not *the* largest terror attack on American soil. How would he go down in the history books if he allowed that to happen under his brief watch? How would it look if he resigned immediately afterward? Putting Joanna Barkley behind the desk wouldn't be perceived as a heroic move. It would look like cowardice. He would be the man who spent thirty-something days in office and managed to let the Russians trample right over them before putting it all promptly behind him.

Rutledge shook his head like a wet dog. He had never been one to back down before, he reminded himself, and he wasn't about to give in to the pressure of the position just yet. He dialed Tabby's number and considered how to explain that they needed to evacuate more than three million people from Manhattan.

Chapter Twenty Two

"No, no, *no*," Angela scolded as she waved her arms like an air-traffic controller. "You cannot put designer handbags that close to the entrance. It'll become a chokepoint. We want to get people in the door and moving, direct the flow of foot traffic."

Her young employee, Chloe, simply blinked at her. Chloe was twenty-three, an absolute wunderkind at accessorizing—but unfortunately had about as much common sense as a housefly.

"We're creating a lane here," Angela explained gently. "People that risk Third Avenue on Black Friday are coming here to find something specific, so the hot-ticket items go over *there.*"

"Right," said Chloe. "Of course. Sorry, Angela."

"It's fine, kiddo. Just get it done."

Angela stepped back and sighed as Chloe worked to wheel the rack away from the entrance. She wished she had more help; even with the offer of double time and a half, there weren't many people that were willing to put in hours on the evening of Thanksgiving to make sure the store was ready for the Black Friday onslaught. After all, they would be all-hands-on-deck before sunrise.

Some of them, like Chloe, had no idea what to expect. You couldn't, not really; not until you'd seen it with your own eyes. But Angela had been on these front lines for most of her life, having spent the last twenty-two years in retail. In fact, aside from one glorious year when she'd been vacationing in Riviera Maya over the holiday, she had worked every single Black Friday since the time she was Chloe's age.

And every year, it felt like they opened earlier and earlier, which meant coming in to finalize their setup while the taste of turkey and cranberry sauce was still on her tongue. Even two hours earlier, when she'd arrived to unlock the store, there had already been a trio of women camped outside, sitting in folding chairs with blankets over their shoulders and sharing cocoa from a thermos.

Unreal, she thought. If she didn't have to work it, there was no way in hell she'd ever venture out on Black Friday.

"Missy, hey." Angela snapped her fingers twice at a thirty-something blonde who worked in women's. "Help Chloe with those handbags, yeah? And I want scarves moved over there, closer to the registers. It's supposed to be a rough winter; they'll be a great impulse buy."

"Sure thing, boss."

Boss. Angela bit her lip to keep the smile off her face. It had been a struggle, proving herself to be worthy of her title, but she earned it. Assistant manager to one of New York's biggest and best department stores—maybe *the* best, if she could say so herself. If all went according to plan, she might one day have Tom's job, and run the whole place.

Then I won't have to be here doing this anymore, she mused. The general manager of Macy's, Tom Spitz, would be there by midnight when they opened their doors, but at the moment he was still home with his family.

Angela crossed her arms, scanning for anything out of place or amiss. She still had to deal with the store's second level, but here, just beyond the entrance, would be ground zero come time. Getting people in the doors and properly dispersed was integral—

Her phone buzzed suddenly in her back pocket, accompanied by a shrill, blaring screech so loud that Angela jumped a little. It took her a moment to realize it was an emergency alert. Usually that meant an update on inclement weather or, god forbid, an occasional Amber alert for a missing child.

And she wasn't the only one that got it. From several directions around the mostly empty store she heard the screech of the alert as her employees received it too.

Angela pulled out her phone to check it.

Her face fell slack.

"What the hell…?" she murmured.

"Angela?" Chloe called to her hesitantly. "Is this real?"

She didn't answer, not at first. She was still in disbelief at the message. The emergency alert stated, in no uncertain terms, that the police were evacuating Times Square and its vicinity.

She knew that it was real; it had come through the emergency alert system, and yet her first instinct was to disregard it. It was nearly Black Friday, for crying out loud. They couldn't just leave.

"Angela?" Chloe called again uncertainly.

"Hang on," she snapped as she dialed the manager's number. But all she got in her ear was another blaring tone, this one telling her that the call couldn't connect. "Missy?" She snapped her fingers twice. "You have Tom's number? Try his cell."

Missy did so, but after a moment she shook her head. "Won't go through. I bet everyone in a ten-block radius is on their phones right now, trying to find out what's going on."

"Yeah," Angela muttered. *Why in the world would we be evacuated?* She needed to know the nature of the emergency if she was going to be expected to make a judgment call. She opened the browser on her phone, but the connection was slow. "Somebody try to check Facebook or Twitter, see if anyone is talking about this."

"Oh my god." Chloe's hand flew over her mouth, the other clutching her cell phone as she lifted her wide-eyed gaze to meet Angela's. Apparently the girl had been one step ahead of her. "Someone just tweeted ... they're saying it's a possible terror attack."

"Who said?" Angela demanded.

Chloe shook her head. "Everyone. It's all over. There was a leak from the mayor's office."

That was all Angela needed to hear. A tingle of fear ran up her spine. She was a lifelong New Yorker, remembered 9/11 all too terrifyingly well. Black Friday be damned; if there was even a chance that something like that could happen again, she wasn't about to endanger herself or the lives of her employees.

"Missy," she ordered, "get the guys out of the back room. Chloe, let everyone on the second floor know. We're leaving." The two women scurried off as Angela cupped her hands around her mouth and bellowed: "Everyone! We're locking up and getting out of here! Grab your things and meet at the front in five!"

Despite her warning, it took nearly ten minutes for the seventeen employees in the store that evening to stop what they were doing, gather their belongings, run to the restroom, whatever else needed doing. But after a brief eternity the group huddled near the exit and around Angela.

It was only then it occurred to her that she didn't know where they were supposed to go. "Chloe, did anyone say where we're evacuating *to?*"

The girl shook her head. "They only said to get out of the city."

Angela scoffed. *And go where? Jersey City? Queens?* She had an aunt in Staten Island, but wasn't even sure the ferry would be running.

Chatter rippled through their small crowd, nervous talk of hurrying home for loved ones and pets, trying to get through to relatives elsewhere in the city. Despite whatever responsibility she felt toward them, Angela knew that she couldn't be accountable for her employees; as soon as the doors were open, they would go their separate ways, at least until whatever this turned out to be was over.

"Listen up," she said loudly. She was divorced, no pets, no children; no one she had to run home for. The job was her life—and in that moment, it made her desperately sad.

"I understand a lot of you have family that you're worried about. Me, I'm going to my car and heading for the Lincoln Tunnel. I can fit four others. Anyone who wants to can come with me."

At first no one took her up on the offer, gazes averted and murmurs rising about family and friends. Then Chloe slowly raised her hand.

"I'll come. I ... don't have anywhere else to go."

Angela nodded. "All right. I'm in the parking deck on the next block. Everyone else, be safe. Be careful. And ... I don't know. Check in when you're able." She took the ring of keys, unlocked the tinted front doors, and pulled them open.

They were met immediately by a cacophony of sound. An orchestra of car horns blared from bumper-to-bumper traffic, backed by the stampede of pounding feet as people strode briskly or even jogged down the choked sidewalks, bags slung over their shoulders and children in their arms. Hundreds of voices shouted to one another, most panicked and frightened, others angry and confused.

"Jesus," Angela murmured. It had been barely more than ten minutes, maybe twelve, since they'd received the alert. But things were different now. If there was a threat, no one was sticking around to see if it would happen.

Her employees brushed past her, joining the chaotic throngs and disappearing into them, the night swallowing their features so that she quickly lost sight of them, just another moving part in a writhing mass.

"Chloe," she said as she locked the doors again behind her, "you go first. Walk in front of me so I can see you."

The girl did, joining the foot traffic with Angela right on her tail. They kept with the pace of the crowd—thousands of people, as far as she could tell—walking quickly as she wondered just how in the hell they were supposed to get anywhere in this traffic. And where were all these people planning on going? It wasn't as if they could all just hike over the bridge ...

"Oh!" She gasped as something gave way beneath her foot. Her heel snapped, twisting her ankle painfully. She stumbled forward, scraping her knees and palms on the concrete. Her purse tumbled to the ground. She tried to stand quickly and was met with someone's knees to the small of her back, forcing her back down again.

"Chloe!" she shouted.

"Angela?" The girl's voice sounded distant already.

"Move!" she shouted angrily to the sea of surging pedestrians. But they kept coming, no one paying her any mind, no one helping her up. She pulled off the broken shoe, and then the other for good measure, and tried to stand again. A man rushing past her bumped roughly into her shoulder, spinning her halfway around and almost forcing her again to the pavement.

She cursed at him and reached for her purse, but two hands scooped it up quickly.

"Hey!" she shrieked. "That's my purse! Stop!" Angela pushed against the current of people, craning her neck to see who had snatched it up. "Somebody has my purse! Stop!"

A few people looked at her, but no one stopped.

"Chloe!" she shouted. She couldn't see her anywhere. She was jostled again, shoved left and right. Finally she pushed her way through until her back was to a storefront window. Her vision blurred with tears. Everything was in that purse; she'd lost her wallet, her phone, her car keys, even the keys to the *store*... and now she'd lost Chloe too.

She had no idea where to go or what to do.

She winced as glass shattered somewhere, not far off. Shouts rose from the crowd. Angela hugged her arms over her chest, suddenly a lot more afraid.

Things were going to get far worse before they got any better.

Chapter Twenty Three

"Arms up," Samara ordered in Russian.

Mischa put her thin arms up straight overhead, and Samara tugged off the blue hooded sweatshirt with the word BROOKLYN across the front. The girl stood there in her jeans and white T-shirt, a small amount of blood staining the collar from a superficial cut on her neck. Her arms were bruised, and likely her chest as well from the seatbelt. But it didn't appear that anything was broken.

"Leg out," Samara said. Mischa lowered her arms and put her left leg out in front of her, and then slowly back to the floor. "Good. Now the other."

The girl winced slightly as she lifted her right leg, and then gritted her teeth quickly to try to hide it.

"What is it? A cut?"

"It's fine," the girl murmured. "Just hurts."

Samara nodded curtly. "Go wash up."

Crashing the truck had not been part of the plan. She had fully expected the Americans to locate the missing grocery truck, but not as quickly as they had. Her plan was to head north, to lead the authorities to Springfield, Illinois, and abandon the truck there—not only to waste their time and efforts, but in the hope that they would draw some wild parallel between it and the small town in Kansas, lead them on a false lead that other Springfields might be the next attack.

But they had located her quickly. What they did not know was that she had a frequency scanner in the truck, and had heard the correspondence to a local Air Force depot requesting an immediate helicopter. From there she had been forced to improvise.

After the crash, she and Mischa hurried from the scene, cutting across two residential backyards and hiding in a pair of garbage cans alongside someone's garage. The police would expect her to flee, she assumed; they would set up roadblocks, check vehicles, be on the lookout for the Russian woman with the fiery red hair. So they waited, long enough for Samara's legs to cramp in the stinking trash can, crouching in an inch of muck at the bottom of it, taking shallow breaths through her mouth.

She heard cars passing by. She heard the squawk of a radio as police searched the neighborhood. No one thought to peek inside the garbage cans, and Mischa stayed utterly silent. At long last, after about two hours, Samara dared to lift the lid. Night had fallen, and there was no one in sight. She helped Mischa out of the other can, and the two of them clung to the shadows as they stole among the homes. She spotted one with no lights on inside, jimmied open the back door easily, and held her breath—but there was no alarm.

Once inside, she located a telephone and made a call to a number she had memorized. She told the man on the other line the address at which they could be found, and then she checked the girl over for injuries.

They had been very fortunate that neither of them was seriously injured. And their plan had still worked, as far as it could have; the Americans would find the cell phone she had left in the truck and would believe that New York City was their next target.

As Mischa washed up in the bathroom, Samara went to the kitchen sink and splashed water on her face. They left the lights off, in case of vigilant neighbors. By her best guess, this home belonged to a couple with one child, a girl, likely a bit older than Mischa. It was far more house than three people needed.

So disgustingly American.

She wondered briefly what had happened to the man who was clinging to the grocery truck in the moments before the crash. The lunatic had leapt out of the helicopter and onto their roof. Even after all Samara had been through, she had never quite seen anything like that. With any luck, he had been thrown from the side, injured or possibly killed.

"Are you hungry?" she asked as Mischa reappeared in the dark kitchen.

The girl shook her head as she stared at the tiled floor. Something was bothering her, and Samara could guess what it was.

"You missed the helicopter. You had a clear shot."

"It moved," the girl murmured.

"Yes," Samara said flatly. "Helicopters move. What have I taught you? What have we trained for?"

"Aim where your target will be. Not where it is."

"That's right. And you lost the gun as well. If they recover it, they will have your fingerprints. They will be on file with the Americans forever."

Mischa reached a small hand into the pocket of her jeans, and then opened her fist. The Tootsie Roll, the one Samara had picked up at the parade, lay in the palm of her hand. She held it out, giving it back.

"No," Samara said. "Eat it."

Mischa hesitated.

"Go ahead."

But the girl did not. Instead she closed her hand around it and returned the candy to her pocket. It was a test, and they both knew it. She did not deserve the treat.

"They'll be here soon," Samara told her. "Go upstairs. There is a girl's room. Find different clothes. Be quick."

Mischa turned and dutifully headed up the stairs. Samara desperately wanted to turn on the television, to see what was happening, but she didn't dare. Instead she went to the foyer and rifled through a coat closet until she found a dark suede jacket and a baseball cap with some sports team's logo on it. She put on both. A minute later, Mischa returned wearing fresh jeans and a thick green sweater that was slightly too big for her.

The two of them stood there in the dark foyer in silence, watching through the front window for another sixteen minutes, until a truck rumbled to a stop directly in front of the house. It was another box truck, this one brown with yellow letters on the side—a package delivery company.

Samara opened the front door carefully and glanced about. She didn't see anyone. The two of them strode quickly to the truck, where the Asian man behind the wheel, dressed in a brown uniform, nodded stoically to them. They brushed past him and climbed into the rear as the truck pulled away from the curb.

Their other three cohorts were there, wearing their black masks with dark tinted lenses, seated on stacks of undelivered packages. In the center was a box much larger than the rest.

The weapon was not in New York, nor was it headed there. It had never left Illinois.

"You are hurt," one of the masked men noted in Russian. Samara had taught them fluency, but their accents would still sound strange and non-native to a trained ear.

"It's none of your concern," she snapped. "We're fine. We continue as planned." She held out a hand. "Phone."

One of the men handed her a smart phone and she immediately opened the browser. Then she smiled. "Mischa. Come see."

The girl peered over her shoulder, reading the news article at the same time. The authorities were attempting to evacuate New York, at night on a major holiday—and it did not seem to be going in their favor. More than a million people were fleeing in droves, jamming the bridges and tunnels. Just as many were refusing to leave. There were photos as well, of surging crowds and panic. There was a picture of a multi-car accident and even a fire. The National Guard had been deployed, but it did not seem to be helping matters.

Samara glanced over at the girl. She had a thin smile on her lips.

It was absolute chaos.

Beautiful, absolute chaos.

Samara smiled too as the truck headed southeast, toward their destination.

Chapter Twenty Four

Zero sighted in on the rifle-mounted scope, adjusting his trajectory by a few degrees to account for the afternoon's unusually high winds. He stood on one knee, the butt of a bolt-action TAC-308 tight against his shoulder. The blinds were lowered and closed, except for the bottommost three and a half inches of the open window, through which the barrel was aimed.

He breathed evenly, finger resting on the trigger. Any moment now.

He did not have to worry about being interrupted; the owner of this apartment was currently in police custody. Another agent had followed him on the street and slipped a small bag of cocaine into his pocket, and then tipped off the cops anonymously about being a dealer. Zero had all the time he needed.

He was on the third floor of the building, his aim directed slightly downward and across the street at the glass-fronted entrance of the Windsor Hotel in Dubai. For several minutes now he had maintained his aim, holding the rifle aloft, waiting for the precise moment. He scanned every face of every person that exited those doors, through his scope. Not one was aware they had, however briefly, been in his crosshairs. Not one of them knew that a single slip of the finger would have been their end.

He didn't know his target's name. He didn't even know what he had done to deserve such a fate. It was not his job to ask questions; it was his job to pull the trigger. He knew only that it was a matter of international security. If the CIA said jump, he would jump.

If the CIA said shoot—well, he would shoot.

He didn't know the target's name, but he knew his face. Zero had studied a high-resolution photo for more than an hour, memorizing every feature. The curl of his gray hair. The curve of his jaw. The neatly trimmed beard, slowly turning white at the corners of his mouth. When the time came, he would have mere seconds to identify and execute. There was no margin for error. There was no excuse for a miss—or worse, for an erroneous shot.

This man, this Dubai businessman, he was what they called a "domino hit." It meant simply that while his death would be fairly insignificant in the grandest scheme of things, it would lead to something bigger: the toppling of a regime. The surrender of an insurgent. A terror operation that failed to bankroll. That was his division's specialty, finding the smaller fish that seem paltry until they're no longer a part of the equation. And eliminating them.

The doors of the hotel swung open. Zero's heart rate remained steady, even as the time drew closer. A doorman held the glass door for a young woman, olive-skinned and stunning in red. Zero watched her through the scope as she headed toward a black town car.

Focus. The door swung back slowly. But just before it closed, someone pushed it again from the other side. A man in charcoal-gray suit. Curly gray hair. A neatly trimmed beard, turning white at the corners of his mouth...

Zero pulled the trigger. There could be no second-guessing or waiting. Before he had fully exited the hotel, the man's head jerked backward. Even before the report of the rifle cracked and echoed, the back of his head exploded into the lobby.

Zero did not wait to watch the body fall. The man was dead. He opened the chamber and the spent cartridge popped out. He caught it deftly and stuck it in his pocket as he stood. He stuffed the rifle into a long black bag made for tennis equipment, slung it over his shoulder, and was out of the apartment before the screams could float up to the partly open window.

"Zero? Hey. Wake up, pal."

He opened his eyes and sucked in a breath. Todd Strickland was standing over him quizzically, one hand on Zero's shoulder.

"You all right? You were tossing and mumbling."

"Yeah," Zero murmured. "Fine."

You're on the jet. Headed to New York.

The assassination had been a dream. But even as he thought it he realized that it wasn't quite true. It had been so vivid, so real—just like the resurfaced memory of the Bosnian boy.

Did I kill a man without knowing what he did or who he was?

That wasn't him. At least that wasn't who he was now. He would never just pull the trigger on someone just because the CIA told him to. If he did, if he *ever* did, then he would be no better than John Watson, who had killed a woman because he was told to. Watson had no idea at the time that the woman was the wife of Reid Lawson.

Zero rubbed his forehead. He had a powerful headache coming on, likely a product of all the questions clogging his brain. "Are we there?" he asked hoarsely.

Across the aisle from him, Maria had her nose buried in her tablet screen. "Almost. ETA is twenty minutes," she told him. "But the evac is *not* going well. Word got out, someone in the mayor's office spilled about the possibility of a terror attack. The whole island is trying to get out at once. Reports are coming in all over Manhattan of riots, looting, car accidents ..."

I need to see Dr. Guyer. His only hope was that the Swiss doctor could tell him if these memories were real or not. But Guyer's conference wasn't for another two days, and there was no way Zero could just abandon the op.

"Are you listening?"

He looked up to see Maria glancing expectantly at him. Had she kept talking? He wasn't sure. "Yeah. Sorry. I missed some of that."

"Two people have already been reported dead in this evacuation mess," she said somberly. "Many more missing. Stores are being mobbed for emergency supplies. Others are being looted. Homes, broken into." She shook her head.

"Well. New York is a bad idea," he said shortly.

Maria gaped at him, her brow furrowing at the same time. "Are you kidding? You told the president you agreed with me that we should evacuate."

He had said that. In the moment, it felt like the right thing to do. But now he was far less than certain. "I changed my mind. I think New York is a distraction. We won't find anything."

"Oh. Great." Maria scoffed loudly. "Hear that, everyone? Kent changed his mind. We can just pack it in, turn the plane around. No need to even investigate."

"Don't you see this is what they wanted?" he shot back. "The panic in the streets, the looting and mobs, *this* is what they're after. When the dust settles and nothing happens, people are going to be pissed off. And the next time we have a legitimate lead, they're going to think we're crying wolf. It'll be that much harder to get anyone to take it seriously."

"They'll spin it," Strickland cut in. "The White House will tell people that the evacuation scared the terrorists off, forced them to abandon the plan."

"Yeah, but they'll have nothing and no one to show for it," Zero countered. "No matter how you spin it, if there's no attack in New York tonight, we've lost. We'll have nothing to go on. They could be anywhere. There could be another attack happening, right now."

"Then we'll find them," Strickland said adamantly. "If they act, we'll get there, and take them down."

Zero shook his head. "Don't be simple."

Strickland's eyebrows rose precipitously. "Excuse me? Who are you calling simple?"

"They won't let us just find them," Zero argued. "They are *toying* with us, and it's working—"

"Enough!" Maria stood from her seat, staring him down. "You asked me earlier if my head was clear." Her tone was low and tight. "Is yours?"

"Yeah," he muttered. "I'm fine."

"Because the Kent I know would not ignore a threat. He wouldn't leave any stone unturned. He would use his head and figure this thing out. We are going to New York because we have a legitimate lead on an attack in New York, and we are going to see it through. Now unless you have anything of substance to add, sit down, and shut your mouth."

Zero sighed and sank into his seat. They couldn't see it. Not like he could. But she was right; he had nothing else to add, nothing to go on. Only their twisted mindset.

"We're over New York," the pilot said over the intercom. "Buckle up back there."

Zero pulled on his seatbelt, but he didn't feel the usual anticipatory flutter of excited and anxious nerves like he usually did on an op. He felt nothing—because he was certain there would be nothing to find. The next attack would most certainly be somewhere else, and he had no idea where.

Chapter Twenty Five

The West Point campus was nearly empty. The place was a veritable ghost town: unusually still, silent, most of the lights off, hardly anyone around. But Maya didn't mind. After all, that was how she had spent her entire first year there; she hadn't gone home for the holidays then, and had used the alone time to remind herself that she didn't need anyone else, that she was strong. That she could get by just fine, even better than fine, on her own.

The dean of West Point, Brigadier General Joanne Hunt, knew who her father was. It was, quite possibly, the reason that Maya had even been admitted. Whether that was true or not, she didn't really want to know. Even if she patched things up with her dad she was still determined to prove herself, to distance herself from whatever legacy he might have.

And she had been. Maya excelled in every subject. She had the second fastest fifty-yard dash in the school, and regularly made fools out of guys much larger and older in her extracurricular judo class.

Yet there was a significant downside to all her achievements.

It was night out by the time she arrived at the campus and back to her dorm, the air growing brisk and chilly. She unpacked her bag and tried to read for a short while, but found herself a little stir crazy. Though the flight from Virginia to New York had been brief, she needed to stretch her legs. Or maybe do more than just stretch her legs.

She changed into shorts and an old T-shirt and headed down to the gym.

The halls were eerily silent, only half the lights on so that shadows fell in corners. Maya passed by an open classroom doorway and saw Melvin, an older gentleman and janitor who didn't have any family to speak of but seemed to enjoy his work at the academy. He smiled and said hello as Maya passed. She headed downstairs, her sneakered footfalls echoing in the stairwell. The gym was on the first floor and on the opposite side of the building from the dorms. She was just glad she didn't have to go outside into the blustery cold to get there. She could hear the wind picking up, howling and rattling windows.

As she neared the gym entrance, she saw movement down the shadowy corridor and frowned. There was a boy, slight-framed and looking very much like a first-year, standing stock-still and no more than twenty-five yards from her.

"Hi." She gave him a small wave. But the boy didn't respond. Instead he spun and strode quickly the opposite way.

Weird. But she didn't pay him any mind. He probably thought he was alone in the halls and got freaked out.

Thankfully the gym was unlocked, and clearly empty since Maya had to turn the lights on. She started with stretches, taking care to tune up her quads and hamstrings, and then put earbuds in before mounting the treadmill. She kept her pace loose and leisurely for the three-mile jog, averaging just under nine minutes per mile. Then she slowed to a brisk walk for another mile, wiping sweat from her forehead. She wasn't really in the mood for weight training, so instead she wrapped her hands and went to work on the heavy bag, practicing her footwork and her punches while her mind cycled through the major points of the Russo-Japanese War, which would be the subject of a history exam come Monday.

She paused to catch her breath and laughed at herself. It was a holiday weekend; there would be plenty of time for studying later. Instead her thoughts turned to Sara. She wanted to call her, to make sure her little sister had settled in okay at the rehab center.

No, she decided. *Give her some space, at least for one night.* Maya would call her tomorrow evening, after she had some time to acclimate to Seaside House.

She went back to work on the heavy bag, practicing a jab-cross routine while twisting her upper body into the hit. Funny; when she was younger she never would have imagined herself here, smacking at a punching bag in a military academy. Yet it was cathartic.

She couldn't help but imagine her ex-boyfriend's face with each solid, satisfying thud of knuckles against canvas. Greg Calloway was like the unofficial prom king of West Point: tall, blond, handsome, well-liked ... as well as superficial, self-important, and leaning hard on the dynastical nature of his wealthy family to propel him through life.

How she had ever allowed herself to be smitten by him, she couldn't remember. Their relationship, if she could even call it that, was all about status to him; she was the top female at the academy, and he the top male. But things soon began to shift, and Maya was surpassing him not only academically, but physically as well. She knew that it bothered him, but he never admitted it aloud. His pride wouldn't let him.

Then, about five weeks earlier, came the trip home to try to reconcile with her dad. Maya had brought Greg along as a buffer and, in a fit of anger directed at both her father and her boyfriend, she got in the car and sped back to New York alone, abandoning Greg in

Virginia. Rumors ran rampant across campus after the break-up and included just about everything except the actual truth, but one thing was universally known: she had made a fool out of Greg Calloway, West Point's golden boy.

And his friends, all those that looked up to Greg as their leader, the kind of guy they aspired to be, they didn't care much for that.

They were problems that Maya didn't want to burden her dad or Sara with. When they had asked her how school was, she simply told them it was fine, but that wasn't exactly the case. There had been some hazing. Boys she didn't even know had called her a bitch, a whore, and worse. There had been whispered threats in the halls—"Watch your back, Lawson," or "You might want to sleep with one eye open." Twice she'd scrubbed graffiti from her dorm room door.

Through it all she kept a straight face and didn't give in, didn't lose her cool. She was certain she could take Greg or any one of his cronies in a fair fight. She also knew that if it came to that, it wouldn't be fair, and if she knocked a few teeth down someone's throat she would be summarily dismissed from the school.

She could have gone to the dean. She could have reported the abuse. But this was her problem, and she would solve it in her way. She didn't need anyone coming to her rescue.

Still, she couldn't shake the feeling that despite her outward indifference, the hazing and threats were continually getting worse. Her refusal to acknowledge them was causing escalation, rather than wearing them down.

Maya smacked the heavy bag with a right cross and immediately winced as skin scraped away. The athletic tape and gauze wrapped around her hand had come loose. She stuck her bleeding knuckle in her mouth and decided that was enough of a workout for one night.

The locker room was just as dark and empty as the gym. She flicked on the lights and stowed her clothes in a locker, but didn't even bother closing it. There was no one else there. Then she stepped into the shower and turned the water up as hot as she could tolerate. She took her time washing her hair, letting the hot water cascade over her sore muscles, the steam billowing in waves.

Then—the lights went out. She was plunged into complete darkness in an instant, her breath catching in her throat.

"Hello?" she called out. "Someone's in here!"

The lights did not come back on. She fumbled in the darkness for the faucet and turned it off, listening intently for any indication that she wasn't alone. But she heard nothing other than the errant drops of water from the shower head and her hair.

It was pitch black; there were no windows in the locker room, no sources of any natural light at all. Luckily Maya knew the layout well. She reached for the hook where she knew her towel to be, wrapped it around herself, and took small, shambling half-footsteps. It felt like it took quite a while, and twice she bumped into something. She wasn't afraid of the dark, but she was keenly aware that someone had to have turned out the lights. It was probably Melvin, the janitor, but the very notion that she might not be alone was enough to set her teeth on edge and keep her breathing shallow.

At long last she reached the switch panel, near the entrance to the locker room, and flicked them on. The lights came up instantly; Maya squinted in the sudden brightness.

There was no one there. No one that she could see, anyway.

Must have been Melvin, she decided. *He probably pulled the door open, saw the lights on, turned them off and left right away.* She reached for the door to see if the janitor was still around, maybe in the gym...

The door budged about an inch, but refused to open. Maya frowned and pulled harder, but it was stuck fast. It wasn't locked, she could tell by the slight movement.

It was barred from the outside somehow.

A cold chill ran up her spine. She slapped her palm twice on the door and shouted, "Hey! Is anyone out there? Hello!"

She scurried to her locker to get dressed. If she was going to figure a way out, it wasn't going to be dripping wet and wrapped in a towel. The locker was ajar a few inches, just as she'd left it. But her clothes were gone. The locker was empty.

"Son of a bitch," she murmured.

And then the laughter began. A slow tittering, so unexpected that Maya's shoulders jerked in a startled quiver. The voice was definitely male, young, and bounced around the empty locker room, making it difficult to tell where it was coming from.

Time was that Maya would have been scared witless, standing there in a towel and unable to escape. But that's not who she was anymore. Instead her fists balled at her sides as she loudly demanded, "Who's there?!"

"What's the matter, Lawson?" the voice taunted. She didn't recognize it and couldn't quite tell where he might be.

"Can't find your clothes?" A second voice. Then more laughter—there was at least two of them. Maybe three.

She padded on her bare feet to the end of the row of lockers and quickly peered around the corner, just in time to hear the squeak of a sneaker and see a flash of someone stealing out of view. They laughed again. Her first instinct was to give chase, but she stifled it and took a deep breath. There were four rows of lockers, plus the showers and bathroom stalls. Too many places for them to hide.

Instead she stood her ground, there at the end of the row of lockers with a view of the shower entrance. "Don't tell me you guys actually stayed behind and skipped the holiday just to mess with me," she taunted. "That's pretty pathetic."

"Pathetic?" the first voice repeated. "Says the girl who never goes home."

"We actually thought you'd left," said a third voice. There were three of them. "That would have been a real kick to the balls. But then you popped up, didn't you?"

She didn't bother to tell them that she *had* left, and had just returned early. It didn't matter, in the scheme of things.

But how did they know...? Suddenly Maya remembered the boy she'd seen in the corridor outside the gym, the skinny first-year. He had seemed spooked to see her and scurried off fast—probably to tell these guys he'd spotted her. Maybe he was even the one who barred the locker room door from the outside.

A now-chilled drop of water slid down her back, reminding her that she was wearing only a towel, locked in there with three vindictive boys. She was already angry, and the sudden vulnerability of her awareness only made her angrier.

"You don't scare me," she declared, her voice loud and even. "So you can keep hiding. Or you can come on out, and we can settle this."

From down the row of lockers, a boy stepped out. Maya glared at him; he was a couple inches taller than her, with a buzz cut and a thick neck. She recognized him as Randolph something-or-other. One of Greg's third-year pals.

Something long and white dangled at Randolph's side, hanging from his right fist. It took her a moment to realize it was a long white tube sock, half as long as her arm, the end of it weighed down with something...

Locksocking. That's what this was. It was a form of hazing made popular by a Kubrick war movie back in the eighties, in a scene where an unruly cadet gets beaten with bars of soap stuffed into the ends of tube socks. But usually the victim was immobilized, held down with a blanket...

Or a bath towel. The only thing she was wearing at the moment.

There was movement to her right as a second boy stepped out from the showers. He was taller, lankier; a fourth-year that she had seen around, but didn't know. He too held a long sock weighed down with soap. And then to her left, the third voice, a dark-haired boy a bit on the chubby side that Maya didn't recognize.

Greg wasn't among them. Whether he had sent them to do this or if they were just trying to gain his favor, she didn't know. It didn't matter much either. She directed her attention forward, to Randolph, as he took two steps toward her down the row of lockers. His lips curled into a cruel smirk as his gaze swept from her eyes downward, past the towel, to her legs, and back up again.

"Greg was a lucky guy," he said, taking another step forward.

She stifled a shudder. Suddenly it wasn't a beating she feared from these three. She did not at all like the way Randolph was looking at her, the way they had waited until after she'd showered, and stolen her clothes, and locked her in there with them ...

They wouldn't, she told herself. *They're just trying to scare me. They wouldn't dare.*

"You know, there are no cameras in here," Randolph said casually, as if reading her mind. "No faculty around. Hell, there's nobody in this whole half of the building. Someone could scream bloody murder and no one would hear it." He smirked again. "No one but us."

He took another small step forward. He was close enough that if Maya took one big stride, she could reach him with a fist. But she didn't move, not yet. She caught a whiff of something acrid and strong—whiskey? Something alcoholic on his breath. These boys had been drinking. That could make them unpredictable, more dangerous.

"I won't," she murmured.

"Sorry?" Randolph sneered. "I didn't catch that."

She glared at him as she repeated louder, "I won't scream."

He grinned. "We'll see."

The tall fourth-year boy made the first move. He took a sudden step forward, his gait long, and brought the sock-cudgel up over his shoulder. Maya didn't hesitate. Instead of moving out of the way, she stepped forward and stopped his swing with one hand. With her right, she rabbit-punched him in the throat with two knuckles.

The boy sputtered as he staggered backward. Behind her, Randolph was moving fast. Maya spun and struck out with a fist, but the stout boy kept moving and she missed him by an inch. He swung the sock into her ribs.

She cried out as it struck her, the pain intense and immediate, sending her to her knees. It was not a bar of soap inside the sock; it was heavier, felt like lead. As her knees hit the tile, the tucked corner of her towel came loose. She grabbed at it, holding it over her chest as she scrabbled away from them, pushing her feet against the floor and sliding backward on her butt.

"Doug, you idiot!" Randolph scolded as the fourth-year boy coughed and held his throat. "I told you to be careful!"

Maya slid backward frantically until her back hit the other wall. She was mere feet from the door, but she knew it wouldn't open. As the three boys advanced on her, she tucked the towel back in and started to rise to her feet.

As she did, she spotted the scars on her bare calf. The thin white lines that had healed but would never go away, in the shape of letters where she had carved a warning to her dad, just before being drugged by human traffickers.

A memory surged through her head, powerful and visceral, one that she had worked so hard to keep back.

She flailed her arms and legs, her eyes closed tightly, as the man clambered atop her. Some of her blows connected, but her limbs were still weak from the drugs and they bounced off harmlessly. He pressed his body weight upon her, forcing her legs still. His hands scrambled to keep hers steady.

The man leered down at her, a maniacal glint in his eyes. A pit of horror solidified in her stomach...

The train. The traffickers. A man had attempted to rape her, and she had told herself then: *Never again.*

When she looked up, she saw a similar maniacal glint in Randolph's eye. The boys' shadows fell long over her, a wall at her back. Nowhere to run. They weren't giving her a choice.

But she wouldn't be the victim. She wouldn't be the one screaming.

Hello?

Maya blinked. Her hands hurt. The locker room around her was hazy.

Someone in here...? Jesus Christ.

No, it wasn't hazy. Her eyes were blurry with tears. She was crying.

Are you okay?

The voice sounded distant, but familiar. Then someone was in front of her, crouched beside her. A shape... a man.

She shoved him away frantically and scrambled backward, her back hitting the wall.

"Wait!" He put his hands up defensively. "Hey. It's me. It's Melvin."

Maya wiped her eyes. The old janitor was there, wide-eyed and very confused. He'd opened the door to the locker room. He saw...

Randolph was on the floor on his back, bleeding from his nose and mouth. His eyes were clenched shut and his breathing was shallow. One of his friends, the chubby one, was on his side facing away from Maya and sobbing in soft moans. The third boy, the fourth-year, was behind her. He was on his stomach with his arm twisted behind him at a wholly unnatural angle that made her nauseous. She couldn't tell if he was breathing.

"What the hell happened here?" Melvin asked in disbelief.

"Is he …" Maya's voice was tremulous and weak. "Is he alive?"

Melvin quickly knelt and checked the tall boy's pulse. "Yes." He pulled out a cell phone and dialed 911. "We're going to need an ambulance …"

She held the towel loosely over her. There was blood on it. Was it hers? She looked at her trembling hands. The knuckles were raw and bleeding.

She had blacked out. She had made the conscious decision not to be a victim again, and some kind of animal instinct had taken over. She could not remember anything about what had happened, what she had done, or how much time had passed. It felt like it could have been hours, but her hair was still damp, clinging to her shoulders. Minutes at best.

"Hey," Melvin said gently. "They're on their way. I'm going to have to call the dean. Are you hurt?"

"I-I don't think so," she said in a whisper.

At least not physically. But she hadn't felt so unsafe, so violated, since being kidnapped. And in a place where she was supposed to feel secure. Even worse, she had lost control. She could have killed someone. In the moment, she wasn't worried about the dean, or what the academy might do. She was afraid—afraid of herself, what she was capable of, and the darkness she now knew was inside her.

CHAPTER TWENTY SIX

"Still nothing!" Zero reported over the headset, half-shouting over the gusts that blew in through the open side door of the Sikorsky HH-60M, the late November wind chilling him to the bone. The helicopter was a decommissioned Black Hawk, now serving as a medical evacuation chopper on loan from New York Presbyterian. Maria sat in the copilot seat and Strickland in the rear behind Zero as they swept as low as the pilot dared over Times Square.

Zero held the sonic detection meter that Bixby had given them, the device that looked like a miniature radar gun with a scooping plastic dish aimed downward toward the city. It was tuned into a low-frequency range that would pick up the ultrasonic weapon—but only if it was actually there, and only if the perpetrators were using it.

The evacuation efforts had been declared an utter catastrophe and all but abandoned. Anyone who wanted to leave the city could try, but the bridges and tunnels were still clogged, no thanks to several accidents from fleeing citizens. The National Guard had been pulled back. They weren't forcing anyone to leave who didn't want to—especially since the ensuing panic had caused four deaths, potentially more as reports came in, and that wasn't to mention a currently incalculable amount in property damage.

Zero and his team had been in the air for two hours now, scanning and finding nothing. On the ground, FBI agents from the Jacob K. Javits office did sweeps on foot, with help from whoever the NYPD and fire department could spare.

No one had found a thing, not a scrap of evidence to support the potential terror attack. Yet Zero held his tongue. An "I told you so" wouldn't do anyone any good; he knew Maria would already be torturing herself over it.

"We should sweep outward," Strickland suggested into the radio. "Spiral pattern outside the Times Square area, in case they've moved on, changed their plans ..."

"Negative," the pilot replied. "Winds are picking up. There's a storm front moving in. We're going to have to set it down, at least until this passes."

"We can help with the ground search in the meantime," said Strickland. Zero knew the young agent was eager, maybe even overzealous to find these people after their argument on the jet. It was beginning to feel like each of them had something to prove.

"No," Maria countered. "We've got more than two hundred people on the ground looking. The three of us aren't going to make much of a difference. We need to get some rest, and when the storm passes...we'll pick it up then." Her gaze flitted over her shoulder at Zero for just a moment.

He was well aware what was going on in her head. They wouldn't be getting back on the helicopter after the storm. He had been right; the phone in the truck was another distraction, intentioned to force them into action and incite panic. It had worked like a charm.

No matter how he mulled over the details they knew, he could not for the life of him determine where these people might go next. All he knew was that it wasn't New York.

Then where the hell are they?

The helicopter returned to LaGuardia as the rain began to fall, and the three of them holed up in one of the dozen or so hotels surrounding the airport. Zero wasn't even paying enough attention to heed the name of it. There were three rooms waiting for them, though he had seen over Maria's shoulder that she'd nearly booked only two on her tablet before recognizing her mistake and getting him his own.

They split off down the corridor, agreeing to reconvene in three hours, which was the best approximation of the storm passing. It wasn't until he was inside with the door closed behind him, in the still and silent room with its welcome and well-made bed that he realized just how exhausted he was. It was not yet midnight and they had gone from Virginia to Vegas to Illinois to New York in the span of a single day.

He set down his gear bag, pulled off his jacket and shoulder holster, and sprawled onto his back on the bed. A shower would have been nice, but he didn't think he could muster the energy. Instead he closed his eyes for a brief respite from the outside world.

As soon as he did, an image of the Bosnian boy flashed through his mind. It came involuntarily, unwelcomed and intrusive.

In his crosshairs, the boy stooped to pick up a coin. A fortunate find, mere moments before he would be murdered.

And then there was the Dubai businessman, the back of his skull spattered across a hotel lobby in half an instant.

Zero sat up as the rain began to come down heavier, lashing at the window. He wouldn't be able to sleep. Not until he knew more; not until he could ascertain whether these were actual memories or his fragmented mind playing tricks on him. If they were real, then there must be something in his head to connect them, something to make sense of what he was doing and why.

He had tried meditation before, back when most of his memories of the CIA were still lost to him. He had gotten fairly adept at it; if nothing else it helped to calm his mind, and on a couple of occasions had even helped him recover fragments of lost memory. Zero arranged himself as comfortably as he could in an upright position on the bed, legs crossed beneath him, and took a long, deep breath. He let it out slowly as he relaxed his muscles, feeling the tension run from his shoulders. He counted to ten, and then tried to blank his mind...

A crashing peal of thunder startled him back to reality. Outside the wind howled and the rain fell heavier. He wasn't going to have much luck meditating in a violent storm. With a groan he rose from the bed and went to the small bathroom to splash water on his face—but he paused, glancing down at the bathtub. It gave him an idea, though he wasn't sure it would work.

He plugged the tub's drain and turned on the faucet. As it filled with warm water, Zero took off his clothes, leaving them and the Ruger LC9 on the sink. When the tub was half-full, he turned the water off, closed the bathroom door, and turned off the light.

There were no windows in the bathroom, so he was immediately plunged into darkness. He took two small, careful steps and climbed into the tub, lying back as comfortably as he could with his legs bent and his knees up. The temperature was near perfect on his sore muscles, and he felt himself relaxing almost instantly.

He had only ever read about sensory deprivation and its effects on the mind, and he knew just as well that his makeshift setup was less than ideal—but still he had to try something. The basic concept was that the removal of stimuli from multiple senses (in this case, sight and sound) and by creating a uniform stimulus to his senses of scent and touch, his mind would be more conducive to meditation.

At least he hoped.

He reclined carefully in the tub, leaning back until his head was in the water, and then up over his ears. The sounds of the raging storm outside fell away, replaced only by the dull roar of his own blood rushing through his head. He didn't close his eyes, but he didn't need to. He stared straight up, where the ceiling was overhead if he could see anything at all in the pitch dark bathroom, and focused in his even breathing.

Finally, in spite of himself, he forced his mind to return to the memory. The burnt-out building. The rifle against his shoulder.

He rounds a corner four blocks north. He's walking home alone. Eyes cast downward at the ground. You have the shot—

In the dark and deafening silence, Zero could almost feel the trigger under his finger.

The boy's face lights up as he spots something on the ground and bends to pick it up. It's shiny. A piece of metal—a coin, perhaps. He looks pleased as he sticks it in his pocket.

You have the shot.

He could see the boy's soft brown eyes through his crosshairs.

You know from your briefing package that he is nine years old.

Your finger compresses the trigger. You take your shot...

The gunshot echoed through his head, as sudden and startling as the crashing thunder outside, and with it came an explosion of light. His field of vision turned from black to white in an instant, fading slowly and leaving a vague afterimage that turned yellow, and then red, and the purple.

As the bizarre, hallucinatory burst of light faded, the memories surged through his head just as powerful as the violent storm over the city.

The Dubai businessman, shot from an apartment window across the street.

An Irish woman, the sister of an IRA terrorist.

A semi-retired accountant in Des Moines who handled the accounts of a holdings company that funded illegal arms smuggling in Kuwait.

The Bosnian boy.

Memories of a dozen assassinations swirled through his head, maybe more, all of them at his hand. He saw himself, years younger, strangling a college-aged student as he walked alone through a parking lot so that the CIA could capture the kid's neo-Nazi uncle in a sting operation at the funeral. In his mind's eye he slipped a knife between the ribs of an ailing Iraqi patriarch and framing a rival insurgency group so that two warring factions would eliminate each other.

He remembered them all, in what might have been an instant or could have been an hour. He remembered them, and more.

You are not employed in any official capacity by the CIA or the US government.

Before Maria, before Alan Reidigger, before being a full-fledged agent. Before being Agent Zero.

If captured, we will disavow any and all knowledge of you. Your files will be permanently deleted. You will be forgotten and left to be tried as a criminal.

Years earlier, at the dawn of his career, he had been recruited not as a field agent, but as something else. A CIA assassin. A glorified hitman.

A dark agent.

The phrase flitted through his head before he truly understood what it meant. But once it had, he knew—that was how he had begun his career in the CIA. As a "dark agent," one who carried out assassinations of carefully planned targets that would imbalance a bigger equation.

Not targets, he told himself. *Victims. They were your victims.*

He was told who to kill, and he killed them. A whole part of his own past that was locked away in his head now came flooding back—and as soon as it did, he wished it didn't. The memories barely even felt like his; they felt as if they belonged to someone else, some darker and younger version of himself that had far fewer scruples and everything to prove.

And worst of all, this darkness in him hadn't come at a low point in his life. He remembered it clearer with every passing moment. He was recently married to Kate. Purchasing their first home. A child on the way. They would name her Maya. And while his wife attended doctor's appointments and bought baby clothes, Reid Lawson murdered for money.

"No!" He sat up quickly, splashing water over the side of the tub. He clambered out, nearly slipped, water all over the tiled floor. His hands groped in the darkness. One of them found the wall and slid around desperately for the light switch. His other grabbed onto the edge of the sink, feeling along its surface. He felt the Ruger under his grip as he flicked on the switch.

A second sudden explosion of light, this time from the daylight bulbs of the vanity. He winced as it blinded him. He panted before the mirror, naked, hair plastered to his forehead, tears in his eyes.

He didn't like the person he saw there.

Zero squeezed them shut. Behind his lids was no better; he saw the younger version of himself, the kind that killed indiscriminately simply because he'd been told to. Through the turmoil, a vague realization struck him; he'd never stopped to wonder how or why killing came so easily to him. He told himself it was necessity, that it was a natural fight-or-flight instinct, that it was his extensive training as an agent…

But now he knew the truth.

"I'm sorry." His voice was hoarse, something between a whisper and a whimper. "I'm sorry," he said again, to everyone and to no one.

At last he opened his eyes to face himself, the person he couldn't pretend not to be. He hadn't realized he had grabbed the gun, couldn't remember picking it up … but there it was, in his right hand, and pointed at his own temple.

CHAPTER TWENTY SEVEN

Zero dropped the gun as if it was red-hot. It clattered into the sink as he jumped back, hands trembling.

I'm not okay.

Tears stung at his eyes no matter how much he tried to will them away. He couldn't trust his brain. He couldn't trust his memory. He couldn't trust *himself*. Though he was still dripping wet and his hands still shook, he managed to wrestle into a pair of jeans. He frantically tugged on his T-shirt, ignoring the damp spots that sprouted instantly against the fabric. Whether it was cold sweat or bathwater, he didn't know.

Zero tore open the door to his hotel room and staggered into the hall, catching himself against the opposite wall.

I need help.

For a moment he couldn't recall Maria's room number. He glanced back over his shoulder at his own door—206. Right. She was in 209. Barefoot and hair clinging to his forehead, he smacked against her door with the flat of a palm.

"Maria!" He needed help, and he needed a familiar face. He couldn't be alone right now. His breath was coming faster—a panic attack was coming on. Perhaps a full-blown breakdown. He slapped at the door again. "Maria!"

"Hang on," came the sleepy reply. The lock slid aside the door opened.

Zero took a step back in confusion.

The woman's light eyebrows knit in the center. "Kent! Are you okay?"

He knew Maria. Of course he knew Maria. He knew her laugh. He knew her voice, her mannerisms. He even knew the feel of her skin on his.

But this woman before him, looking increasingly concerned, was a stranger to him.

"Kent? Why are you wet? Were you out in the rain?"

This blonde-haired stranger, her eyes somehow vibrant despite being the gray of slate, was utterly foreign.

"I-I need help," he managed.

He had forgotten her face. Just like he forgot Kate's name, or how to load a pistol. He could conjure every detail about Maria, down to the birthmark on her right thigh—but not her face. It was a blank in his mind, somewhere in there yet impossible to grasp, like a misplaced word right on the tip of his tongue.

"Come in," she urged him. "Come on, tell me what's wrong." He flinched slightly as she reached for his elbow, but he let her guide him into the hotel room. It was identical to his, but everything was opposite. Like a parallel dimension, a mirror of this one. Maybe this Maria wasn't the same Maria. Maybe it was a doppelganger from this opposite place...

I'm losing my mind.

"Talk to me, Kent." Her voice was gentle, oozing with concern.

"Wait. Just wait." Zero squeezed his eyes shut tightly. He thought of Rome. The apartment overlooking the famous *Fontana delle Tarterughe*, the Turtle Fountain. That's where he had found her. She'd thought he was dead. She opened the door, her eyes wide and surprised, dropping the coffee cup in her hands. "Tell me you're Maria."

"What?" she asked incredulously.

"Please," he insisted. "Just... just tell me."

"Kent." He felt both her hands envelop one of his. "I'm Maria."

He opened his eyes slowly. As her face came into focus through the hazy blur of his moist vision, so did the memories. He breathed a small sigh of relief; he recognized her. It was Maria. "Okay," he said in a breathy whisper. "Okay."

"What's happening to you?" She said it as if she already knew, or at least suspected, that something was amiss.

His hands were still trembling. "I don't know how to explain it." How could he? How could he make her understand what it was like to forget in an instant the face of your closest friend and former lover? How could he explain opening his eyes and seeing his own hand holding a gun to his head?

"Try."

He nodded and took a breath. "I've been having... problems. Forgetting things, simple things. But meaningful things." He paced as he spoke, his cadence growing more rapid. "I think my brain is damaged. And memories—new memories are coming back. Of killings."

"Killings?" Maria repeated.

"Murders. Assassinations of people who, who may or may not have been innocent. A boy. A woman. Before all this, before becoming a field agent... I think I was an assassin. A CIA killer." He stopped abruptly and looked her in the eye. "A dark agent."

"Okay," Maria murmured. She reached for him again, this time taking him by the shoulder and directed him to the edge of the bed. "Sit." She lowered herself beside him. "Hold my hand. Good. Now listen to me. Dr. Guyer told you that certain things might manifest in your mind, right? Fears, delusions, fantasies. What seem like memories, but aren't real. Didn't he?"

"He did," Zero admitted quietly. "But these were so real. So vivid. Like I was there—"

"They wouldn't seem like memories if they weren't," Maria countered. "Remember when you were convinced that we were having an affair before Kate..." She paused. "While Kate was still alive?"

He nodded. She was right again; he had once been utterly convinced by a fantasy-turned-memory that he and Maria had started their tryst long before Kate's murder.

"Furthermore," she added, "I'm a deputy director now. So I can tell you with some authority that there is no such thing as a 'dark agent.' That's a CIA fairy tale. We don't hire assassins to kill innocent people. If we did, I would know about it, don't you think?"

"Yeah," he muttered. Maria was only one step removed from the head of the most clandestine arm of the entire Central Intelligence Agency. She knew things that even Zero didn't know.

But then...

"But you didn't know about the Russian," Zero pointed out. "The guy in Vegas, the one trading nuclear secrets for amnesty."

"Well...no." Maria stared down at the bedspread as if it might hold a satisfactory answer.

"You said it was 'above your pay grade'..."

"Those kinds of secrets could cause an international crisis—" Maria argued.

"Like an American assassin killing children on foreign soil," Zero said flatly.

"Kent!" Maria dropped his hand and threw up her own in exasperation. Thunder clapped outside, as if punctuating her outburst. "There are no dark agents, okay? You didn't kill people for money! You got your memories back; you think you would have forgotten your own background?"

"I don't know." He stood again, thinking clearer now that Maria had calmed him to some degree. "Maybe. Maybe I did. You and I both know that the agency has been working on mind control and memory suppression since the seventies. The CIA invented the memory suppressor that was installed in my head. Bixby worked on that tech himself." He looked up at her sharply. "What if those memories, those assassinations were intentionally repressed, even before I became a field agent? Maybe the agency did something to me back then, but they're still in there, and now that my limbic system is completely fucked, they're coming back…"

"Jesus, Kent, listen to yourself. You're sounding like a conspiracy nut."

He scoffed. "After everything we've seen, everything we've done—everything we've kept quiet! You really think it sounds crazy?" She couldn't dissuade him from seeing the truth of it now. The memories had shown him.

He was no better than John Watson, killing an innocent woman on the street without asking as much as her name.

"I'm not sure what to think anymore." Maria pinched the bridge of her nose and sighed. "But I do know that I can't keep you out here like this. Once this storm clears up, I'm sending you home."

Home. Yes. That was what he needed. Out here, he was a liability. He could forget how to drive a car and endanger lives. He could forget how to shoot and get his teammates killed. But…

He realized grimly that there was no one waiting for him at home. Sara was at the rehab facility. Maya was likely heading back to school, if she wasn't there already. And Maria would be out here, in the field. Zero wouldn't burden Alan with his problems when he had his own. At home, he would be alone with his thoughts. And he couldn't trust himself.

When he looked up again, Maria was gazing at him through narrowed eyes. "Why not?"

"Huh?"

"You just said you couldn't trust yourself."

Zero blinked. Had he said that aloud?

"Kent, are you having… harmful thoughts?"

"What? No. Of course not." He shook his head adamantly. He wouldn't tell her about the gun he'd held to his own head. That was a fluke, a bizarre physical reaction to emotional trauma. Or so he told himself. If he copped to it, she'd never let him stay. "No," he insisted again. "And I want to stay. I want to see this through. I need to. Afterwards, when we're done… I'll figure all this out after."

Maria didn't quite look like she believed him. But if he knew her, and he did, she was thinking the same thing he was: that the best place for him was here, with her, under her watchful eye. "We'll just have to be careful then."

"Yeah," he agreed. "Careful."

She patted the spot next to her on the bed, and he sank into it. She wrapped her arms around him and guided his head to her shoulder, not caring that his hair was still dripping. He felt safe with her. Protected. This was where he should be. Not at home alone with his thoughts. For the briefest of moments, he even let himself believe that the memories of assassinations were false. She ran her fingers through his wet hair and held him. They stayed like that for several minutes, until Zero's heart rate finally slowed to normal, until his hands stopped trembling. Until he let himself remember that even if he was a killer and a liar, someone still cared.

But then the fingers stopped running along his scalp. Maria's grip fell slack, and when he glanced up, she was looking past him. He followed her gaze. Zero hadn't even realized that the television was on, tuned to the news and muted. He saw what she saw, the ticker along the bottom of the screen.

A.M. SPECIAL SESSION CALLED TO VOTE IN VP.

He blinked at the words for a moment as his exhausted brain struggled to grasp meaning. A special session—that meant Congress was being convened. In the morning. To vote in a new vice president...

He finally caught up to what Maria was undoubtedly already thinking.

"That's it," she said in a whisper.

"The target," he murmured in agreement as he sat up straight.

The group they were after had phoned in a threat on the most populous city in the United States that had all but proven to be a red herring. And while all eyes were on the tumult in New York, the next sonic attack would cripple the country by targeting its leaders.

CHAPTER TWENTY EIGHT

"Ouch!" Sara exclaimed as she pulled her thumb from her mouth. She'd chewed every nail down to the quick before circling back around to her left thumb, and now a narrow crescent of blood blossomed from the tear she'd bitten in the tender nail bed. She stuck the thumb back in her mouth and sucked on it as she checked the time on her phone.

It was two fifteen in the morning. Good enough. She'd planned on waiting until three, but her skin was crawling. Anticipatory sweat was prickling on her forehead. Despite being physically tired, exhausted even, she was mentally alert and awake. Her brain was excited.

She was jonesing hard.

After her meeting with Dr. Greene, Sara had made the definitive decision to leave this place, this Seaside House, and go home. She started to create an escape plan that didn't involve the rehab facility knowing she was even gone. But then something else had happened in her mind: a taste of freedom had loomed. And with it came an urge, a craving, more powerful than any she'd had in weeks.

She had some cash, gifted to her by Maya, and after she made her escape she'd have hours before anyone knew she was missing. Not her dad, not the doctors. She could do whatever she wanted. And that's when the darkness in her, that duplicitous voice, started in.

You could do it. Score just one hit. That's all it would take, you've been off it so long.

One hit. One high. Then back home.

No one needs to know.

Ever since that tiny thought had sprouted in her mind, she could seemingly think of nothing else. It would be like a farewell party, one more for the road—and then she would get serious about her recovery. Do things on her own, the way she knew she could. She was stronger than her addiction. But just one more taste wouldn't hurt anyone.

Sara climbed off the bed and put her plan into action. It was all conceptual at this point; she had no idea if it would work. It was time to see. Her room at Seaside House was situated like a hotel room, with a bed and a bureau and a small writing desk, an attached bathroom decorated in seashells, and a decent-sized closet.

She went into the bathroom. The tub was a little small, but hanging over it was a cloth curtain with the pattern of a coral reef, a plastic liner behind it. It was suspended from twelve metal loops around the shower rod. She reached up and carefully opened each loop, taking down the curtain.

Then she went into the closet. There was a metal bar hanging there for clothes. It was stronger than the shower rod would be, so she reattached the twelve rings to the closet bar. Then she bunched them up, all twelve of them close together, the shower curtain tight between her hands. She held on tight as she could and suspended herself there, lifting her feet off the floor.

There were cameras in the halls. She'd noticed them walking back to her room after the meeting with Dr. Greene. There were cameras at the main entrance and every other exit to the building. There were cameras covering the front of the place, and there was a man sitting guard just inside the facility's lobby, watching the comings and goings. She couldn't as much step foot into the hallway without being seen, much less walk out through any doors.

But if all went according to plan, she didn't actually have to leave her room.

As her feet left the ground, the shower rings bent slightly—but they held. If she'd only used a few of them, they might have broken. But all twelve together held her slight frame.

Perfect.

The metal pole in the closet was a tension rod, so pulling it loose didn't require any tools. Sara pushed the ends together, freed the rod with the rings and curtain still attached, and closed the closet door.

She quickly set about bunching up sheets and pillows beneath the blanket in a form that she hoped looked like a sleeping sixteen-year-old girl. She made sure she had her phone, her charger, and her backpack of clothes and the meager personal items she'd brought along.

Then she went to the window.

Sara's room was on the second floor, a straight-down drop onto grass that she figured to be about eighteen to twenty feet high. She was five-two. The shower curtain was six feet long. That left a nine-foot drop onto grass—a cinch. Or so she hoped. She had spent a long time looking out the window earlier, trying to spot any cameras and seeing none. The spotlights that lit the back lawn had clicked off on an automatic timer around one a.m.

No one would see her. She was sure of it.

But now came the hard part. She opened the window about two feet and positioned the closet rod lengthwise across it, parallel to the window so that the wood of the frame held it in place, keeping tension on it so it wouldn't clatter to the floor. She trailed the shower curtain out the window. It fluttered slightly in a soft breeze.

Sara looked down. Suddenly eighteen feet looked a lot longer than she thought. But she couldn't back out now. She couldn't just give up and go to bed, pretend it never crossed her mind.

You're so close.

A tingle went up her spine in anticipation of her goal.

Just a little further.

Sara held the bunched-up shower curtain in one fist, keeping tension on the closet rod against the inside of the window frame as she carefully swung one leg out. She ducked low to maneuver herself out of the opening. This was the moment of truth. With one leg out the window and against the façade of the building, she held her breath and slowly brought her other leg off the floor.

The shower rings held. The closet rod held.

Then she was out the window, feet against the side of the building, praying a thousand times per second that the shower curtain didn't tear, that the rings held. She lowered herself inch by inch, trying hard not to audibly grunt with the effort for fear that someone might hear her. It was harder than she thought, climbing down the length of curtain; after only seconds her hands ached, and the darkness below still looked dangerously far.

After a few minutes she was nearly at the end of the shower curtain. Now would come the hardest part of all. There was a window ledge a couple feet to her right; she reached for it to steady herself, taking a deep breath.

She pushed off from the side of the building and made a whipping motion with her arm, shaking the shower curtain in the hopes that the closet rod, braced against the window frame, would come free. For a moment it seemed like she would fall, but then the rod slammed against the frame again. Her grip nearly slipped, but she held on tightly, gasping for breath with the thrill of nearly falling.

Sara set her teeth and tried again. This time she moved her arm up quickly, giving the closet rod some slack, letting it fall away from the window frame, and then whipped the shower curtain out.

Then she was falling. Some part of her brain remembered what her dad had taught her, and as her feet hit solid ground she let her knees bend so that they would only absorb some of the shock as she fell backward.

Still, pain jolted up her ankle as she landed. She half-rolled backward, onto her butt and back. The curtain and the closet rod came tumbling down beside her as she lay there, hissing breaths through her teeth, fearing the worst. If the ankle was broken, she wouldn't be going anywhere.

After a few moments she dared to stand. It hurt, but it didn't feel broken. She tested her weight on it. Pain shot up her leg—but she could put weight on it. Not broken. Just sprained. She rolled her eyes at her failure to execute a decent landing.

But still, she was free. She wasn't expected to be anywhere until nine o'clock the next morning. And even then some employee of the rehab facility might come to her door, check on her, and see what she hoped looked like her sleeping form. The window would be slightly open, but there would be no other evidence of escape. Maybe they would decide to let her sleep a little longer. Maybe they would try to wake her and discover the ruse. It hardly mattered. The shower curtain and closet rod would be deposited in the nearest dumpster, and she would have hours before anyone would even come looking. By then she could be far away.

Sara hobbled across the dark lawn, doing her best to ignore the pain in her ankle. She headed toward the beach. Toward freedom.

Toward just one last fix.

CHAPTER TWENTY NINE

Zero felt as if he was running on fumes.

He hadn't slept a wink in New York. The edge of the horizon turned purple with the first hint of dawn as the jet swooped down rapidly into Ronald Reagan Washington National Airport. Zero had been awake for nearly twenty-four hours straight, though the physical, mental, and emotional turmoil he'd endured in that time made it feel more like forty-eight. The escapade in Vegas felt like it had been a week ago and not yesterday. But there would be no sleep. Not yet.

"Hey." Across the aisle of the jet, Strickland held something out. A small blister pack containing a pair of white pills. "A little pick-me-up. Just caffeine pills, nothing serious. Better than coffee."

Apparently I look just as bad as I feel. Still Zero took them appreciatively. "Thanks." He popped them from the pack and downed them with half a bottle of water.

Maria jabbed at her tablet in the seat in front of him. Ever since seeing the announcement about the special session of Congress, they hadn't spoken any further about what happened in the hotel. Despite his exhaustion, Zero did feel better—only by virtue of forcibly pushing the newly discovered memories, or perhaps delusions, out of his head.

As long as I don't remember those, or forget anything else, I'll be fine. He almost laughed at himself for such a ridiculous thought.

"Twelve minutes," the pilot announced.

"Here's what we're looking at," Maria told them as she held the tablet aloft for him and Strickland to see. On its screen was a map; in its center was a long gray rectangle that Zero figured must be the Capitol Building. A circle of roads enclosed it, with Constitution Avenue running parallel across the top of the map, nearly tangential to the arcing Northwest Drive.

With two fingers, Maria zoomed out of the map. A red square demarcated an area approximately three blocks in every direction, equidistant from the US Capitol. "Using Bixby's specs and what we've seen the sonic weapon do, this is the best approximation for maximum damage," she explained. "The weapon fires in a conical formation. Any further out and they'd risk diminishing the effects. So this square represents our best guess for the weapon's greatest potential. We start there and create a perimeter. Remember that this thing can fire through stone, wood, and glass. It's not only possible, but likely that they're hidden indoors somewhere."

"Possibly even a vehicle," Strickland added, "like the box truck in Kansas."

"Right," Maria agreed. "We've got just under two hours before the session is scheduled to begin. Not enough time to sweep every building. But we'll have help—a handful of FBI agents in plainclothes. We'll divvy into three teams with one of us on each. We want to keep this discreet. We *don't* want this group catching wind and running away. We want that weapon, and we want these perpetrators alive."

She turned to Zero. "You'll have the sonic detection meter. If we get close to time and haven't found anything, I want you on the ground. Earplugs in and meter in hand."

He nodded once. She didn't have to elaborate on what that might mean. If they failed to locate the weapon before the session was set to begin, they might find themselves at ground zero of an ultrasonic attack—which would then become their best bet of finding it.

It also meant they would have to do so fast enough that casualties and damage were kept to an absolute minimum. It was a horrible thought, knowing that the best way of finding the weapon was if the weapon was used.

How did the saying go? *You can't make an omelet...*

At the very thought of it, the Bosnian boy swirled through his mind again.

No. Not now. Focus.

"A few of our FBI friends should already be posted to street corners as we speak, keeping an eye out for any suspicious activity," Maria said. Then she added in a stage murmur, "With any luck, we're going to nail that Russian bitch *today*."

There would, of course, be no special session of Congress that morning. As soon as they'd boarded the jet, Maria had made a phone call—only one, but the only call that mattered. She had contacted CIA Director Shaw and told him their working theory about an attack on Congress. Shaw ordered them to get to Washington ASAP, and promised he would take care of the rest.

Zero was at least vaguely aware of what "the rest" meant. The session would be secretly cancelled. Every member of Congress would already know not to arrive at the US Capitol that morning. The CIA, perhaps with help from the Feds, would make sure that cars still came in and out of the circular Capitol property, to stage the appearance of the session still occurring. But anyone of import—politicians, visiting dignitaries, foreign leaders—would be spirited away to a secure location outside of DC. The president was most likely on a plane or helicopter, heading either to Camp David or to a secret bunker somewhere, depending on the Secret Service's determination of the situation's severity.

But there would be no public announcement. No media. No warning to the people. They needed this group to believe that the session was still going to happen, which meant that outside of those deemed important or a potential target, no one would be aware. And that was what made that horrible thought all the more horrible—in order to find the people responsible, they might have no other choice than to let a few eggs crack.

As soon as the plane rolled to a stop, the three of them leapt out and rushed to a waiting black Crown Vic, the engine running. Behind the wheel was a stoic man in a dark suit and sunglasses. Whether he was CIA or FBI or Secret Service didn't matter and he didn't offer. The driver knew their destination, and as soon as all arms and legs were inside the vehicle they were off like a shot.

Ronald Reagan Airport, Zero knew, was only a fifteen-minute ride from the Capitol Building, twenty with light traffic. But he also knew that there were restricted-access roads available for just such an occasion, and the driver was equally aware. He weaved in and out of lanes expertly, occasionally flicking on a siren just long enough to let out a jarring *whoop-whoop*, alerting a stubborn driver to an emergency vehicle. Then they turned onto a restricted road that would take circumvent 395. There were no gates or guards at its mouth; only several posted signs that threatened drone surveillance and prosecution to the fullest extent of the law.

But the laws don't apply to us, Zero thought bitterly as they roared along the empty access road. The memory came again, as swift and unstoppable as a gust of wind: the businessman in Dubai, spotted through crosshairs. *Bang*—his brain scattered across a hotel lobby.

He breathed a soft but ragged sigh. Maria glanced over her left shoulder at him from the passenger seat, just for a moment, but with obvious concern.

Zero resisted the urge to tell her that he was okay, because that might signal to the others in the car that at some point he had not been. As far as he knew, Strickland was not privy to the events that had transpired in the hotel only a few hours earlier. The young former Ranger might not be as understanding as Maria was to know that his teammate was potentially compromised.

The driver eased down on the accelerator, inching the speedometer up past ninety. There was no one else on the restricted road, likely wouldn't be between there and the Hill.

"Two minutes," the driver muttered. It was the first words he'd said since they climbed in, and the only words they'd hear him say.

Zero secured his gear bag on his shoulder and checked the Ruger. He knew it was loaded; he hadn't touched it since holding it to his own head, other than to holster it. He was mostly just ensuring that he hadn't suddenly forgotten how to use it. But it was all there, in his head. The familiar sensation and the knowledge of what it could do.

"Sending the maps to your phones," Maria told them from the front seat, tablet in hand. "Strickland, your team will start at the northeast corner. Zero, you'll take three guys and sweep the buildings to the..." She trailed off, leaning forward slightly and staring straight ahead through the windshield. The Crown Vic slowed, and Zero craned his neck to see around the driver's head.

"What the hell..." Maria murmured.

He saw what she saw. The gray, almost white dome of the United States Capitol loomed ahead, the height of it cut off by the windshield. Access to the semicircular Southwest Drive was blocked by no fewer than eight police cruisers, parked at odd angles with the red-and-blues flashing. Accompanying them was a cavalcade of black SUVs, a few unmarked white interceptors, and a scattering of other emergency vehicles.

Uniformed officers scurried about, setting up sawhorse barricades and stretching caution tape and hastily escorting people in suits away from the scene.

They were evacuating the Capitol Building.

Men in blue jackets and matching baseball caps directed foot traffic and squawked into radios, their features indistinguishable from the next. The bright yellow letters on the jackets' backs told Zero precisely who he was looking at: FBI.

"That's not good," Strickland muttered.

Maria had the passenger door flung open before the car could skid to a stop. An FBI agent turned at their arrival, taking off his hat and impassively running a hand over his dark hair as she strode quickly up to him, practically shoving her credentials in his face.

"Deputy Director Johansson, CIA," she rattled off quickly. "What the hell is going on here?"

"CIA?" The agent's brow furrowed. "What are you doing here?"

"What am I... what am I *doing*?" Maria's cheeks flushed with anger. "This is my operation!"

The man shook his head. "We weren't made aware of any CIA involvement. There was a threat made on the Capitol, and we don't take that lightly. I'm sorry ma'am, but I'm going to have to ask you to step back behind the barricades ..."

Maria threw her hands up in frustration. "This is beyond bullshit," she said through gritted teeth as she pulled out her phone. "Our plan is completely blown. I'm getting to the bottom of this." She put the phone to her ear. "Director Shaw, please." Her lip curled in a snarl directed at the unfortunate soul on the other end of the line. "Then put me through to his personal cell!" she snapped.

Zero and Strickland exchanged a glance. Neither had to say anything; they knew what this meant. Very few people were even aware that the president had authorized a small, covert CIA team to locate the sonic weapon.

Rutledge, it seemed, had lost the faith.

A three-person team of FBI agents strode quickly by them, two men and a brunette woman—chattering about a sweep and gesturing to a device in her hands. Zero frowned.

The device was familiar. He had one exactly like it in his gear bag. It was a sonic detection meter, and if he had to guess, it was similarly capable of picking up ultra-low frequencies.

The picture formed in his mind. Director Shaw had promised to take care of things. And he had—by providing Bixby's CIA tech to the FBI. Undoubtedly an effort to save face in light of his team's failure.

"Yes, sir," Maria muttered behind him. "I understand, sir." As she spoke on the phone, her voice sounded defeated, but her nostrils flared angrily. Zero couldn't imagine all the things she wished she could say at the moment.

She ended the call and her arm fell slack at her side. "We're off it," she told them without looking at either Zero or Strickland. "We're done here."

Zero shook his head. The police and FBI presence was probably noticeable from a quarter mile away. It was still long before the appointed time for the special session to begin. If the ultrasonic weapon had been here, it was long gone by now. If they hadn't arrived yet, they wouldn't dare to even get close.

And that was assuming it was ever going to be there at all.

CHAPTER THIRTY

Maria sat heavily on a bench across the street from the Capitol Building. She watched as scores of officers and agents went about their business like ants swarming over a dropped crust, carrying the sonic detection meters that Shaw had so generously provided for them.

An olive branch, as it was, for her failure.

But they wouldn't find anything. Of that much she was certain. The weapon was nowhere near here. About twenty yards to her right, a news van was double-parked, reporting on the possible threat to the Capitol from a distance that was either safe or the ideal shot or both. To her left, Kent and Strickland stood with their arms folded as the talked quietly between themselves. She wondered if they were still planning, despite the news that they'd been pulled.

They had nowhere to go but home.

She had been pulled from ops before, but it didn't lessen the sting. They had failed. *She* had failed. They failed in Illinois, and in New York, and now in DC.

Her phone rang.

It was an undisclosed number. Someone important, no doubt. Someone else to remind her of what she already knew.

"Johansson."

"Deputy Director," said a male voice that she had trouble placing at first.

Maria winced. "Mr. President. I want you to know that I take full responsibility—"

"For canceling a special session of Congress?" Rutledge interrupted. "For having me whisked onto Marine One, en route to some underground bunker?"

"Yes sir." It was all she could think to say.

"New York is still an absolute mess. And there was no attack. The US Capitol is evacuated and being carefully swept. But they have found nothing, not a shred of evidence to support your claim. I don't know if you understand the ramifications of shutting down the US government for even a few hours, Ms. Johansson, but I can tell you that they are extensive."

Rutledge's tone wasn't particularly harsh or angry; it was rather calm, passive, like a tired parent repeating themselves for a hundredth time. "The media is reporting. The internet is abuzz with rumors. People are starting to notice, to connect the dots here. The entire point of involving you and your people was to keep that from happening. Now that it's happened, responsibilities are being transferred."

"Yes sir."

"The FBI will be handling this matter," he told her. As Shaw had already told her. As the confused agent who had no idea about CIA involvement had already told her. "Please make sure they have any and all intelligence, evidence, or communication that your team has gathered."

Shaw's words, no doubt, coming from the President of the United States. Rutledge knew nothing about gathering intelligence. It seemed that the CIA's new director had less of a spine than Maria had previously thought. He wasn't one to get his hands dirty; he was one to offer up CIA tech and promote cooperation and relay messages via a more powerful figure.

Her jaw ached. She hadn't realized she'd been clenching her teeth so hard.

"Yes sir."

"Doesn't make sense," Todd Strickland said quietly, his thick arms folded over his chest. "This fit. It all fit."

"No." Zero shook his head. He realized now they'd been too hasty, too distracted, too overzealous in assuming the Capitol would be the next target. It was certainly the most attractive target—but that was exactly why it didn't fit. "If this was the plan all along, then the random attacks in Havana and Kansas would have been pointless. They showed their hand for a reason; *this* reason. To make us paranoid. To make us scurry to safety. To disrupt the status quo. It's working."

Todd shook his head. "To what end, though?"

Zero could only shrug. "Maybe … maybe to this end. Maybe to no end. They've vanished, and they don't have to resurface, ever. Or maybe they show up somewhere randomly again, some place that doesn't make any sense, just to keep us guessing. To remind us that they can be anywhere …" He trailed off as a thought formed in his head. They *couldn't* actually be anywhere. The group responsible had no idea who was pursuing them, who was aware. Now that they had entered the US with the ultrasonic weapon, they weren't leaving. They couldn't risk it.

"Hey." Maria approached them sullenly. She looked drained. "Just learned the hard way that having the most powerful man in the western world remind you that you failed is quite a blow to the ego."

Strickland blew out a short breath. "We didn't fail. We found the truck. We saw the woman. We almost had…" He stopped himself. Zero knew that it was for his benefit that Todd didn't finish his statement; Zero was the one who had let her and the little girl get away.

We almost had her.

"We're the only ones that saw her face," Strickland continued. "Or Zero is, anyway. We're still in a unique position to help."

"And what?" Maria countered. "Go rogue? Defy orders from the President of the United States?" She snickered bitterly. "There was a time when that might have been my move. Kent's too. But not this time." She gestured with her head. "Come on. We're going home."

Maria trudged off, back toward the waiting black car that had brought them, and Strickland dutifully followed. It was almost laughable to Zero, a total boy scout like Todd suggesting that they keep going, ignore orders. Still, he wasn't wrong. Zero *had* seen her face, in detail, through a rifle scope.

The boy stoops to pick something up. A piece of metal. A coin, perhaps…

"No." Zero shook his head. He couldn't go home. He couldn't stand to be alone with himself right now. Not with this tempest in his head. Not with the knowledge, however manufactured it may be, that he was a hired killer.

"Kent?" Maria paused and looked over her shoulder. "What'd you say?"

But he didn't answer. Instead he was stuck on something else that Todd had said, or had nearly said.

We almost had her.

Following the truck crash, Zero had the woman dead to rights. He was going to shoot, to wound her—but then the little girl had appeared.

He couldn't do it. He couldn't pull the trigger.

"Earth to Zero?" Strickland's voice sounded far away.

He still didn't know if the memories were his actual past or some manifestation. But one thing was perfectly clear, made so by a psychopathic Russian woman and her adolescent companion: he wasn't that person anymore. He wasn't an indiscriminate killer. If he was, he would have pulled that trigger without a second thought.

But he didn't. He couldn't.

People had the capacity to change. He'd proven that in his own life, even in ways he actually could remember. Time was that he and Strickland were enemies. Time was that he and John Watson were friends. Time was that Maria Johansson would have laughed at the very notion of her being CIA management.

People could change. There was darkness in his past, he was damn sure of that, and possibly much more than he even realized. But that was something he would have to deal with. Overcome. And move on.

"No," he said again, louder. "We're not done."

Strickland grinned. "Finally, someone around here is talking sense."

Maria sighed. "We have no leads. Nothing to go on."

"That's not entirely true." Just before Maria had approached, right after her call with the president, Zero had been on the precipice of a thought—and now it came back to him. "I think I have an idea."

CHAPTER THIRTY ONE

Sara dug her bare heels into the sand. It was cooler than she thought it would be, but felt welcome on her throbbing ankle. She hugged her arms over her chest and shivered slightly. Even on the beach with the rising sun shining on her face, a late November morning was still chilly, and a breeze blew in from the ocean.

But that wasn't why she shivered.

After her less-than-elegant escape from the rehab facility, she'd hobbled across the lawn of Seaside House and toward the beach. She kept to the shadows, eyes forward and alert, managing to avoid any trouble. It was late enough at night that the drunks, revelers, and thugs had all gone home. Still she stayed cognizant, and ducked back at any sign of headlights for fear that a curious cop might wonder what a teenage girl was doing out that late at night.

She reached the beach while it was still dark and walked a short ways along it, until the pain in her sprained ankle was too much to bear. She found a bench and set herself on it, finding relief in taking her weight off the injured foot for a short time. Despite her quest and the persistent nagging in her brain, she was exhausted, and couldn't help but curl up with her backpack in her arms and nod off.

When she woke, the sun was just cresting on the horizon. Sara rubbed sleep from her eyes, stretched, and sat up—then cried out at the shockwave of pain that ran from her ankle up as she set the foot down on the ground. It was tender and swollen, turning purple.

She tugged off her shoes and socks and limped down to the sand, where she sat on her butt and dug in her heels until the cool sand sifted over the hurt ankle. It felt nice, though she could feel a strange warmth in the injury, and a pulsing sensation like her own heartbeat.

But she hadn't forgotten her goal. She could have been back in Bethesda by now, back to her dad's apartment by bus. Yet she was still in Virginia Beach, barely more than a few miles away from Seaside House.

She wondered if they'd look for her, the staff at the rehab facility. Would they call the police, on account of her age? They would certainly contact her dad—though, come to think of it, she had no idea if he was even back home or not from whatever derring-do the CIA had him on.

Derring-do? She almost laughed at herself. *Thanks, Maya.* Just another bizarre term she must have heard from her well-read sister. Sara wondered if they might try to contact her if they couldn't reach her father. Maya would worry, but there'd be little she could do about it from New York. Sara had her cell phone on her, but she had turned it off. Her dad could track it. She didn't know if anyone had tried to call her since her escape. It was likely they weren't yet aware of her own derring-do.

And much like her dad, she was on a mission. Seated there on the beach with her feet bare and half buried in the sand, Sara glanced around. She was close to a skinny pier, maybe a football field's length to her right, an old wooden thing that was more for the seabirds than for people, judging by the layer of white poop drying in the sun. Beyond the rickety old pier, she could see the hazy silhouette of the boardwalk less than a half mile in the distance, bathed in early morning fog.

Bingo. Boardwalks were attractive for two types of people: tourists and homeless. Virginia Beach had both in spades, and as much as she hated to stereotype, she knew that a hit wouldn't be far or that difficult to acquire. She still had the fifty bucks in cash that Maya had given her. Hopefully it would be enough. Then she'd be broke, and she'd have to hitchhike back to Bethesda.

The more troubling concern was that she didn't exactly know the protocol for this kind of transaction. Sara had always gotten her stuff from her former roommate, Camilla. She'd picked up on some of the lingo here and there, but she didn't know how to ... approach a vendor, so to speak.

Excuse me, sir? Good morning! Do you happen to sell drugs?

She laughed aloud at the thought.

Behind her, a middle-aged man and woman jogged by. A short ways down the beach, a scruffy-looking man with an unkempt gray beard dug through a wire trash bin. A young guy walked hurriedly through the sand, just out of reach of the incoming surf.

Sara arched an eyebrow at the youth. He looked to be just a few years older than her, with dark hair and olive-colored skin. Hispanic, perhaps, or maybe just deeply tanned. Despite the November weather he wore sandals and a gray hooded sweatshirt with the sleeves cut roughly off at the shoulders, exposing wiry arms with amateur tattoos down their length. He kept his hands in his pockets and glanced around constantly.

As he passed by Sara, his gaze flitted to hers. The boy had dark bags under his eyes. The time was very early for most, but she got the impression that it was simply very late for him—so late that the sun had irritatingly rose again.

Something sparked in her. She recognized that hurried walk, that nervous glance. The facial twitch that made his cheek jump almost imperceptibly when he had looked her way. He was walking parallel to the surf because no one could approach him from that side. He was heading straight for the rickety old pier.

Whether he was strung out or homeless or perhaps a combination thereof, Sara didn't know. But she picked herself up, acting casual as possible, and brushed the sand from her butt. She slung her backpack over her shoulder and carried her shoes in her hand and she followed the boy. The pain in her ankle was immediate and throbbing. Her limp was pronounced.

But she had a strong feeling that this boy would have what she was after, and the need was stronger than the pain. The need was stronger than common sense. The need was stronger than the realization that if she was wrong, or if he was dangerous, or if he wasn't alone, she was an unarmed sixteen-year-old girl who would not be able to run away.

Maya ran.

She ran every morning that she was able. But most days she ran at a brisk jog, enough to maintain an eight-minute mile. Building stamina and strength. Conditioning her body.

Today she *ran*.

She didn't time herself or count the laps as she sprinted around the West Point track. She simply ran. Her muscular legs sprang powerfully with each step, clearing several feet with every bound forward. The cold air whipped at her face, tears stinging her eyes.

It was the cold air. Nothing else.

The events of the night prior were a bizarre, vague haze. Three boys had accosted her in the girls' locker room after a shower. She blacked out. She came around when Melvin the janitor barged in. He found the boys badly beaten and broken. He found Maya, in only a towel that used to be white, covered with blood that wasn't hers.

Then she cried. Her vision blurred with tears, and when it cleared again she was in the dean's office alone. It was quiet. It was dark. She was in shorts and a gray T-shirt. Someone had brought her clothes. Some of the blood had been cleaned from her. It was still there though, on her hands, in the wrinkles of her knuckles and the creases of her fingernails.

Not her blood.

There were voices, adult voices, stern and low. In the hallway. Their words were lost to her.

She cried again.

She hated that, the crying. It was weakness. Even before West Point, Maya had always hated crying in front of people. It told them she was vulnerable.

She told herself all manner of stupid things. That the tears were the weakness leaving her body. But that wasn't true. She was a dichotomy: a foolish little girl who thought she knew everything when she knew nothing. A monster who let the demons of her past overwhelm her to the point of nearly taking a life.

Those boys, they had made threats. They had assaulted her. Her ribs still ached from the one successful blow they had gotten in. That was one thing that she remembered from the night before: the dean told her that the weapons those boys had, they were long tube socks each with a heavy padlock stuffed in the end. It seemed they had taken locksocking quite literally.

When it was still night, she had cried and cried until she couldn't cry anymore. She was alone; there was no one around to see her tears. But still she hated it.

Eventually the dean, Brigadier General Hunt, came in. She wore jeans and a green sweater. She sat down. She patted Maya's knee. Maya remembered thinking, despite everything, how strange it was to see Dean Hunt in anything other than her uniform.

The dean asked: "Who can we call?"

Maya thought about it.

"Don't call anyone."

She was an adult. This was her life. Her fight. Her dad, if he was around, would come running. Swooping in and saving the day. Unless he was still out there somewhere, swooping in and saving someone else's day.

She didn't need saving.

"Don't call anyone," Maya had said.

At some point she'd fallen asleep. When she woke, she was still in the dean's office. Still alone. Her back ached from the uncomfortable position she'd slept in, curled in the seat of a leather armchair.

She didn't know if she was allowed to go anywhere. She didn't know what would happen to her. Would there be charges? Would she be allowed to stay in school? How bad was it, what she had done to those boys?

Even though she was only in shorts and a T-shirt, Maya went outside. There were no guards, no MPs, no administrators keeping her there. She shivered in the early November morning cold. She walked out to the empty oval track.

Then Maya ran.

Sweat poured from her brow. She gulped cold air like a fish out of water. Her legs continued to bound forward even as the muscles shrieked in protest. But she ran. Tear stung her eyes. She screamed then, as she ran, the sound of it both breathless and full at the same time.

Then she slowed. She walked. The pain came now, fresh and raw. A burning in her side. Her throat. Her lungs. Her legs. Her ribs, where a padlock-stuffed in a tube sock had smacked her.

Even if there were no charges, and even if she was allowed to stay in school after what happened... even if she was completely exonerated of any wrongdoing because she had been attacked, what sort of life would she have there? She'd already gone and pissed off half the male population of the academy. Those boys had friends. The events of last night might very well go and piss off the other half. She'd be a pariah.

It was infuriatingly unjust. All she wanted to do was excel and mind her own business. Yet it seemed that everyone wanted to step in her way. All because some petty jealousy had congealed into anger in the wrong people.

If she stayed, there would be more to come. She knew it. Dean Hunt could make the worst example of those three. She could expel them, or even bring criminal charges against them. She could bar them for life from any sort of military service in the United States. Ruin them and their futures.

She would do little but make martyrs out of them.

It wasn't fair.

Maya heard a chiming sound, a strange sort of high-pitched ringing that was as familiar as it was jarring. It took her a moment to realize that it was her ring tone. But she didn't have her cell phone. Did she? She patted her shorts before realizing dully that they had no pockets. She followed the sound, jogging to a nearby bench.

Her phone sat there, still ringing, the screen lit with a number she didn't recognize. For a moment she just stared at it. She had brought it to the locker room with her last night. Had someone brought it to the dean's office for her? Had she brought it out here with her? She couldn't remember.

You're cracking up, Lawson.

"Hello?"

"Hi, is this Maya Lawson?" It was a young woman with an irritatingly peppy voice.

"Speaking. Who's this?"

"My name is Penelope, calling from Seaside House Recovery Center."

Oh no. Whatever Penelope had to say could not be good.

"What's happened?" Maya demanded.

"First, I just need to confirm your relation to our guest, Sara Lawson. You are her sister, is that correct?"

"Yes."

"You're listed as the second point of contact for Sara. The first contact person, Reid Lawson, wasn't available, so we've contacted you—"

"What's. Happened?" Maya demanded again, punching each word from her mouth.

"Well. Um…" This Penelope paused. "Sara has, uh, left our facility."

"Left," Maya repeated blandly. The rehab center had made it perfectly clear that their program was voluntary; Sara could walk out the door any time she wanted.

"Yes. To be more specific, she, uh… well, it appears that she climbed out of a second-story window."

Maya let out a deflating sigh. "When?"

"Sometime during the night? We're not sure. She wasn't in her room, and had disguised it to appear that she was still asleep…"

Penelope kept talking, saying something about a shower curtain and a twenty-foot drop, but Maya's mind was racing. Sara was not held there against her will. She could have walked right out the front door. But if she climbed out of a window in the middle of the night, that meant she didn't want to be seen. She didn't want anyone knowing she had left. Maya had left her some money, a meager sum of cash, but still possibly enough…

A knot of panic gripped Maya's stomach.

"Ms. Lawson?" said Penelope.

"I'm sorry, what was that?"

"I said, we don't ordinarily involve law enforcement unless the family believes that the guest may be harmful to themselves or others."

"Yes. Do that." Maya hung up. Maybe the police would find her. But she wasn't about to leave it to chance. Maya scrolled through her contacts until she found the number labeled as "Third Street Garage."

"'Lo," answered a grunting male voice. "Third Street."

"Alan. It's Maya."

"Oh. Hey, kiddo!" The guttural, monosyllabic persona of Mitch the mechanic fell away, replaced by the affable Alan Reidigger. "How are you? You okay?"

"Not really. Long story. Can you track Sara?"

"Sara?" he repeated with some alarm. "What's going on?"

"She fled rehab. Climbed out a window and scaled a wall or something in the middle of the night."

"Christ. Okay. Uh, if she has her phone and didn't turn it off, yeah. I can find her. But I think we both know your sister is a bit smarter than that. If she doesn't want to be found..."

"You know I hate to ask it," Maya said cautiously.

"I'm already putting on my jacket. Text me the address of the place she was at, I'll track her down myself."

"Thank you, Alan." Maya breathed a short sigh of relief.

Then she glanced around. The gray sky. The empty track. The academy, still and silent with the long holiday weekend. The sweat was cooling on her brow. She shivered.

"Do you know someone who can get me to Virginia Beach?" she asked. "I want to help."

"Of course," Alan told her. "Do you want fast, or do you want legal?"

"Fast as possible."

"I'll text you where to be." Alan ended the call.

Less than fifteen seconds later, her phone chimed. A text from Alan with an address not far from West Point property. Maya jogged toward the dorms, intending to change clothes quickly. She wouldn't have time to scrub the dried blood from her fingernails.

Her life, as far as she knew, was in shambles. Her head was a mess. Her fate was in the hands of administrators. But she'd be damned if anything was going to happen to her sister.

CHAPTER THIRTY TWO

*M*ore than a billion devices in the continental United States alone.

Those were the words that were stuck in Zero's head as the dark-suited driver drove them back to Ronald Reagan Washington National Airport. Bixby had said that just yesterday, though it felt like it might have been a month ago.

He could tell that Maria wanted to ask questions by the way she fidgeted in her seat. But she didn't dare ask, not when they didn't know the identity or affiliation of their driver. So she remained quiet, squirming, for sixteen minutes until they arrived back at the airstrip. The Gulfstream was there, the pilot lingering nearby, talking on his cell phone and smoking a thin brown-wrapped cigar.

As soon as they were out of the car Maria whirled on him. "Why are we back at the jet? We're already within spitting distance of home, and our last lead."

"We're going somewhere," Zero answered vaguely.

"Where?" Strickland asked.

"I don't know yet," he said candidly. Zero motioned to the pilot, whirling one finger in small circles. "Wheels up, ASAP."

The pilot frowned. "Destination?"

"Not sure," Zero called back as he ascended the ramp. "For now? Just up."

Inside the cabin, he pulled out his cell phone, made a call, and put it on speaker.

I really hope I'm right about this.

"Bixby," answered the engineer.

"It's Zero."

"Zero! Oh, man. Look, I'm sorry. I didn't want to give the Feds those sonic meters. Shaw made me do it. Now every Tom, Dick, and Harry is going to know we're dealing with a sonic weapon..."

"Bixby," Zero snapped. "Shut up a second. Calm down. I have an idea." He was keenly aware that Maria's and Strickland's eyes were upon him. That Bixby was listening intently.

The caffeine pills that Todd had given him earlier were working, maybe too well. He felt wired, almost jittery. Zero rubbed his face, trying to organize his thoughts in a coherent way that didn't make him sound like a madman.

"Okay," he said. "Here it is. This group we're after, they don't know what we know. They don't know that the president authorized a small CIA team to pursue them. For all they know, every cop and FBI agent in the country is looking for them. That means they have to operate completely under the radar. They're being careful. They attacked during a holiday; they're staying off of phones and radios."

Maria nodded slowly. "With you so far."

"It also means they won't leave," Zero continued. "They have to assume that every airport, seaport, train station, bus terminal, and land border is going to be crawling with cops. They know we have video of Kansas. They know I saw the Russian woman's face. They got their weapon in here, and they got the element of surprise, but now they're here. They're not leaving. They're stuck here."

Strickland frowned. "I think you're losing me."

Zero let out an exasperated sigh. How could he elucidate what was going through his head when his pulse was pounding and his thoughts came jumbled? "I thought this was about panic and chaos. And it is, at least somewhat. But that's ancillary. You don't send that kind of weapon and a crew into a foreign state on what will ultimately be a suicide mission without a masterstroke. They haven't gotten there yet, but I think they will. So far we've been seeing an attack a day—Havana, Kansas..."

"But nothing yet today," Strickland noted.

"Right. There will be. I'm sure of it. The Capitol didn't fit because it was obvious. Wherever they're going to hit won't be."

"But we don't know where that might be," Maria argued. "And if it won't be obvious, we have no way of knowing until it happens."

"Exactly!" Zero said. "We have the sonic detection meter to give us a location, but it's too short-range. We'd have to be in the thick of it for that to work. But again, they don't know what we know. They don't know what we *have*."

One of Maria's thin blonde eyebrows arched precipitously. "And what do we have?"

"We have OMNI."

"Oh no." Bixby's murmured sigh through the phone told Zero that the engineer had already picked up on what he was suggesting.

But Maria shook her head. "OMNI failed us."

"It didn't fail," Zero insisted. "It just led us to the wrong place. The parameters were too wide." He looked at the phone in his hand. "Bixby, you said it yourself: OMNI is like a search engine for sound."

"Uh-huh." Bixby sounded defeated. "I did say that."

"And currently there are more than a billion devices in the continental United States alone that OMNI could pick up on—because it's tuned to a frequency range. But tuned to the *right* frequency, there's only one device in the whole country that will match what we're after."

Maria's eyes widened as she came to understand what he was suggesting. Strickland touched his chin and nodded.

"So?" Zero asked the phone. "Can it be done? Can OMNI be calibrated to pick up on the ultrasonic weapon's frequency, like you did with the sonic detection meters?"

There was silence from the phone, for an uncomfortably long moment.

"Bixby?"

The engineer cleared his throat. "Zero, look. I want to help in any way I can. You know I do. But we're talking about a machine that cost tens of millions just to create, let alone network appropriately. A machine whose very existence is not only objectionable, but objectively immoral. Security clearance on this thing goes higher than yours, a covert CIA operative. Not to mention that any alterations made to it can be immediately traced to me—"

"But can it be done?" Zero interrupted.

"I mean... theoretically? Yeah. I don't know if it can be reversed, though. It might cause permanent damage to OMNI's central processing unit—"

"Bixby," Maria said sternly. "As deputy director, I'm authorizing you to recalibrate OMNI to the frequency of the ultrasonic weapon."

"No offense, Johansson," Bixby said quietly. "But we both know you don't have that authority."

Maria set her jaw angrily, but held her tongue.

The plane's engines whirred to life. The pilot lifted the ramp and secured the door as Zero chose his next words carefully.

"I know you," he said into the phone. "You're a good man. But you're not in the field. You don't see this kind of stuff firsthand. Sometimes good men turn on the news, and they see that a bunch of people were hurt or died because of this or that. It happens every day. I bet in your long career, there have been a few times that you've turned on the news and saw that some people suffered at the hands of something you knew about. Maybe something you were tangentially involved in. But right now, I'm telling you that you could have a direct impact. You can choose to help, or you can choose to stand by. And if you stand by, and then you turn on the news, and you see that some people were hurt or died because of something that you could have had an active hand in stopping... how is that going to feel, Bixby? Are you going to sleep soundly that night? Because I'll tell you. I don't sleep soundly much these days."

The silence over the phone stretched long enough for Zero to think that the call had dropped.

"Aw, hell," Bixby said in a half-whisper. "Okay, Zero. I'll... I'll do it."

Zero held back his sigh of relief.

"I'll have to take it offline briefly—which means that if anyone is paying attention, Shaw and the NSA might be clued in that something is up. I'll route the results to Johansson's tablet. But after that, I'm gone. I'm not going to be of any more help to you. I'm not going to stick around and wait for them to come for me."

Zero wasn't sure what Bixby meant, if he would just leave the lab or actually leave. OMNI was a dangerous thing just to know about, let alone use or tamper with. But he decided not to ask for clarification.

"Thank you, Bixby."

"Give me fifteen minutes. Godspeed." The engineer ended the call.

"Tell the pilot to get us in the air but not to log a flight plan," Zero told Maria. "Keep us close until we know something." The jet's CIA clearance allowed them to circumvent FAA regulations during a crisis. They didn't need to tell anyone where they were going.

"That clearance will only last until someone decides to check in with the agency and confirm it," Maria pointed out.

"Even if there's a deputy director of Special Operations aboard?" Strickland asked.

"We're not supposed to be on this op or this jet." She shrugged. "But we're also not supposed to tamper with top-secret computers that are capable of spying on the entire country, so hey." She maneuvered toward the cockpit to talk to the pilot.

Strickland lowered himself into a seat and buckled up. "If this works, we'll get a location, just like we did with the Russians in Vegas. Right?"

Zero nodded. "Right."

"But what if it's on the other side of the country? What if they're in California or something by now?"

"We'll still have their location," Zero said. "We can alert local authorities, let them know exactly where they are. And we'll be in an advantageous position to get there quickly if we're already in the air."

Strickland nodded. "Sounds like a plan."

A plan. It was a plan, but not the one that Zero wanted. Earlier he'd had the harrowing thought that a new attack would be their best way to find these people and their weapon.

But now, another attack was their *only* way of finding it.

CHAPTER THIRTY THREE

Samara adjusted the baseball cap over her head, pulling her red hair into a ponytail behind it. She smirked to herself, imagining that she looked like a ... what was the term? Ah, right—"soccer mom." With Mischa in tow, she probably looked like an American soccer mom.

Just a woman and a girl and their team of elite black-clad commandos.

Samara stretched her arms in the morning sun. The air here was fresh and invigorating with just a hint of salinity from the nearby Chesapeake Bay. They were nearly there. But first, they had to introduce a bit of chaos.

This place, this town, had an amusing name. Prince Frederick, it was called. Samara had never been here before, but she knew it well, very well—perhaps better than most of the twenty-five hundred or so people that called the small town home. It was established in 1734 and named after the then-Prince of Wales. It was the county seat of Calvert County, situated on a peninsular stretch of rural Maryland that jutted downward into the Chesapeake.

It was just under forty miles from Washington, DC. And it was less than eight miles from their destination.

Mischa stood nearby, leaning against the side of the brown delivery truck, wearing the oversized green sweater and craning her neck slightly upward. The girl's eyes were closed, her features passive, face bathed in sunlight. After hours hiding in garbage cans and driving through the night in the rear of the boxy delivery truck, the girl seemed to enjoy being out of doors.

She was a weapon. A spy. An operative. But in some ways, still very much a child.

Samara checked the internet on her phone. She was well aware that the chaos in New York was still continuing. The evacuation measures had ceased and the government had given an all-clear on the potential threat, but people were not resting easy. There had been much damage, panic, chaos. Even a few deaths. It would take weeks to return to what passed as normal in such a place.

And then there was DC. The capital of the United States. Samara could have laughed at how well that had gone—she, in fact, had done nothing to facilitate it. She and her team had had no idea of any special session of Congress and frankly could not care less. But the powers-that-be had determined it a possible target, and hoped to catch them there.

Their current location, forty miles from the Capitol Building, was the closest Samara would ever dare to get to the lion's den. They had another destination in mind.

She glanced around the parking lot of the strip mall. The delivery truck was parked in a rear row of what passed for a commercial hub in Prince Frederick. There was a grocery store, a Chinese food restaurant, a post office, a deli, and a mattress store. Morning shoppers came and went without any idea what was about to happen. The power of the sonic weapon would ensure that even those inside, perusing produce or selecting breakfast cereals, would feel its effects.

"Mischa," she called.

The girl opened her eyes and dutifully rounded to the rear of the truck. One man was up front, posing as the driver. Five more were in the rear with the weapon. Samara glanced about casually, making sure that no one was watching, and then she tugged the rolling metal door upward about halfway.

Four black-masked faces turned to her. The fifth was pale with dark hair. His almond-shaped eyes widened in alert at Samara's sudden presence. He reached quickly for the black mask he had removed, the mask they had been ordered to not take off, not ever. Not until they were dead or done.

"What are you doing?" Samara asked calmly in Russian as she stepped up into the back of the truck.

"Nothing," the man said rapidly. "Fixing. That is all."

Samara was fairly certain he meant "adjusting," but the word in Russian must have alluded him. He pulled the mask over his face as Mischa joined them and pulled the rolling door back down again.

There was something about the features of these men that Samara found interesting. The Russians of her native land, the land that she had turned her back on, were typically hard and unyielding. They looked as if they were hewn from wood, or perhaps carved from stone. These men, the men in the truck, these commandos that had been awarded to her for this purpose, were soldiers. They followed orders explicitly. Each and every one had at least eight confirmed kills in their careers. They knew that this was most likely a one-way trip. Yet she found their features to be softer, as if they had been molded from clay. It was not a fault or shortcoming; quite the opposite. It was an attractive quality, if Samara was being honest. She had long ago disposed herself of "the Russian way," and the thought of associating herself with them in any way other than heritage was sickening.

With the man's mask secured again and the door closed behind them, Samara tapped twice on the metal frame just behind the driver's seat. "Get into position," she instructed. The truck's engine rumbled to life.

She reached into her pocket for the two small bean-shaped objects there. "Ear plugs," she told Mischa. The men followed suit. Two of them lifted the large rectangular cardboard box that stood in the center of the truck's rear, the bottom cut from it, and revealed their weapon.

In moments they would activate it. The Americans would be aware immediately that there had been a new attack on another seemingly random place. They would draw their parallels between this and the other attacks. If all went according to plan, police and investigators would assume that the perpetrators had already fled, as they had twice before. Hurried to another state, or onto a plane or a boat.

No one would suspect they were a mere eight miles away. Hiding in close proximity.

Prince Frederick. Samara smirked to herself as she powered up the sonic weapon. *What a strange name for a place.*

Chapter Thirty Four

Zero paced the narrow aisle of the Gulfstream. It had been sixteen minutes since Bixby's call, but they hadn't yet been connected to OMNI. He worried that the engineer had changed his mind. Or been caught in the act. Or that someone had been listening in on the call. Any number of things could have gone wrong—or perhaps nothing. Maybe it was just taking longer than Bixby expected.

The jet was at twelve thousand feet, staying low to keep out of commercial flight paths and on its second lazy circle of the DC Metro area, careful to avoid planes coming into Ronald Reagan or Dulles.

Maria fidgeted. Strickland cracked his knuckles. Everyone was anxious. No one had answers.

The shrill sound of a ringing phone made Zero start. He was jumpy.

"This can't be good," Maria murmured as she answered the call. "Johansson."

She put it on speaker in time for the back half of Director Shaw's statement. "—think you're doing, but you are to land that plane and report back to Langley, now."

"No," Maria said plainly.

There was a moment of stunned silence. "Excuse me?"

"Sorry," Maria replied quickly. "I meant to say, no *sir*. We have a lead. A way to find these people. We're going to see it through. Unless, that is, you're going to dispatch someone to shoot us down?"

"I have half a mind ..." Shaw growled.

The intercom crackled. "FAA is demanding that we land." It was the maverick pilot from the cockpit. "Shall I tell them to kindly bend over a barrel?"

"This will cost you your badge, Johansson," Shaw threatened.

"Management hasn't been suiting me all that well anyway," Maria muttered.

We're not going to pull this off. They were out of time. Shaw might not have known about their plans with OMNI yet, but he knew they were up to something and defying orders.

The FAA knew they didn't have flight clearance. Zero was all too aware that further defiance could even mean jail time for all three of them.

"I need a heading or something back there," the pilot said. "I can't keep circling."

"You are refusing a command that came from the President of the United States," Shaw said firmly.

The screen of Maria's tablet lit to life. She snatched it up and smiled broadly, turning it to show her teammates. It was a map, a GPS map of the entire lower forty-eight states. In the lower-left corner was a yellow blip moving in a tight, slow circle. Indicating a scan, it seemed. And in the upper-right corner were four tiny white letters: O-M-N-I.

"I'm sorry, Director Shaw," Maria said. "But we have a job to do, and we're going to see it through."

"You failed," Shaw retorted. "It was transferred to other hands because you failed—"

"No." There was a hard edge to Maria's voice. "We didn't fail. We just didn't finish yet." She ended the call. "So. That went well. What do you think he'll send to shoot us down? F-16? Maybe an F-22?"

"Hello back there?" the pilot's voice came through the intercom.

Maria pressed the intercom button. "Need a minute."

"They're making some pretty interesting threats up here," the pilot replied. "I'm not sure we have a minute."

Zero shook his head. The pilot was right; they were out of time. "I appreciate you back me up on this, Maria. But it's over. We should land, hand over the tablet to the FBI. Tell Shaw what we've done. Or else this is going to get worse for all of us." If it was just him, he would gladly defy orders and keep fighting the fight. But it wasn't just him; Maria, Strickland, and even their pilot would all go down for his idea.

"It's not over," Maria said adamantly. "Not yet. And I'll decide how bad I want things to get for me, thank you very much."

Strickland shrugged. "Spent my whole life following orders. It's kind of fun to see how you do things for once."

Zero smirked. How often he'd found himself here, against the world with little to no support but for a few good friends. It made all the difference—

Ding. Maria's tablet made a noise, a digital chime like a single small bell. It was so disconcertingly euphonious that for a moment, none of them could place what it was or what it might mean. It was not a blaring alarm, or a siren, or a shrill red-alert.

But the map on the tablet was zooming rapidly.

"Jesus," Maria murmured. OMNI zoomed onto the Eastern seaboard. "We've got a hit."

"On the weapon?" Strickland asked as he stood from his seat.

The map zoomed farther, faster. On...Annapolis? No. It swung south, pinpointing the location of the frequency it tracked.

"It's close," Maria breathed. She frowned. "In Maryland. Some town called...Prince Frederick? Just off the western shore of the Chesapeake."

The map zoomed even further, and then stopped.

"A shopping center, it looks like." Maria blinked at the screen, seemingly in awe.

"This is in real time," Zero prodded. "It's happening. Right now."

Maria snapped out of it. She smashed her hand on the intercom's button. "Prince Frederick, about thirty-eight miles southeast of here. You know it?"

"I do." The plane's wing dipped suddenly as it turned, so suddenly that Zero had to grip the back of a seat to keep from stumbling. "ETA six minutes. Maybe less."

"These attacks don't usually last more than a few minutes," Strickland noted.

"And we'll have to find a place to land," Zero added. Even with their devil-may-care pilot and a suitable strip to land on, descent and taxi could add ten minutes to their arrival time.

"So we jump," Strickland said. He suggested it as simply as someone might say, *Hey, let's go out for dinner tonight.*

So we jump.

"We jump," Maria agreed.

"Sure," Zero muttered. "We jump. Why not."

"This is insane," Zero remarked as he secured his chest strap.

"You mentioned that once or ten times." Strickland grinned. The younger agent already had his rig on and secured. He double-checked his leg straps. "Make sure your harness is snug first before the leg straps, or else they'll ride up on descent."

"Thanks for the tip." Zero was nervous. He'd done this before, jumped out of airplanes. But it had been quite a while, and he wasn't exactly in a rush to do it again.

"Todd, stow my straps," Maria said as she tapped on her phone. Her rig was on, parachute container high and tight against her back as Strickland knelt to tuck the hanging strap ends. "We need to tell someone what's happening and give a precise location. I won't be able to contact Rutledge, since he's been moved to a secure site."

"Two minutes," the pilot told them.

"FBI is likely already aware, but they won't get there as fast as we will," Zero noted. "Same with local PD." According to OMNI, the frequency was still ongoing. The assault on the small town of Prince Frederick had lasted four minutes now—which was roughly the length of the attack on Springfield, Kansas. They had precious little time to get there.

"We're closest. We've got protection. We've got weapons." Strickland secured his gear bag to his chest by the straps to keep it from interfering with the parachute on his back. "There's no one to call. It's up to us."

The jet dipped in altitude, suddenly and significantly. Zero felt the sensation in the pit of his stomach.

"One minute!" the pilot said over the intercom. "I'll give the go-ahead when we're over the coordinates you gave me. On my mark, make the jump!"

This was really happening. They were going to leap out of a speeding Gulfstream and try to land in a shopping center in Maryland during an ultrasonic attack in the hopes of finding the weapon and detaining the people responsible.

Just another day at the office.

"Ear plugs in!" Maria ordered. "We won't be able to communicate, but they'll protect your hearing against the frequency. Let's keep it tight and get there in one piece!"

Zero fit the tiny, kidney bean–shaped ear plugs into each ear. Instantly all sound was drowned out by a slight whine, a high-pitched frequency that felt as if it was coming from inside his own head.

Maria opened the cabin door. Wind whipped about, tearing at his clothes, stinging his eyes. He was certain that it was deafeningly loud, but he heard none of it. Only the whine in his ears. It was remarkably eerie.

Suddenly the lights went out in the plane's cabin. They wouldn't be able to hear the pilot's voice; this was his mark. Go-time.

Strickland leapt out without hesitation. Maria followed on a two-count. Zero edged to the door. The world looked very far away.

You've done this before. It's just been a couple years.

That didn't make it any easier. But somewhere down there, very far away, people were being hurt and worse at that very moment.

He took a breath, and he jumped.

Chapter Thirty Five

Zero was floating.

At least that's how it felt. With skydiving, there wasn't that sensation of plummeting as there was with shorter drops, like the first hill of a roller coaster or, say, leaping out of a helicopter and onto the top of a box truck. He held the arch position as he fell: elbows out, hands flat in front of his face, knees slightly bent and head back. Without looking at the rushing ground and without the sound of the wind tearing at him, he could have been floating in place.

It was oddly serene. Any fears or anxieties he had a few moments earlier, back on the plane, were gone. But then he did glance down at the oncoming Earth. He had to remind himself that he was aiming for ground zero of a new attack.

He kept his left arm out for stability, to keep him from spinning, as he reached back with his right for the deployment cord. His fingers closed around it. In the instant before he pulled, he saw a parachute open below him and slightly to his left, what he presumed was just a bit west. It blossomed like a flower, though he couldn't tell if it was Maria or Strickland beneath it.

Then another opened, white in color but a disconcerting distance to Zero's north. How had the three of them gotten so scattered so quickly? It must have been the speed of the Gulfstream, and the few seconds of hesitation before he made the jump.

Zero tugged the cord. Again there was no sound as the shadow billowed out over his head. His shoulders were tugged upward as his descent slowed. He didn't know where Maria or Todd would land and there was nothing he could do about it. He could only concern himself with his own landing. Glancing around to get his bearings, he saw the vast and glistening Chesapeake Bay to his right—which meant he was facing north. He gripped the control lines and brought himself down steadily as he scanned the oncoming ground. This place, Prince

Frederick, was a lot of green, dotted with homes on sprawling rural properties. He looked for a downtown, for the commercial shopping center.

He spotted an L-shaped arrangement of beige, flat-topped buildings. A wide parking lot beyond it. And... was that smoke? Even from his height he could see it, a dark plume rising up from the lot. A car accident, perhaps, in the wake of the sonic weapon's effects.

Zero tugged on the control lines, steering the chute as best he could to land him at the far edge of the lot. As he touched down on asphalt, he kept his legs slightly bent and broke into a jog upon impact, slowing himself as the parachute landed behind him.

He tore at the chest harness and leg straps as quickly as he could and swung his gear bag over a shoulder. Then he glanced around.

It didn't look like anyone had noticed his arrival, that a man had mysteriously parachuted into the parking lot. They were, it seemed, more preoccupied with surviving.

People ran across the lot. Some winced as if they were in great pain; others had their mouths opened in a silent, yawning scream that Zero did not hear. He was right about the source of the smoke; there was at least one, perhaps more, minor collisions around him. Across the parking lot he could see people falling over, writhing in pain. Some not moving at all.

Near the buildings, the strip mall stores, people clambered and fought to get inside, thinking erroneously that it might help alleviate the ill effects they were feeling. It wouldn't, and the people already inside were thinking the opposite, fleeing and getting to the outdoors. Fists flew and arms shoved and legs trampled.

Zero noticed all of this in seconds after landing, though it was entirely silent to him. He heard nothing but the high-pitched whine in his ears. It was unnatural and chilling. Without sound, he felt detached from it all, as if he was merely watching a disaster film on mute.

And then—he felt it.

At first it didn't feel like much of anything other than the vague sensation of knowing that he wasn't quite right. Then it was the thundercloud of an oncoming headache in his skull. Then a bad hangover after a night of heavy drinking.

His head swam with dizziness. Nausea roiled in his stomach. Zero knew all too well what this was; he had parachuted directly into the range of the ultrasonic weapon.

His vision blurred and he stumbled forward. A pedestrian ran by, a hazy and silent shape that whirled him. His balance was thrown; his equilibrium was off. He lurched and put out both hands to steady himself.

Now he understood keenly why the weapon was not only dangerous, but terrifying. He had no idea which direction it was coming from. No way to tell where it might be hidden.

But that's not true, he reminded himself. The sonic detection meter was still in his gear bag. But it might as well have been locked away in Bixby's lab in Langley for all the good it would do him now.

Zero hit the asphalt with both knees. He couldn't see anything but fuzzy shapes and colors that bled into one another. The infrasound was vibrating his eyeballs in his skull. He couldn't stand. Bile rose in his throat. He didn't dare try to move. An attempt to get out of the weapon's range might accidentally bring him closer to it, and Bixby had warned about the effects at the closest ranges.

Ruptured organs. Internal bleeding. Death.

He could do little but ride it out like a storm, and hope against hope that Maria and Strickland had landed a safe distance away, that they weren't dealing with the same as him at that moment.

And then—if by some miracle, the sensations waned. The dizziness subsided. The nausea faded. He could see again, his vision returning to focus as if someone had slipped a pair of eyeglasses over his forehead.

They stopped.

The attack, by his best guess, had lasted less than two minutes since he'd landed in the parking lot. But it had felt much longer.

They stopped.

He was grateful for it. But he also panicked. If the attack had ended, he and his team had little chance of finding them again. They would escape. They would run again. Unless they were actively using the weapon, they wouldn't be able to track them.

Zero reached for his gear bag. As he did he wobbled unsteadily on his feet. He was still dizzy. He was still off-kilter. The realization struck him swiftly as he yanked out the yellow and black handheld device and powered it on.

The effects were slight. Zero hadn't moved, but still what he felt suggested that he was in the longest-range zone of the weapon. Maybe the attack hadn't stopped. Maybe the attack had simply waned. And that meant...

Yes. The sonic detection meter had a signal. A blip, barely a reading—but it meant the device was still powered on. Zero whipped the meter left and right in a semicircle, pointing the plastic dish in various directions, trying to lock onto a location.

There. A digital number flashed on the small screen at the rear of the device, behind the handle and above Zero's thumb. It read "270."

The perpetrators, and their sonic weapon, were two hundred seventy meters to the southeast. The number vanished, a moment later replaced by another: 290.

Then it, and the blip of the signal, was gone. He wasn't sure whether they had shut the weapon off or had moved beyond the detection meter's range. But he knew they weren't far. And he knew the direction in which they were heading. And he knew that they would need a vehicle large enough to transport their team and the weapon.

He had to find something smaller and faster.

Zero dared to tug his earplugs out and sucked in a breath as he was instantly and unceremoniously reintroduced to the world of sound. The aftermath of the sonic attack on the parking lot of a strip mall in Prince Frederick was horrifying. Pained moans, confused shouts, and terrified shrieks filled the air, an accompaniment to the sirens of various emergency vehicles that converged on the lot.

But Zero had no time to waste. He couldn't linger and help anyone here; he had to make sure this didn't happen anywhere else. He spotted a motorcycle on its side, a classic chopper in black and silver, and ran to it, pushing it upright with a groan. He let out a small sigh of relief as he saw that the keys were in the ignition, and a quick murmur of thanks to the patron saint of stupid luck when the engine turned over and nothing was seriously damaged.

Then he swung a leg over the bike, shifted, and roared out of the lot to the southeast.

He weaved in and out of traffic as he rushed to try to catch up to the perpetrators. He reasoned they must be in a truck, like the grocery box truck from Illinois, or perhaps a large van. He blew through a red light to catch up to a white windowless contractor van about fifty yards ahead. The local cops would certainly have their hands full with the attack that had just gone down and plenty better things to do than chase him.

Zero came up alongside the van and peered in through the driver's side window. The bewildered driver was a man with a beard in his forties or so. No redheaded woman. No child. No sketchy-looking Russian sorts.

Damn it! Where'd they go? So far this woman and her comrades had tried so hard to stay under the radar. But now they had initiated a new attack, fled with the weapon still in use, and judging by how far ahead they had gotten, had as little regard for traffic laws as Zero did at the moment.

Why? There was nothing to the southeast but more rural land and, eventually, the vast Chesapeake Bay.

He saw another truck up ahead and raced for it. It was the only tactic he had; pausing long enough to contact Maria or Strickland wasn't an option. But then a sign to his left drew his attention. It was a simple sign, advertising that this town, Prince Frederick, was the county seat of Calvert Cliffs.

That was all. *Now leaving Prince Frederick, County Seat of Calvert Cliffs.*

But it was enough for Zero to squeeze the motorcycle's brakes so hard that the rear wheel came off the street. He turned it and expertly put the bike on its side as it came to a screeching, squealing stop.

He knew where they were going. And now he *had* to make time to contact Maria.

Zero tore the radio from his bag and hissed into it: "Maria? Todd? Come in! Anyone? Can you hear me?!"

A hiss of static gave him his answer. Maybe their sonic protection, the earplugs, were still in. It could have been that they didn't know the attack was over, that they'd landed too far away and were making their way to the parking lot and plaza, where they would find no terrorists and no Zero.

And then they'd check.

He pulled out his phone and rapidly punched in a frantic text message, one that he hoped not only made sense but immediately told them where he'd gone and what was happening.

He wasn't entirely right. There was something more to the southeast of Prince Frederick, built right at the edge of the peninsula, overlooking the bay. Zero had never been there, but he'd heard of it. Knew of it.

Calvert Cliffs nuclear reactor.

That's what his text to Maria said.

The first of the two-unit reactor at Calvert Cliffs was opened in 1977, owned and operated by a joint venture between American and French energy companies. The second had opened sometime in the nineties, along with a full update to the facility.

There was one other thing that Zero knew about Calvert Cliffs. Despite it being built on a bluff overlooking the Chesapeake, nearly three million people lived and worked within a fifty-mile radius. The city of Annapolis. Some parts of Baltimore.

And Washington, DC.

The sonic weapon was never the point. It was a means to an end. A distraction. The redheaded woman and her people, they were planning to cause a meltdown. The ensuing fallout wouldn't claim just dozens of lives like the attacks had so far. It would kill millions.

Chapter Thirty Six

Zero pushed the motorcycle to the limits of what it was capable of as he raced southeast, following the green signs that pointed the way toward the Calvert Cliffs reactor. He wanted desperately to stop, to contact someone, to tell them what he now knew—the CIA, the FBI, the National Guard. Anyone. But he couldn't drive the motorcycle one-handed while using a cell phone, and he couldn't bring himself to stop. He was the closest. Anyone he could contact would take too long to get there.

Maria would see his message. She would understand. She would send the cavalry.

He turned the bike onto an access road that led to the facility. Signs warned him that this road was by authorized access only, yet he realized grimly that no one was trying to stop him.

He understood now why they had attacked on a holiday. No one would expect something like this. The reactor's staff, and by extension their security, would likely be on a skeleton crew.

The motorcycle slowed as he reached a small guard house protecting a chain-link gate with barbed wire over the top. The guard lay on the ground, torso and upper half out the open doorway to the small square structure. There was no blood, no gunshot wounds, yet the man was discernibly dead.

Zero didn't have to be a nuclear physicist to tell what had happened here. The unsuspecting guard had seen the truck or van or whatever sort of vehicle they were in approaching, and in the next moment had gotten a point-blank blast from the sonic weapon.

They never turned it off. That's how he had been able to track it with the sonic detection meter in Prince Frederick, until they'd left its range. They drove right into the reactor site with the sonic weapon powered up, silently and invisibly blasting anyone in their way. As for the physical barriers, the gate was twisted and crumpled, obviously rammed by something large enough to flatten it.

A short burst of automatic gunfire jarred him out of his thoughts. It was short-lived, five or six rounds, and then all was silent again. Zero scanned the facility beyond the gate.

There was a second checkpoint, another crashed gate, and then an expansive lot. Beyond that was the assortment of buildings that made up the nuclear facility, one of them standing dominantly larger and boxy over the rest, and behind it the two wide, domed white structures that were the reactor units.

Zero brought up the sonic detection meter and scanned. The blip registered a signal and told him: 240. Two hundred forty meters from his current location.

He fit the electronic earplugs into his ears. As he kick-started the motorcycle again, there was no sound; just a high-pitched whine in his head and the rumble of an engine beneath him. He tore across the parking lot, keeping his eyes open and his hands tight on the handlebars.

A thought occurred to him, possibly too late: his motorcycle was loud. Anyone would hear it coming—assuming they could hear anything at all. The perpetrators, the people behind the sonic weapon, would need ear protection as well.

But if there was more shooting, Zero wouldn't hear it. If anyone was taking shots at *him*, he wouldn't know unless he was hit.

As if to illustrate his point, a man ran into view not a hundred yards in front of the motorcycle. As Zero rounded the corner of the parking lot that took him adjacent to the buildings, he saw the sandy-haired man running from the large, boxy structure. He wore a white lab coat, its coat tails billowing behind him as he flat-out sprinted toward the cars.

The man dared to glance over his shoulder, right at Zero for just a moment. He must have heard the motorcycle engine. There was no sound, at least not to Zero, as the man's body jerked. Blood blossomed into the air like a mist and he fell forward, onto his stomach and face, as silent bullets pounded into him from behind.

Zero slammed the brakes and put one foot on the asphalt. There was little question to the source of the shots. A brown delivery truck sat double-parked at the curb outside the largest structure, in the fire lane. A man stepped out from behind it. He wore all black, head to toe, including a mask and visor. He held a long, dark assault rifle in his hands, barrel pointed downward as he strode toward the downed researcher.

The assailant prodded him with the gun, making sure he was dead.

He didn't even look at Zero. He couldn't hear the motorcycle.

So Zero gunned the engine and flew at the black-clad commando with a mounting speed that matched his fury at shooting an unarmed scientist.

The motorcycle was less than thirty feet away when the commando finally saw the movement in his periphery, limited as it was by the mask and visor he wore. It also kept Zero from seeing the panicked expression that was likely on the man's face in the final seconds before impact, but he could imagine it. He'd seen it before.

Then two hundred forty pounds of steel slammed into the commando, throwing him an impressive several yards and bouncing over him a second time as Zero leapt and rolled away from it, keeping his arms clutched close to his body.

The impact hurt, but he didn't waste a beat. Zero pulled the Ruger from its ankle holster as he jumped to his feet and fired four shots into the delivery truck, punching tiny holes in its side as he ran parallel to it and the entrance to the administrative building beyond.

Three more black-wrapped commandos jumped out of the back of the truck. One gripped his upper arm where Zero had tagged him with an errant shot. The other two gripped automatic weapons.

Dammit.

Zero threw himself forward, tucked into a roll, and dragged his knees into his chest behind a concrete planter perpendicular to the building entrance. He knew they were shooting at him. He couldn't hear it, but he could feel the chips of concrete flying by, stinging his face.

Silence is going to get me killed.

He wouldn't be able to hear if they stopped shooting or resumed shooting. He wouldn't be able to hear if they were planning to flank him or if they were shouting at each other to take cover or retreat or toss a grenade.

He had no choice. He had to do it.

Zero tugged the sonic earplugs from his ears. Then he winced immediately, ducking his head and covering his face at the report of a short burst from an assault rifle. It was a sound he'd heard a thousand times, maybe more, but would also scare the hell out of anyone going from near-absolute silence to ear-splitting gunfire.

A male voice called to him. "Come out now! Move here!"

Zero frowned. The man spoke Russian, and sounded passably fluent, but his word choice and odd accent told him that the speaker was not native.

It hardly mattered. He was outnumbered, out-gunned, and most definitely not coming out. He gripped the LC9 in a sweaty hand, waiting for another burst of shots. Waiting for an order for the three men to flank him, take him out. To toss a grenade.

But no. Instead came a simple and direct order in Russian: "Turn it on him!"

Zero's eyes widened in shock as the meaning behind those words registered. He scrambled for his earplugs, but he couldn't find them. They'd bounced from his hand when he'd taken them out and the shooting began.

He'd been in firefights. He'd been in raids with bombs going off in every direction. He'd been aboard boats that were torpedoed and helicopters struck by RPGs. At least in those scenarios, there was something to see, something to hear—something to potentially avoid.

The sensation struck his body in an instant. His muscles seized as a seemingly unnatural force, as invisible as it was silent, reverberated through him. He wanted to cry out but his throat constricted, his mouth wide open as if in a yawn. He tried to focus but his eyes vibrated intensely, blurring the world into a smear of vague, bland colors.

His insides roiled. His stomach flipped with nausea. He fell to his hands and knees. He was vaguely aware that he'd dropped the Ruger as he vomited. He felt as if his entire body was about to be vibrated apart into a million pieces.

This is it. This is how I die. Not with a bang, or a blast, but in utter and complete silence.

Then there was a sound—no, there were *sounds*, out there, somewhere, but they were distant and distorted, as if someone had slipped earmuffs over his head. The sounds didn't matter. He was in agony, at the mercy of the sonic weapon and completely unable to do anything but roll over and die.

He thought of Sara. Even though he couldn't see, her angelic face filled his mind's eye as if she was there. It was strange, in that moment, that he was capable of any sort of lucid thought, but despite the pain permeating every part of his being, a calm came over him and he thought only of her. Maya would be all right. She was strong and capable. In that moment before what he was certain would be his death, he thought of Sara, and he sent up an unsaid prayer that she too would be happy, healthy, and safe.

CHOOM!

He definitely heard that. A coughing chug erupted, the unmistakable sound of a powerful gun.

CHOOM! It came again, thunderous and deep despite his waning hearing. There was something else there too, a rattling sound, like a snare drum behind the deeper and intermittent bass drum of a gun blast.

And then, as if the heavens themselves had seen fit to answer him, he sucked in a gasping breath. His body collapsed onto pavement. His eyeballs ceased their frenetic vibrating, and though nausea still racked his gut, the dizziness began to subside.

The attack stopped. Or *was* stopped. And the sounds that came back suggested a fierce firefight.

Zero reached up shakily and gripped the edge of the concrete planter, still crouched behind it for safety from bullets. He dared to peek out. A black car had arrived, its doors thrown open, stopped not fifteen yards from the brown delivery truck. Two figures took cover behind it. A flash of blonde hair. A shorter, stocky man.

Maria.

Todd.

She had the downed Russian's assault rifle in her hands, providing cover fire on the truck and the commandos. Strickland held a twelve-gauge shotgun, police-issue by the look of it. He racked the slide and pulled the trigger.

CHOOM!

Buckshot peppered the side of the truck, and Zero sluggishly put it together. They'd received his message. They'd come running. Strickland must have hit the ultrasonic weapon, incapacitated it enough to cease the attack on his body.

He couldn't have been in the sonic blast for more than a few seconds for him to still be alive. Yet it had felt like an eternity.

From his vantage point, he saw a black-clad commando rounding the truck near the front fender, trying to get the drop on their assailants. Zero stood suddenly. He was wobbly on his feet and nearly fell, but grabbed onto the planter for support. He had no idea how many rounds were left in the LC9, but brought it up anyway.

Track your aim to the right, he reminded himself.

He fired two shots. The gun bucked in his hand. The first shot struck the man in the neck. The second, in the side of his black helmet. He fell limply.

The shooting ceased. He saw four bodies. He had struck one with the motorcycle. Were there more? He had no idea.

"Zero!" Strickland shouted. He racked a round into the shotgun, grabbed it by the meaty stock, and hurled it into the air. It somersaulted twice lazily in a high arc as the last black-helmeted man standing jumped from the back of the truck. He brought the automatic rifle up, aiming straight ahead—straight at him.

Zero dropped the Ruger and caught the shotgun in his arms. He flipped it around and fired it once, one-handed. The recoil stung his arm. The stock jumped back, glancing off his ribs. The commando took the shot straight to the chest. His body flew backward as if he'd been hit by a car, right back into the rear of the truck.

Silence again.

Zero waited. He cautiously glanced left and right. There was no movement, no sound.

"Clear." His voice came out choked and hoarse.

The rear doors of the truck were open, and beyond them, amid cardboard boxes that had never been delivered, was the root of their problems. It was an admittedly ugly thing, a wide dish welded to a steel dolly that also held a large cube with leads extending from two terminals.

A battery. It must have been. Blue sparks crackled from the terminals where Strickland's shot had damaged it.

Zero pumped the shotgun once more and aimed it point-blank at the battery. The gun coughed. The battery exploded in a white flash that left black spots in his vision for several seconds.

"Are you okay?" Maria's voice, behind him.

"Yeah." The spots subsided, but Zero didn't turn just yet. He was distracted by the body lying on the floor of the truck, the man he'd blasted in the chest with the shotgun. The man's black visor and mask had come off partially when he fell, askew on his face. Zero reached for it and tugged it off.

He blinked at the face for several seconds.

"Zero...?" Todd asked cautiously.

The commando was not Russian. He was clearly Asian—and by Zero's more-than-educated guess, he was Chinese.

"Check them," he said. It hurt to talk. "Not Russian. Chinese."

Maria frowned as she knelt toward the nearest dead commando. "He's right. They're not Russian."

"This is a set-up." Zero hopped down from the back of the truck as he put it together. The Chinese, the trade war with the US that threatened their economy...the Chinese were attempting to frame the Russians with the sonic attack. To what end?

To instigate a war. The Chinese had weapons and supplies that the Russians would want. Nothing was as profitable as being on the paying end of a major conflict.

The woman. He had seen her himself, and she was most definitely not Chinese. He looked around frantically for her amongst the bodies that lay strewn around the truck. He saw three downed guards in green fatigues, guns still in their hands. Their unmarred bodies suggested they had received the full brunt of the ultrasonic weapon—and their horrified death masks suggested they had not died well.

"The woman," he said. "We have to find her."

"Wait," Maria insisted. "You're bleeding." She gestured toward her mouth.

Zero gently touched two fingers to his own mouth and they came back smeared with red. Suddenly he was aware of the copper taste at the back of his throat. Something inside him was bleeding, but there wasn't time to determine what.

"Backup?" he asked.

"I called everyone there is to call on the way over here," Maria said quickly. "They're en route, but no one can get here fast enough. Local PD was advised to deal with the Prince Frederick situation—they're out of their depth on this one."

Zero grunted. They were, as it tended to happen, on their own.

"Split up. Find her. I think she means to force a meltdown. There's a girl with her." It pained him to say it, both literally and figuratively, but he did anyway. "Consider both hostile. Maria, take the administrative building." He gestured to the boxy structure before them. "Strickland, to the east. I'll take west. Radios on. If you see something, say something."

They didn't need anything more than that. Zero passed the shotgun back to Todd. Maria switched her assault rifle for one from the dead commandos. Zero unholstered a nine-millimeter Beretta from one of the downed guards, and they split up to find the redheaded woman before Calvert Cliffs' twin reactors caused a catastrophic meltdown.

Chapter Thirty Seven

Fukushima.

Chernobyl.

Three Mile Island.

Those were the names that ran through Zero's head as he stole quickly around the western edge of the administrative building, gripping the borrowed Beretta and keeping a keen eye out for any signs of life.

It seemed that the perpetrators, the now-dead commandos and the redheaded Russian, had been thorough. They had attacked the facility the day after a national holiday, when it seemed that the reactor was working on a skeleton crew. They'd blasted the facility with the ultrasonic weapon, the frequencies passing through concrete and steel. His own experience with it had been awful beyond compare, but he at least had the minor advantage of knowing what it was. These people—the two more bodies he passed along the way, not to mention whoever might have been on duty inside at the time—would have had no idea. They simply would have felt it, and fallen to it, their last thoughts being terror and confusion and panic, with nowhere to hide or run to.

Zero knew a lot about a lot of things, but he didn't know much about the inner workings of nuclear energy. He did, however, know that Three Mile Island's partial meltdown and subsequent radiation leak was the largest nuclear disaster in US history. He knew that there was still much of Chernobyl that was uninhabitable to humans, let alone plant and animal life. He knew that the Fukushima meltdown was caused by an earthquake, which led to an electrical failure.

Could she do that? he wondered. *Could she force an electrical failure, or cut power to the cores and purposely melt down the reactors?*

His palm was sweaty at the very thought of it. If the Russian woman was successful, it wouldn't matter much for him—he would be at ground zero, and likely dead in minutes, if not sooner. He had at least been right about one thing: their plan was always going to be a one-way trip for the black-clad commandos and the woman.

But then there was the child. He didn't know where she fit into all this, but she was just a child. Despite his warning to Maria and Strickland to consider her hostile, he wasn't sure he could convince himself that the girl was anything but innocent in all this.

He wondered what, if anything, was happening in the outside world. Where was their backup? Was the FBI or CIA en route in helicopters? Would the National Guard roll up in Humvees and Jeeps? Had they initiated evacuation protocols for the nearest towns and cities?

Or had Zero and his team cried wolf too many times, in Illinois and New York and Washington?

So much of his professional life was spent asking questions that he couldn't answer.

The structure to the west of the administrative building was squat, one-story and concrete, with a flat roof and smooth facades and thoroughly unremarkable. Behind it the white-domed reactor units rose like massive dunes, not only dwarfing the building but looking all the more intimidating with the slow-blinking red lights that flashed slowly at their peak.

Zero looked for a way inside, sticking close to the concrete wall and moving quickly. His guts still ached. He hoped he hadn't suffered any long-term damage. His hearing and vision seemed to be fine, as far as he could tell ...

He almost passed it by. To his right was a steel door with no knob or handle, just a door interrupting the smooth concrete, and he nearly passed it by because it looked closed. But he paused and frowned.

It wasn't quite closed. He could see just the shadow of the jamb, and when he knelt to examine it, he saw that the steel door was open just an inch, if that, propped open with a smooth pebble that looked like it had been plucked from the same concrete planter behind which he'd taken cover.

Zero looked it over. The door was accessible by a keypad to the left. Three words were stenciled in white paint across the steel: AUTHORIZED ACCESS ONLY. Someone had not only accessed it, but had then wedged the pebble in the jamb.

To ensure a quick getaway, if needed.

He put one hand flat on the door to push it open, but hesitated. It could be another distraction. It could be a trap, set for anyone who came pursuing her. But there was simply no way to know other than to go through the door.

Zero let out a breath, and he pushed it open. The Beretta was up in an instant, tracking left and right. There was no movement, no signs of life. The passage beyond the door was dimly lit with caged bulbs in the ceiling. The walls were the same smooth concrete as the exterior, nondescript and utilitarian.

This was not the sort of building that visitors and administrators frequented. This, he reasoned, was a place where strict and somber business was conducted. He left the pebble in the steel door and quietly stole down the corridor.

At the first turn he found another body. Another guard. He'd been shot in the head at point-blank range with a small-caliber pistol. Zero shook his head. The guard was young, likely barely out of his twenties. And this was the day after a major holiday. The young man might have come into work a bit hung over, or still drowsy from the festivities. He might have been somewhat disgruntled to be working that day at all, or looking forward to the weekend. He would have heard someone access the steel door, but it hadn't been forced. No cause for alarm. But the corner was blind. Whether the Russian woman came around, or if he peered out to see who was approaching, was unclear.

The only thing he could say for sure was that she'd been within arm's reach when she'd shot him.

He stayed absolutely still and silent for a long moment, and when he heard nothing he dared to speak into his radio. "I've got a dead guard here, in the western building, concrete, single story."

The reply was a hiss of dead air.

"This is Zero. Does anyone copy?"

"…copy," Maria's voice came through, though just. "Breaking … way."

His nostrils flared. The thick concrete was blocking out the signal. He wondered if that was by design, but could only hope that Maria's message was that she was on the way to his location.

Suddenly he heard a clatter, like something metal falling to the concrete floor. Zero stood straight up instantly, listening intently, not sure he could discern a direction as the sound echoed down the corridor. He decided to go left, past the dead guard, and soon came to a set of steel stairs leading downward.

Down. That meant subterranean. Now he understood why the pebble had been jammed in the door—it was very possibly the only way out in a hurry.

He rushed down the stairs. No matter what he did to try to stifle the noise, every step clanged heavily. He was broadcasting his arrival, but he couldn't stop. At the bottom was another hall, shorter than the one above him, with doors lining the eastern side.

The first two were closed, sealed by the same sort of keypad he'd seen from the outside. With the Beretta up, he whipped around to the first open doorway he came to. It was filled with a dizzying array of discerning scientific equipment, the function of which he couldn't begin to guess at.

And one woman.

Zero actually took a step backward, surprised as he was to find her there. She stood facing him, her blazing hair falling in waves around her shoulders as she regarded him with a small smirk. Slowly she lifted her hands, palms toward him.

At her feet was a silver pistol. The noise he'd heard. She dropped it. There was no weapon in her hands. She wasn't actively trying anything.

This is a trap, a voice screeched in his head.

The pebble. The pipe. An unarmed woman whose team was dead.

"Freeze," he said, though he felt immensely foolish as soon as the word came out. She wasn't moving. "Step away from the gun."

"It is empty." The words came out softly; they didn't need to be spoken loudly in the silence of the place. Her English was perfect, though the guttural Russian accent on her consonants was clear. "You've got me."

Zero glanced over his shoulder, checking his six, certain there must be someone behind him trying to get the drop. But there was no one there.

"Hands behind your back," he told her sternly.

Her smirk spread to a grin, but her hands didn't move. "Tell me," she said slowly. "Are you the crazy one?"

"Crazy...?" Zero wasn't sure how to answer the question.

"The man who jumped from the helicopter. The one who caused the truck to crash."

Oh. That *crazy one*.

"Yes," he said, for lack of a better response. Then he repeated: "Hands behind your back."

The woman cocked her head slightly to the side. "You do not want to just shoot me?"

"I'd like very much to shoot you," he told her plainly. "But someone has to answer for what you've done. Your team is dead. We know they're not Russian." He paused a moment. "But you are. Aren't you?"

Her gaze swept the floor in what appeared to be the first genuine gesture he'd seen from her. "I was. Though I suppose that part of me is inescapable."

"And now you work for the Chinese," Zero postulated. "To frame Russia for the attacks. Why turn on your own people like that?"

"Why?" she repeated in a breathy sigh. "For what they did to me."

What did they do to you? he was about to ask, but the words stalled on the tip of his tongue. The woman was plain-featured enough to be nobody and anybody at the same time.

There was a slight exoticism to her, the shape of her eyes and the curve of her chin, that was just enough to be attractive yet not enough to stick in the memory. He could imagine that with makeup and a fitted dress she could be stunning. In a sweatshirt and jeans she wouldn't get a second look.

"You're a sparrow," he asked, though it wasn't said like a question. An elite female assassin. Reared from a young age to be completely indoctrinated to the cause of country. A spy, a killer, a negotiator, a lover, a thief—sparrows were trained for years to be anything they needed to be.

"Was," she corrected him again. "No longer."

Zero scoffed. "You consider this a promotion? They sent you here to die."

"I volunteered," she said simply. "I defected to those who treated me like a person instead of a weapon. To those who gave me genuine purpose."

Zero shook his head. "Killing people? Causing chaos and panic? That's your purpose?"

She smiled again. "Can you say differently about yourself?"

"I don't…"

He trailed off. He was going to argue it, to tell her that he didn't kill innocent people, that he didn't cause chaos and panic—but then the Bosnian boy appeared in his memory again. The Dubai businessman. The Irishwoman.

Can I say any differently about myself?

He forced the thought out of his head. He had enough tumult swimming through his mind; he wasn't about to revisit his past or consider the role he played in the grand scheme of things at the moment.

He'd save that for tomorrow.

"Hands behind your back," he said again. "Next time I have to say it, you're getting a bullet in the thigh."

At last the hands came down, albeit slowly, past her chest and toward her hips. "Is that what you think I've done?" she asked him. "Caused chaos and panic and killed indiscriminately?"

"I *know* that's what you've done." He held the Beretta with his left hand as his right slipped into the gear bag slung over his shoulder, fishing for a zip tie.

Her hands paused as her head cocked slightly to one side. "You have not figured it out yet?"

Zero paused. *Figured what out?*

"I had you pegged from the beginning," he said, trying to sound confident, though her slight smirk was causing his conviction to shrink by the second. "Chaos. Panic. Dissension. That was your MO. Hit random targets and keep us guessing."

"Hmm." The noise came out like a half-chuckle. "Random. Yes. It would seem that way, wouldn't it? But tell me, if this was our plan along, the reactor, why would we waste time in Kansas, or Havana?"

Zero's throat flexed. She had a point. If they had a sonic weapon, why show their hand well before their masterstroke? He had assumed that it was to make the attacks appear arbitrary and unsystematic.

But they only wanted it to look random.

"Chaos was a beneficial side effect," she said, her voice a breathy purr. "Keeping your people on edge, wondering the significance of the locations, if there was one...that was merely a game. But the real reason was elsewhere. A nuclear scientist's vacation suite in Cuba. An engineer on holiday in his hometown in Kansas, spending Thanksgiving with his family. An employee of this very facility in Prince Frederick..."

Zero's gaze flitted quickly to the floor and back again as he realized what she was insinuating. The ultrasonic attacks had seemed like random targets intended to cause panic and to keep them on the defensive—but they were a diversion. The panic, the injuries and deaths, distracted him and his team from the real goal.

"You needed information," he said quietly. "To access the reactor. To get in here."

The Russian woman smiled. "The attacks were front-page news. No one even noticed a missing phone here, a hacked laptop there. A stolen keycard. Of course, smaller and more talented hands than yours or mine handled that part."

Smaller?

The girl.

He'd been wrong. The little girl was not innocent in this at all. She was as indoctrinated as the woman standing before him, maybe even more so.

The redheaded woman took a small sidestep. Behind her was a monitor in black and white, showing the unmoving outside of the very building they were in. The steel door, the only access point Zero had seen.

She had seen him coming. She knew he was alone.

Which meant she was stalling him.

"Where is she?" Zero demanded. "The girl you were with."

"Mischa. Her name is Mischa."

"Where is she?!" he growled.

"By now?" The woman shrugged one shoulder. "I imagine I've kept you here long enough that she has successfully shut off the coolant flow to the reactor cores. The heat generated by the reactors will melt the fuel elements, liquefy the cladding, and release massive amounts of heavily contaminated steam into the air. The winds of the Chesapeake will spread radioactive material north by northwest far faster than any evacuation can occur. Simply put? You're too late."

Nausea was already roiling Zero's insides, but now it doubled. The Russian woman knew he would come looking for her, and not the girl. So she'd sent a child to melt down a nuclear reactor.

He couldn't be too late. He needed to get out of there, to find the girl and stop her. But he couldn't just leave the Russian woman there.

Shoot her.

He set his teeth in grim determination.

She smiled as if she could read his mind. "Go ahead," she prompted. "I can see that you want to."

His finger twitched. He wasn't an assassin. Not anymore. This woman should answer for her crimes. Yet there were so many lives at stake.

He made a decision. Past, present, and future, he was a killer.

Zero squeezed the trigger.

"*Oomph!*" A force like a hurled bowling ball struck the small of his back. He hurtled forward as the Beretta barked. The shot struck a computer bank. Sparks flew as Zero sprawled to his stomach on the concrete.

A small shape tucked into a roll and rose in front of him. The girl. She'd struck him with what felt like a knee to his back. Zero was winded; it was a powerful blow. He struggled to breathe as he rose to his elbows. A small foot kicked out and caught the side of his face, turning him on his side. A second kick left his hand stinging and sent the Beretta clattering away.

"Kill him," the redheaded woman said in Russian. "I will finish it."

Zero saw stars. Behind them the redheaded woman rushed past. He reached for her ankle, trying to trip her up, but not fast enough.

"Maria," he coughed into the radio. "Strickland. Anyone!"

There was no response.

The girl stood a few feet from him, perfectly still, arms at her sides. She regarded him impassively, her face a smooth mask. She looked like she was waiting for something—for him to get up, perhaps.

So he did. With some difficulty he rose to his knees, and then his feet. His face stung and there was pain in his spine. He held out one hand.

"Wait..." he told the girl. Or tried to.

"Yah!" she shrieked as she flew at him in a flurry. Tiny fists and feet buffeted him, impossibly fast and stronger than he would have thought possible. It was all he could do to keep his hands up and protect the soft spots she targeted. A blow landed in his kidney and he winced. A foot struck the nerve in his thigh and he fell to one knee.

A small fist came straight for his nose in a jab. He managed to get an arm up, to deflect it an inch from his face. He grabbed hold of her forearm and twisted it, bringing his other elbow up—

The girl cried out, and Zero instinctively let go of her.

Her childlike cry of pain sent a memory ringing through his head. Sara, when she was only twelve, had been stung by a bee on a walk through a park. Her anguished cry sounded exactly the same.

Zero took a quick step back, panting heavily.

The girl rubbed her arm as she pushed out her bottom lip.

She murmured in English: "Please don't hurt me."

She barely resembled Sara, save for the blonde hair. But now that was all Zero could see. She was a little girl, barely more than twelve years old herself, downright swimming in an oversized green sweater.

He didn't want to hurt her. He wasn't sure he could even bring himself to hurt her. Every memory of everything his two daughters had been through because of him came swooping into his brain, colliding into one another like a traffic jam.

The girl, Mischa, bent slowly, not taking her eyes off of Zero. Even as crocodile tears formed in her eyes, she picked up the Beretta at her feet.

Chapter Thirty Eight

Maria kept the stock to her shoulder and her finger on the trigger of the stolen AK-12 as she hurried out of the administrative building and toward the western facility. This group had been thorough; not only had they learned Russian, but they'd even made sure to acquire Russian-made weapons, and good ones at that. The AK-12 was a newer Kalashnikov model, based on the AK-400 prototype and only put into production in 2018.

But now was hardly the time to appreciate their choice in weaponry. All she'd heard from the static-filled partial message she'd received from Kent was that he'd found someone dead, which suggested he was on the right track.

"Todd," she said urgently into the radio, "I'm en route to Kent's location. He found something. You copy?"

"Copy," Strickland replied. "I've got a survivor over here, but she's in bad shape. Should I ...?"

Maria could tell by the hesitation in his voice that he didn't want to suggest aloud that he abandon the woman. "Do what you can there," she ordered. "Then get here. Backup should be here any moment."

"Roger," Strickland confirmed.

She didn't actually know if backup would be there any moment. Their nearest resources were in DC, and even by the speediest helicopter it would take at least twelve minutes for them to arrive. It had been no more than half that since she'd made the call.

With the AK-12 at the ready, Maria stole quickly along the smooth concrete of the one-story structure to the western side of the facility. She spotted a steel door with no handle and a keypad entry. It was closed. She grunted in irritation and rounded the corner, but there did not seem to be any other entrance point.

She cursed aloud, wishing Kent would radio in again. With no other recourse, she doubled back to the steel door, put a palm against it, and gave it a small push.

To her surprise, it gave way.

"Clever," she whispered to herself as she noted the tiny pebble that had been lodged in the jamb. The door had appeared to be closed, but however Kent had gotten in, he must have had the foresight to prop it open in an almost imperceptible way.

"Steel door on the southern façade," she told Strickland in the radio. "It looks closed, but it's propped open. Get here as soon as you can."

She didn't wait for a reply. She shoved the door open and led with the assault rifle. The corridor was dimly lit and seemingly empty. After making sure the pebble was still in place, she headed quickly down the hall as quietly as she could, taking shallow breaths through her nose.

The corridor stretched on straight ahead, but there was a corner coming up on her left. She wished she knew which way Kent had gone, could track him somehow…

A shape flew around the corner mere feet away from Maria, startling her. She hadn't even heard the footsteps—but she recognized in an instant the shock of blazing red hair.

It's her. The Russian.

"Stop!" Maria cried.

The woman froze for an instant, her eyes as wide and surprised as Maria's must have been—but the woman didn't hang around. She sprinted for the straightaway beyond.

She didn't know why she even bothered to shout. They never stopped.

As much as Maria wanted to take the woman alive, she couldn't risk losing her again. She took careful aim and squeezed the trigger.

The woman sprawled forward as a burst of automatic gunfire tore the air. Her body fell roughly to the concrete floor. Maria's ears rang; the shots sounded twice as loud in the echoing corridor.

I got her.

She advanced slowly, keeping the assault rifle aloft as she approached the body. The redheaded woman was on her stomach, arms and legs splayed akimbo, unmoving.

Maria frowned. The lighting was dim, but not so much that she couldn't tell there were no bullet holes torn in the woman's back.

She didn't see the foot until it was too late. A heel came up, bending at an unnaturally flexible angle, and kicked at the barrel of the assault rifle. Maria's torso twisted with the force of it, and before she could right herself the Russian woman flipped over and sat up, at the same time sending a fist into Maria's right thigh. The blow buckled her knee and she fell down upon it, smacking her patella painfully against concrete.

She missed. The woman had flopped to the ground a mere instant before the bullets would have shredded into her.

The Russian rolled swiftly backward and sprang to her feet. Maria didn't bother standing; she twisted back around as she brought the rifle up again. Not aiming, not even bringing the stock to her shoulder, just pointing forward and pulling the trigger—

Click!

The magazine was empty. A surge of dread washed over her as Maria realized she'd grabbed up a weapon that had only a few rounds in it. In her haste, she hadn't even checked.

But it was still a weapon.

As the redheaded woman leapt forward, Maria stood and swung the assault rifle around like a club. But the Russian twisted with it, taking a weak slap across the chest and grabbing onto it with both hands. For a moment they struggled against each other for possession of it.

Then the Russian let go.

Maria staggered back a step, enough to put some space between them, and enough time for the redhead to deliver a chopping blow to her left supraspinatus, the muscle atop her shoulder. Her entire arm involuntarily went limp, and the Russian yanked the assault rifle away from her.

Before Maria could get her hands up, the stock of the weapon came flying at her forehead.

The strike knocked her flat on her back, but she barely felt the impact. Her brain rattled against her skull. Stars swam in her vision, and all Maria could do was wait for the next blow, for the stock to come down again on her head.

But it never came. Maria forced herself to sit up, pain throbbing in her head. Her vision was blurred, but she saw the flash of red hair sprinting away down the corridor.

The redheaded woman wasn't interested in waiting around and killing her. She apparently had more important things to do—like melting down the reactor.

Maria staggered to her feet and gave chase. She shook the fuzziness from her head and commanded herself to focus. The hall turned to the right, and then opened into a wide, well-lit circular room.

The first thing she noticed was the Russian, with her back to Maria, at a control panel on the farthest side of the chamber. All around her, encompassing the entire round room, were control panels of hundreds of buttons and levers, monitors and keyboard, diodes and dials.

There were two bodies on the floor, both wearing white lab coats.

"Stop," Maria demanded again, knowing it was a futile order.

The Russian had her hand on a black lever. She half-turned to Maria with a smirk on her lips. "You are too late. The coolant flow has been stopped. And now..."

She pulled the lever. The white lights overhead blinked out. For a moment Maria's breath caught in her throat as they were plunged into darkness. Then red lights in the wall flashed on, throwing the room into an eerie glow.

"Backup power has been shut off," the Russian told her. She brought the stock of the assault rifle up in both hands, and then smashed it down upon the control panel, snapping the lever cleanly off. "It cannot be restored. You cannot stop the meltdown. In two to three minutes, we will both be dead."

Maria's throat ran dry. If that was true, two to three minutes wasn't enough time for any help to arrive. Or they would, just in time to experience the fallout firsthand. If there was any way to stop it, she wouldn't have the first clue which of the thousands of keys and dials around her might do that.

Her first instinct was to run, to get out of there, get in the car and speed away. But she couldn't do that. She couldn't leave Kent and Todd behind.

She wished he was there with her. She wished she knew where he was. If they were going to die there, she could only wish that he would be in her arms when they did.

She still loved him. That much was clear. And that longing, along with the knowledge that she might never see him again, congealed into rage.

"Well," said Maria. "In two to three minutes, one of us will be dead. The other will be sooner than that." She balled her fists and charged at the Russian woman.

Zero watched as the girl bent and picked up the Beretta near her feet. Some part of his brain screamed at him: *Stop her. She's going to kill you.*

Yet another part froze him into inaction. The part of him that was a father who had hurt his own daughters—not directly, but through his deeds, through his absences, through his lies.

He barely saw the girl's face. He only saw Sara. And he could never hurt her.

Mischa took her time. She seemed to be fully aware that he wouldn't stop her. He had the feeling she'd done this before, used this tactic. Without taking her eyes off of him, she leveled the Beretta. The gun looked comically large in her tiny hand.

"You don't have to do this," Zero told her. He kept his voice even and gentle. "You're just a child. You're not a killer."

"I've killed," the girl told him. She didn't say it ruefully or boastfully; she said it as simply as stating that the sky was blue. Her accent was difficult to place, just barely tinged with Russian but also something else.

"You're not a sparrow," Zero ventured. "And that woman ... your mother?"

"Not my mother."

"You don't owe her anything. If you listen to her, you'll die down here with the rest of us. You do know that, don't you?"

The girl's gaze flitted away from him, just for an instant, but long enough for Zero to recognize a glimmer of emotion. She did know it, and she did not want to die.

"This is our purpose," the girl said quietly.

"No," Zero said firmly. "Your purpose is to be a child. To ... to grow up, and have a life of your own. Not this."

The girl sighed softly, as if she'd grown bored of the conversation. "Goodbye." Her finger came to rest on the trigger.

Suddenly an earsplitting burst of automatic gunfire echoed through the facility. Zero winced instinctively. The girl whipped her head around to see if it had come from behind them.

Zero had a chance. He leapt forward and grabbed her wrist, shoving it and the gun upward. Mischa gasped in surprise as he wrenched the Beretta away from her. But she wasted no time twisting her arm out of his grip and responding with a swift back-kick to his abdomen. As he doubled over, she threw herself forward, rolled, and grabbed up the silver pistol that the redheaded Russian had left on the floor.

It was up in an instant, and this time the girl did not hesitate. She pulled the trigger.

The Russian hadn't been lying. The gun was empty. Mischa frowned deeply at it as if it had personally offended her.

Zero trained the Beretta on her, though he kept his finger resting on the trigger guard. "That's enough. Stop this."

The girl tossed away the useless pistol. "Or you will shoot me? I am, as you said, just a child."

Zero's heart pounded in his chest. If he didn't do something, she would come at him again. He could see in her eyes that she knew damn well he wouldn't shoot her. And all he could see in her face was ...

Wait a second.

He stared at the girl. A moment earlier he could only see his daughter's face in hers. But now, he just saw a stranger, a passive-masked girl who had tried to kill him and wouldn't make the same mistake again.

It had happened again. Just like with Kate's name, just like with Maria's face ... he couldn't see Sara anymore. He tried to conjure her to his memory, but he failed. He'd forgotten what she looked like.

And while any other time that might have induced panic, he actually felt something else. Relief. At least for the moment.

The girl let out a shriek and leapt at him. Still Zero did not pull the trigger. Instead he brought the gun straight up, not bothering to deflect the blow that was coming. When Mischa was within arm's reach, her small yet powerful fist struck him straight in the gut. At the same time he whipped the Beretta down.

He doubled over and grunted, taking the full impact of her strike, as he brought the grip of the gun crashing down on the top of her head. The girl's body went rigid for a moment, and then crumpled in a limp heap at his feet.

Zero panted, catching his breath. He quickly knelt to confirm that he hadn't cracked her skull. "I'm sorry," he whispered. Then he sprinted out of the room as fast as he was able. His body was sore; his muscles screamed in protest. His insides still hurt. But the Russian woman had run off in a hurry, and someone had fired that burst of gunfire.

The only person he'd seen with an automatic weapon was Maria.

Zero made his way to the steel staircase and bounded up them, not caring about the loud clanging of his footfalls. He was halfway up when the lights suddenly went out. He sucked in a breath as he stumbled forward, nearly falling but catching himself at the last second. A moment later, red lights in the walls clicked on.

That can't be a good sign.

He picked his way quickly but carefully up the rest of the stairs, down the concrete corridor and past the dead guard. He didn't know where they might have gone, Maria or the Russian, but he didn't dare call out.

He didn't have to. From down the hall came the telltale sounds of a struggle. Female grunts. A shriek of pain. A cry of attack.

Zero sprinted toward the sounds, turning another corner and finding himself in a wide, round room surrounded on all sides by control panels. On the floor were several bodies. It took him a moment, in the dim red glow, to recognize that two of them were dead, and the other two were locked in combat.

The contents of Maria's gear bag were spilled across the ground. The Russian had the strap of the bag around Maria's neck, her teeth gritted as she pulled back with all her might. Maria writhed, struggling to pull the strap free with one hand while clawing at the Russian's face with the other. But her flailing arms were weak, quickly losing strength.

Zero lurched forward and kicked at the redheaded woman. He planted his foot in her side and she tumbled away, rolling twice and coming up on her knees. She stared up at Zero with unadulterated hate in her eyes, accentuated by the red glow of the lights. She reached for something on the floor near her—a thick black shard of plastic, it looked like, broken off of something. It had a nasty jagged edge to it that she wielded like a knife as she rose to her feet.

Maria coughed and sputtered as Zero trained the gun on the Russian.

"Don't," he warned. "I *will* shoot you."

"If you were going to," she sneered, "you would have by now." She held the jagged piece overhead in a stabbing position.

She's going to make me do it.

Three things happened at once. The Russian rushed at him, a primal scream on her lips. Something else rushed past him from the left, through the circular room's entrance.

And Zero pulled the trigger.

In the thunderous, echoing boom that reverberated through his head, Zero realized in horror that the something else was Mischa. She hadn't stayed down long, and she threw herself in front of the Russian as he fired.

The girl fell. The redhead stood.

No!

The Bosnian boy came back into his mind. He smiled, and stooped to pick up the coin from the dirt in the moment before his death.

The redheaded woman's mouth fell open. A rivulet of blood, black under the red glow, trickled from the small round hole in the left side of her forehead. Her jaw worked up and down slowly, as if she was trying to say something. Then she fell to the floor.

Mischa rolled over and got to her hands and knees. She looked down at the dead woman before her, her face as impassive as ever.

He didn't hit the girl.

Your aim tracks to the right.

He'd forgotten to compensate for his injured hand, and missed Mischa by what couldn't have been more than an inch.

Maria grabbed a zip tie from the spilled contents of her bag and forced the girl to the ground. Mischa did not fight back as Maria tied her small wrists behind her back. Then she stood and faced him.

"Thanks." Her voice was raspy and hoarse from nearly being choked to death. "But…we're out of time, Kent. The reactor is melting down. We can't have more than a minute left. Not enough time to get far enough away."

Zero stared at the girl on the floor, lying on her stomach with her hands zip-tied behind her. Even if they had the time to flee, he wouldn't leave her there to die. The girl could not take her eyes from the dead Russian woman beside her, the pool of blood slowly creeping toward her fuzzy green sweater.

Their plan had worked after all. Even if they couldn't frame the Russians, they could still cause the biggest nuclear disaster in US history. They could still kill millions.

"There must be something..." he started to say, but even as the words tumbled out he knew they were useless. They were surrounded by equipment the likes of which neither had ever seen. It was futile.

"Hey." Maria took his hand in hers. "There was never going to be a happy ending for us, you know? Not in this line of work. But... as weird as it sounds, I'm glad you're here."

He nodded slowly. His brain felt numb, only barely aware that he would never see his girls again. That they had still failed to stop the meltdown in time. That the little girl on the floor was still going to die.

Yet he understood. It was some solace that Maria was there. He knew a lot about a lot of things, and one of them was that at this proximity, it would be quick. They'd be dead in seconds once the radiation began leaking from the core.

He drew her into a tight hug, and she put her arms around him. They stood like that, just holding each other, and waited for the end.

Chapter Thirty Nine

Sara followed the olive-skinned young man down the beach. She took her time, trying not to look like she was following him, walking barefoot in the surf and watching as people went by. Occasionally glancing out at the sea. But always keeping him in her peripheral vision as he walked with his hands shoved in his pockets.

The urge was stronger now. Her throat prickled, goose bumps rising on her skin at the very thought of getting a fix. But still she kept it together as best she could.

The youth in the cut-off gray hoodie passed the old rickety pier and kept walking, heading toward the Virginia Beach boardwalk in the distance. Sara let him gain enough of a lead that he wouldn't think she was trailing him, but not so far that she couldn't keep an eye on him. After about twenty minutes of strolling in the wet sand, she finally saw him pause, look around cautiously, and then vanish in the shadows beneath the boardwalk.

She hesitated. Though the day was bright, the expanse beneath the pier was not. It wasn't pitch-black, not by a long shot, but there were plenty of thick, round wooden beams for people to hide behind. Plenty of shadows to creep from. Plenty of opportunity for someone to prey on a sixteen-year-old girl who was in the wrong place at the wrong time.

But the need was stronger than logic, even stronger than her fear. With her shoes in her hand and the cash burning a hole in her pocket, Sara clenched her jaw and headed beneath the boardwalk.

For the first several yards there was nothing but odd bits of trash, random soda cans and potato chip bags, pizza crusts and cigarette butts. Then there were bodies—just a few, but enough to freak her out. People sleeping in the sand that would stay dry until high tide. Whether they were homeless or junkies or both, she couldn't guess. But she picked her way further, looking for the young man with the wiry frame and the amateur tattoos running down both arms.

She heard voices before she saw him, and quickly ducked behind a wooden pillar. When she dared to peer out she saw the boy, not ten yards from her, in the further shadows beneath the boardwalk. He was talking in low tones to a dirty man with a patchy brown beard and a rat's nest of hair stacked upon his head. They shook hands, or at least it looked like they did.

Sara recognized a hand-off when she saw one. Drugs and money were exchanged in that handshake, though both parties were well-practiced enough that no one watching would have seen either.

She had been right about him. And now the urge became an itch, one that could only be scratched in one way. A heat rose in her chest and up to her throat at the very thought of it, and to her own surprise, her mouth actually watered.

Still she waited, at least until the man with the patchy beard stalked off. The youth was alone. He looked around again, and then surreptitiously counted the few bills in his palm. He nodded to himself once, apparently satisfied.

Then Sara stepped out from behind the pillar. "Hello?" she said cautiously.

The young man took a step back, surprised as he was to see her. But then his eyes immediately narrowed into a look of distrust and anger in equal measure. "What you want?" he demanded.

"I want..." She cleared her throat. "I need a hit. Just a little something."

The young man glanced left and right again in suspicion. "You kiddin' me? Get yo' ass back to the suburbs, girl."

"Please." She reached into the pocket of her jeans and pulled out the cash that Maya had given her. "Whatever I can get for fifty dollars. It's all I have."

She held it out for him. The young man raised an eyebrow and at first didn't move. After a long moment, he slowly walked toward her and snatched the money out of her hand. Sara bit her lip hard, fully realizing that there would be little she could do if this guy decided to walk off with her money.

Instead he reached into the breast pocket of his sleeveless hoodie and produced a tiny baggie of white powder. He showed it to her. She reached for it. But he pulled it out of her reach.

"You gotta do it right here," he told her.

Sara glanced around. She didn't like being under there, in the shadows beneath the boardwalk with the strewn trash and the bodies lying around. But the urge was stronger than her doubt and unease.

"That way I know you're not a narc," the boy added.

"Fine." Her voice was tight and came out timid. "I will."

He handed it to her, and then he took two steps back as he tucked her money into his pocket. Her fingers trembled as she carefully untied the knot in the top of the bag. As carefully as possible, she poured the contents onto the back of her hand, on the fleshy bridge between her thumb and forefinger.

It wasn't a lot. She wasn't sure of the going rates of street drugs, but it looked paltry for the fifty dollars she'd given him. Still, her brain yearned for it. Her stomach twisted in knots in anticipation. Besides, it had been weeks since she'd had anything but caffeine. This would do the trick, she was certain.

She brought her hand up to her nose, plugged one nostril, and sucked it up in one snort.

The young man grinned at her. "Shit, I had you pegged all wrong. You a pro, huh?" He chuckled as if he'd told a joke.

But Sara ignored him. She tilted her head back, her eyes closed, her lips slightly parted as the drugs altered the pleasure centers of her brain and flooded her skull with endorphins.

Yes. This was what I needed.

But then—her eyes opened suddenly. A wave of dizziness swept over her like a rogue wave. She teetered on her feet, barely catching herself before she tumbled right over.

She didn't understand. It was such a small amount. There was no way it was too much for her...

Unless...

The young man chuckled again. The ground tilted as Sara saw him pull out a cell phone.

They're laced.

The drugs are laced with something.

Whatever they were mixed with was far more powerful than anything she was used to. She staggered again, catching herself on a wooden pillar. A splinter pierced her palm, but she didn't feel the pain. Her brain was active, alert, crying out for her to flee, but her body wouldn't respond.

The young man put the phone to his ear. "Yo. Go tell Big Man I got one for him. Under the boardwalk. Blonde girl, teenager. Real white-bread. She ain't going nowhere for at least twenty minutes, but be quick."

No.

Her knees hit the sand even though she didn't realize she'd fallen forward.

No.

The young man had called someone to—to come get her.

Get up!

Her legs felt like jelly. Her mouth was dry as cotton, though her stomach wanted to vomit. There was no misunderstanding the young man's intentions. He was handing her off to someone.

Traffickers.

The thought came like the shriek of a ghost from her past. She was vaguely aware that she was rocking, her arms folded over her chest. Her face was wet. Was it wet? She touched the tears that fell from her eyes, her fingers leaving gritty flecks of sand on her cheek.

"Dad," she murmured. "Dad, help me." At least she thought she said it aloud. Maybe it was just in her head.

"Yo. This the girl?" A new voice. Deeper.

"Man, you see any other white girls whacked out of their minds?" the young guy said quickly. "Hurry up, before someone sees."

Oh my god. How did they get there so fast? It had only been seconds—hadn't it? Maybe it had been minutes. It could have been an hour for all she knew.

"Come on, girlie," said the deep voice. "We're going for a ride."

"No," Sara protested, though it came out a whimper. Her vision was blurred, but she saw a large man ambling toward her, wearing a black tank top and a gold chain. He reached for her.

"No!" she screamed.

"*Unh!*" The big man's body suddenly jerked. He fell to his knees in front of her.

"What the fuck?" shouted the younger guy. "Bitch, you better not—" His protest was cut off by a wail of pain that didn't even sound human, let alone male.

Sara could do little but quiver in the sand. The big man tried to get up, but his head jerked violently, and he fell on his side in front of her. His eyes were open but glazed. Behind him, the young guy tried to run. Someone was on him in a second, much faster. But smaller than him. They grabbed the young man around the neck from behind, twisted, and full-on choke-slammed him into the sand. He gurgled and sputtered as he struggled to breathe.

Sara squeezed her eyes shut.

Hands were on her then, grabbing her shoulders. She shrieked and squirmed away, but they held fast.

"Sara!"

What? How...?

She opened her eyes. Tears welled immediately, blurring her vision all over again. She knew that voice, though she couldn't see clearly.

"Maya." She tried to say it, but her tongue felt too thick for her mouth.

"Come on. It's okay. I've got you." Her sister put one of Sara's arms over her shoulders and supported her waist as she hefted her to her feet.

It seemed impossible. She was hallucinating, she was sure of it. But she could hear Maya's steady breathing, could smell her familiar scent. After a few moments they were in the sunshine again, warm on her face, and Sara looked.

It was her. Maya was really there, and Sara was crying all over again.

"They ... they tried to ..."

"Shh," Maya said soothingly. "I know. But they didn't. I'm here." Then she had a phone to her ear. "Alan, I found her. Pick us up at the mouth of the boardwalk."

Alan was there too, somewhere nearby. "How?" Sara managed to ask.

Maya let out a sigh. "I love you," she said, "but you are really damned predictable."

I love you too, she wanted to say, but her mouth was desert-dry. Or maybe it wasn't just in her head. Maybe she had actually said it aloud. The beach tilted left and right as Maya helped her shuffle through the sand, and when Sara's head lolled and came to rest on her sister's shoulder, she left it there.

It felt safer that way.

Chapter Forty

Zero held Maria tightly against him, breathing in her scent for what would be the last seconds of his life. Any moment, the reactors would melt the fuel elements, releasing deadly radiation and a contaminated cloud that would spread into town and cities up and down the Chesapeake's coast.

He didn't want to think about that. He wanted to think of the good times, with Sara and Maya, with Kate, with Maria, with Alan. Vacations and dinners and inside jokes. That's what he focused on, forcing his mind to daydream, to not think about if it would hurt, or how long it would take to kill him ...

Then there was a grunt.

A shuffling of feet.

Maria looked up, frowning. Zero did too. He blinked in confusion at what he saw.

Todd Strickland entered the round control room, and he wasn't alone. He had one arm around the waist of a dark-haired woman, her arm slung over his shoulders.

"What the hell are you doing?" Maria asked in shock. "You should have gotten the hell out of here!"

"Well, excuse me," Strickland muttered, obviously out of breath, "for trying to save the eastern seaboard."

Zero still couldn't believe what he was seeing. The woman was professionally dressed with her dark hair pulled back into a ponytail. Her eyes were unfocused and glassy, and he could see a thin streak of dark blood trickling from her ear. She grimaced with each step in obvious pain. It didn't look like she could stand on her own; Zero assumed she had ruptured an eardrum and it had thrown her equilibrium out of balance.

But she's a survivor.

This woman had clearly bore the brunt of the sonic attack—and she had survived.

"Card." The woman gestured toward one of the dead bodies on the floor of the control room. "Keycard."

"What?" Zero asked dimly.

"Find the keycard, Zero!" Strickland barked.

"Right." Zero fell to his knees and rooted around the dead man's white lab coat. He located a plastic card clipped to the inside of it and yanked it free.

The woman's fingers trembled as she took it and pointed to a console. Strickland helped her to it, and with some difficulty, she slid the keycard into a slot above a keyboard. A monitor blinked to life. With Todd supporting her, she typed in a command—excruciatingly slowly, one key at a time, hunt-and-peck style, swaying all the while.

Maria's fingers found his and squeezed tightly. Zero closed his eyes.

He heard a slight whir from overhead.

When he opened them again, white lights blinked to life in the control room.

He let out the breath he hadn't realized he'd been holding in a long whoosh.

"I don't understand," Maria said. "The Russian told us there was no way to stop it…"

"Not…for you," the woman managed to say.

Zero understood. The Russian thought that their sonic weapon had taken out the employees of the facility. There was no way for Zero or Maria or Strickland to stop the meltdown—but a trained nuclear engineer would know every failsafe in the facility.

"Coolant…is flowing," she winced. "But we should go. Radiation…"

"There still might be a leak," Strickland finished for her. "Let's go!"

Maria rushed forward and hauled Mischa to her feet. She held the girl by the elbow and led her quickly out of the room. As she did, something small fell from the girl's fingers. Zero glanced down at it quizzically.

It was a candy. A Tootsie Roll. But he didn't have time to wonder about it. Instead he supported the engineer from the other side. She yelped slightly as Strickland and Zero lifted her between them, and they half-jogged out of the room and down the corridor.

Maria held the steel door open, and as Zero exited he kicked the pebble out of the jamb. The door slammed closed behind them with a resonant clang.

The sun felt good on his face. After everything he'd been through, everything he'd done, he'd almost been killed in silence—twice. But out here, it was anything but silent, and he was glad for it.

The thrum of no fewer than six helicopters filled the air in a buzzing roar. National Guard trucks surged into the parking lot to the south, filled with personnel fully dressed and armed to the teeth for a battle that wouldn't be coming.

Maria held Mischa by one arm and waved her CIA credentials aloft with the other as soldiers swarmed toward them. "CIA!" she shouted over the din. "The meltdown has been averted! Hostiles are dead! Keep that door closed! There's still risk of radiation leak!"

Strickland and Zero passed the engineer to a pair of National Guard medics, but not before the former leaned forward and whispered something to her. She nodded, and smiled an exhausted smile back at him before letting herself be carted off for care.

"What'd you say to her?" Zero asked.

Strickland grinned sheepishly. "I said, 'thanks for saving our lives.'"

Zero returned the grin and clapped the younger man on the shoulder. "Hey. Thanks to you too for saving our lives. You could have gotten out."

Strickland shrugged. "Life would be a lot more boring without you around."

"Heads up!" Maria called to them. She gestured with her chin at one of the helicopters as the skids touched down on asphalt. The door slid open, and a discerning man in a suit stepped out.

Edward Shaw, director of the CIA, spotted them immediately and made no attempt to hide the urgency in his gait as he approached them.

"Director," Maria nodded to him as he neared.

"Who's this?" Shaw asked point-blank, nodding to Mischa.

"She was with them."

"The Russians?" Shaw asked.

"The Chinese," Zero corrected.

Shaw frowned at that, but only slightly. Then he nodded once as he came to an understanding. "Evidence?"

"Dead commandos," Maria told him. "The agency should be able to ID them as Chinese nationals."

Shaw beckoned two dark-suited agents over, and then pointed to the girl. They took her from Maria, each holding a shoulder. Mischa's face remained as impassive as ever, even as the agents began escorting her roughly away.

"Hey, wait." Zero stepped forward as the agents paused. "She's a little dangerous, but she's just a kid. Remember that, would you?"

Mischa looked up at him. Her eyebrows met low on her forehead in a look that suggested she was trying to figure him out.

"Sorry about the bump to the head," he told her.

"I..." Mischa glanced to the sky, as if there was something written there. "I'm sorry I tried to kill you," she murmured.

"Where will she go?" Maria asked as the two agents escorted the girl away.

"For now? Langley holding cell," Shaw replied. "Until she feels like talking."

"And, uh... where will *we* go?" Strickland asked cautiously.

Shaw's nostrils flared. There was plenty of reason to fire them on the spot, or arrest them, or even have them shipped straight to H-6. But there were just as many reasons not to.

"Home, Agents," he said at last. "You'll go home. Right after you're medically cleared and debriefed." Shaw turned on a heel toward the waiting coterie of agents that would serve as a clean-up crew for the mess that waited beyond.

"Sir?" Maria called after him. "One moment. I ... I want to step down."

Shaw paused. "This can't wait until later, Johansson?"

"No, it can't. I want to return to field agent status. Immediately."

He waved a hand impatiently. "Fine. Done. I think we're all better off that way anyhow."

Zero bit back a smirk at that. But it faded quickly as he remembered one last thing. He trotted after Shaw, leaving Strickland and Maria out of earshot. "Director. What about OMNI?"

Shaw's eyes widened. He looked around rapidly, as if Zero had just uttered a curse in public. "You don't say that name outside of Langley, do you understand? In fact, you can forget you ever saw it. Or there *will* be repercussions, Agent—"

"But I did see it." Zero stared the director down defiantly. "And I want to know what became of it."

Shaw sighed tightly. "Well. Thanks to the 'modifications' made to it, the *device* appears to be irreparably altered. And our mutual friend has locked everyone out."

Bixby.

"But he could fix it," Zero said. "If he wanted to."

Shaw shrugged slightly. "I'm sure he could. If we knew where he was. Now, if you'll excuse me." The director turned once more and stalked off, faster this time, before one of them tried to stop him again.

If we knew where he was? Bixby said he would be gone, but Zero didn't think that meant he'd go dark. The engineer knew just as well as the rest of them that OMNI was an immoral machine, and he knew what the agency might do if they knew he'd damaged it. So he locked out the CIA, and he vanished.

Zero felt a small pang of guilt at that. But then, Bixby had spent so much of his life in that lab. Maybe he would go somewhere, see the world. He struggled to imagine the eccentric engineer on a non-extradition beach sipping Mai Tais, but stranger things had happened.

"So," he said as he rejoined Strickland and Maria. "Back to being a field agent, huh?"

She shrugged. "Management just isn't for me. I see that now."

"I get it. You save my life, I save yours, and now you're feeling like you're missing out on the action—"

Maria grabbed his face in both hands and kissed him deeply. He was hardly surprised, and didn't pull back. Instead he leaned into it, putting his hands on the small of her back.

"Move back in," she said simply.

He smiled. It sounded nice. But he had too much on his plate that she didn't need to be burdened with. "How about dinner? And we see where things go from there."

She smiled back. "Deal."

Strickland scoffed as he headed toward the nearest helicopter. "I'm putting in for a transfer. I am *not* third-wheeling it with you two."

President Jonathan Rutledge sat behind the Resolute desk in the Oval Office, his elbows on its surface and fingers tented in front of his mouth.

He had a lot to think about.

For starters, he'd doubted himself. He'd doubted his ability. He'd doubted his own leadership. And then he'd doubted Deputy Director Johansson and her cohort, the mysterious and oddly disarming Agent Zero. But they had gotten the job done—even after they'd been told not to—and came through. Sure, they'd made mistakes. Big ones, in fact. But at the end of the day, a major disaster had been averted. The perpetrators were dead or in custody. The ultrasonic weapon was destroyed, its remnants in the hands of the CIA.

There's probably a lesson to be learned in there somewhere, Jon, he told himself sarcastically.

Barkley would still be voted in as his vice president at the next special session of Congress, but Rutledge would not be immediately stepping down. He'd changed his mind. He was not going to be bullied into shying away, even if the bully was himself and his own insecurities. Someday Barkley would make a terrific president. It just wouldn't be this week.

There was a knock on the door to the office, and Tabby Halpern poked her head in. "We're all set, Mr. President. We can patch you in whenever you're ready."

"Thank you." The door closed again. He was alone in the Oval Office, a rarity these days. There were only two lamps on, the furniture casting long shadows across the floor.

Rutledge placed a hand on the receiver of the telephone in front of him. If he was going to go through with this, then there was a necessary first step.

He lifted the receiver. At first there was silence. Then he was patched through, and the line began to ring.

"President Rutledge." The male voice on the other end of the line was smooth, a bit high-pitched, with a heavy accent. "I hope that you can imagine my surprise when my people told me that your government was on the telephone. These sorts of conversations are usually planned well in adv—"

"Let me stop you there," Rutledge interrupted. He did not bother with pleasantries or formalities. If the Russian president could call Rutledge out of the blue, then Rutledge could do the same—except that the man on the opposite end of this call was Chinese President Li Wei. As a young leader, Wei's ambition for China's prosperity was as widely known as his disdain for the United States, especially illustrated by the recent tariffs and impending trade war.

"This is not a social call," Rutledge told him. "This is a demand."

"I'm sorry?" Wei said, surprise registering in his voice.

"Grab a pen and jot this down. You're going to cease imposing these ridiculous tariffs and economic sanctions on our exports. In fact, we're going to have a summit, you and I. A very public one. And we're going to reach an agreement that is *very* agreeable to the United States. Tariffs will be lower than when you first came to office."

Wei scoffed. "I do not believe you are in a position to demand such—"

"Actually I am," Rutledge said loudly. "Because we know what was attempted. We know what was ordered. And if my request isn't subtle enough, you will find the Seventh Fleet in Taiwan by week's end. You won't have to worry about a trade war on your hands, Wei. You'll have a *real* war."

"This is preposterous!" Wei growled. "You would threaten us with war?! I have no idea what you are talking about—"

"You do, Wei." Rutledge lowered his voice to what he hoped what his own threatening volume. "You do know. Now, my people are very good at keeping secrets. But me, not historically so. If you give me reason to, I will make the news public to the world about what happened here on American soil. But I don't think that has to happen. You and I are going to become friends, Mr. President. Because President Ilyin and I are already fast becoming friendly, and I don't think he would appreciate what was tried here today. Certainly not enough to side with China in a major conflict."

Rutledge paused meaningfully, but Wei said nothing in response.

"You decide," the President of the United States concluded. "I'll expect a response tomorrow."

And he hung up the phone on the Chinese president.

The Oval Office was silent, dimly lit. Rutledge decided he liked it that way. He scooted back his chair a bit so that he had room to prop his feet up on the desk. It was a nineteenth-century relic, one behind which many of the most powerful men in the world had sat.

He was one of them. He could put his damned feet up if he pleased.

CHAPTER FORTY ONE

Zero ran his hand through his hair and sighed. "Tell me again."

Maya scoffed and shook her head, though there was a smirk on her face. "No. I'm not going through it all again."

"But how did you know where to find her?"

"I…" Maya shrugged. "Intuition, I guess. I just put myself in her shoes and thought about where the most likely to go would be. And lo and behold."

Zero couldn't help but smile despite the situation. "You'll make a terrific agent."

The two of them sat on the tiny patio outside Zero's Bethesda apartment, sipping coffee despite the late hour and trading war stories of the past forty-eight hours. It was nice, he decided, having someone in whom to confide—and well past the time that he felt the need to keep things from her.

Just that same morning he had nearly been killed in a nuclear reactor. He and the team had been flown back to Langley, where they were inspected and debriefed. He was banged up, bruised all over—for the most part, the usual. The bleeding that he'd experienced from the ultrasonic weapon was the result of a minor tear in the lining of his stomach. Nothing that some medication and a couple weeks on a soft diet wouldn't be able to heal.

He wasn't supposed to be drinking coffee, but he felt he deserved it.

It was hours later before he was allowed to access his personal cell phone, and when he did he was thoroughly alarmed and perturbed to see missed calls from the Seaside House Recovery Center. He'd almost called them back, too, before he saw the text message from Maya that read: *Sara's with me. At your place. All is okay.*

He'd rushed home to find Sara fast asleep in her bed and Maya dutifully awake. She'd told him the story, and then a second time when he asked for it, all the while amazed that Maya had taken such measures to locate her sister. Alan had helped her get there, and had even helped her look, but ultimately it was Maya who had found her, incapacitated a drug dealer and a would-be human trafficker, and rescued Sara. Then they had taken her to the hospital to get checked out, and she'd been sleeping it off ever since.

"I don't know what to say," Zero admitted. "Except that I'm proud of you. Of the person you're becoming."

"Thanks," Maya said quietly. She sipped her coffee and stared out into the night sky.

There was something more to be said, he could tell. What it was, he wasn't sure.

"For what it's worth," he offered, "I'm sorry. For everything. All of it. Your mom, the lies, the job…"

Maya shook her head. "Nothing to be sorry about." Then she chuckled a little at herself. "Scratch that. You're not getting off the hook that easily. There's plenty to be sorry about—but that's behind us now. I think that as I get older, I'm starting to see it."

"See what?"

"Why you did it. Why you tried to… protect us from all that. I can't say I wouldn't have done the same."

He felt a lump in his throat but swallowed it. It meant a lot to hear that from her. It meant *everything* to hear that from her. He was by no means faultless, but that simple acknowledgment at least told him that he hadn't completely screwed everything up.

Yet Maya still had that thousand-yard stare.

"What is it?" he prodded.

She smiled thinly and just shook her head. "Nothing."

"Come on. I'm telling you about confidential matters of international security, and you can't tell me what's bothering you? I know you're an adult now, and you can handle your problems. Whatever it is, I promise. I won't interfere. It just helps to talk."

Maya sighed. "Sure. Okay. Here goes."

Whatever it was, it was obviously difficult for her to talk about.

"There was an incident at school," she began. "Three boys cornered me in the locker room. They assaulted me—rather, they tried to."

Zero sat up in alarm, going instantly into protective-father mode. "Jesus, are you okay? Did they hurt you?"

"No. I'm fine." Her voice lowered. "They're not." She looked over at him, her gaze boring into his. "I blacked out. I beat them—badly." Her gaze swept the floor. "I almost killed one of them, Dad."

He nodded slowly in understanding. While he was no stranger to violence himself, he had hoped that the trait wouldn't be passed on to his daughters. Though, if he was being honest with himself, he would much rather that violence be inflicted on would-be perpetrators of violence on them than against them.

"I suppose," he told her, "we all have some darkness in us. I certainly do. Your sister does. And ... and you do as well."

Maya nodded, but said nothing.

He reached over and gently squeezed her knee. "You know, there's a quote I like. It goes, 'Everyone you meet is fighting a battle you know nothing about.' I can't fight your battle. We can't fight Sara's. You can't fight mine."

"No," Maya agreed. "But we can be there. For each other." Her voice trembled slightly. She wiped an eye and scoffed at herself.

"Of course we can. We have to be." They both sipped their coffee, letting the moment sink in. "So what now?" he asked.

"Well, I got a call from the dean today," Maya said. "All three of those boys are being expelled. I could press charges if I wanted, but I think beating the shit out of them and ruining their academic lives was enough for me."

They shared a small laugh.

"But at the same time," Maya continued, "I don't think I'm ready to go back just yet. I requested a leave of absence. I want to stay here, with you and Sara, through the holiday. I'll go back in January, after the break."

Zero wanted to protest. He wanted to tell her that she had to live her life, to do what was best for her—but he held his tongue. She'd made this decision herself. She had decided already that this was what was best for her.

"Okay," he said. "That would be great."

"Good. Maybe between the two of us, we'll be able to keep an eye on our resident escape artist." Maya looked into her empty coffee cup. "I need a refill. How about you?"

"I'm good. Thanks."

Maya rose and headed inside. Zero leaned back in his chair and stared at the night sky, the stars above. He had his girls' backs. That was no small miracle. But there were still the new memories to contend with, the assassinations and his potentially sordid past. The forgetfulness he had been experiencing. He would be seeing Guyer in two days in Baltimore.

It couldn't come fast enough.

"Hmm."

"Mm-hmm."

"Huh."

It very much seemed to Zero that much of Dr. Guyer's neurological examination consisted of sporadic grunts and brief under-breath comments, the meaning of which he could not begin to translate.

The two of them were in an admittedly very posh office at Johns Hopkins in Baltimore. It hardly even resembled any doctor's office that Zero had ever been in, with leather sofas and soft earth-toned walls. Yet that didn't detract from the fact that he'd been there for seven hours and still had no answers.

Guyer had performed a full battery of tests on him. Out of what he could recall, Zero had endured a mini mental status examination to test for alertness; an NIHS stroke scale test for cranial nerve function and motion sensation; a full assessment of cognitive function, which included identifying pictures, associating language, and performing basic memory tests; and both an MRI and MRA with contrast. There were others, the acronyms of which had been lost on him as soon as the doctor had uttered them.

Now he sat across from Guyer at a wide oak desk as the Swiss doctor reviewed the results, occasionally grunting or letting out a "hmm" or "huh" without bothering to share his findings. Guyer was undoubtedly brilliant; he was sixty-one, but his piercing green eyes were as keen and alert as a man half his age. His hair was entirely white, trimmed neatly and impeccably parted. His white coat was spotless and he wore an Italian tie that likely cost a month's rent of Zero's apartment.

"Huh," said Guyer.

Zero's irritability mounted. "Okay, Doc, you're going to have to start telling me something here. It's been hours. Anything at all would be helpful."

Guyer smiled at him over the desk.

Zero knew, not only from his training as an agent but just his experiences as a person, that it was not a pleasant smile. Guyer did not have good news for him.

"Reid," he said. "There is no easy way to say this."

"Give it to me straight. I'm sure I've heard worse."

Guyer's smile vanished. "No. You haven't."

A knot of dread gripped his stomach.

"Please keep in mind that you are one of a kind in this regard. There has never been a patient quite like you, and there may never be again—"

"Doctor," Zero pressed.

"Yes. Of course." Guyer made a motion of straightening his tie, even though it was perfect already. "From what I can tell, your limbic system is more severely damaged than previously thought—perhaps even irreparably."

"Okay," Zero said slowly. "What does that mean?"

"It means that you may start losing memories even while gaining new ones," Guyer explained. "Short-term memory should not pose a problem. But the part of your brain responsible for storing long-term memories is chaotic and unpredictable, like ... well, forgive the metaphor, but it is as you Americans might say, Swiss cheese."

"Losing memories is nothing new," Zero said. "I told you earlier, I've been losing memories on and off over the last several days—"

"I mean permanently, Reid."

Zero stood. He didn't know what else to do in the moment. He stood from his chair with enough force to push it backwards. The very first thing he thought about was forgetting Sara's face, during the fight with Mischa. It had come back to him soon enough, just like Kate's name and Maria's face ...

But permanently?

"I am sorry," Guyer told him. The doctor's voice dripped with conviction. "There is nothing I can do for you currently. This is ... beyond modern science."

"So what's going to happen to me?"

"Unclear," the doctor replied. "If I had to guess, based on what I know, I would say it is very likely that your memory will continue to degrade, but I cannot say how quickly it will happen."

"How?" Zero's voice came out hoarse. "How will it happen?"

"Again, this is working off of my best educated guess, but what I am seeing is a physical deterioration of the part of the brain responsible for storing memories. I suppose if I had to compare it to anything, I would say it is ... akin to Alzheimer's."

Zero drew a deep sigh. "People die of Alzheimer's."

"Yes," Guyer agreed quietly. "They do."

"So ..."

A silence spanned between them like a vacuum.

"Yes," Guyer said at last. "It will likely kill you. But whether you have two years or twenty, I could not say." The doctor closed his eyes. "I am truly, truly sorry."

"Yeah. Me too."

Guyer rose from his seat, and they shook hands across the table. "I do hope that I see you again, Reid. With regular check-ups, I may be able to ascertain the rate of atrophy. But I do not trust it in the hands of any other neurologists. It will have to be me."

"Okay. Yes. Thank you." It was all he could think to say.

Outside, on the streets of Baltimore, Zero walked. He wasn't heading to his car. He wasn't heading anywhere. He walked until he didn't know where he was, and then he walked further.

He passed faces. Some smiled. Others laughed. Some argued, and some minded their own business.

Everyone is fighting a battle you know nothing about.

He wondered if any of these people had just discovered that their battle was a losing one.

His own brain was going to kill him, and he had no idea when.

What would he tell his daughters? What would he tell Maria?

Nothing, he decided. Both of his girls were at home waiting for him. Tomorrow he had a dinner date with Maria. He had a head full of memories as an assassin that he still wasn't sure were real or not. He clearly did not know everything there was to know about himself, and he might not ever, at this rate.

He was going to start forgetting things permanently. And not just how to load a gun. The faces of those he loved. Maybe their names. The time spent with them. The very memories he had clung to in what he thought would be the final moments of his life, in the nuclear facility.

And all that would happen before he died.

Zero stopped. Across the street was a bag lady, a nest of gray hair heaped atop her head, shopping cart at her side, holding a cardboard sign aloft for anyone who would pause to read it.

It said: THE END IS NIGH.

"It certainly seems that way," he murmured.

All the more reason to enjoy the time he had left with those he loved. He could have died a hundred times by now, maybe more. He should have died a few times just in the past week.

Zero made a vow to himself at that very moment: he would spend his remaining days doing whatever he could to make the world a better place. Not just for him, but for those who came after. For his daughters. For the survivors, like Maria and Alan and Strickland.

If his battle was going to be a losing one, then he would do whatever he could to make damn sure the war was won.

Now Available for Pre-Order!

DECOY ZERO
(An Agent Zero Spy Thriller—Book #8)

"You will not sleep until you are finished with AGENT ZERO. A superb job creating a set of characters who are fully developed and very much enjoyable. The description of the action scenes transport us into a reality that is almost like sitting in a movie theater with surround sound and 3D (it would make an incredible Hollywood movie). I can hardly wait for the sequel."

—Roberto Mattos, Books and Movie Reviews

DECOY ZERO is book #8 in the #1 bestselling AGENT ZERO series, which begins with AGENT ZERO (Book #1), a free download with nearly 200 five-star reviews.

A new, high-tech railgun is invented, with a capability of firing an indefensible missile, seven times the speed of sound—and the fate of America is at risk. Who or what is the target? And who will be behind its launch?

In a mad race against time, Agent Zero must use all of his skills to track down the source of this unstoppable weapon and figure out its destination before it is too late.

Yet at the same time, Zero learns of a shocking new development in his mental condition, one that might sideline him for good. Can he save the world—and can he save himself?

DECOY ZERO (Book #8) is an un-putdownable espionage thriller that will keep you turning pages late into the night.

"Thriller writing at its best."
—Midwest Book Review (re *Any Means Necessary*)

"One of the best thrillers I have read this year."
—Books and Movie Reviews (*re Any Means Necessary*)

Also available is Jack Mars' #1 bestselling LUKE STONE THRILLER series (7 books), which begins with Any Means Necessary (Book #1), a free download with over 800 five star reviews!

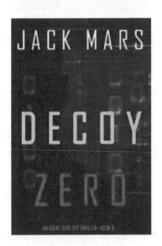

DECOY ZERO
(An Agent Zero Spy Thriller—Book #8)

21100247R00152